WRITTEN IN DUST

MEL A ROWE

Also by Mel A ROWE

COPYRIGHT

**Caveat:* As a courtesy, since there may be some sparse language choices in this story that may represent an obstacle for the reader, I am offering this warning. Please note this language and cultural references are purely for fictional purposes only and not designed to offend any individual persons, culture, or religions implied.*

The Following Is Written in Australian English

I consider the ELSIE CREEK SERIES a love letter to the unique individuals that continue to shape the Northern Territory into a truly amazing part of Australia.

My dad would've loved it.

ZERO

It was one of the most spectacular electrical storms Rowan Peddler had seen in years. Would it be his last?

Lightning strikes of skeleton-like fingers stabbed at the dark clouds, to then spark and explode, brightening the skies. The whipping wind carried the scents of outback dust and rain. It led the rumbling thunder to roll like a dozen road trains, only to detonate with a flash of twenty hand grenades.

He winced as a flashback bit at his mind, of a place with walls of rain and humid air as thick as soup. A place of mosquitos and gun fire.

'It's just a storm.' Rowan stood on shaky feet, wiping sweaty palms on jeans that had seen better days.

With a rattly breath, he gazed over his front steps, shaded by the deep verandah. It was his favourite spot in this two-storey house. Part of the infamous Peddler Property, that creaked loudly of his loneliness.

He sniffed at the air as more lightning arced across the sky. It was one big storm front and his house was in the middle of it.

He rolled his shoulders, unable to ease the tight sensation digging deep into his spine, staring into the darkness.

Nothing was out there, just the outback.

And that storm.

He reached for his tobacco pouch, sitting on a small table beside a bottle of bourbon and a glass. The highly polished wood stock of his loaded shotgun reflected the lightning, where it rested against the wall beside his favourite chair.

He flicked open the soft leather pouch, rolled his smoke and lit it in one well-practised move.

Only for his lungs to squeeze a ring of fire.

He slammed his hand against the dark house as he coughed and coughed, heaving for air. He had to hang on. He had to make it. For her.

Finally, the coughing subsided enough for him to take shaky breaths, scowling at the smouldering cigarette in the ashtray.

It was the waiting that was the worst. The guilt was crippling him, knowing she'd hate him for it, but he had to tell her. He had to right his wrongs.

Collapsing back into his cane chair, which moulded perfectly to his frame, his long legs crossed at the ankles, he sipped on his bourbon and waited for the squeeze in his lungs to subside.

As he watched the storm towering over the wide flat land, his limbs grew heavy, and his eyes closed, he hoped for a sleep free from nightmares.

Suddenly ripped from his sleep, forced back in his chair, his arms were thrust against his body. 'What the—'

'Morning, Peddler. Napping on the job, again?'

Rowan's head pounded, his throat rough, his tongue furry. He grimaced at the ropes wrapped around his arms, strapping him to the chair, still on the front porch where the hallway light streamed through the screen door.

He never turned on the lights, not while he was on watch.

Damn, he fell asleep on the job. This illness was killing him on all levels, when he used to be able to hear the soft footfalls of a bronze quoll crossing the outback dust, except now someone could sneak right up on him and tie him up, no less.

He gave up straining against his bindings.

It was over.

This was it.

'So, you finally fronted, huh?' Rowan narrowed his eyes at the tall man in dark camouflage military cargos. Kempsey. 'You still look the same, just skinnier. Still got that barbie-doll blond mop.'

'Hides the grey.' Kempsey tousled gloved fingers through his hair. 'Due for a cut. I see you're still sporting that number one.'

'Hides the grey.' They shared a grin.

Rowan paused. 'Why are you here?'

'You knew I was coming.' Kempsey sat at the small table, cranking open Rowan's shotgun to remove the live shells. 'So where is it?'

Rowan sniffed at the pre-dawn air, crisp from the storm that was more puff than power. Still, the sprinkle of rain was enough to settle the outback dust. 'It's gone. All gone.'

'Bull, it is.'

'Can't you tell I'm living like the king of the outback?'

Kempsey rummaged in his top pocket to remove a packet of cigarettes, lighting a coffin nail before pouring himself a bourbon.

How dare that prick make himself at home, sitting back to face the dawn, which was nothing but a fine ribbon of light on the distant horizon. The sky was full of stars, so deep they floated like coral dust in an endless sea of silent witnesses keeping the secrets of men.

'Get it over with,' snapped Rowan, 'or give me a damned cigarette.'

Kempsey chuckled. 'Sure.'

Rowan leaned against the ropes biting into his chest, but he damn well needed this, using his teeth to snag the cigarette.

A flick of the lighter, and Rowan took a long drag. *Damn.*

The smoke never made it down his lungs before he was hacking all over the place.

He coughed and coughed, heaving for air. Wiping the spittle on his shoulder, leaving a trail of bright crimson blood staining his shirt. He hated that. Especially when he had a cloth in his pocket.

'You should quit smoking if that's what it does to you.' Kempsey held out a shot of bourbon to Rowan.

'So they tell me.' Rowan swallowed deep, letting the heat of the liquor douse the fire in his chest while washing away the metallic taste of blood.

He scowled at the cigarette lying on the verandah's floorboards. Reaching out with his boot, he soon gave up when he couldn't stretch far enough.

Kempsey plucked the cigarette from the floor, dusting it before holding it out to Rowan. 'You still—'

'Yeah, I'm dead anyway.' The coffin nail hung from his lips as he tried to distract himself from his itchy chin. 'Am I the last one?'

'Yep.'

'So, why are you here?' Rowan took a smaller drag of his smoke, forcing down the urge to cough.

'You know why.'

'Not a mind reader, mate. But I heard Smithy died of a

heart attack and Tolser died in a boat accident. All by natural causes. You're getting good at it these days.'

'What gave me away?'

'Tolser was afraid of water. So for that man to drown first, then Smithy …'

'Smithy did that to himself. His panic attack turned into a heart attack, right in front of me.' Kempsey shook his head, exhaling a stream of smoke. 'He never could control his nerves, not after that trip.'

'Yeah.' Both men sighed, staring at the dawn inching higher in the sky.

'Tolser didn't have it,' said Kempsey, 'cried like a baby trying to sell me his wife and kids. Smithy didn't have it either. None of them did. So, it must be you. You had the box.'

'A block. I didn't know it was a box that opened. It was Tolser who passed it to me in the first place, mate, so I reckon Tolser had it and sold it. How else did he make his millions?' Rowan scowled bitterly back at the house. 'And me. Living here on my military pension in the old family home that's falling down around me. Do you honestly believe if I had the stupid thing, I'd still be sitting here?' Rowan spat out his smoke and watched it roll down the porch steps. Taking a shaky breath filled with fiery rage, as the first tweet of the birds' morning song began.

'Well, I've got a theory …' Kempsey stepped off the porch, dropped his smoke alongside Rowan's, barely squashing them into the dirt with his boot.

Rowan hated leaving rubbish lying around, especially cigarette butts. 'Didn't give yourself a headache thinking up this theory, did ya?'

Kempsey grinned, his teeth as white as his hair. 'I reckon you've got it stashed somewhere. Holding onto it for a rainy day.'

'Rainy day, mate!' Rowan's bitter laugh echoed around the verandah. 'If I did, I would've sold it and spent it on my last hurrah before the big C has me bedridden. I'd get the penthouse in some ritzy five-star hotel, gorge myself on food, wine, and women, to gamble the lot away.'

'About ten years ago, I would've believed it.'

Rowan shrugged against the ropes. He deserved this for what he'd done.

He cleared his throat, his voice wavering as he said, 'I'm hoping you'll do the same for me. A bloke can't live like this. Not when all I've got to look forward to is getting my tucker through a tube, and bed sores from being too crook to move except stare at a ceiling.' He looked up at the dimming stars, a ceiling that was alive.

'Are you sure? Haven't you got any family left?'

'It's just me. I'm the last of the Peddlers.' Rowan heaved in air, craving another cigarette and a bourbon chaser. 'Just don't mess up my face. I always wanted an open casket to scare the townspeople away. Not that there'll be anyone at my funeral.'

'Sure, mate, sure …' Kempsey's boots never made a sound as he stood in front of Rowan. 'Do you think they'll let a prick like you into heaven? Or are we both destined for hell?'

'Dunno? But I'll find out shortly.' It's a question he'd been asking a lot lately. It's why he'd been racing against time to make things right. But had he done enough?

'Why not tell me where it is now, so I don't tear your place apart?'

'Haven't seen it. Haven't got it. Always thought Tolser had it and sold it.' Rowan sighed at the soft salmon pink sky, inhaling the crisp scent of the fresh outback dawn. 'It's sure going to be a pretty day …'

ONE

Detective Sergeant Marcus Moore stood in the shade of the front porch, watching the sapphire sky turn red from the churning dust caused by an incoming car.

It parked behind the ambulance, which stood among the scattered police cars, shaded by the two-storey farmhouse. Home of the infamous Peddlers.

'Hey, Marcus.' Dr Stewart Mannen Junior grabbed his medical pack and slung it over his shoulder.

'Stewart. Thanks for coming.'

'Rowan Peddler was a patient. Who found him?'

'Two-dollar Darryl and his nephew, Chopper.' Marcus nodded at the two Aboriginal men leaning their backs against a flatbed truck on the far edge of the bush. Chopper was just a kid, who obviously wasn't taking it so well, while Two-dollar Darryl scrunched his wide-brimmed hat in his hands.

'Did they say what happened?'

Marcus pointed at the cane table and chair set by the front door. 'They found Rowan sitting in that chair, thinking he was napping. He didn't sleep in the house, apparently, just napped.'

'Rowan told me he was an insomniac.'

'Anyway, they gave him a nudge on the shoulder to

wake him up and he fell.' Marcus and his crew had taken photos and scoured the area for clues, but the rain had washed away all tracks, except for Two-dollar Darryl and Chopper's truck.

'Won't they come inside?' Stewart nodded at the Indigenous men by the truck.

'Nope. Not until the place gets smoked …' It was a big house that was too quiet. To die alone like that, the thought made Marcus' stomach squeeze.

'What do you think happened?' Stewart gently peeled back the sheet to lean over the body.

'There were no signs of a struggle, but there's an empty bottle of bourbon, half-smoked cigarettes, a loaded shotgun, and a tonne of empty pill packets.' It looked like a suicide, textbook style. Yet something wasn't right. 'Those pills have your name on them and that's a lot of medication, Doctor. High-end opiates at that.' If they were in the city those pills would sell for a fortune to druggies on various street corners. Marcus wasn't having that kind of market in this town. 'How many meds did you give him?'

'A bit. Rowan came in for a cough he couldn't shake and wanted some cough mixture to get rid of it, only to discover he had terminal lung cancer. He should've been carrying an oxygen tank, not cigarettes.' Stewart read the medication labels.

'That's no good.' Marcus adjusted his cap. Rowan Peddler was a quiet man who'd kept out of Marcus's way — considering what the Peddlers did for a living.

'It was only last week that I told Rowan he had about six weeks to three months to live.'

Marcus rubbed at the back of his neck. Even if Rowan Peddler lived notoriously on the wrong side of the law, it was a horrible way for anyone to learn of news like that. To die alone was sad, and so slowly like that even worse. It was far better to go out in a shootout—you didn't have to think about it then.

Stewart stripped off his gloves. 'Has he got any next of kin?'

'Don't you have that in your medical records?'

'Rowan said he was the last of the Peddlers. Told me to call Two-dollar Darryl if there was an issue. But that's his employee?'

'You could say that.' Marcus narrowed his eyes across the ochre dust to where Two-dollar Darryl and Chopper waited. But there'd be no record of anyone ever having been paid to work for the Peddlers.

Senior Constable Porter strolled through the front door. 'I wonder if the town's hermit has a will?'

'There'd have to be one,' said Stewart. 'Rowan told me this land's been in his family for generations.'

'The Peddlers have been around a while.' Marcus hooked his thumbs into his police belt. 'Porter, give Otis a call and see if he has any details of a next of kin for Rowan Peddler. Stewart, can we send Mr Peddler to the morgue?' The poor man had been outside too long already.

Stewart nodded.

'The cause of death is?' Marcus asked, waving over the waiting ambulance officers.

'Can't say until I complete the autopsy. I'd better grab the rest of his medications from the house.'

'I was going to suggest that.' Marcus led the way. 'What do you know about Rowan Peddler, from his doctor visits?'

'Ex-military guy who took his pension and came back to look after his mother, like someone else I know.'

Marcus shrugged. 'Anything else?'

'Rowan struck me as a smart man, but very private.' Stewart paused, with eyes widening. 'What happened in here?'

Inside the farmhouse the staircase stretched ahead to

the upper levels. To the right stood the large office. On the left it opened to the living room where furniture was tossed in all directions with stuffing strewn everywhere like fake spider webs at Halloween. Pictures were off the wall, tables knocked over, and bookcases emptied.

'On first impression, it looks like Rowan, or someone else, was looking for something. But with his medical condition ...' Marcus wasn't so sure this was a criminal investigation.

'Terminal patients have been known to have fits of rage when first dealing with their imminent death. But Rowan was neatly dressed, had his boots polished and he was rather tight-lipped or spoke in riddles.'

'How did Rowan react when you told him he only had a short time to live?' News like that sent chills to scurry across his broad shoulders.

'Nothing. The man showed no emotion. I told him to keep his meds in the fridge because of the heat.' But to get to the kitchen they had to get past the pile of books scattered across the floor, all from the same author. Stewart picked up a book. 'Look at all these romance novels.'

Marcus smirked. 'How do you know it's a romance?'

'Jenny's got these novels at the nurses' station. She shares them with the nurses and patients, and you should hear them *swoon*.' Stewart chuckled. 'They do this rating on the male hero of each book, kind of like our dating-ratings game.'

'Hmph.' Marcus scooped up a paperback. 'Do women really go for this?' He'd never bothered with romance because he never had time for women who wanted relationships. Work was his life.

'Ooh, look, it's the complete collection.' Tanisha squealed, pushing back her police cap to eagerly snatch up the books.

'How do you know?' Marcus asked Tanisha, who

rarely left the station. Yet Tanisha had been the first out the door to see inside the Peddlers' house. A house no one had been allowed to visit in decades.

'I read.' Tanisha flicked through the pages, only to squeal again. 'Oh my word, they're autographed.'

Marcus flipped open the paperback to find a delicate handwritten note:

Rowan, I hope you'll enjoy this book.
Maybe learning how to romance a woman might help you lose
your bachelor tag!
All my love TT.

'He knew Taylor Timms?' Tanisha's eyes were so wide and bright, Marcus braced himself for another squeal. 'Wait until the girls hear about this.'

Marcus dumped the book onto the nearest empty shelf. He didn't have time to read fiction, only crime reports, the latest in police investigation technology, and the pile of paperwork waiting at the office.

'Oh-oh-oh, he's got *Lambert's Gold*! Squee!' Tanisha hugged the book. 'I've been trying to get a copy of this for *centuries*. This book's worth hundreds. No, it's probably worth thousands!'

Marcus rolled his eyes at the big-hearted Tanisha with her flair for dramatics.

Porter scooped up a paperback from the floor. 'Tess reads these.'

'So she should, they're the best romantic adventures *ever*.' Tanisha squeezed the book against her generous chest, as if holding a precious child. 'Can I take this, Sarge? Pretty please.'

'No.' Marcus tugged the book free from Tanisha's hands and tossed it onto the bench.

Tanisha's face fell in absolute horror.

'Get to work, you lot. Tanisha, you can head back to the station to man the phones.'

'But someone should stay behind to guard these books, Sarge.' Tanisha again reached for *Lambert's Gold*. 'I'll do it. No over-time, Sarge. You can count on me.'

Marcus grumbled. 'Since when do we guard books at a crime scene?' Technically this may not even be a crime scene, if the poor man died of ill health.

'Tanisha might be right, Marcus,' piped in Porter, flicking through a paperback. 'If word gets out they're here, I reckon Tess's grandmother will close up the craft shop and make Tess come hunt them down.'

Marcus rubbed at his eyes. *This was not happening.*

'If any of these books go missing, and I find out who the thief is, I'll throw the book at them.' Marcus snatched the book out of Tanisha's hands again and haphazardly threw it at the bookshelf to prove his point.

Days like this, he missed big city policing. Instead, he was stuck in this small town, dealing with staff who were more like a group of girl guides!

Nothing too exciting ever happened in this town.

Well, not since his best mate Connor came back, and they had that bomb scare at the school a few weeks back.

That school scene was history now, because the outback rumour mill would be churning at full speed, spinning the story of how the small-town hermit of the notorious Peddler family scored a collection of romance novels and died.

TWO

'Oh, for the love of vodka! I can't believe we're in the middle of the outback. It's the middle of nowhere!' Felix's shrill voice bounced off the interior of the car. 'And they have cows. Real cows! I'm expecting someone to start milking one any minute now. And those toilets at that last roadhouse must be where cleaning products go to die.' Felix snatched up the hand sanitizer from his man bag and rubbed on the clear liquid.

'You didn't have to come with me.' Wren gripped the steering wheel. They'd been driving alongside a train line for hours, chasing down the highway's white line that disappeared in the curve on the horizon. It was the only sign of civilisation among this arid countryside of olive-green and silver-leafed scrubby trees punching through the ochre dirt, pinned by a towering blue sky. The enormity of the surrounding outback made them seem so small. What's worse, they hadn't seen another vehicle for hours.

'Listen, Toots, I will not leave you alone in this time of need. You need me, whether you like it or not.'

'I would've been fine.' She was used to roaming solo.

'Now you might be, but later …' Felix wagged his finger at her. 'I'll be there to hold your hand. To pick you up when you fall, and to make coffee in the morning. I'm here to protect you from who-knows-what is out here in the middle of nowhere.'

'You? Protect me?' Wren smiled. Her first smile in days. 'The queen who squealed from the roadhouse toilet because of an incy-wincy spider.'

'It was horrid! That spider was huge. You could've put a saddle on it to ride out on the filth of the place,' Felix said with wide eyes. 'I'm not like you, Toots. I don't do rugged adventures into the wilderness that involve hazardous outback loos or fighting off man-eating spiders. I'll die if I see any snakes. Just die.'

Wren's smile grew into a wide grin, almost feeling an urge to laugh. She was glad Felix had barged his way into this car, refusing to leave. 'Did you pack the coffee?'

'I packed that first, my hand lotions second. Who knows what they'll have here—wherever here is?' Felix tossed his thumb at the wide, flat countryside. 'It's a shame you wouldn't let me bring the coffee machine. It wouldn't have taken up much room.'

She glanced to the backseat, crowded with matching suitcases. 'I brought two bags. You, my glamour queen, brought eight.'

'Hello, I didn't know what I was packing for. I believe in being prepared.'

'You could have stayed in Sydney.'

'Toots, we never get to spend any quality time together, what with us both being so busy with life. And this is what best friends do — support each other.'

'I appreciate it.' Even if guilt was killing her for not being here sooner; she couldn't be late, not now. Wren rolled her shoulders. She'd been on edge ever since she'd heard the news that began the race to get here.

But for Felix to leave his home, that was huge. It still

surprised her that Felix had crammed all his luggage into the car without an invite. 'Why did you insist on coming?'

'I needed a break. A time out.'

'The club?'

He squeezed a dab of moisturising cream on his hands and began to methodically rub it in working on the nails, cuticles, then through to the back of his hands. 'The club. Reggie. Everything. Even if I'm so out of my comfort zone in—where are we again?'

'Northern Territory.'

'It's big ... And empty.' They stared out the window as the road rolled ahead. 'Why did you decide to come out here?'

'I promised Rowan I would. I was originally going to be here a few weeks from now, just ...' This was nothing like they'd planned.

'How come you never told me about this guy?'

'I did.'

'You told me he was your male advisor.'

'He is—was.' Wren gripped the steering wheel tighter.

'I know you prefer flying solo and rarely get close to people, but this guy must mean a lot for you to catch a boat, a helicopter, two decent planes, and one tiny god-knows-how-that-thing-flew for an aeroplane. Crossing countless time zones and oceans just to get here.' Then he breathed.

'We're not there yet.' Again, she checked her gold watch. The days all seemed to roll into one, ever since the phone call that seemed like a century ago. But in three days— well, four considering the time zones, she was here. 'I don't want to be late; I owe it to the guy.'

She grabbed the map for the hundredth time, driving along the one and only highway that cut through the Northern Territory. Surely, they couldn't get lost, could they? Ha, it was pretty much the story of her life, getting lost to find a story.

'*We have a sign!*' Felix's voice bounced around the compact car's interior as he pointed to the road ahead. 'Please tell me it's civilisation?'

The tall sign said:

WELCOME TO ELSIE CREEK

Wren leaned closer to the steering wheel. Beyond the small rise in the road, shining like a single solar panel in the sun, was the small town of Elsie Creek.

They were here.

A siren blasted the air as blue and red lights flashed behind them from a slick police car. It moved fast, considering her own speed.

'Where did that cop come from?' Wren slowed down. 'Felix, you're supposed to be keeping a lookout.'

'Don't blame me for your speeding. They really must hide behind the bushes out here because I didn't see that car.'

'Dammit.' She hit the steering wheel as she pulled to the side of the road. 'We're going to be late!'

'Calm down, Toots. You don't want to get arrested. People go missing out here and get chopped up into meat pies or—'

'Felix, enough!' Wren scowled at her side mirror, because she hadn't been able to look at her rear-view mirror ever since Felix claimed the passenger seat.

'*Hubba-hubba.*' Felix fanned his face while staring at the rear-view mirror.

'I can't believe you said hubba-hubba.'

'Blame it on all this outback dust I'm sniffing, but that ...' Felix pointed at the officer coming alongside, '... is one heavenly hot tamale.'

As the electric window rolled down, she had to recoil

from the ferocious wave of scorching heat that rose from the tarmac. It was potent.

'Your driver's licence, please,' requested the policeman.

'Well, hello there, Officer.' Felix waved his fingers in the air as if playing an imaginary piano.

Wren dug around in her bag and pulled out her international driver's licence and the rental car details. After handing them over she sat drumming her fingers on the steering wheel. She didn't have time for this.

'Any reason for the speed, Miss Sumney?' The officer riffled through her paperwork.

Wren removed her sunglasses and faced the officer. He was huge, broad shouldered, with a police cap and dark sunglasses. She couldn't see much more than that because the sun was in her eyes.

'A funeral.' She knew she'd done wrong, so why not cop it sweet from the cop. 'Look, I'm sorry I was speeding, I just don't want to be late.'

'Whose funeral?'

'Rowan Peddler's.'

'That's not on until two o'clock.'

'It's one-thirty now and I don't know how far it is to get there.' She frowned at her watch, ticking away every precious second.

'No, it's only twelve-thirty.'

'It can't be. I changed my watch when we landed at the airport.'

'You're probably jet lagged and mucked up the times, Toots. You should've let me drive and navigate with that map thingy.'

Wren whipped around to face Felix. 'You haven't driven a car since you got your licence. And you don't know how to read a map unless it involves a floor plan of the Dolce & Gabbana spring collection.'

'I have too driven since I got my licence.' Felix lifted his chin. 'Once. It was that drag queen's pink Cadillac.'

'In the deserted car park next to your club.'

'You wouldn't know what day it is without me.'

'I do too. Today's the funeral!' She slammed her hand on the steering wheel.

'*Okay, you two, cut it out!*' The police officer's voice was powerful and full of authority, snapping them into silence. 'Out of the car.' He opened the driver's door. 'You both need to cool off.'

'Well, that's a bit ironic ...' mumbled Wren, getting out of the car, feeling the full brunt of the outback heat. Were they going to get arrested? And what was it that Felix had said about getting chopped up into meat pies?

THREE

'Tourists who aren't used to driving long hours need to take a break and stretch their legs. Otherwise, they get hypnotised by that white line on the road, suffer with fatigue and cause an accident.' Marcus had attended way too many accidents caused by road fatigue.

Marcus marched the pair of tourists to the space between their rental car and his police car. 'Stay right there.'

He went back to his car, scooped out the ticket book. Glancing back, he watched the pair dressed in black fancy city clothes, like funeral clothes.

But the woman.

The woman …

Wren Sumney was a stunning mirage on a deserted outback highway. He had to be dreaming.

In a black dress that perfectly outlined every smooth curve of her body, man, that lady had curves that went on forever. Her blonde hair in a twist, with a few loose curls surrounding her fine face. But her eyes. Damn.

It'd been a long time since he'd seen a woman like that. Especially out here.

And for a man who was used to surprises as part of his

job, nothing could have prepared him for this.

Breathe, buddy, she's just a ticket.

'Are you going to arrest us?' The male passenger asked, clutching onto Wren's hand, using her body as a shield.

While Wren just openly glared at him.

'No.' Marcus suppressed his grin. 'But you'll get a ticket.' He forced himself to look away from the woman, to flick open the ticket book. 'I need an address if you're staying in town.'

'I'll get it.' Wren had a walk that made his heart stop. With her heels click-clacking on the highway, her sashaying hips and long legs were worth the watch.

'I'm Felix, by the way. From Sydney ...'

Marcus ignored the other man. His head tilted as Wren leaned into the car, the hem of her dress rising. Everything else was forgotten...

The door slammed shut, ripping him awake from his daydream.

'Here's the printout of my booking. It's a B&B something.' Her soft perfume was like a cloud of feminine heaven.

'That's Mrs Ludcombe's place. Are you staying there?' He had to know more—no, he needed to know everything. 'Are you really going to Rowan Peddler's funeral?'

'Yes, to both. Is it really twelve-thirty?'

Again, he had to tear his eyes away from her to show his watch face. 'It's twelve-forty.'

Wren removed her fine gold-banded wristwatch to adjust the time. Same as her passenger. They were telling the truth.

'How do you know Rowan Peddler?'

'Well, sugar, it's a long story—'

'Sergeant.' Marcus was no one's sugar, especially another man's.

'Isn't it unusual for a sergeant to do traffic? Out here …' Wren's voice was sweet and syrupy like honey, but it probably hid the deadly sting of a thousand bees.

'Normally.' Marcus had only come out here to do paperwork in the car, because the station's chatter was all about Rowan Peddler's funeral today, wondering if any strangers would show …

He inhaled her feminine scent. He'd never forget it; if only he had the words to describe it.

Then he realised she'd changed the subject on him. Marcus ripped off the yellow ticket sheet, passing it to Wren. 'How do you know Rowan Peddler?'

'Six hundred and twenty dollars! Are you kidding me? How fast was I going?'

'You were doing one-sixty clicks.'

'It's an open highway, no speed limit.'

'That ended ten kilometres back, coming down to one-ten.' Everyone ignored that road sign, especially when they saw no signs of civilisation. 'So you were doing fifty over the speed limit. Just down the road it drops to eighty, then forty because of the pesky town water buffalo.'

'Water buffalo?' The tourists asked.

'It wears ribbons, you can't miss him. Cecil's harmless, and no one wants to see him hurt.' Damned buffalo was getting super-pampered after his gun wound.

'Okay … But why so much?' She waved her ticket at him.

'I could send you to court, where you'd lose your international licence and pay a minimum of five thousand in court fines. I'm doing you a favour, lady.'

'Okay, okay …' Trying to control her anger, her daggered look just got sexier. And with the sun reflecting off her hair like a halo, she was a damned hot, angry angel. 'I can pay for it now if you have some credit card machine handy.'

'You can do that at the station. I'd appreciate it if you paid before you left town.' Surprised at how calm he sounded, considering how the heat was getting to him. Or was it her?

'So, am I free to go?' She slipped on her sunglasses, crossing her arms over her chest, which only made her cleavage deepen.

Down, boy.

'Yeah …' Marcus cleared his throat. 'Be sure to watch the speed limits in town.'

'Oh, we will, Sergeant. You can count on us, Sergeant.' Felix pushed Wren towards the car, opening the driver's door for her. 'Thank you, Sergeant. It was nice to meet you.'

Wren said nothing, slamming the driver's door shut. The car pulled away and through the side mirror she flipped him the bird.

Marcus chuckled. It wasn't the first time.

But again, she'd avoided answering his question—how she did know Rowan Peddler?

FOUR

The small chapel rose from the sunburnt soil, its normally empty car park was packed with utes, bikes, tractors, four-wheel drives, boat trailers, and even some saddled horses.

Marcus watched over it all as he stood with Porter by the chapel's front doors.

'Hi, Marcus.' Emelia, the perky blonde, waved as she skipped up the path to the church.

'Emelia.' Marcus rolled his eyes behind his dark sunglasses.

'It's a great turnout for the hermit—I mean, a man who didn't talk to anyone.' Emelia waved at others as if this was the social event of the century. 'What's going to happen to the Peddler property, and to Sandfly?'

'Not my concern.' Marcus stepped away from her.

'Otis never told me if there was a will,' Porter said. 'He was too busy to answer the door.'

Marcus frowned. 'What time did you go around?'

'Just after lunch.'

'Otis doesn't talk to anyone when he's watching *Days of Our Lives*. Everyone knows that. He hasn't missed an episode in ten years,' said Emelia in that irritating know-it-all tone.

Marcus took another step away from the perky blonde.

'But how does a man like Rowan Peddler end up with those autographed romance novels?' Emelia tapped her chin like she was working on some Einstein theory. 'It has everyone talking ...'

Marcus shook his head, watching the locals. People from all walks of life had shown up in their cowboy hats, church hats, straw hats, and assorted baseball caps. The farmers, cattle station owners, stockmen, and assorted townies were all here. But what was unusual in the mix was the large number of fishermen.

Deep from the mangroves they'd emerged, the commercial crabbers and the net-hauling barra fishermen, along with the many serious anglers who loved the sport of fishing. They'd all shown up wearing deeply tanned leathery skin, assorted polarised sunglasses, board shorts, and long-sleeved protective fishing shirts along with the Territory's staple of the double-plugger thongs. Although some bothered to wear shoes for the occasion.

It was a big turnout for someone who never talked to anyone.

Stewart weaved through the crowd, shaking hands and patting backs, then jumped up the steps to join Marcus. 'Nice uniform.'

Marcus checked his tie. It'd been a while since he'd worn the full-dress blues. The jacket was too hot, and the peak cap was just as bad for this climate. But he wasn't the only one suffering in full-dress uniform. Nearby, showing off his assorted service medals, was the town's fire chief, Jax, and some of his crew. 'I see you dragged the tie out, too, Doctor.'

'Let's hope Kat doesn't give me another lecture on it.' Stewart stroked his necktie, nodding towards the crowd. 'I've only seen the crabbers once, when they all got food poisoning from their new cook. I can't believe they're here. Isn't it fishing season?'

'Mm-hmm.' Marcus watched everyone from behind his dark shades.

'Wait, dumb question. It's always fishing season in the Territory's Top End. Home to the mighty barra.'

Marcus gave a quick chuckle. 'You sound like a tour guide.'

'I'll always be the tourist around here, counting down the days until my contract ends,' said Stewart. 'Did you find the next of kin?'

'Nope. But there are a couple of strangers in town.' Marcus nodded at the hire car, just parking by the front gate.

'Whoa …' Stewart paused the slow rock on his boot heels. 'Who is that?'

'Wren and Felix from Sydney.'

The strangers wove through the assorted cars, trucks and horses, then through the crowd that stopped talking to stare. A few men angled their heads as Wren climbed the steps in that dress that showed off every smooth curve of her beguiling body.

'Miss Sumney.' Marcus nodded, grateful for the sunglasses and police hat, allowing him to have a really good look. He loved that dress.

'Sergeant. Is the open casket still …' Wren grimaced at the church doors.

'It's open. Do you want to go in?'

She barely nodded.

The handle was hot against his palm as he opened the door for her.

'Thanks.' She paused for a moment, then with a deep breath, she walked inside with Felix beside her.

'How do you know her?' Stewart asked.

'I gave Wren a speeding ticket when she drove into town.'

'Are you insane?'

'She was speeding. And it's my job.'

'How do they know Rowan Peddler?'

'Don't know, she keeps avoiding the question. But I aim to find out.'

FIVE

'That sergeant's hot. And so was that blond next to him. What did you think?' Felix asked Wren as their eyes adjusted to the dim light.

'I didn't notice.' But she noticed this small church with its hard wooden floors, and the open casket waiting at the front.

'You what? Are you blind?'

'In case you hadn't noticed, we're at a funeral and not at a nightclub to pick up.'

Felix's eyes widened. 'I'm not going near no dead body. No siree. Not me. You said a funeral, not a viewing.' He grabbed her arm. 'We can wait back here with the sergeant.'

'I have to do this.' Wren pried Felix's fingers from her arm, then took a shaky breath. She didn't want to do this either, but she had to. Each step was like walking on a tightrope over a steep canyon in a dance with destiny.

But then she saw him, Mr Rowan Peddler.

'I made it, like I promised, but you were supposed to be waiting for me. You were supposed to play tour guide for me, not this …' He looked so peaceful.

She hiccupped as sorrow filled her chest; gravity had never felt so heavy.

Wren unclasped her long necklace, which held a small black bauble. It was a compass that never worked. Hanging like a black Christmas ornament, it spun on the end of the chain reflecting the light streaming through the stained-glass windows.

She placed the compass between his hands. 'My gift, from the girl who enjoys getting lost, hoping this will help you find where you need to go, so you'll never lose your way …'

Gently, she kissed Rowan's forehead. Tears squeezed from her eyes as she nodded at the waiting priest.

Felix held out some tissues as she sat beside him in the front row, as the last of the locals filed in and the service began.

It was a short service, the priest inviting those gathered to say a few words. But nobody did. Then the sergeant, in full dress blues, with other police officers and firemen, gathered around the casket.

Cupping her hand over her mouth, again the tears spilled when the sergeant shared a soft yet sad smile with her as they carried the casket from the chapel.

She was kicking herself for being rude to the guy over the speeding ticket, when he was only doing his job. But how was this part of their job description?

The rest was a blur as tears welled and the casket was lowered into the ground. Someone else spoke, and then it was done.

With head down, her shoulders ached, she was so, so tired. The guilt of not being here sooner made her stomach churn. 'Have they all gone, Felix?'

'Most of them have, yeah.' Felix dabbed at the corner of his eyes. 'Funerals are so sad.'

Wren dug around in her bag and pulled out a packet of tobacco, papers, and lighter. She dropped them on top of the casket. 'Here's that drink and smoke I promised you. Even though I'd been telling you to quit smoking for years.' She unscrewed the lid on a hipflask and poured a nip onto the casket, then a sip for herself. 'Felix?'

'Heck, yeah.' Felix snatched the flask and drank deeply, only to gasp in horror. '*Ugh*. It's bourbon. You don't drink bourbon. Rum and vodka, yes, but not bourbon.'

'Rowan loved his bourbon.' She took another sip, then emptied the rest on the grave. 'Told him I'd have a drink at his funeral.' But it wasn't supposed to be like this, not when she'd expected to share another four decades with the guy, because fifty-seven was way too young for an active man like Rowan.

'Er, excuse me, Miss?' The Aboriginal man removed his wide-brimmed hat, to rake fingers through his black curls streaked with grey. 'You're Wren. He told me you'd come. He said you would.'

'I promised Rowan I would.'

He pressed his hat against his chest, and pointed at the gravesite 'Like I promised him somethin' too, Miss. My name is Darryl. Two-dollar Darryl.'

'It's nice to meet you.' She shook his hand.

'You gotta second?'

'I'll be over here trying to find a mobile signal.' Felix graciously gave them space with a look that said, *you have to tell me everything after.*

'How can I help you, Darryl?'

'I'm here to help you. I swore to the man I would.'

'Why?'

'I live on the Peddler property. I've been workin' for the Peddler family for a long time.'

'I'm sorry for your loss.'

He shared such a sweet smile, marred only by the sadness in his eyes. 'Did you know he was sick, Miss?'

'Rowan never told me. Did you know?'

Darryl nodded. 'He talked about you all the time, but he also wanted to keep you hush-hush.'

'What do you mean?'

'He didn't die of no natural causes, Miss. He was counting down the days for your visit.' Darryl paused to check they were alone, then stepped in closer and whispered, 'Sorry to say this, Miss, but the man was murdered.'

Wren tried to swallow the hard lump stuck in her throat.

'Rowan gave me a letter to give to you if he didn't make it, but you can only get it if you come to Sandfly. It's what he wanted.'

'How do I get there?' And what was Sandfly?

'When you come to the house, we'll show you. It's what he wanted, Miss.' Darryl pointed to the coffin. 'He was family to me; a brother, who asked we keep this a secret until I give you that letter. I'll come find you at the house in a day or two.' He put on his weathered cowboy hat, gave a quick nod, and walked away.

Felix scooted over to tug on Wren's sleeve. 'What was that all about?'

'I don't know?' Did she hear that right? Rowan Peddler was murdered?

SIX

'Do we have to do this, Felix?' Wren was still spinning over the conversation with Darryl.

'Yes, we're here now.' Felix pulled open the heavy front door of the outback pub, which towered over the town's main intersection. It sat opposite the railway station and across the road from the hardware store that led to the main street of Elsie Creek. And what a tiny town it was, she could see the last shop where the road disappeared on the horizon, where she had to fight against the urge to jump into her hire car and forget everything Darryl had said.

Sadly, there was still more work to be done. 'I'm meeting some guy named Otis here.' Removing her sunglasses, she entered the Elsie Creek Hotel.

Felix froze, with his wild eyes darting around the room, gripping onto her arm. 'You've got to protect me here, Toots. At all costs.'

'Huh?'

'Me, against them.' Felix nodded at a sea of cowboy hats.

'I've never seen so many cowboys, except for rodeos.'

'I luv 'em, but I don't think they'll love me.' Felix pursed his lips together. For the flamboyant man, this was well out of his comfort zone. It's why he never left Sydney.

'I've got your back, babe. You'll surprise yourself and fit right in.' She hooked her arm through his. 'Let's find a quiet spot at the bar. Or better yet, let's leave.' She turned around and bumped into the large chest of another man. 'Sorry,' mumbled Wren, when she looked up and frowned, recognising the sergeant without his uniform. 'Sorry, Sergeant.'

'Still ticked at me about the ticket?'

She winced. What possessed her to give this cop the bird like that? 'I'm sorry, I'm just cranky from the lack of sleep.'

'Jet lag?'

'I think so. Look, I understand you were just doing your job, Sergeant.'

'Please, call me Marcus and this is Stewart. He's one of the town's doctors.'

Wren hadn't even noticed the other guy; all she saw was Marcus. Big. Strong. Marcus. The inner strength and power just emanated from the guy like some unseen force. It was deliciously intoxicating. She had to look to her trusty friend for some sort of rescue.

Felix dived right in with his smile lighting up the room. 'Hi, I'm Felix from Sydney, and this is Wren. Well, you already knew that didn't you, Sergeant? I mean, Marcus.' Felix eagerly shook the two men's hands.

'Did you know Rowan Peddler?' Wren asked the doctor.

'He was my patient.'

'Huh …' Wren narrowed her eyes at the men. Grief was clouding her judgement—or was it what Darryl had said earlier? 'So, we have the investigating officer and the man who signed the death certificate.' Did she have the courage to dare ask about the details of Rowan's death?

No, today was about celebrating the life of a man. 'I need a drink.'

SEVEN

'You really ticked her off with that speeding ticket,' Stewart muttered to Marcus, watching Wren walk away.

She had a walk that made Marcus want to follow. Which was unusual, because Marcus followed no one—unless it was for work.

'Oh, don't mind Wren,' piped in Felix. 'She's a tonne of fun once you get to know her. When it doesn't involve funerals and …' Felix's face dropped as if the mask had melted.

'Are you okay, Felix?' Marcus had seen Two-dollar Darryl talking with Wren at the gravesite. It had been a short conversation that had left Wren somewhat stunned. 'Did you know Rowan Peddler?'

'Me, no.' Felix shook his head, stepping away from them. 'I'll go find that drink now. Tootles.' Felix scurried away like a rabbit, weaving his way through the crowd towards Wren.

At the bar's far corner, Wren was in a lowered head conversation with the menacing front bar manager, Mean-Rene, with her heavily inked arms crossed over her leather vest, frowning at Wren.

But it was more of a surprise when Mean-Rene nodded and smiled at Wren while taking a white envelope. Then, without missing a beat, Mean-Rene poured a beer with one hand while passing the white envelope to the young publican, Samantha.

Samantha opened the envelope, then slid it into the back pocket of her jeans and gave a nod to both Mean-Rene and Wren.

What was the deal there?

Marcus made his way to the bar, keen to find out.

Wren got her drink and passed one to Felix as Mean-Rene pointed towards the back doors that led to the beer garden. And just like that, Wren disappeared outside.

Again, the temptation to follow her was strong. Marcus wanted answers to the questions Wren was avoiding.

Instead, he paused to lean his arm against the bar. Wren wasn't a victim of crime, and he had no reason to think she was a criminal. He just didn't know who she was, or why he was so keen to follow her.

'Hello, Marcus. It's a rare day to see you in my front bar.' Samantha, the young publican, placed a cold schooner in front of him.

'The wake's here.'

'So, it is. Did you have much to do with Rowan Peddler?'

'No. You?'

Samantha gave a wry smile. 'It's a small town, Sarge.'

Some days it was too small. 'Can I ask what that woman gave you in that envelope?'

'Wren?'

Marcus nodded.

Samantha pulled out the envelope and opened it up. 'A thousand in cash.'

'What for?'

'To anyone who wants to have a drink for Rowan Peddler. Consider your next beer on the lady. I heard you and your other officers carried the coffin. Why?'

'The priest called me. Rowan was the last Peddler and a veteran.' As soon as he'd heard no one was there to plan Rowan's funeral, Marcus volunteered to be there with full-dress blues, putting out the call to see if anyone would join him. Rowan Peddler deserved some show of respect for serving his country.

'That Wren must be a someone to the Peddler family to do this ...' Samantha held up the cash filled envelope.

Marcus frowned and grabbed his beer, determined to find out.

EIGHT

'Toots, where are we going?' Felix followed Wren past the shady verandah and pool tables, to where large tables and chairs were scattered across a lush green lawn that met dusty paddocks and distant sloping hills.

Various groups of men, women, and children of all ages happily mingled. It was obviously a tight-knit community where everyone knew everyone else.

'I needed to get away from the bar.' Too many people were staring, and Wren hated being in the limelight. 'The barmaid told me to check this place out.'

Felix screwed his nose at the tall fence that contained some sort of a pond. 'Tell me this isn't some special outback beauty bath for tourists?'

'It's a croc cage.'

'What?' Felix took a step back as Wren stepped in closer. 'At a pub?'

Wren pointed to the attached sign that said *Karma, the saltwater crocodile.*

'Why are they keeping a man-eating crocodile where children are playing?' Felix pointed at the children on the lawns, their laughter echoing across the grounds. 'Oh, I love the tutus. I've never seen so many.'

Wren grinned at the assorted boys and girls, playing like children do, but all of them were wearing tutus. 'That's so cool.'

'Makes me want to fetch my tutu and tiara from the cupboard, kick off my shoes and go play with them.'

'You can.'

'Er, no. Not with this crowd. So, what's with the penned beast? Can you see it?' Felix peered through the mesh to the large circular pond, its calm surface reflecting the sky.

'It might be at the bottom? But I've heard about Karma.'

'Did Rowan tell you?'

Wren nodded. 'They found Karma in a private dam that didn't have much food left, just water. So the townspeople came together and built this pen to keep him safe.'

'Why, if it's a wild animal?'

'He's missing a front foot, and being injured like that, the other crocodiles fighting for territory would've killed him.'

'Is that why he hid in that dam?'

Wren shrugged, peering at the water. 'Look at the bottom, he's just lying there.'

They leaned against the mesh to peer at the mammoth beast resting on the bottom of the pond like a cement statue.

'Is he dead?' whispered Felix. 'He looks dead. There's no bubbles, nothing.'

'You've gotta be a flamin' Peddler,' said a male voice behind them.

'Excuse me?' Wren turned to face an old man wearing a felt hat. He reminded her of a forties jazz player, complete with snappy suspenders he hoisted higher onto his shoulders.

'You're a Peddler.' He swaggered closer, wagging his

stubby finger at her. 'I can see it in you, girlie. You've got that same tall lanky build and them dead straight shoulders, just like Rowan Peddler. And just like Ol' Pop Peddler, too.' He leaned in close with sparkly eyes among the deep sun-kissed crinkles. 'Are you as cunning as the rest of the Peddlers?'

'Wren's smart,' said Felix. 'But she's not a Peddler.'

'I'm a Sumney.'

'Nah, you can see it. You're a Peddler, you've even got their nose and blue eyes. Like pale sea-glass blue. They all had it. I know …' He tapped on his nose. 'I kept thinking you looked familiar, wondering where I'd seen you before. It's because you're a Peddler. Am I right?'

Wren grinned. 'I'm Wren. Rowan was my father.'

Felix snorted for air. 'Why didn't you tell me?'

'And me when I asked earlier?' added Marcus.

Where did Marcus come from? 'Would I have gotten out of that speeding ticket?'

He shrugged and sipped his beer.

'It's a pleasure to meet you, Wren. We were worried there were no Peddlers left.' With both hands, he heartily shook Wren's hand. 'I'm Billy. I live here at the pub, I'm the yardie who does the cleaning up after this mob.'

'You must be up at dawn,' said Felix. 'The cleaners in my club start at daylight.'

'I am. Is this ya fella?' Billy shook hands with Felix.

'I'm Felix from Sydney, I'm the best friend who feels like I'm missing something.'

'Later. Promise,' she whispered to Felix, returning her attention to Billy. 'Did you know my family?'

'Everyone knew the Peddlers. Your grandfather, Ol' Pop Peddler was a proper rascal. He would've kept your hands full, if you'd been working as a cop in this town back then, Marcus.'

'How long ago are we talking about?' Marcus asked.

'Long time. Ol' Pop Peddler didn't mind a tipple or two and would have Two-dollar Darryl to drive him home.'

'Do you know this Darryl?' Wren asked, 'Is he someone to trust?'

'Heck, yeah. Two-dollar Darryl would do anything for the Peddlers, and the Peddlers trusted him like family.' Billy pointed at the crocodile's enclosure. 'It was your father who gave the largest donation to build this fancy croc-cage. We all built it. But then he went and surprised the heck outta us by showing up with a mob of rocks that he personally planted on the roof of the croc cave.'

'Why?' Wren asked.

'Rowan reckoned that this croc needed a cave, complete with a rock garden to make him feel at home, like in the wild. Only prettier. Your grandmother had a thing for bromeliads, that's what's planted there. Did you meet her?'

Beyond the pond, stood a domed concrete cave with rocks making up the rockery roof garden. Striped and spotted patterns spread across the tropical plants stiff leaves that looked like the spiky heads of a pineapple. From their centres they gave a showy display of unusual flowers in bright bold colours to beautify the home of a deadly animal. 'No, I didn't meet her.'

'Mrs Peddler was a good woman who lived a hard life. Lung cancer got her, same as your father.' Billy removed his hat. 'I'm sorry for your loss, Miss.'

'Thank you.'

'If there's anything you need, you come see me. I didn't mind Rowan Peddler, he helped me out a lot over the years. Never asked for anything back or said anything to anyone. He was a quiet man, that one.' Billy plonked his hat on his head and flicked his suspenders higher onto his shoulder. 'Do you wanna see him?'

'Who?'

'Karma?'

'Sure, I'm keen.'

'Didn't the Park Ranger put Karma on a diet and restrict his feeding times?' Marcus leaned his beefy shoulder against the fence, in a T-shirt that showed off the outline of his complex muscles. His cologne was such a fresh and spicy scent of woodsy cedar and a peppery lavender, Wren had to stop herself from leaning into his body heat to inhale deeply.

'You're not in uniform now, Sarge.' Billy wore a trickster's shine to his eyes, pulling out a plastic ziplock bag from his back pocket, filled with dark brown strips like dried bacon. 'Me and this croc are the same age, accordin' to the local croc wrangler.'

'How old's that?'

'Never too old to dance with the ladies.' Billy gave her a scamp's wink.

Wren smiled; it came easily this time.

'Now me and Karma are old mates, on account of my homemade beef jerky.' Billy shook his plastic bag.

'Did you make this?' Felix pointed at the bag.

'You wanna try some? It's nothin' fancy. My brother, Mickey, and me made big mobs. Here.' Billy held out the open pouch and Felix daintily grabbed a slice. 'Miss?'

'Sure.' Wren took a piece. Surprised at the rough dry texture that had a strong smoked hickory beef flavour. 'Yum.'

Marcus also took a piece. 'Billy makes a good jerky. You smoke it with your brother?'

'Yep, out back of the airport hangar. It's a family recipe. Karma loves the stuff.' Billy raised his finger to his lips. 'Shh, don't tell anyone or they'll all be doing it, and then we'll have that new park ranger on our backs over an obese crocodile.'

'Can crocodile's get obese?' Felix asked Billy.

'Who knows? But Karma is special, he can predict the future.'

'Nooo,' gushed Felix.

'Karma picked the winner of the AFL grand finals, the winners of the Melbourne Cup, and our local Stockman's Cup.'

'Is that true?' Wren asked Marcus, who was heartily tearing at his jerky.

'You have to see it to believe it.'

Felix waved his slice of jerky in the air. 'Ooh, can we ask him if I'm going to marry Reggie?'

Wren struggled to swallow down the jerky. How self-absorbed was she to not know this. Felix didn't do adventures, preferring his silk pillows on his own bed, and super soft bath sheets in his massive bathroom. Felix never strayed past the surrounding suburbs of his club, until now. Felix was running away. 'Did Reggie ask?'

'He's hinting at it. But I don't know if it's for me, or the club.'

Billy looked around. 'Can't do that today, too many people. Another time we can.'

'You're on, Billy. I love my tarot card reader, so I'm down for a fortune-telling crocodile named Karma. Oh, and more of this jerky, it's divine.'

For the first time in days laughter bubbled inside Wren, she even smiled at Marcus, who smiled back. He was sweet. And big, broad, and just a beautiful man to carry her father's coffin like that. And he was mega-hot!

But she couldn't think like that. Not now.

'Here, watch this.' Billy rattled the fence and the large saltwater crocodile, resting on the floor of the deep and clear pool, shifted its long nose.

'Up you come, old fella. Come and meet the long-lost Peddler, her family paid for your plush palace.' Billy held out a thick slice of beef jerky over the water.

The crocodile pushed off the pond's floor to lazily swim in circles. The pond was deceiving, it was a lot deeper and wider than she realised.

'Should you have your arm over the fence like that, Billy?' Wren pointed to the sign that said *Danger! Man-eating Crocodile*.

'I don't keep it here for long. Karma's lightning quick and as cunning as your grandfather. He can jump higher than the rocks your father laid on the roof of that cave. *Here, fetch,* you great big lizard.' Billy tossed the jerky across the pond to land on the far side. 'That'll keep him busy.'

Karma was huge and scary enough for Felix to clutch onto her hand.

Effortlessly hauling his massive body out of the pond, the crocodile stretched over five-and-a-half metres long. His glistening thick scales, which ran from head to tail, wore a myriad of battle scars. Karma was terrifying.

'How heavy is Karma?' Wren asked Billy.

'Almost a tonne in weight, with the power to chow down on a human skull or them rocks like an ice cube.'

The beast had rows of teeth within its long jaw as it tossed the jerky into its mouth.

'They don't chew, you know,' Billy said.

'But all those teeth—' Felix pointed his piece of jerky at the crocodile.

'Nah, they swallow pebbles to do the digestive work in their guts. Your old man knew that.' Again, Billy tapped his nose. 'That's why Rowan Peddler delivered all of them rocks to help this croc digest his tucker, because their teeth are only designed for taking down their prey.'

'I've seen some of the local river crocs take down a full-grown water buffalo in seconds,' said Marcus.

Karma the crocodile lay in the sunshine, his mouth open, with the jerky resting on his tongue.

'What is he doing?' Wren leaned in closer, with Marcus and Felix doing the same.

Billy gave a low chuckle. 'Karma's sucking on it like a lolly.'

'No way.'

'He likes the flavour of it on his tongue or somethin'. It's the weirdest thing.'

'Who can blame him? This jerky is so delicious,' said Felix. 'Where can I buy some more?'

'Here, I've got plenty.' Billy thrust the plastic bag into Felix's hands. 'You can shout me a beer later.'

'You're on.'

'How long does Karma stay like that?' Wren was fascinated by the prehistoric beast.

'For hours. I reckon he meditates, like one of 'em Tibetan monks.' Billy again made her smile; he was the breath of fresh air she needed to lighten the heaviness of the day.

'Miss Sumney?'

Did everyone know who she was? She turned to face a middle-aged man with a sweaty face, pushing his round-rimmed glasses along his nose.

'I'm Otis. You're a hard woman to track down. I'm glad you made it.'

'Me, too.' After the four-day non-stop race to get here, she just wanted to be still for a moment.

'Can we talk?'

No. Wren wanted to chill with Billy, to drink beer, eat jerky, and watch a crocodile meditate. But she had to go.

'But, but …' Felix whined, sliding the pouch of jerky into his man bag. 'What about me?'

'Can't leave you behind.' She hooked her arm through Felix's. 'Thanks for that, Billy, and to you too, Marcus. I've put some money behind the bar for those who want to have a drink for Rowan. Please?'

'Don't mind if I do, Miss.' Billy tapped at his hat. 'You should come and have a beer with me and the Triple Js later, in the pub. Or you can find us at the hardware store during the week, cheating at cards. We've got plenty of stories to tell about the Peddlers, specially about that rascal Ol' Pop Peddler.'

'That sounds good, Billy.'

'Are you coming back?' Marcus asked her.

'I'd like to. But ...' She paused to glance back at Otis. 'I'll see how we go with this.'

NINE

After leaving Otis's home office, Wren and Felix strolled down the main street of Elsie Creek. A lone orange pedestrian crossing was the only set of traffic lights on a main street that hosted a small supermarket, a hardware store, a hairdresser, a craft shop, and a post office. No one else was around.

Music and assorted voices greeted them as they stood on the street corner by the hardware store, facing the towering pub. It was packed, as if the whole town was inside. 'Can we skip the pub?' Wren asked Felix.

'Why? I'm not scared to go inside anymore, we know people now.'

'I've had enough noise and people talking at me for the day.' Especially after Otis's dull drone, it was just like a high school teacher you struggled to listen to without falling asleep. Worse, when she needed to remember what he was telling her about Rowan's will.

What she remembered the most was that she was all that was left of her family.

Felix hooked his arm over her shoulders and gave her a squeeze. 'Look, there's a bottle shop on the corner. Let's have ourselves a little boozy picnic in the park by that train museum thingy.'

At the drive-thru bottle shop, rock music blared from the speakers, where a man stood in the main thoroughfare, feeding a water buffalo.

'What is that?' Felix gripped Wren's arm, pulling them to a stop.

'Oh, hey.' The guy with a deep suntan gave a crooked grin. 'You're the long-lost Peddler. Wren, right? I'm Luke, everyone calls me Bottle Shop Luke.'

'Hi, I'm Felix from Sydney.' Felix waved, while hiding behind Wren.

'What is that?' Wren pointed at the big black buffalo dressed in red and black ribbons like a mascot leading a street parade. Was this what Marcus had warned her about earlier?

'This is Cecil, who loves the ladies and has a thing for flowers. Go on, you can feed him, he's harmless.' Luke held out a handful of daisies.

'I'm keen.' Wren took the limp daisies and held them under the big shiny black nose of the water buffalo. Red ribbons wrapped around his blunted horns, with chalk writing along his sides that read:

Farewell to Rowan Peddler.
You'll be missed by all.

Tears welled as she grimaced a smile at the buffalo, his long, soft, black lashes shading sympathetic eyes. Cecil nudged his large forehead ever so gently against her arm, coaxing a giggle out of her.

'Hello, Cecil.'

The water buffalo sniffed, then plucked at the daisies to chew like a cow, never taking his eyes off her.

'Felix, do you want a go?' She held out the last of the daisies to her friend while stroking the buffalo's forehead.

'No. I'm fine over here, thank you.'

For a moment Wren forgot all her problems, as she hand-fed a water buffalo who licked at the white daisy petals spilt across his black lips. 'Does Cecil have a home, Luke?'

'Cecil belongs to my grandmother. We tried to keep him at home, but he's an escape artist who loves being with people. Cecil used to be a nuisance, until they gave him the job of sharing the town's news.' Luke's smile faltered at the chalked words spread across Cecil's broad back. 'I'm sorry for your loss.'

'Thank you. Did you know Rowan?'

'Rowan was a good man, he helped me out heaps.' Luke hooked his thumbs through the belt loops of his jeans. 'I had some trouble with my outboard and got stuck down river. Rowan was the only one in radio range that day and came in his boat with a case of cold beer to tow us all the way back to the town's boat ramp. Rowan never asked for anything in return. He refused. So if you ever need anything, Wren, let me know.'

'Thank you, Luke.'

'Hey, you're a Peddler, and they've been here for generations, so that makes you one of us. Besides, you've got the Sandfly. I'm sure we'll be good mates in no time.'

Luke gave Cecil a pat on the rump. 'Sunset big fella, time to head home to grandma.' With ribbons swinging off his long black tail, the water buffalo meandered down the road.

'So, um ...' Luke raked his fingers through his dusty brown hair. 'It might be too soon to ask, but what are you going to do about the Sandfly?'

She shrugged. 'I don't know what this Sandfly is.' Otis never mentioned Sandfly at all in the will. 'Two-dollar Darryl said he'd show me.'

'Well ...' Luke again shared that easy grin, showing the

dimple in his deeply tanned complexion. 'I'll leave that surprise for Two-dollar Darryl.'

Wren wanted to know now.

But then again, did she really need to know everything, considering the questions Darryl had raised over her father's death?

Murder, in this small town? A place that saved crocodiles and allowed pet water buffalos to wander its streets.

'Are you heading into the wake?' Luke asked Wren.

'We did earlier. I'm not in the mood for crowds after that long drive to get here.'

'I get you. Here, let me fix you up. Name your passion.' Luke tossed his thumb back to the row of glass-door fridges

'Oh, let's indulge. We are on holidays.' Felix opened fridges, as Luke loaded up a small foam esky with ice and drinks, even scoring them some glasses. What a champion.

They waved goodbye to Luke, crossed the road to the train station where there was a long stretch of green lawn beside a vintage train.

'Let's drink from the train.' Wren slipped off her heels and climbed the black metal ladder. 'This is so cool. I wonder if we can get to the roof?' She peered around the locomotive to find another small ladder. 'Pass me the esky.'

'I'm not built for mountain climbing, Toots.'

Wren pushed the esky along the short roof of the driver's cabin. 'Come on, I know you'll love it.'

Felix huffed and puffed, rolling up the cuffs on his shirt before slowly climbing. 'I don't even do the stair master at the gym, now look at what you have me doing.'

'But look at this view.' She pointed to town. 'Check out the roofs.'

'I-I-I … for once in my life have no words.'

They stood on the roof of the vintage locomotive,

which was situated on a small rise, giving them a grand view of the town's roofs spread before them, covered in spectacular two-dimensional cartoon-like characters.

'Is that a Mad Hatter having a tea-party on the train station roof?' Felix pointed to the nearby building that stood at the end of the lawn.

'It is …' Wren leaned down to read the large sign on the wall and laughed. 'It says *Tea-house Museum*.'

'So that snail racing over the roof with an envelope in its mouth is …'

'*The post office*.' Their laughter echoed within the deserted train station.

'The cracked spanner …' Wren pointed to the simple tool that was massive. 'It must be for the hardware store.'

'Oh, I love that retro woman in curlers. I bet that's for the hairdressers.' Felix shaded his eyes with his palm and pointed like a sea captain searching for land. 'Can you see that? Way over there. That's a Dalmatian peeing on a fire hydrant.'

'That must be where the fire station lives.' She loved the details in the artworks and the enormity of these hidden treasures.

Beside the fire station was a larger-than-life image of a man's bulging bicep, wearing a police uniform, nabbing a masked burglar.

'That's got to be the police station,' said Felix.

'The strong arm of the law.' And Marcus had very nice muscular arms indeed.

They sat on the metal roof of the train, still warm from the dying sun, legs dangling over the side, gazing at the scenery. Beyond the station's empty stockyard and the town's painted roofs, there was nothing but the open outback in all directions, with a massive sky displaying an impressive sunset.

'It's beautiful here.' Wren loosened the pins in her hair and let her shoulders relax.

Felix passed her a drink. 'Surprisingly, it is. I love those roofs, and the quirky croc, and that pretty painted buffalo that had eyelashes I'd kill for.' He then waved his cocktail at the sunset. 'But that is spectacular. An uninterrupted view of art and the outback. '

'It's impressive indeed.' It was like an outdoor museum that changed with the setting sun, which was slowly becoming nothing more than a distant ball of fire.

'How come you never told me Rowan was your father?'

She stirred her ice to mix her drink. 'I tried to tell you many times, but you were having some major drama with your father, banning all conversations to do with fathers, and Father's Day and—'

'Oops.'

'All good, we're allowed to have selfish moments.' She took a deep mouthful of the lemony vodka. 'Even though my mother made me believe that my father never wanted me, I always wanted one, hoping one day Mum would find me one.'

'Sorry, honey, but your mother was a nun against all things fun.'

Wasn't that the truth. No laughter, noise, or smiling were allowed within that humble abode.

'How did you find out?'

'When I went through the paperwork, cleaning out my mother's apartment.' It was another funeral with Felix by her side. She gave his hand a squeeze. 'It was on a private detective's report. I think Mum was going to contact Rowan, but chickened out.'

'What did you do? Call this guy up and say, *Hey, I'm your kid?*'

Wren grinned over the rim of her glass. 'With a bit more tact than that. We agreed to do a paternity test before we even met.'

'Why?'

'Because I didn't want to get emotionally attached to someone I wasn't related to.' She was so used to being a loner, with only Felix to report to, until Rowan came along. For the past ten years they'd shared a different kind of friendship, and now she'd been left behind to deal with the guilt and grief—it wasn't fair.

'And the tests came back ...'

'Ninety-nine point nine per cent positive. As soon as they confirmed the results, Rowan flew out to meet me in North Queensland. We hung out at Port Douglas, drinking rum at this bar overlooking the beach, getting to know each other.'

'Did you ever call him daddy?'

'Never. Dad, yes, but it took a while. I mean, it was a word I never thought I'd call anyone.' She sighed so heavily her shoulders slumped. 'I'd planned to visit this place in a few weeks. Rowan was going to take me fishing and four-wheel driving and other stuff ...' For some reason Rowan always flew out to see her.

'Did Rowan know your mother well?'

'No. He did say he remembered her, but I think he did that more to be polite. Come on, it was a one-night stand, and he'd been on a big drinking binge after some heavy training to get into a special forces division. Rowan finally got accepted and was celebrating before he left for his new posting the very next day.'

'Sounds special, this unit?'

'All I know is they did bunkers and tunnels or something in the jungle. Rowan didn't like to talk about it much.'

'Did he know about you?'

'No. My mother never told him.'

'But if Rowan did know ...' Felix let the question hang in the air.

'Rowan swears he would've provided for me; said he would've even shown up to my school graduations and stuff with my grandmother before she passed.' Everything she'd wished for as a child.

'Aww, that's so sweet.'

'Rowan was a sweet guy. I'll miss him.' Wren raised her glass to the last of the sunset. 'To Mr Rowan Peddler, a champion among men.' She patted her throat, naked without her compass. 'May you find where you need to go to rest in peace.'

They sipped their drinks, watching the last of the sunset. When darkness descended to reveal a supercity's skyline of stars.

'I've never seen so many stars, except for all those self-proclaimed stars in my club.' Felix craned his neck. 'What's the plan, Toots?'

'Tomorrow, I'm to collect the keys from the police station. I'd like to stay at the farmhouse.' She'd inherited the Peddler farm, a property that had been in her family for generations. Rowan had told her plenty of stories about the place, some not so good. Was that why he kept coming up with excuses to stop her from visiting sooner?

'How long are you planning on staying?'

'I don't know.'

'At least there's enough eye candy in this place to keep us entertained. Tell me you noticed Bottle Shop Luke? He was cute.'

'I didn't notice.'

'Are you serious?'

'I was patting a water buffalo, feeding him daisies. Not like that happens every day.'

'But what about the doctor, and the sergeant?'

'Meh.' Oh, she noticed Sergeant Marcus Moore all right. How could she miss his deep chest, broad shoulders, and muscular arms? But she couldn't afford to look any closer. She couldn't.

'It's obvious you're not yourself, Toots. So there's no way I'm leaving you all alone out here.'

'You don't have to.'

'I'm here now.' Felix nudged her with his elbow. 'Besides, I want to see what Karma predicts about Reggie.'

'Do you want to marry Reggie?'

'The pressure …' Felix groaned, dragging his hands down his face. 'He's talking about it all the time. I don't know if I'm ready.'

'You've been together for a while and Reggie makes you happy. But do get a pre-nuptial before you take the plunge.'

'Do you think I should?'

'That's up to you, but if you're hesitating now …'

'Ha. Look at me, taking relationship advice from the girl who practices the art of getting lost as a way to avoid committing to a long-term relationship.'

'Don't want one.' She preferred going solo. Less emotional stress that way.

'Liar.'

'Fine. I do want that special someone, I'm just scared of getting hurt.' *Again.*

'Listen, Toots, you just haven't found the right man strong enough to keep up with you. You'll want someone rugged enough to toss you over their shoulder like a caveman and grunt *mine*.'

Their laughter carried across the deserted train station, hidden in deep shadows.

'That's what *you* want.' Honestly, Wren didn't know what she wanted, which was probably why she was always searching for a home.

'I do. Yet, Reggie is as much of a weakling as me, and we have a lot in common. But you …' Again, his elbow gently nudged into her side.

She didn't want to think too far ahead, already emotionally drained as it was. 'Do you think we'll have fun in this town?'

'We've always made our own fun, wherever we go.'

'Yes, we do …' She raised her glass at the sleepy town. 'Hello Elsie Creek, it's so nice to meet you.'

TEN

'Now you be nice to the police sergeant and take a good look at the man while we're here.' From the passenger seat, Felix wagged his finger at Wren as they arrived at the police station. 'It's time you took the edge off the ice-queen routine.'

Wren gazed at the station's roof, unable to see the painting of the Strong Arm of the Law from this angle. 'Ice queen?'

'Cold and unemotional. The cook at the B&B told me over breakfast your father was like that.'

'I'm shy, not cold. And I like my privacy, not like you, my glamour queen.'

'Why hide my fabulousness?' Felix waved his hand in a flourished bow as the sliding doors opened to the station. 'Now you play nice Kitty Kat and for the love of vodka and cherry-lime, check him out.'

'The long-lost Peddler returns. Hi, Wren, and Felix from Sydney. I'm Tanisha,' said the Indigenous officer seated behind the counter, with a wide smile and plump cheeks. 'I was hoping to talk to you at the wake, yesterday, but you disappeared.'

'Big day. Lots of driving,' said Felix.

'Here to pay for your speeding ticket, Wren?'

'Oops, I nearly forgot.' Wren dug around in her bag for the yellow ticket.

'Wren's also here to check out the sergeant of hotness.'

'I am not.'

'And so you should.' Tanisha arched her perfectly manicured eyebrows at them. 'Marcus is damned fine to look at.'

Plonking his elbows on the counter, Felix rested his chin on his hands. 'Ooh, I'm hearing ya. Those arms. And that steely stare, it's sexy!'

'I hadn't noticed.' Wren swiped her credit card along the machine that Tanisha presented to her.

'Did your heartbeat and pulse die too?' exclaimed Tanisha.

Wren's jaw dropped at the comment from the woman she'd just met.

'Wren's had a lot on her mind lately, I'm sure she'll look today. Won't you, Toots?'

Wren grimaced at the pair.

The pay machine hummed, and a green light blinked on its dashboard, sending the printer to whirl into action.

'Here's your receipt. Please take care driving in town, we have a precious pet pygmy water buffalo to watch out for.'

'We met Cecil last night,' said Felix. 'He's got the most divine eyelashes I'd kill for. But yours are just as luscious, Tanisha. Real or extensions?'

'They're all mine.' Tanisha fluttered her long lashes with pride. They were impressive.

'Can I speak to the sergeant, please?' Wren wanted her keys. 'I believe I'm expected. Otis made the appointment.'

'Only if you promise to check him out.'

'I told Wren she also had to check out that hunky

doctor, too.' Felix nodded like his head was on a stick.

'The Hot Doc is what we call Stewart. They're both single, you know.' Tanisha jumped off her stool from behind the high reception desk.

It was a small station with their staff room in the reception area, where assorted magazines and newspapers rested on an old boardroom table, surrounded by chairs of various ages. Floor to ceiling cupboards ran along the back wall, with room for a kitchen sink and a bench for basic coffee and tea supplies, with a silent television sitting on top of the tall fridge.

Tanisha knocked on the office door, opening it. 'Hey, Sarge, the long-lost Peddler, Wren, is here to see you.'

Admittedly Wren had been lost more than once in her life, which is why her father had given her the compass. She sorely missed it. And her father.

'Marcus will see you now,' said Tanisha with a smirk. 'Can I come visit, Wren? I'll be more than happy to help you settle in. I'll bring over my famous chicken empanadas.'

'Oh, that sounds absolutely delish,' called out Felix from the front counter. 'Say yes, Wren. You can never turn down home cooking, not in the country, it's impolite.'

Since when did Felix, a guy who'd never left his 'burb, know about food protocols in the country? 'That's very generous of you, Tanisha. Are you coming, Felix?'

'Oh no, Toots. You can handle this one on your own. I'm happy to talk with Tanisha, I'm dying to know where to shop in this town. Now, don't forget to smile and take a good look at the man.'

'Felix is right, Marcus is worth looking at, honey.' Tanisha practically pushed Wren into the office then promptly closed the door.

'Hi.' Wren didn't want to be here. Alone.

'Hi, Wren. Otis told me you were coming.' Marcus

smiled, getting up from behind his desk and held out his hand. 'I think we should start again after the speeding ticket yesterday.'

'Agreed. And I just paid for my ticket.' Wren shook his hand and checked him out, as instructed. She knew she'd be getting the third degree from Felix, suspecting Tanisha would want a full-blown police report on the sergeant's looks, too.

His hands were large, strong, and warm, making her own seem so tiny.

'Please take a seat, Wren.'

'Thank you.' Taking the nearest seat, she glanced around the small office to avoid any eye contact with the man who had so much presence.

There were a few postcards and plaques on the noticeboard. In a photo frame, resting on top of the filing cabinet, was an image of two men standing side by side, one of them wore a police uniform. They looked like brothers.

The large desk was messy, yet it seemed to have an order to the chaos. Her eye caught the name on the open file. *Peddler, Rowan.*

Marcus slammed the file shut and hid it under a pile of papers.

'Otis said you had the keys to the Peddler house.' An entire house and land package with an undisclosed sum of cash in the bank. It still hadn't sunk in.

'Yes, I do.' Marcus rummaged around in his drawers.

Doing as promised Wren took in the details, and she had an eye for details. Starting with Marcus's tanned forearms that were ink-free and strong, without too much hair.

The biceps were big and tight, their shape perfectly outlined by the short sleeves of his uniform, which suited his wide shoulders and broad chest. His short thick black hair had a sexy tousled look that was begging for her fingers to ruffle it some more. On to the strong jawline with its hint of a five o'clock shadow that gave him a determined handsome profile. His lips were symmetrical, shapely, and thin. Licking her own lips, she made her way to his dark brown eyes that were dreamy, yet smouldering, holding her gaze. *Holy mother of milk*, the man had a steely stare that was sexy!

'Here they are.' He put the keys down in front of her.

She held her breath to take a good look at the entire package.

Holy hot tamale, gimme an ice bath and a fan!

The man was so super-sexy, steam surely had to be pouring from her ears.

'Are you okay, Wren?'

'Can I get a drink of water, please?' She croaked like a dry cane toad frying on the outback highway.

But it got worse!

As Marcus stood and turned to get a glass of water for her, his broad shoulders emphasised a narrow waist, leading to a tight set of buns she wanted to beat like a drum. Her heart hammered as the blood rushed all over her body, with her eyes glued to his glutes as he got her some water.

'Thank you.' She gripped the cold glass, gulping it down, scared she'd spill it down her shirt.

'Are you sure you're okay?' Marcus returned to his seat behind the desk, where he was the grand commander in charge of everything. Including her pulse.

Get a grip, girl.

'You might be jet lagged or something. I heard you came in from the South Pole?'

'South Pole?' One of those embarrassing girlie giggles burst free from her lips, as if she was a fumbling teen all over again. She pinched her thigh to wake up. 'Where did that come from? There's nothing but ice and penguins in Antarctica. Oh, and the weather station for scientists.' Yet, taking a swan dive off the edge of a glacier and into icy seas sounded pretty good about now.

'The town is quick with the gossip.'

'I must remember that.' Suddenly remembering her other reason for coming today. 'Can you tell me exactly what happened to Rowan?' Didn't that just stop all her female fantasies of ripping off his shirt to see if he had a six-pack.

'I thought you might ask that.' Marcus sat back, wearing his serious police face. It was the same one he'd worn when they'd first met, and at the church.

The man was on the job.

And she needed him to be. 'Who found him?'

'Two-dollar Darryl. He's—'

'I know who he is.' And she was going to speak with Darryl soon to sort out this mess, because a night of tossing and turning over the possibility of a murder was not good.

'The town's doctor—'

'That's the Hot Doc, Stewart?'

'Yes. Stewart conducted the autopsy, concluding Rowan's death was from natural causes.'

'His lung cancer?'

'Yes. Did you know about it?'

'No. Rowan didn't tell me, even though I'd only spoken to him the day before he passed, making plans for me to visit.'

'For when?'

'In two weeks. Marcus, how long did Rowan know he was sick?'

'A week before he passed.'

It was a like a swift punch to the stomach. She gulped at the air, clutching her belly. 'Why didn't Rowan tell me?'

'If he had?'

'I would've done exactly what I did to get here—caught the first plane out.' Too ill to even drink, she plonked her glass onto the desk.

'Maybe Rowan didn't want you to make a fuss.'

'I still would've been here. It would have been better than him dying alone.' She glared at him. Then blinked, sitting back in her seat. 'Sorry, I didn't mean to off-load on you like that.' Cupping her face in her hands.

'It's okay, Wren.'

No, it wasn't. She had no right to be rude.

'I'm sorry for your loss.'

'Thank you.' There were no tears this time. Just tiredness and raw feelings, with a smattering of bitterness towards Rowan for not telling her.

'Why didn't you say Rowan was your father when we met?'

'Would that have gotten me out of the speeding ticket?'

'Probably not.'

She shared a fleeting grin. 'Good. That shows a strength of character, not letting someone con their way out of trouble.'

Marcus's eyebrows shot up in surprise.

'Are you copping some flak from the locals over it?'

He shrugged one of those big shoulders. Since when did a shoulder shrug become sexy?

'Um, so, they found my father …'

'On the front verandah with a loaded shotgun, a tobacco pouch beside an empty packet of pills and an empty bottle of bourbon.'

Did the guy memorise the file or something?

When the implications of the scene he'd described hit, her stomach plummeted in a sickening spiral. 'That sounds like a suicide.'

'The doctor said it wasn't the pills. Rowan's lungs gave out. He died of natural causes.'

'Do you agree with that finding, Marcus?'

'I'll let you discuss that with the doctor.'

'I didn't ask for the doctor's opinion, I asked for your professional opinion, Sergeant.' She kept her icy gaze steady on the uniformed officer of the law.

'Well, I haven't completed my findings just yet.'

'Do you think there's more to this?' Could Two-dollar Darryl be right?

'I didn't say that. I'm just dotting the Is and crossing the Ts. But if I do find out anything—'

'Yeah, yeah. You'll let me know.' She snatched the keys off the desk, tossing them into her handbag, annoyed at the lack of answers. 'Well don't be shy in letting me know if there's anything you need from me, Sergeant Moore.'

'*Detective* Sergeant Moore.'

'Detective, huh? From Melbourne?' She narrowed her eyes at the plaques on the wall. 'So, you'd know your stuff?' She hoped.

Again, he gave her another one of those sexy shrugs. Not fair.

'Well, there is something you can help me with, Miss Sumney.'

The formality of his tone, and loss of first-name basis, was irritating.

'I do have some questions. If you wouldn't mind, I'd like to escort you to the Peddler property. I'm hoping you might be able to give me some insight into Rowan Peddler's personality. We can go now, if that suits you?'

She sighed, dissolving all that bitterness in a puff of smoke. Marcus was only trying to do his job, which made the guy off-limits. Her father deserved that much.

'Sure. I'm happy to assist, Detective Sergeant. I'll follow you, so I don't get lost from here to wherever the house is.'

'Well, I hear it's this way ...' He opened the door for

her as the corner of his lips curved for only a moment, but the cheeky glint in his eyes twinkled.

The cool air-conditioning from the main station room was refreshing, even if it was mixed with ink and coffee. She needed air. 'Ready, Felix?'

'Where are we going, Toots?' Felix was lounging at the large conference table, having a coffee with Tanisha.

'The detective sergeant is kindly going to escort us to the premises.'

'Oh, is he now?' Tanisha arched her perfectly plucked eyebrows at Marcus stalking across the foyer.

'I'll be on the radio if you need me, Tanisha.' As Marcus headed for the front door the three behind the counter tilted their heads.

'You could start a Conga line following that butt.' Wren again sighed at Marcus's magnificent rear end. Even his back was impressive, with a set of thick thighs she could happily latch on to.

'You looked!' Felix spun around to face Tanisha and threw his arms in the air. 'She looked. For the love of vodka and cranberry, I believe the Ice Queen is starting to defrost.'

'Hallelujah, the girl has a heartbeat,' shouted Tanisha.

'Since when did my perv become such hot news to the both of you?' With hands on hips, Wren glared at Tanisha and Felix.

'Oh, Toots, I was worried you'd given up on men.'

'I wish I could, it'd make my life so much easier. But, sorry, no, I haven't given up on men, and I'll admit Marcus is hot.'

'How hot?'

'So-sizzling-hot-you-could-burn-your-finger-touching-him kind of hot.'

'Come on, Toots, you can do better than that. How hot?'

'Marcus is so hot he'd scorch the sun to make the moon burst into a thousand falling stars that'd plummet to earth and start a billion bushfires. Satisfied?' But she wasn't going to touch Marcus, he had a job to do, and who knows how long she was planning to stay. At the moment she was just taking it day by day.

'Ah … Wren?' Tanisha made short stabbing motions with one long red fingernail with sparkly diamantes on the tips.

'Ooh, I like your nails.'

'Thanks. But sweetie …'

Wren turned in the direction Tanisha was pointing.

It was Marcus, standing right behind her.

Wren swallowed the lump in her throat. 'Please tell me you didn't just hear all that.'

Marcus smirked at her as his eyes sparkled. Sparkled!

'Oh, no …' She buried her fiery face in her hands, wishing the floor would crack open a crevice and swallow her whole.

'After you, Miss Sumney.' Marcus opened the doors for her.

'Um, yeah.' With head down, she scurried towards the sunshine.

'I thought an Ice Queen's skin would be blue, not cooked-mud-crab red.' Marcus gave a low chuckle, with Tanisha and Felix's laughter echoing behind her.

ELEVEN

Forty minutes out of town, following a widely graded red dirt road, Marcus turned his highway pursuit vehicle down a well-maintained track. Rows of barbed wire topped the high fence that ran on both sides of the driveway in dead straight rows.

He pulled up to the closed gate with its thick heavy chain and sturdy padlock. The large sign, tied to the mesh read:

WARNING:
TRESPASSERS WILL BE SHOT
ON SIGHT
WITHOUT QUESTION!

The chain clanged loudly, and the double gates moved whisper quiet to stand like sentries guarding the smooth track ahead. It led to a two-storey farmhouse with its rooftop rising above the scrub. Within the large clearing, surrounding both the house and shed, Marcus parked his car near a small pile of ash.

More piles of wood ash were set around the farmhouse perimeter, the wood smoke still lingering as he climbed out of his car as Wren pulled up behind him.

'Here, you can open the door.' Wren tossed the keys to Felix.

'Why not have the *He's-so-hot-he-could-burn-your-finger-and-start-shooting-stars* sergeant open it for us?' Felix's laughter bounced across the surrounding outback, where a few black cockatoos mimicked a reply.

Marcus hid beneath the brim of his police cap and sunglasses, suppressing a smile. No one had ever described him like that in his life.

'Just open the door. It was embarrassing enough.' Wren wrapped her arms around herself, staring up at the house.

Felix skipped up the stairs. 'You've gone all Ice Queeny again.'

'What is this ash for, Marcus? There are piles everywhere …' Wren pointed to the nearest heap of black charcoal with grey, white ash.

'I'd say Two-dollar Darryl did a smoking on the place.' A few wallabies in the long rolling paddock raised their heads.

'A what?'

'Smoking ceremony. It's an Aboriginal custom to cleanse the place, especially after a death. Some say it's to help send those who've died on their journey, and with Rowan's health …'

'That's so nice.' With glassy eyes, Wren faced the house.

'Have you been here before?'

'No. Always wanted to. My father kept putting it off, saying it was easier for him to meet me.'

'How often did you see him?'

'Four times a year, sometimes more. Rowan was a live-in-the-moment kind of guy and would meet me for a weekend just for the hell of it. But we'd regularly phone each other.'

Why didn't Rowan Peddler want Wren to visit? The daughter Rowan told no one about—except for Otis, who worked on the man's will. Two-dollar Darryl had said nothing, and Wren had no father's name on her birth certificate—he'd checked. There was nothing in the system to even connect Rowan as her father.

This whole *long-lost-Peddler* story and Rowan's passing just kept bringing up more and more questions. Today he was hoping to find some answers.

On the front porch, standing near the outdoor setting, Wren shivered as goosebumps squirrelled up her arms. 'Is this where he …' Her voice faltered. '… was found?'

'Yes.' There was no shine in her eyes, her humour gone, leaving only a fragile daughter who had lost her father. He reached out and gave her shoulder a tender squeeze. 'Are you okay?'

Wren nodded as she examined the floorboards that made up the deep verandah. Her eyes narrowed at the cane chair, and the side table by the front door, holding an ashtray and bourbon bottle.

'I've got the shotgun at the station, and the doctor took all of the meds. Do you have a gun licence?'

'Rowan helped me get one. Dragging me to rifle ranges, or those paintball escape rooms. He was good at it, we'd win every time.' She gave a fleeting grin at some memory, picking up the leather pouch to inhale the tobacco aroma. 'Rowan only smoked this one type of tobacco. I gave him this pouch, even though I'd lecture him constantly about the perils of smoking. But he said he'd been smoking this brand since he was a kid.'

'Mm-hmm.' Didn't Wren know about the Peddlers' history? 'Do you know much about this place?'

She shrugged. 'Rowan had his stories, told me my

grandfather was a scary man. Did you meet Pop Peddler?'

'Once. He chased me and my friend, Connor, away from this front porch when we were kids.'

'Why?'

'We needed money for bike parts and asked if he had any work. Haven't been back since, except the other day ...' Was that why Rowan kept Wren away from the place? Because the Peddlers had a very colourful history.

'He died out here all alone.' Her slender fingers pressed against her full lips, as if holding back a sob. While Felix rattled around inside like an elephant.

'You don't have to do this today, Wren. We can go back to town.' Marcus rubbed her shoulder with a need to see her smile. Not this soul-depressing sadness that made his heart ache.

'I'm good.' She stood tall, swallowing her tears, and stepped through the front door, only to stop short. 'What the hell?!'

The chaos of upturned furniture was everywhere.

'Did you execute a search warrant on this place?' Her frown was fearsome, but at least the spark was back in her eyes.

'No. This was how we found it. Did Rowan live like this?'

Didn't that just make her scowl deepen.

'Hey, you'd be surprised at the way some people live.' Marcus pointed at the room. 'But I also agree with you, because my first impression of this place was someone was searching for something.'

'You do?'

'*Did.* Doctor Mannen said some terminally ill patients are known to lash out like this soon after they learn the news, especially when they have mere months to live. Less.'

Her clever eyes took in the details of the room. Billy

was right, they were a pretty, pale sea-glass blue.

He followed her into the dining room with its mat pulled up, the dining chairs knocked over, the cupboards lugged away from the wall. A mix of cups and plates spilled into a mosaic of cracked crockery across the floor.

It was the same for the kitchen, where Felix rifled through the cupboards.

Wren made her way upstairs. Marcus followed.

She was like a ghost, gliding from one room to the next, never saying a word. Her summer dress outlined her curves, and her long hair rested softly past her shoulders. He wanted to wrap one of those loose curls around his finger, just to see how soft her hair was.

Shoving his hands into his pockets, he followed her as she entered her father's room. Nothing had been moved since he'd come in search of a suit for Rowan's funeral.

In the bedroom Rowan's clothes were haphazardly flung across the floor, pockets were torn from jackets, and paperwork was everywhere. The double bed mattress leaned against the wall and piles of linen sat beneath the half-hanging curtains. It looked more than just a tantrum; this looked like a search. Was it from looters? Or was it something else?

Wren picked up the military uniform from the floor, brushing off the dust, and held it against her chest.

Her muffled whimpers tore strips off his soul. Without hesitation, Marcus wrapped his arms around her slender frame, pulling her into his chest and let her cry.

Her sadness was infectious. Even with her soft hair against his cheek, her feminine aroma, and soft skin, those tears hurt. All he could do was hold her, and he'd keep holding for as long as she'd let him, stroking her hair, gently rocking her until her tears subsided.

Then Wren took a deep breath, using the heels of her

palms to brush away the tears staining her cheeks. 'Thanks, Marcus.'

'Any time.' But something had shifted inside his chest. The desire to protect and comfort her was strong, he'd do anything to stop those tears.

'Sorry, it just hit me, seeing this ...' She gently laid Rowan's uniform across the empty bed frame, her fingertip tracing along the medals. It was a duplicate to the one Marcus had selected for Rowan's funeral.

The man had a score of medals, which meant Rowan had seen some serious combat. 'Do you know much about Rowan's military service?'

'He did some tours overseas—Timor, Fiji, New Guinea, other places. He enjoyed it.'

'Why did Rowan leave?'

'To come home and look after his mother when his father had passed.' She picked up a photo of four boys and shared a soft smile.

'What else do you know about Rowan? What was he like?' Marcus leaned against the open door jamb while Wren plucked a few items from the floor.

'Rowan was rather fastidious about things, precise in his dress and the way he lived. *Everything has its place and everything in its place*, he used to say to me.' She grinned at the memory.

'Is that how he'd make you keep your room clean as a kid?'

'No. We didn't have that kind of father-daughter relationship. I wish we had. I was almost twenty when we met. Rowan was more of a friend.'

She paused in the middle of the room. 'If I did this out of anger, I would've ripped those curtains off the wall to cause the most amount of impact. And why push the cupboards away from the walls instead of pushing them over? Why place the pictures on the ground and not smash their glass frames?' She whirled around and faced him with fire in her eyes. 'Someone was searching for something.'

'How can you be so sure?'

'Because there's no way Rowan would've done this. He had pride in everything he owned. Rowan treasured things like that photo of his brothers. I also know he avoided going near his mother's and his brothers' rooms after they died.'

'Why?'

'Because Rowan was waiting for me to help him. We were planning to go through every room together, where he was going to tell me all about the family I'd never met.' Wren pointed at the picture of the four young men, recognising Rowan. 'Somebody else did this.'

Well, didn't that change everything.

'What would they be looking for, Wren? Can you tell if anything's missing?'

'I haven't been here before.'

'No one has. The Peddlers were private people.' Marcus pointed to one of the dresser drawers lying on the floor. 'That's almost three thousand in cash there, and there's more in the kitchen. There's some jewellery, that I'm assuming is your grandmother's, still sitting in the other room. If it had been a robbery, that'd be the first things stolen.'

She looked at him bewildered as they headed downstairs. 'Did you dust for prints?'

'We did.'

'Were there any other prints? Rowan's been living on his own for eight years.' She faced Marcus from the bottom of the stairs and jabbed her finger into his chest. 'You found more than one set of prints, didn't you?'

'Now hold on a second ...' She'd caught him off guard, unlike anyone he'd ever met. Was he that transparent to the lady?

'You did. Were you going to hide that from me? When you said that if—'

'I know what I said.' With palms up, he tried to calm her down. 'Look—'

'Don't you dare give me some lame departmental brush-off, Marcus. I'll gladly tell you anything you want to know, but you have to be straight with me, too. Don't you think I deserve that?'

'Only if you'll stop looking at me like I'm the enemy.'

And just like that, she'd doused her inner fire. 'Sorry. I'm ...' She threw her hands in the air as if in defeat. 'I'm not normally this emotional.'

He held her upper arms gently, lowering himself to meet her eyes. 'It's an emotional time for you, Wren. You have nothing to be sorry for.'

She rewarded him with such a sweet smile it damned near melted him on the spot. 'Promise you'll be straight with me? Please.'

How could he refuse that look?

He checked around for Felix. 'Okay, but this is for your ears only. Can I trust you on that?' He shouldn't even be doing this!

'Absolutely, it's a two-way street. But why all hush-hush?'

'Because I'm going on a hunch, not evidence. But I believe you.'

Damn, it was another one of those sweet smiles.

'Believe me, I'm not telling the drama queen anything if that's what you're worried about.'

'Really?' He arched an eyebrow at her, because girls talked.

'Felix's not built for anything too dangerously dramatic, he'd have a hissy fit and run back to Sydney.' She then gripped his wrist, her touch so soft and warm, making his blood rush beneath his skin. 'Tell me about the other prints, Marcus.'

'I can't believe I'm telling you this …' What was up with that touch? A touch. A single hand on his wrist.

'Tell me.' Now both hands held his arms, and she stood squarely in front of him and all he saw was Wren. Dear god, she was gorgeous.

He stepped back, wiping at his mouth that didn't know if it was thirsty or about to water any second now.

'Marcus?'

Focus. Do your job, mate.

He stared at the messy room, anything but her. Looping his thumbs through the clips on his belt that held his sidearm, pepper spray, and cuffs. He was good at his job and knew that this was more than just a hunch. 'There was a separate set of smudges, not prints, like someone was wearing gloves.'

'Where?'

'Everywhere.' He pointed to the hallway mirror where smudges showed along its edges. 'Did Rowan have any enemies?'

'No. Well, only his father.'

Pop Peddler had a reputation as a cruel bastard, but he hesitated in saying that, as this was Wren's family. 'Can you think of anyone Rowan may have mentioned from his past?'

'No. Rowan had lost touch with those he'd served with. He told me missed the military lifestyle, but was happy to leave it behind too.'

'What did he mean by that?' Marcus followed her as she continued her slow tour of the house, through to the office at the base of the staircase.

'Rowan joined the Army to get away from his father.' She dropped her head, rubbing her upper arms. 'Rowan said his father hated him, called him the runt of the litter, said that he was stuck with him.'

'That sounds like Pop Peddler.'

'Really?'

'You should take up Billy's offer to meet with the Triple Js at the hardware store. They'll tell you anything you want to know about the Peddlers.' Should he warn her it might not be pretty.

'I might do that.' She moved from the office to the main foyer, giving him another one of those fleeting smiles.

Marcus cleared his throat, following her into the living area. He wasn't surprised to find the romance novels neatly placed on the bookcase. Tanisha hadn't stopped nattering about those books, in between concocting some lame excuse to get back inside this house.

'Wren, did Rowan really leave because of his father?' Did the Peddlers have enemies?

'And to see the world beyond his backyard. You must've done the same if you were a detective in Melbourne? How did that happen?'

'Long story.'

'Think you'll tell me sometime?'

'Do you really want to know?' Because, somehow, she'd woven a spell over him. He'd tell her anything she wanted to know. What kind of truth serum was this?

'I happen to like stories.' She glanced at him over her shoulder, sharing another of those sweet smiles, only wider.

Was Wren flirting with him?

'Oh, for love of vodka and pineapple, this will not do.'

'What's wrong, Felix?' Wren headed for the kitchen.

Again, Marcus followed, taking in the view of that hip sway of her skirt and those shapely legs.

Felix slammed the fridge shut. 'There's no coffee machine. No plunger. Nothing.'

'Rowan was a black tea only guy. He didn't do fancy.'

Felix waved his forefinger in the air like a wand. 'I'm talking about us staying here. I can put up with this being a shambles, but not without decent coffee.'

Wren gave Felix a hug, patting his back like he was a small child who'd fallen and scratched his knee. 'We'll be fine my big, strong man. We'll survive.'

'Damn straight, we will. I'm starting a shopping list. We need furniture, linen, crockery, and some paint to spruce up the place, because no one deserves to live with that lime paint. But topping our list is a coffee machine.'

'Anything to keep the cocktail maker happy.' Wren giggled. 'You've put booze on that shopping list?'

'Oh, my sweet BFF, as if I'd ever forget the necessities.'

'The stores in town have a limited choice. I doubt they'd have a coffee machine.' Marcus never needed one. His coffee got delivered.

'We don't do limits, handsome, we call friends.' Felix whipped out his mobile phone from his man bag. 'I have no range out here! I need to call Reggie to get Jimmy Chow's help.'

'Who?'

'Jimmy Chow, the conservative decorator by day and a fabulous drag queen's stylist by night. And style is what this house direly needs. You called your father weekly, Toots, so he must have a landline somewhere.'

'I saw it by the hallway stairs, it's sitting under the knocked-over side table. I'll get the cases while you pick which room you want us to attack first, Felix.'

'It'll be the kitchen. How many bathrooms are there?'

'Three. One down here, two upstairs. You can have your own bathroom, just be sure to put silk bed linen, and those big soft bath sheets you like, on the shopping list.'

Marcus coughed at the thought of Wren and silk

sheets.

Felix puffed and panted like he was in some soap opera, patting his hand over his heart. 'You'd better not be teasing me, Toots.'

Wren shook her head. 'We have the budget.'

'Well, I'd better get my booty moving and make those phone calls.'

Marcus shifted aside to let Felix flounce out of the room.

'Sounds like you're moving in.' Did his heart just flip at that thought? Hold on! He couldn't. This would make it tricky because Marcus didn't do long-term relationships, and Wren had inherited the Peddler property that came with a tonne of complications.

Too hard, man, walk away now.

She smiled, tapping his arm as she walked past. 'Looks like we'll be part of the neighbourhood for a bit.'

'Want a hand with the luggage?' What was he saying? He had work to get back to. He had a file to pull out and images of this house to troll through. But here he was, carting luggage like a bellboy at the Peddler Palace.

He'd only do this for Wren. Anyone else and he'd have made an excuse to leave.

But if he'd known it was all Felix's luggage, he would've just left. How can one man own that much luggage?

Wren was crouched by the front porch steps, chewing her bottom lip, deep in thought.

'Did you drop something?'

'Rowan only smoked handmade rollies.'

'He's a Peddler, of course he did.' Did he dare tell her why?

Wren skipped over to the small table where the ashtray sat. 'There are tailor-made cigarettes among the hand-rolled ones. Do any of your officers smoke?'

'Porter used to, but he wants to date Tess, who runs the Post Office. Tess hates anyone smoking, so he quit.' The hell Porter was going through just to date Tess, it was sickening to watch. But Porter kept saying Tess was the one for him. How could Porter be so sure Tess was *the one*?

But a certain blonde, with her heavenly feminine scent, had his eye, even if it was to watch her carry an ashtray down the porch steps.

Too bad it was a woman who came with a tonne of complications.

It was obvious she had no idea what she was walking into.

Did he dare intervene?

'Look at the ground, Marcus, it's regularly raked. Rowan was very particular about leaving rubbish; he'd carry a plastic bag for cigarette butts to not litter anywhere. See, there's no butts or rubbish anywhere, except there ...'

Two tailor-made cigarette butts lay side by side in the dirt. Was it something or nothing?

The place had been swarming with first responders, it could have been anyone's.

But there would be DNA on that evidence—if this was a case.

He unclipped the pouch on his belt, pulled out a plastic glove and evidence bag. 'Look, I don't want you jumping to any conclusions—'

'I'm not. You have hunches, I have theories. But can I assume you're going to have them tested?'

He never discussed cases with civvies, especially when they were this close to the victim of a crime—if there was a crime. 'I'll investigate it. Just don't—'

'I won't.'

Damn, woman—she was already finishing his sentences. 'You didn't even know what I was going to say.'

'I bet you were going to say that you're just dotting the Is and crossing the Ts before you close the case. Am I close?'

Too close. 'Are you a police officer, too?'

'No. Just a product of watching too many cop shows.' She lifted her dainty chin letting rip a cheeky grin that matched the glint in her eyes.

He chuckled, so tempted to ruffle the top of her hair.

The radio on his hip squawked with static. 'I'd better head back.'

She grabbed him by the wrist, stopping him. 'Thank you, Marcus.'

'For what? Carrying all of Felix's luggage up those stairs?'

Her sweet laugh made him smile with her. Marcus didn't smile much, yet it came so easily with her.

'That, and for being straight with me. I'm glad you can see what I see about the house. But I was thanking you for what you did for me upstairs.'

'My pleasure.' He patted her small hand that held his wrist, tempted to link their fingers together. 'If you ever need anything, just call me?

Seriously, he should cut his losses now, get in the car and just nod to the woman on the street in passing—just like he did with all of the other Peddlers in the past.

'Will you keep me informed of any developments?'

'I will. You?'

She barely nodded, but the way her lips curled into a smile—it was better than any handshake. They had a deal.

Marcus opened his squad car door, while she watched him like an angel under the sunshine, dwarfed by a big house that had once housed the devil of dust.

'I think you'll fit in just fine, Wren. Especially with Tanisha and her friends.' Tanisha would be good in this situation, not Marcus, he needed to keep a professional distance.

'Why do you say that?' Felix asked, flouncing down the front steps to join Wren.

'They all want to see Rowan's collection of romance books by that author Taylor Timms.'

'Who?' Wren and Felix looked at each other and shrugged.

Maybe it was another surprise she'd find going through the Peddler Palace.

In the side mirror's reflection, he chuckled at Felix and Wren doing some weird rain dance in the dust out front of the house, before racing each other inside.

His smile disappeared when he glanced at the evidence bag lying on the passenger seat. His hunches had always paid off in the past. He knew there was more to this case. It felt like a case. But did he dare dig for dirt on Rowan Peddler's death, when the evidence, so far, had showed no foul play?

TWELVE

Wren carried another box to the verandah, sliding the old baseball bat next to the other sporting goods by the front door. They'd been making good progress on the house, packing everything into boxes. Clothes and knick knacks were in one pile. Broken and irreparable furniture in another. Pretty soon they could start painting.

A large, dusty flatbed truck, towing an eight-foot freezer trailer, parked in front of the farmhouse. The truck's doors opened and closed. Two-dollar Darryl adjusted his well-worn cowboy hat as his boots stirred up the dust crossing the car park.

Darryl's offsider adjusted his snapback cap, then brushed down his shiny hip-hop street-style shirt. He'd only be about nineteen, with a rich burnt-caramel skin tone, much lighter than Darryl's.

'Mornin', Miss.' Darryl took off his dusty Akubra at the verandah's steps, raking fingers through his tight black and grey-flecked curls. 'This is my nephew, Chopper. He's stayin' with me from the city.'

Wren shook their hands, dreading this visit.

'You've really gotten into it.' Darryl pointed to the piles

spread along the verandah.

'I always have trouble sleeping in a new house. I nap a lot.'

'Your father was the same. He'd nap on that chair all the time. It was his favourite place.'

The silence was deafening.

'Saw the copper here, yesterday.' Darryl scuffed his boots in the dirt.

'Marcus escorted us to the place; he had the keys.' It was a huge set of keys for a house that didn't have that many doors to lock.

'Just so you know, there's three gates we always keep locked.'

'And that sign out the front?' Who has a *shoot first ask questions later* sign on their gate, complete with rows of barbed wire?

'Your grandfather put that up. It might be best you keep it there for a bit, Miss.'

Felix pushed open the front screen door, tucking his feather duster into his pink apron, adjusting his long pink gloves that had fur on the cuffs. 'Oooh, we have visitors. Hello, I'm Felix from Sydney.' He thrust his fancy-gloved hand out to the young man.

'Chopper,' he mumbled from beneath his fitted cap still sporting the authentic sticker on the flat brim.

'Why?'

'Coz he got his ear half-chopped off,' replied Darryl.

Chopper tugged his cap's brim lower to brush down his black hair.

'That's why he's here. Got into some trouble, so my sister sent him to me to sort him out.' Darryl tapped the kid's chest. 'Show some manners, you take your hat off when you're around the ladies.'

'That's okay.' Wren could see the guy was upset.

But Chopper did it anyway, sharing a shy grin as he kicked at the dirt with his sneakers.

'Chopper's good, Miss. Bin a big help, he has. 'Specially since the man got sick.' Darryl's eyes darted towards the cane chair by the front door.

'Were you close with my father?'

'Known him a long time. He was a good man. No matter what anyone tells you, Miss, the Peddlers are a good mob. They always did right by me.'

'Do you want to come inside?'

'Nah, Miss, I wanna show you the place.'

'Where are we going?'

'Just like that Felix from Sydney wants to ask, we're going on a tour.' Darryl's white teeth were such a contrast to his dark skin, it only made his smile shine even more. 'Grab a hat and let's go.' He made quick work of the distance between the house and the truck. Leaving Felix and Wren with little choice, except to grab a hat and sunglasses, and race after the cowboy clambering into the truck.

Wren and Felix sat in the front cab with Darryl, while Chopper rode on the back of the truck as they followed the track deeper into the Peddler property. The bushland stretched along both sides of the long paddock. Its short yellow grasses ran like a corridor that stretched for miles.

'How big is the property, Darryl?'

'Your grandfather wanted a hundred hectares of land and water. So we got it for him.' Darryl gave a sly grin as he steered, their shoulders swaying over the dusty road's corrugations. He tossed his thumb towards the bush that ran on his right. 'Elsie Creek is over there. She connects with the rivers and takes you all the way to the ocean. For town you go the other way. But it's quicker by road.'

'Does this property have river views?' Felix asked.

'Better than that, mate. The Peddlers' own an island.'

'Toots, you own an island. An entire island.' Felix gripped her arm. 'Can we see it? Does it have a beach, and tropical palm trees? We could get a cabana and sip cocktails all day on your very own island.'

'They didn't tell ya, Miss?' Darryl slowed down the truck, then started reversing into the clearing between gum trees and prickly pandanus.

'No one's told me anything.' The crisp air carried a sweet blend of eucalyptus, honey, dust, and fresh water.

The brakes on the truck hissed and the engine was silenced. Darryl poked up his hat's brim to lean over the steering wheel. 'Didn't your dad—'

'Rowan told me nothing. Didn't even tell me he was sick!' She winced at her words that came out louder than expected.

'Well, Miss, you're the boss-lady now. You can ask me anythin' and I'll tell you, plain as can be. I promised the man I would, he wanted you to know all of the Peddlers' secrets.'

'Thank you, Darryl.' Surely there weren't that many family secrets in this outback town?

'Come on, out ya get.' Darryl's wide smile was reassuring as they clambered down.

'What do they grow here?'

'Stock feed only, these days.'

'I'm not a farmer, Darryl. Is that a lot of work?'

'Nah. It's only cos we get the long grass after the wet season.' Darryl pointed to the long yellow paddock. 'It used to be all tobacco.' From behind the driver's seat Darryl passed her a small tobacco pouch. 'Chop-chop.'

Wren's eyes widened, recognising the scent as the brand her father smoked.

'OH, FOR THE LOVE OF VODKA AND PEACHES,' Felix's voice was like a sonic boom across the field sending grazing wallabies fleeing. 'That's illegal tobacco. Are you for real?'

Darryl bobbed his eyebrows up and down.

She read that as a yes. 'No way.' Rowan had packets of the stuff in his bags. She'd never given the brand a second thought, because she didn't smoke. 'Does everyone know about this?'

'Small town, Miss.'

'Who did they sell to?'

'Everyone and anyone. But mostly the fishermen and stockmen buy it. It's top-class tobacco, but cheap coz of no tax.'

'When did this all start?'

'Back with the war when they had that big mob of American soldiers camped on the other side of the Elsie Creek train station. They only got so much rationed to them, and their supplies were regularly delayed. So your great-grandfather grew it, chopped it up in the shed here, then your great-grandmother would sell it on her day trips to town when she'd fetch the mail and groceries.'

'You mean to tell me the Peddlers have been growing illegal tobacco for eighty years?'

'It wasn't illegal back then. Not until this government man with a tie and these silly shorts and long socks, came round carrying his clipboard like he was some king. He was telling Pop Peddler he had to pay money for a licence to grow the tobacco that had been growing on the Peddlers' property for decades. You should've seen Pop Peddler, all calm and polite like, squinting at that government man yakking and pointing at his clipboard.'

'What did Pop Peddler do?'

Darryl chuckled. 'That government man left pretty quick on account of that sawn-off shottie your grandfather liked to carry, and I heard him saying to that government man he was gonna shove that clipboard in a place where the sun didn't shine on Sundays.'

Holy second-hand smoke, what was this outback world—a kingdom of its own accord? 'Why was Pop Peddler carrying a shotgun?'

'For the crocs.' From the freezer, Darryl helped Chopper load boxes onto a small trolley.

'Crocodiles? Where?'

'Show you.' Darryl hoisted a large box onto his shoulder, then led them down a wide cemented slope, Chopper followed with his loaded trolley.

'Is this a boat ramp?' Wren paused on the crest, which overlooked the wide river.

'It is. I helped them make this. No more getting bogged in the wet.' His boot scuffed over a set of indented handprints captured in the cement with the names *Rowan, Pop, and Two-Dollar Darryl.*

'Do you have a boat?'

'Miss, you own four of 'em. One's up at my place, two are in the shed.' Darryl pointed to a long, boarded walkway that stretched across the water where a fancy racing boat was tied to the dock. 'And that's your dad's toy.'

The boat was sleek and shiny with gold words on the hull that read *Sandfly.* Huh, was this what Bottle Shop Luke was talking about, he liked the boat? 'It looks like a ski boat.'

'Barra boat. Your father liked his fishing. I should drag it out and put in the shed.'

'Do the Peddlers own any yachts? You know, to go with her island, sand, and palm trees?' Felix leaned over the railing to peer at the murky river waters.

'I wouldn't do that if I were you, mate.' Chopper gently pulled Felix back from the edge. 'Look.'

'Is that a log?'

'That's a croc, mate. That's King. Watch 'im. He's a cheeky fella that one.'

King had to be the body-builder's version of a salt water crocodile with a torso as wide as a dozen wooden planks. With dark armoured skin, he floated on the water, watching everything with sharp eyes, only to slowly sink out of sight.

Felix grabbed Wren's hand. 'Is King like Karma the crocodile? At the pub?'

Darryl chuckled, unlocking a high gate with strings of barbed wire running along the top. 'Always, keep this gate shut, Miss.' He tapped on another blunt sign that read:

SHUT THE GATE OR WE ALL DIE

'King is a cunning bugger. This part of the river is his territory, where he keeps his harem of women. Don't ever trust him, and always keep this gate closed, coz King likes to get in here and have a sticky beak. It's a bugger to get him out.'

'Where does this path lead?'

'Goat Island.' Darryl led them down the sturdy boardwalk, which felt like a swaying bridge over crocodile-filled waters. Wait, there really were crocodiles—scaly, long-nosed monsters with mouths full of sharp teeth, lying along the far bank like statues in the mud.

'That's the island?' Felix screwed up his nose. 'Where's the palm trees? The beach sand? The cabana … It looks like Alcatraz.'

Large boulders made up the perimeter, where the water met the land, topped with a wooden dwelling that reminded her of a marooned houseboat with solar panels glinting off the roof. Its wide verandah and decking ran all the way around, leading to a sturdy jetty that stretched across the water.

'What is this place, Darryl?' She wouldn't have minded

Felix's idea of tropical paradise.

Darryl unlocked the steel doors, pushing them open. 'Welcome to the Sandfly Saloon.'

Wren gripped her scalp. 'Wait. Darryl, is this bar legit, or is this like the tobacco?'

Darryl laughed, opening the double doors to let the breeze and sunshine stream over wooden barrels set out as tables, surrounded by assorted stools.

'Your family were bad-asses, Toots. Illegal chop-chop, now this.' Felix pointed at Wren, then turned to Darryl. 'Did they have an illegal still too?'

'Used to, they called it Outback Rotgut. But that Bottle Shop Luke, he cuts us a good deal these days.'

Wren met Felix's wide-eyed look. No wonder Luke said they'd be friends!

Darryl lifted a roller door to reveal a full wooden bar with a row of glass-door fridges, beer taps and glasses.

'It's a proper bar.'

'Yeah, just the tax man doesn't know about it. Nobody likes doin' paperwork round here.'

'How? What? When? Where?' She fought for air, pressing her hands to her chest.

'Breathe, Toots, take a deep breath, and have a look. Ooh, you've got a piano?' Felix made a beeline for the upright piano that stood in the far corner.

Overwhelmed, Wren sat on the nearest barstool. Its seat was made from a vintage steel tractor seat, attached to a base that was nailed to the floor.

Like a trophy across the ceiling, fishing nets held up a gigantic saw shark with its long, slender, saw-like snout equipped with sharp, toothlike saw-teeth along each edge. An enormous set of shark jaws, buffalo horns, and a crocodile skull were scattered along the rest of the walls like a rustic museum. There was a pool table, a dartboard, and a really big round table.

'What's that table for?' It was so big compared to the rest of the furniture.

Darryl paused from unpacking a box of rum cans into the fridge. 'Poker games. Two-up gets played in the middle. Pool over there, darts along that wall, and the band plays by the piano. We've had some ripper blues nights too, where the Sandfly is jamming and the dock's full of people.'

'How do the customers get here? Do they drive through the property?'

Chopper dumped his boxes against the side wall. The wheels of his trolley rumbled along the walkway boards as he headed back to the truck.

'No one's allowed on the Peddler property. Pop Peddler was pretty strict about that, your father was the same. People can only visit the Sandfly by boat.' Darryl lifted another roller door, giving them a grand view of the river, with more crocodiles sunning themselves on the distant sand bank.

'Are we really on an island?'

Darryl nodded towards the black and white images on the wall. 'Your great-grandfather started this place. It was nothing but a dirt floor, tin roof, an old tuckerbox for the beer, and a fire pit. But he loved his fishing and wanted a safe space to fish, free from the crocodiles. Your grandfather scored all the building materials by swapping it for chop-chop to build the Sandfly proper. Your grandmother ran the kitchen, making sure people got fed, and we all helped.'

'Even my father?'

'He pushed the mop and washed glasses. He was the smallest of the brothers.'

'Do you know what happened to my uncles?'

Darryl nodded with sadness in his eyes. 'Flash flood got 'em coming back from Katherine, pushed the truck over and gone … That's when your grandfather started drinking that rotgut too much. He got …'

'Mean. My father told me.'

Felix gave the piano's keyboard a dusting, its ebony keys faded, and the ivory worn and yellow. 'You're missing a key.'

'Dunno what happened, one day it was there, then one day gone.'

'This is so out of tune. And that missing key sucks.' Felix ran his fingers up and down the keys, then started playing Queen's *Don't Stop Me Now*.

A generator coughed in the background, settling into a chug-chug-chug rhythm, as the ceiling fans stirred the air. The rumble of the trolley wheels coming down the wooden walkway announced Chopper's return.

'What do you do here, Darryl?' Wren asked.

Darryl helped Chopper remove a beer keg from the trolley and slide it behind the bar. 'We manage the property, Miss. We're here to help you. Chopper, get the lady a drink.'

'Drink, Miss?' Chopper wiped his hands on his shirt. 'Bottle Shop Luke said this vodka was for you and that fella, Felix from Sydney.'

Tempting as it was, it wasn't even lunchtime yet. 'Water, please. I didn't bring any money.'

Chopped chuckled. 'You're the boss, Miss. This your place now.'

'Please, call me Wren.'

Chopper looked back at Darryl, who only shrugged, stacking assorted beers into the fridges.

What was she going to do with an illegal bar!

Chopper placed a bottle of water on the bar. 'Glass?'

'I'm good. Saves washing dishes.'

'Your dad said the same thing.' Chopper's smile was glorious.

'So, what do you do, Chopper?'

'I help my uncle. We collect the mail and whatever the other mobs want.' Chopper fiddled with a lighter, his slender fingers flicking the switch. Instead of a flickering flame, out popped a blade.

'What is that?'

'My fancy box-cutter.' Chopper's mischievous smile widened as he showed off his toy. It was a stainless-steel blade that clipped onto the side of an everyday Bic lighter. 'It's one of 'em tools of the trade.'

'Is it?'

'Sandfly's customers' smoke, and we got all of 'em beer and fish boxes to open.'

'Who are the customers?'

'The fishermen. They radio through if they need supplies.' Chopper pointed at the large VHF radio mounted on the shelf behind the bar. 'They'll offload their fish, crabs, prawns straight into our fancy tucker box.'

'Where does it go from there?'

'We cart it to the Elsie Creek train station, where it goes to the fish markets. The local supermarket and the pub takes some, too.'

'That's why you have a freezer on that trailer?'

'Boats snap-freeze some of their fish stocks,' explained Darryl. 'You see, Goat Island sits in a spot that makes it easier for them to drop in here when they need supplies, than travel all the way round the coast to Darwin Harbour. You've got the mangroves upstream for the crabbers.'

'What?'

'Mud crab. And the barra—'

'That's barramundi?'

'They're downstream on the dry, and during the wet, they'll go way up to the flood plains. And throughout the year we'll get them fancy fishos coming through.'

'Who?'

'Mobs of blokes in fancy fishing boats, like the Sandfly boat there.' Darryl pointed at the sleek black boat floating alongside the dock. 'Bottle Shop Luke calls them anglers. They're recreational fishermen with money to burn on flash boats and tackle. They come in for the big money barra comps.'

Felix plonked down onto the stool beside Wren. 'I give up. You're missing a key on the piano, which is such a shame. Remind me to add that to our shopping list, then I'll study YouTube videos on how to tune it. Ooh, I love these stools.'

'My uncle made them.' Chopper's cheeky laugh carried, as Darryl ducked his head to hide the blush darkening his skin.

'They're fabulous. You should be proud.'

Wren approached the large image on the wall. It was of a group of men of various ages, and a much younger Darryl. 'How old were you when you started here, Darryl?'

'Young. Thirteen, fourteen maybe. I thought I'd scored a free ride on the train, until the conductor caught me. He threatened to call the cops, but your grandfather was there delivering stuff at Elsie Creek Station and stopped them.'

'What happened?'

'He said I worked for the Peddlers. Gave that conductor a few packets of chop-chop and a flagon of Outback Rotgut and told him he saw nothin'. Then he told me to stop gawking and to give him a hand loading his boxes onto the truck. So, I did.'

'Just like that?'

'Yep. Bought me a lemonade at the pub, waiting for his wife to finish shopping, asked me what I wanted to do.'

'What did you want to do?'

'No idea. I wasn't doin' nothing, but I wanted to do something—as long as it wasn't swallowing cattle dust musterin'—just didn't know what. That's when your grandfather asked me if I could keep my trap shut. I said I could coz I didn't know anyone to tell nothing to.'

'What did he say then?'

'Patted me on the shoulder and offered me a job, but only if Mrs Peddler liked me. Which she did, and bought me some tucker, then brought me back here.'

'Are you serious?'

'Yeah. They gave me clothes, food, a wage, and I bunked in with your father for a while, too.' Darryl nodded at the bank where a small shack overlooked the river. 'Your grandmother taught me to read, your grandfather taught me to fish, shoot, and weld those stools. Your uncles taught me to drive the truck, tractors, bikes, and get my licences. Then your entire mob helped build my home, for me.'

'And you work here, in this bar?'

'Everywhere. Sowing and harvesting the tobacco crops in the fields. Helping them in the sheds to dry, cut, and package the tobacco for sale. Move the fences and help run the bar and do trips.'

'When did the tobacco stop?'

'When your father came back from one of his trips.'

'He went legit?'

'Nah. Just stopped growing it. We've still got plenty, Miss, all sealed to never go stale.' Darryl unlocked a cupboard that was full of packaged tobacco. 'The crabbers, fishermen, stockmen, and the town-mob all like its coz it's organic.'

'You know smoking is bad for you?'

'Yeah. Peddlers all got lung cancer.'

'They did?' Her eyes widened at the realisation. 'You never smoked?'

'Never liked it. And that rotgut made good men nasty.'

'Like my grandfather.'

Darryl barely nodded. 'Pop Peddler was always good

to me. Only yelled if I mucked up a bit.'

'Where did your nickname Two-dollar Darryl come from?'

'Because I only gamble with two dollars at a time.'

'Huh?'

'Two dollars on two up, or them pokie machines at the Elsie Creek Pub.'

'You never go past two dollars?'

'Nope. Mum said my dad was a terrible gambler, so I only play with two dollars.'

'I like it. So you don't produce any more rotgut? Or you've got some stashed like that tobacco?'

'Your father and I tipped it all out, then used the barrels to make Sandfly's bar tables.' Darryl pointed to the assorted tables scattered around the room.

'It works for me. So, if they …' She swallowed down the bubbles of fear. 'The police were to raid—'

'*The Sandfly Saloon*,' Chopper announced it like a radio DJ, sliding away his fancy box cutter.

She tried to smile. 'Will I get into trouble for all of that chop-chop?'

'Your grandfather said this island was no-man's land,' replied Darryl. 'Goat Island is free from the taxman coz they don't know it exists and we don't advertise.'

'It'd have to be on Google maps, right?'

Darryl shrugged.

Was this what Marcus was hinting at? Hesitating with his careful questions and answers, and why he'd never been to the Peddler house, not since he was a child.

From the middle of the room, she faced Felix, the man who owned a nightclub. 'What do I do?'

'The question you should be asking yourself, Toots, is what do you want to do with the place?'

'I don't know. I wasn't expecting this.' She sighed from

the weariness strapped heavily across her shoulders. With her fingertip, she dusted a photo on the wall. It was from the first time Wren had met her father in Port Douglas. 'You knew about me?'

Darryl nodded. 'Your father talked about you all the time. He was proud of you.'

'So how come no one else in town knew I existed?'

'Because he didn't talk to that mob. But I'd never seen him so happy when he come back from meeting you the first time. He hung up that picture on the wall and said no more rotgut.'

'Is that why he kept me away from this place? The Sandfly Saloon and the tobacco?'

Darryl's face was sullen. 'No, Miss, there was something else going on. He'd never tell me, but he was worried 'bout somethin'.' From behind a panel, Darryl removed a white envelope. 'I promised him I'd give this to you, only if he were gone before that visit you'd been planning.'

Wren swallowed hard, her fingers trembling as she held the envelope, staring at her name: *For Wren (Peddler) Sumney*. She recognised the writing; it was her father's.

THIRTEEN

Fresh from the shower, dressed in her comfy PJs, Wren entered the large office and sat behind an amazing oak desk with deep drawers she had yet to explore.

But not tonight.

Tonight, she hoped for some answers, and pulled out the letter Darryl had given her earlier.

Dear Wren,

Sadly, I received some bad news on my health. No matter what life throws at you, sometimes you've got to take the Croc by the snout and give it all you've got. You know I'll fight this until the end and never surrender.

We're the same, Wren—we'd never give up without a fight!

I am grateful to have had the privilege of not only being your friend and confidante, even if I was that grouchy old-fashioned advisor, but most of all, I am honoured to have you in my life. I'd never been prouder of someone like you, that even my cranky father would've been proud of the legacy we leave behind.

So, if you have received this letter from Two-dollar Darryl, you should've received the ownership of the farmhouse, the shed and all its toys, and the Sandfly Saloon.

The bar does not exist on paper. Neither does Darryl working for the place. But I have provided him with regular wages in the nest egg I hope he'll accept from Otis. I know you'll get on well with Darryl, he was like a brother to me and can be trusted.

I'd be honoured if you made the house your home. It's been a part of the Peddlers for generations. It should be your home too. It'd be great place to return to from your world adventures.

I'm talking about some of those adventures and challenges that can start from your own home's front door. As your grandmother would say, home is where the heart is, especially in the place I told you I hung out the most!

Good luck, I know you'll succeed in whatever you choose. You have always been an inspiration to me. Your strength and sense of what's right and wrong are admirable, and your uncanny ability to <u>see things outside the box is a gift.</u>

Please enjoy my gifts, and the many more discoveries to come.

Love,
Rowan (AKA Dad)
<u>B1/ C13/ P47/ L8.</u>

Wren wiped at the tears, re-reading the letter. Her skin prickling with goosebumps as the sorrow and guilt became a heavy burden across her shoulders.

There was nothing suspicious in this, just a man saying

goodbye. Maybe the medical reports were true, Rowan's death was due to his health.

'Toots, did you want another cup of tea?' Felix pushed opened the office door and screamed. 'AAAHHHHH. *There's a man at the window.*'

Wren spun around in her seat.

The man's eyes flared, then frowned before he ran off into the dark.

'Felix, stay here.' Wren bolted for the door.

'Where are you going? *Don't leave me here.* ALONE.'

'Lock the door, arm yourself with something, and phone a local friend.' Wren grabbed the baseball bat lying with the rest of the sporting goods by the front door. With the small torch from her handbag, she slammed the front door behind her and gave chase. 'I'll fix that freaking perve.' No one was scaring them away from her father's house.

FOURTEEN

It had been a long day running the roads with his team, closing off sections of the highway to let through a fleet of road trains towing massive mining trucks from the local mine. But all day Wren had been on Marcus's mind.

He stared at the images from the Peddler's farmhouse, spread across his desk. Money and other items normally nicked in a robbery were still there. So what were they looking for in that farmhouse?

Porter rapped his knuckles on the door. 'Sergeant. Tanisha called and said that Felix from Sydney saw a man peeping in at the Peddler house and reckons they're under attack.'

'Where's Wren?'

'Apparently she's chasing the guy with a baseball bat, leaving Felix in the house.'

How fearless was that woman? Marcus snatched up his keys and bolted for his car.

Throughout the entire trip he worried. He didn't have Wren's number to call and check she'd returned to the house. Nothing.

Marcus sped through the open gates, to find every light within the farmhouse sparkling. Yet it seemed so small under the galaxy of stars.

Marcus pulled up with Porter in the police car behind him. Tanisha's compact sedan skidded to a stop next to the verandah.

'Oh, thank god you're here.' Felix pushed open the front door. Gripping a frypan, he rushed towards Tanisha in her pyjamas and dressing gown as Darryl and Chopper rushed up to the house.

'Felix, where's Wren?' Marcus asked sternly.

'She's still out there. Wren hasn't come back yet.'

'What did you see?'

Felix raised his hand above his head. 'This tall man stood right behind her, watching Wren. She chased him around the back of the house, that way.'

'Sarge, we've just come from downriver,' said Darryl. 'We didn't see her, but we heard this one screaming, so we come running.'

'Wren's been gone so long.' Felix clutched onto Marcus's arm. 'You have to find her. I'd just die if anything happened to her.'

'We'll find her.' Marcus peeled back Felix's fingers from his arm. 'Tanisha, help Felix inside and find out what you can. Porter, we'll drive the cars down the back with spotlights on. I want as much light down the back for Wren to see it.'

The two police cars lit up the darkened property. The wide flat corridor of short golden grasses looked white under the spotlights, trapping some grazing wallabies.

But there was no Wren anywhere.

They reached the riverbed, where pairs of floating red dots slowly submerged in the river. Crocodiles.

Did Wren know about crocodile safety and how they hunted at night?

Marcus used his handheld spotlight to scan the

riverbanks. There was nothing.

'We'll split up. Keep the lights on the car, facing back towards the house. Hopefully, Wren will see it. I'll search on foot this way. Porter, you go with Darryl and Chopper in the other direction.'

Marcus's boots crunched on the paddock's dry grass, keeping the riverbed on his left side where a long irrigation ditch acted as safety barrier between the scrub and river. It gave him some hope of Wren keeping a safe distance from the crocodiles.

The moon flirted behind a few clouds, as a group of fruit bats screeched in their flight, with the river trickling as smooth as a slow running tap.

A few twigs snapped behind him. Marcus paused.

'*Gotcha!*' Wren slammed into him with such force it knocked the wind out of him. They grappled, rolled in the dark and down into the irrigation ditch.

Marcus pinned Wren onto her back, but she kneed him in the ribs, wrapping her strong legs around his waist, flicking mud everywhere.

'It's me, Wren. Marcus.' He couldn't breathe under that grip.

She stopped wriggling. 'What are you doing here?'

'Felix called us.' He took a few deep breaths, but the sting between his shoulders was pure fire.

'Sorry, I didn't know it was you.'

'What the hell were you doing out here on your own?'

'I wanted to scare off that perve, to make sure he never came back again. But he got away.' The anger in her voice only maddened him more.

'So why did you attack me!'

'I didn't know it was you. I thought the pervert had doubled back on me.'

Their voices raised as he argued with Wren, while

keeping her pinned on her back in the mud beneath him. 'Why didn't you call us?'

'Because he would have gotten away.'

'Well, he did, *didn't he!*'

'Yeah, he did.' She sighed and all her fire melted away. 'Do you think he'll come back?'

'I don't know.' Marcus tried to simmer down his anger. 'But don't you *ever* run off in the middle of the night like that. *Do you hear me?* You scared the crap out of me, not knowing where you were, and Felix's half frightened to death up at the house.'

'I'm sorry,' Wren replied meekly, only to snap at him. 'Next time I'll take the *shotgun!*' She tried to wriggle free, but Marcus held her wrists. She tightened her thighs around his waist as she tried to push him off.

'I'm not letting you go until you calm down.'

'Come on, it was probably some kid creeping around in the dark. I just wanted to scare him for scaring Felix.'

'Did you see who it was?'

'Not that clearly. It was male, same height as you, with a much leaner build. Felix would give you a better description.'

'Just promise me you won't go off chasing strange men in the dark again?'

'You can't protect me twenty-four-seven,' she mumbled under her breath like a bratty smart-arse.

'Promise me, Wren.' He tightened his grip on her wrists. 'And stop wriggling like that.' His body started to stir in ways it shouldn't. But she had her legs wrapped around his waist, struggling against his groin.

'Okay, okay, I promise. Happy now?' Wren's irritation was loud and clear.

But he didn't care, he wanted her to be safe. 'Are you injured or anything?'

'I won't know until you *get. Off. Me.*' Her body jerked beneath him.

He rolled off to sit beside her, as the blunt pain burned in his shoulders and ribs. 'What did you hit me with?'

'The baseball bat.' She was so smug about it, too.

'Good shot.' He rubbed the burning sensation on his neck.

Wren leaned back on her elbows, grinning up at him. 'I aimed to please. And to think I let you off easy.' She sat up, then winced. 'Ow!'

'What's wrong?'

'My leg. I must've cut it rolling in this mud with you. It's going to do wonders for my complexion.'

'Where does it hurt?' Marcus scrounged in the dirt for his torch.

'So now you have a torch?' Her sarcasm was undeniable. 'Why didn't you use it sooner?'

'Did you have one?'

'I lost mine when I jumped you.'

Marcus shone the torch down her leg. 'Aww, crap.' There was a stick imbedded in her calf muscle. 'Does it hurt?'

'What do you think?'

'Don't talk to me like that! I asked you a civil question.'

'Of course, it hurts. But I'm so full of adrenalin, I'm not feeling anything. You'd be the same, right? Hey, how much do you wanna bet we'll both feel it in the morning, calling each other names we've never heard of?'

Marcus chuckled. 'You have a such a way with words, you know that?' Reaching for his pocketknife, he cut the material of her long cotton pants, exposing her lower leg.

'It looks sore. You'll need stitches, but I'm not pulling it out.' He didn't want her to bleed out and get an infection from the mud. He unbuttoned his shirt.

'What are you doing?'

'I'm going to wrap your leg to keep that stick in place.'

'But there's mud all over your shirt.'

'The inside's clean—unless you want to take your shirt off?' He grinned at the possibility, and at Wren's silence for once, as he carefully secured the stick in place.

'Now what?'

'You are going to behave and at least play nice with me while I carry you back to the car. Then we're going to wake Stewart to fix your leg and to see if he can fix the pain in the neck you've become.' He scooped her up to his chest in one swift move. She was lighter than imagined.

'Is that figuratively or literally speaking?'

'What is?'

'The pain in the neck?' She shared a meek sorry grin. 'I'll behave, because I don't think I can walk with a chunk of wood sticking out of my leg. I may dislike being useless, but I am practical.'

'Good girl.'

'What does it feel like?'

'What?' He carried her up the bank towards the distant car lights. Her arms wrapped around his bare shoulders, holding her close to his chest. He'd describe it as pretty damned good, except for the mud they were covered in and her injury.

'Playing hero.'

'I don't see it as playing hero, and you're certainly no helpless damsel, that's for sure.' Damn, she was pretty, even with the mud.

'You found her, Sarge?' Porter rushed over with Darryl and Chopper.

'Porter, can you get my car? Be sure to radio ahead to the hospital and tell them we're coming in with a leg wound. Darryl, can you tell Tanisha and Felix, Wren's—'

'I'm fine,' interrupted Wren. 'Tell Felix not to panic, I'm

fine.'

'You sure, Miss? That doesn't look too good.' Darryl pointed to her leg.

'I'm okay. But if I know Felix, he'll have had ten panic attacks by now. So can you ...'

'Yes, Miss. You'd better take care of her, Sarge.'

Marcus huffed, with his voice clear and full of authority. 'Just do as requested.'

They all scattered, leaving Marcus to carry Wren.

'Do you usually have people run when you speak?'

'Yes. Except for you.' Marcus adjusted her weight, shifting her higher. Even with all the mud, her sweet feminine aroma was still there.

'I don't mean to do it on purpose, Detective Sergeant.' Wren's arms tightened around his neck, her head resting on his shoulder. It would have been romantic except for the mud and leg wound.

'Do you have trouble with authority?' Like he was having trouble stopping himself from nuzzling into her hair.

'Not generally. You just seem to be an exception to the rule.'

He stopped to stare at the deep pools in her eyes. She was everything against his rules. Everything.

Yet, he couldn't stop his reaction to the wash of warm heat coming from her soft skin against his bare chest. He didn't feel the cold, the mud, or the scratches, just her skin.

The flash of lights broke them out of their trance. It was Porter in his car.

'Oh, for the love of vodka and mango, where the hell are you, Wren?' Felix's screechy voice cut through the darkness.

'I think Felix has shifted from panic attack to attack dog mode.' Wren giggled. 'You can't help but love the guy. He cares.'

'I'm sure Tanisha will bring Felix up to the hospital.' Marcus placed Wren on the backseat to stretch out her leg, handing her the seatbelt. 'Hold on, and no backseat driving.'

FIFTEEN

Marcus carried Wren through the sliding doors of the small bush hospital where Stewart and the head nurse, Jenny, were waiting.

'What happened to you two? Go for a roll in the mud?' Jenny escorted them to the emergency room. 'You can put her down here, Marcus.'

Stewart tugged on his plastic gloves as Marcus placed Wren on the examination bed. 'Where's your shirt?'

'On her leg.'

'What happened to your back? It looks like a bruise forming.'

'Ask your patient. But don't worry about me, fix Wren, please.' Wren may have been playing tough in the car, but she was pale and in pain.

'Is Wren under arrest or something?'

'No.' Marcus frowned down at the wound on her leg. It made his stomach churn.

Wounds had never bothered him before. He'd grown an iron gut from his many years on the job, but it made him ill to see her like this. 'Just fix her, Stewart. Now.'

'Sure, mate, that's what I'm here for. We'll clean the area to see what we have. Can someone please tell me what happened?'

'I thought Marcus was this peeping Tom. It's not my fault you didn't identify yourself in the dark.' Wren frowned at Marcus.

'You shouldn't have been out there at all.'

'Hey, will you pair stop it?' Stewart unwound the bandage and inspected her leg. 'Nurse, we'll need a local to start.'

'It looks sore.' The woman was tougher than he thought. 'Are you in any pain? Stewart, give her something for the pain.'

'I'm with Marcus. What pills do you have?'

'Already on it.' Stewart removed the cap from the syringe.

'You're not sticking that into me, are you? I'll take door number two and choose the pills, please.' Wren was on her elbows, inching her way up the bed.

'It's a small needle, you won't feel it,' said Stewart, approaching with the syringe.

'No, you don't.'

Marcus held Wren in place before she wriggled off the bed. 'You're not scared of needles, are you?'

'Yes. I am.'

'You ran off into the dark after some man and attacked me thinking I was that creep. I'm bigger than you and you showed no fear.' Marcus cupped her cheek to look at him while Stewart did his job. 'That small needle isn't going to hurt as much as that stick jammed into your leg. Which you didn't even feel until we'd finished grappling in the mud.'

'This is different.' The tiniest of whimpers escaped as her grip tightened on his hand, gazing up at him with enormous eyes. 'Ow.'

'Didn't think the Ice Queen could feel anything. But I see you can.'

'I feel …' She swallowed as those sea-glass eyes became shiny again with tears.

'Hey, you'll be okay.' He stroked her hair. 'Stewart's one of the best surgeons around.'

'Brilliant is the word you should be looking for,' piped in Stewart.

'If he's that good, why is he working here, being a prick pricking me with that needle.'

'Because he's a smart-arse who is good at his job.' Marcus stroked her hair as her body relaxed, her grip loosened, and she sank deeper into the pillow on the examination bed.

'I'll give it a few minutes to kick in and we'll clean you up.' Stewart sorted out the instruments on the trolley and cracked the blue icepack. 'Marcus, this is for that war wound on your neck. You can wash up while I work on Wren.'

'I'll be right outside if you need me.' He didn't want to leave her. Yet, if he stayed, he'd be scrutinising everything Stewart did, while suffering with a severe case of heartburn from the worry.

'Mate, I've got this.' Stewart nodded at him, putting on a surgical mask.

Normally, it was Marcus removing concerned friends and family from the room to let the medical team do their work. Not him.

Was he too close to the patient?

'Wren, we're going to take a scan of the leg, and then we'll discuss our options from there …'

Wren gave him a slight nod, and Marcus squeezed her hand. If she asked him to stay, he would.

But she didn't, and he closed the door, leaving Stewart to do his magic.

SIXTEEN

'Where is she?' Felix's voice screeched like a thousand police sirens as he rushed through the hospital doors in his red silk pyjamas, covered with a smoking jacket. Tanisha shuffled in beside him, still in her fluffy slippers and dressing gown.

'Wren's in with the doctor.' Marcus paced the waiting room, holding an icepack to his ribs and another one to his neck. His wounds didn't matter, not while Wren was inside that other room.

Dammit, this was taking too long. Stewart should have finished by now.

'Oh, for the love of vodka and … and …' Felix stopped everything, slapping Tanisha on the arm, with their mouths falling open to stare at the shirtless Marcus. 'You should be on TikTok. Can you dance?'

Marcus scowled at the pair. 'I'm no TikTok cowboy.'

'How do you know about them?'

Marcus narrowed his eyes at the sniggering Tanisha, who was forever showing her phone around at work to display shirtless men dancing like strippers.

'Well, what happened to you?' Felix asked.

'Wren did this. She thought I was the creep.'

Felix and Tanisha's giggles were amplified in the silent hospital corridor.

Arseholes.

'Is Wren okay? Can I see her? Does she have to have her leg removed? Will she need blood? I can donate, you know? Oh, I'd die if she died—'

'Felix, Wren's just getting a few stitches.'

'You left her in there, *alone*?' Felix pointed to the closed doors.

Marcus didn't like being on this side of that door, either. 'They're doing their job.' Like he should be, but he couldn't, not while Wren was still inside that room.

'Did they give her a needle?'

'Yeah. Does Wren hate needles, Felix?'

'They terrify her. Oh, she's gonna hate that doctor now. The only thing she fears is needles. She'll curse his soul to—'

'Felix, shut up!' His head and shoulders hurt, and his ribs ached. He didn't need Felix's drama, not when he was trying to solve the situation. 'Sit down, the pair of you. Now.'

The pyjama-clad duo shuffled in their slippers to obediently sit on the plastic chairs.

'Tanisha, what are the rest of the men doing at the Peddler house?'

'Porter, Two-dollar Darryl and Chopper are searching the property. I tried to get some fingerprints from around the windows, but it looked like he wore gloves. I was going to tape the area off, but Felix screamed at me.'

'You only put out that police tape when there's a dead body. Wren is *not dead*.' Felix then gasped, with hand to his heart. 'Are we safe in that house, Marcus?'

'I'll organise someone to look at the security of the place.' But the Peddlers had high fences and barbed wire, along with a reputation of *shoot first answer questions later*. No local dared to visit the Peddlers.

'I want armed guards on patrol, twenty-four-seven. Oh, and a dog! No, I want a dozen massive, gnarly, vicious attack dogs.'

'Felix, calm down.' No wonder Wren didn't share too much information with the drama queen. 'Let me discuss security options with Wren.' Marcus waited a few beats before putting the next round of questions to the delicate man sitting in silk PJs. 'Felix, can you tell me what happened?'

'I came downstairs to the office. Wren was at her desk reading and this man was standing right behind her with his face pressed against the glass.'

'What did he look like?'

'Tall. About your height, but thinner. Nothing like your set of shoulders and those arms and those—'

Marcus cleared his throat, wishing he'd kept a spare shirt in the car. 'Focus, Felix. What was this man wearing?'

'Sorry, it's just there at my eye height …' Felix pointed at Marcus's abs.

Marcus scowled at the sniggering Tanisha, trying to remind her he was her boss. 'Go on, Felix, what was this man wearing?'

'Um, yes, so this strange man was dressed in black, wearing camouflage face paint like soldiers. I know it was that make-up, because I had this show at the club where all these hot men played Navy SEALs, it was just fabulous.'

'Felix, can we please focus on the guy you spotted at the house tonight? How old was he?'

'Late forties to mid-fifties with blue eyes. I'm not sure if it was blonde or grey hair peeking from beneath the black beanie he had on, but he was so angry, staring at Wren.'

The tendons in his neck tightened as his heartbeat raced with fear for Wren. Why was this happening to her, and in *his* town? 'Would you remember this man if you saw him again?'

'Of course. I'm a man who remembers a man's face, even if they're wearing make-up.' Felix crossed one leg over a knee, smoothing down his silk nightwear.

Marcus wore nothing to bed, unlike Felix. No wonder Felix had eight cases of junk Marcus carted up the stairs.

'Is Wren safe from that man? Is he going to come back and stalk her? Oh for the love of vodka and ginger beer, will she ever be safe?'

'I won't leave Wren in any danger.' Not if Marcus had any say on the matter.

The double doors opened and Stewart entered the hallway. 'Wren's done.'

'How is she, Doctor?' Felix shuffled in his slippers with his silk dressing gown flapping like a cape. 'Is she going to live? Will she be able to walk again?'

'Wren's fine. She's got eight stitches.'

'I hope you were careful on the scar. Wren's got great legs.'

Marcus agreed.

'Please, I'm a professional. You'll hardly notice it when the stitches come out. Wren's being cleaned up, you can see her shortly.'

'Thank you, Doctor, you're a god.' Felix vigorously shook Stewart's hand.

Stewart had to pry his fingers free. 'I'd like to check the sergeant, so if you'll excuse us.' Stewart led Marcus down the corridor. 'How are you feeling?'

'Sore. Wren really belted me.'

Stewart directed Marcus to the examining table in his office and checked out his back. 'You've got a nasty bruise across the shoulders. What did Wren hit you with?'

'A baseball bat.'

'And the ribs?'

'Her knee.'

Stewart chuckled. 'That's what you get for rolling around in the mud together. Then again, you lucky bastard to wrestle with Wren like that.'

'I don't feel lucky, not with this headache.'

Stewart shone his penlight into Marcus's eyes, continuing his examination.

'Is Wren, okay?'

'She's going to be fine. A bit off with the fairies from the pain killers, though. Wren told me she has no drug tolerance, while cussing at me without swearing.'

'What did she say?'

'Something about evil penguins pushing me off a glacier where my soul would plunge to the dark depths of Antarctica, where the sea lions would pluck the flesh free from my bones. Jenny was in hysterics.'

'What were you doing?'

'Giving Wren a tetanus shot. I almost called you back to hold her down.'

Marcus smirked as the stress shifted.

'Was there really someone at her window?'

'Yep. The bastard was standing right behind her, watching her every move.' Marcus gritted his teeth as a rage fired in his chest.

'And you'll be there to protect her?'

'It's my job.'

'Yeah, but that little lady really kicked your arse.' Stewart removed his gloves and unlocked the nearby medicine cabinet. 'Here, take these for the muscular pain and headache. And when my much-prettier patient is no longer under the influence of drugs, I'm going to ask her out to dinner.' Stewart held out a bottle of water.

Marcus stared at the pills in his hand. Normally, he didn't care who Stewart dated, but this was different. 'Felix reckons Wren's going to hate you for the rest of her life because you gave her a needle.' He took the pills and washed them down.

'I'm sure I can charm my way around that. So, are you escorting Wren home, or are you letting Tanisha take her back?'

'I'll be transporting Wren back. I want to see what's happening at the Peddler property.'

'I think I'll visit the patient in the morning after rounds.'

'Why? Are you worried she might get infected from the mud?'

Stewart nodded. 'With Wren's fear of needles, I doubt she'll come back here in a hurry. Are you going to carry her to the car, or shall I?'

'Wouldn't want to mess up that nice clean white coat of yours, Doctor.'

'You may as well be half decent. Take this.' Stewart passed a grey T-shirt to Marcus as they returned to the emergency room 'Try not to stretch it too much with those shoulders.'

'Wow, you could grate cheese on that washboard of a stomach.' Wren shared a cheeky grin while staring at Marcus slipping on his T-shirt.

Felix rushed into the room. 'Oh, my poor princess, are you okay? Can you walk?'

'I'm stoned! That doctor gave me drugs and two needles. I hate needles. But hey, did you see the body on the detective sergeant? Seriously, Felix, you could grate cheese on that man's stomach. It could crush rocks and sharpen diamonds even.'

'Ooh, you are so going to hate yourself tomorrow.' Felix sniggered as he glanced back at Marcus and Stewart. 'She's going to hate the both of you when she wakes up. I hope you have more drugs for her, Doctor? We can share.'

'Felix, drugs are dangerous, they make you feel so out

of control. I'd rather be drunk any day than be like this.' Wren went to pat Felix's shoulder, missing him completely and started falling off the bed.

Marcus quickly caught the glassy-eyed, woozy Wren in his arms.

'Hey you, Detective Sergeant, you.' Wren was high as a freaking kite.

'Let's get you into the car.'

'Why, what are you doing later, handsome?' She was like a drunk trying to pick him up in a bar, lazily wrapping her arms around his neck.

'I'm taking you home.'

'Your place or—wait, I don't have a home, not since I ran away from the ultimate Ice Queen. But you ... I could raffle you off at a cougar's convention.'

'What?' Marcus, struggling to keep up with what Wren was saying, carried her out with her entire lower leg bandaged.

'Now, Toots, be nice to the man carrying you across the threshold.'

'Felix, I'm liable to say anything in this condition. Save me.'

'I'm here.'

Marcus placed Wren into the backseat of the squad car, Felix climbed in beside her.

'What did you give her and how long before those drugs wear off?' Marcus asked Stewart.

'In about four hours, sometimes eight in some patients. I warned you she was off with the pixies. It's obvious Wren has no drug tolerance. But, just in case, give her two of these pills if she wakes up during the night in pain. I'll bring more in the morning when I check Wren's dressings.'

Marcus took the pill bottle. 'Great. Wren can talk to you about her father then.'

'What about?'

'Just bring out Rowan Peddler's medical file with you.'

Marcus wanted another look at those medical reports, this time from Wren's clever point of view. 'Text me when you're on your way, so I can be there. And don't let Wren question you without me.'

SEVENTEEN

Wren woke to a thick bandage wrapped around her calf, throbbing in pain, as if stuck in some nightmare. But it got worse, realising last night's adventure had been real.

She hobbled to the bathroom to inspect her injuries, taping a bag over her stitches, while steam filled the bathroom. Her head hung in shame under the shower as the rush of all she'd said to Marcus and Stewart returned, only to jerk back from the memory of Felix screaming at the stalker in the window.

Determined, she carefully clambered down the stairs to the office where the large desk sat squarely in the centre with its back to the wide window view of the main driveway, the shed, and the track to the Sandfly Saloon.

Why was that man here?

Pushing the heavy chair out of the way, she inspected the window. A shiver ran up her spine, prickling over her scalp, as she saw the fingerprint dust and smudges across the glass panes.

How long had that man been watching her?

Among the pile of discarded sporting goods, the deflated footballs and cricket bats—where did her baseball bat end up? She found a walking stick that might have belonged to one of her grandparents.

Outside, the sky was a pale blue, with the sun barely peeking over the treetops to highlight the sleek police car parked in the yard.

What was that doing here?

Was she going to get arrested for the stash of chop-chop in the illegal bar she apparently owned?

But she could only focus on one thing at a time.

The walking cane was a help, as she hobbled along the front verandah to the office window.

Craning her neck at the fingerprints, the man was taller. So, what was he looking at? Her? The office? Would he be coming back? For what?

'What are you doing up so early?' Marcus stood right behind her in socks, work pants, and grey T-shirt.

She squealed, losing her balance, with her heart hammering.

Marcus caught her arms and held her steady.

But she'd squealed—she never squealed or screamed.

'You shouldn't be walking around on that leg.'

'You shouldn't be sneaking up on me.' She pushed off his solid chest. That T-shirt showed off every muscle, tempting her to slide a palm over every curve and dip along his body, while inhaling his divine cologne.

'How are you feeling?'

'Sore. You?' She winced with guilt at clobbering the poor guy who was only trying to help.

'Sore.'

'Why are you still here?'

'Felix was frightened, and you were too out of it to care. I slept on the couch, which is where you're going.' He scooped her up in his arms before she could protest.

'I can walk, you know.'

'Stewart said you need to stay off your leg until the swelling goes down. Or don't you remember?'

'Um.'

His chuckle carried through to his chest, pressing against her side.

Inside, he placed her on the couch. 'At least you're cleaner than you were last night.'

'You're awake?' Felix flitted down the stairs with his silk dressing gown floating like a cape, to give Wren a hug. 'How are you feeling?'

'Sore. And so is Marcus.'

'Well, you did bash the poor man. I'll make coffee.'

'Here.' Marcus handed Wren two pills and a glass of water.

'What's this?'

'Pain killers. We're on the same ones.'

'I hope it's not the same stuff that doctor injected me with last night, it's made me so foggy.' She washed down her pills with Marcus towering over her, making sure she took them. 'Felix, how did we get home from the hospital?'

'Marcus drove us back. You fell asleep in the police car and Marcus carried you up the stairs and put you to bed,' Felix replied from the kitchen doorway. 'It's so nice to have a strong man in the house.'

'You snore, you know that.'

She scowled up at the big brute, watching her every move. 'They drugged me, and I've had little sleep these past few weeks.'

'You need to put your leg up, doctor's orders.' Marcus grabbed some cushions to raise her leg, propping more pillows behind her back. 'Except for that ticked-off expression, I'd say you look comfy.'

'Are you going to fluff my pillows and fetch my morning papers too? I'll get you a bell and a bow tie for you to be at my beck and call as the butler.'

'Don't push it, princess.'

She had no right to be mean when Marcus was only trying to help. 'I'm sorry for hurting you last night. I honestly thought you were the other guy.' The back of his neck wore a dark nasty bruise. She'd hate to see how his back looked. 'Thank you for the hospital trip and for staying over ...' The guy had such a large presence to him. 'Felix would've been happy knowing you were in the house last night. And, um ... me too.'

His lips curled into a satisfied grin. 'Wow, you really can be nice.'

'I don't know how long I'll play nice for, not with my leg this sore.' It was throbbing.

'You can blame it on that huge log they pulled from your leg,' said Felix, returning with a tray of coffee.

'No, not that. This. Look at what that doctor did to me.' Wren lifted her skirt to reveal the largest black and purple bruise covering her thigh muscle.

'Please tell me I didn't do that to you?' Marcus dropped to his haunches, shaking his head with a look of horror.

'No. You left these marks on my wrists.' His thumbprint was clear on her skin. 'And I deserved these, so please stop feeling guilty about it.'

'Where did that come from?' Marcus pointed to her leg, wincing at the ugliness of it.

'This is from the needle that prick gave me! And to think he wanted to inject my butt! I wouldn't be able to sit for a week.'

Relief spread over Marcus's face, as he dropped into the nearby armchair to slide into his boots. 'Why do you dislike needles so much?'

'They hurt. And I bruise way too easily. Rowan was the

same.' She covered her leg, pulling her shirt sleeves down to hide her marks.

'Are you going to hate the Hot Doc for the rest of your life? He's really a darling, you know.' Felix passed a coffee to Wren.

'Thanks. Only until the marks disappear from my leg.'

Felix passed a travel mug to Marcus.

'Thanks, Felix.' Marcus sipped, nodding in approval at the coffee, which made Felix beam with pride. 'Are you going to hate me, Wren, for putting those marks on your wrists?'

'No. I'm to blame for those.' Again, tugging on her sleeves. 'Hey, thanks for what you did for me at the hospital, for being there ...' She'd wanted him to stay to hold his hand in the hospital room. But he left. Like he was leaving now, sliding on his police cap.

It would never work between them. Not with what was stashed on the Peddler property and what Marcus did for a living. Her attraction towards Marcus had to stop now.

'I'm heading home, then to the station. I'll come back in a few hours when Stewart changes your bandages.'

'Do doctors make house calls out here? How sweet,' said Felix.

'That's unnecessary. You can call this doctor up and cancel. Tell him I'm fine.' No way was she going near the doctor again.

Marcus grinned at her, as if reading her mind. 'I asked Stewart to bring over Rowan's file so you can talk to him about your father's medical history.'

Was the guy going to start finishing her sentences too? Carrying her around the place, organising doctor's appointments ... Hold the phone— 'That'd work.' She had questions for the not-so-good doctor. 'Can you be here when I talk to Stewart, Marcus?' They'd made a deal to share information and she respected his opinion. Last night had to do with her father's death, she was sure of it.

'I'll be here. Look, Wren, I went over the place last night while you were snoring the roof off ...' Marcus grinned. Wren frowned. 'I know someone who can upgrade your house locks and put in some sensor lights around the perimeter of your house and shed. They can come out today.'

Felix nodded at Wren like his neck was on a spring.

'Sure, we'll take whatever you're suggesting for security. Again, thank you for your help, Marcus.' She went to get off the couch, keen to escort the cop off the premises, he was distracting her from getting down to the business of scouting the property to find out how this guy got in.

Instead, Marcus pushed her back into the nest of cushions, giving her shoulder a gentle squeeze. 'Try and stay off that leg, at least until Stewart gets here.'

The care in his deep brown eyes made her surrender with an urge to smile and sigh, free from all of her fears. His touch, his stare, his presence ... all of him was calming. 'I'll try.'

EIGHTEEN

For the third time in under twenty-four hours, Marcus entered the Peddler property where the tall white farmhouse was a stark contrast to the rich ochre soils and deep blue sky.

The assorted furniture, bags and boxes cluttering the verandah were gone.

The hardware store's handyman van was parked haphazardly in the yard. Along with Stewart's car from the hospital, Porter's patrol car because he asked him to meet him here. Tanisha was also here, apparently seeing it as her moral duty to take the day off from work to stay and console her friend.

Through the open doorway, the couch where he'd left Wren was now vacant. No surprises there.

Marcus found everyone in the kitchen, seated around the large table, except one. 'Where's Wren?'

'Gone out. Here, you must indulge.' Felix, in his pink apron, held up a plate of muffins and the coffee pot.

'Thanks, Felix.' He grabbed a fresh cup. 'Gone where? I told Wren to stay off her leg.'

'Wren did just like you told her. Then she put on her boots, went to the shed, found a four-wheel motorbike thingy and rode off. She's really embracing the country life.'

'Which way did she go? No, don't answer that. I know where.' Marcus arched his eyebrow at the uniformed senior constable who was meant to be on the clock. 'Porter, are you coming?'

Behind the steering wheel, Marcus waited for Porter, who rushed out with coffee and two muffins. Stewart jumped into the back seat with his own coffee and cake to go. 'What do you think you're doing?'

'Wren is my patient.'

Marcus shook his head. Retracing their car tracks from last night where the long corridor of dry grass spread out like a golden blanket under the sunshine. He was relieved to see no tobacco was being grown. But he wasn't here for that.

'There's the quad.' Porter pointed at the large bike parked near the irrigation ditch that was a steep barrier to the riverbed.

'Can't see her.' Stewart stood beside Porter scanning the area.

Marcus flicked on the car's siren for a few beats, but it was enough to send flocks of birds fleeing in all directions.

Wren popped her head out of the irrigation ditch and waved.

Her smile was a huge relief. 'I see her.'

In the ditch, wearing long red wellington boots, Wren leaned on her walking stick.

'What are you doing out here? You're supposed to be resting.' Marcus jumped down beside her.

'I did.'

'For about ten minutes, I heard.'

'I'm fine. Honestly, I am.' She patted his shoulder. Her eyes were clear and bright, nothing like last night. 'Stop stressing.'

'Why are you down here?'

She paused, chewing her bottom lip.

'We had a deal.'

'That we do. Look, he was hiding in here. See the boot prints.'

Marcus narrowed his eyes at the pair of prints, then tried to get his bearings. 'Where did—'

'We did our mud roll further down.'

'You have a habit of doing that.'

'What?'

'Finishing my sentences and knowing what I'm going to say.' It was irritating.

She tapped on Marcus's leg. 'Lift. I want to see the tread?'

'Please would be nice.' But she had a point. 'That's a different tread. We all wear the same regulation boots at the station.'

'Whoa, that means I ran straight past him. Twice.' Her fear was real, with her face dropping various shades of pale in the blink of an eye.

He plonked a hand on her shoulder to calm her some. 'Did you find out how he got in?'

'Darryl found a hole in the fence.' Wren pointed to the far end.

Over the lip of the irrigation channel to the far end of the property, the distant fence line, with its rows of sharp barbed wire, glinted in the sunlight. 'Darryl hasn't fixed it, has he? That's evidence.'

'I told him to wait for you first.'

'Good girl, you're learning.' Marcus patted her head like a child, grinning at her screwed-up nose. 'That makes it property damage and trespassing.' The list of charges was getting longer.

'Wren, are you going to stand in that ditch all day? Or can I check out your dressings?' Stewart asked from on top of the ridge, with Porter beside him, scoffing down his muffins.

Wren scowled at the doctor.

'Are you really going to hate me for the rest of your life?'

'Only until the bruises disappear.'

As Marcus helped Wren out of the ditch, an engine rumbled nearby. It was a truck, towing a freezer trailer, with Two-dollar Darryl behind the wheel.

'Porter, take Wren's quad and race over to Darryl and tell him to meet me up at the house. I'll transport the doctor and his patient.'

With Wren and Stewart safely inside the house, Marcus approached Two-dollar Darryl and Chopper waiting in the truck's shade. 'Morning, Darryl. Chopper.'

'Morning,' mumbled Chopper. Scuffing the toe of his sneaker into the red dust. The lad's shiny sports shirt and streetwear styled baggy cargos were a stark contrast to his older uncle in dusty denim, beside him.

With arms crossed over his chest, Darryl gave a short sharp nod of his well-worn Akubra. 'Sarge. You get this fella yet?'

'I'm working on it. Wren tells me you found the hole in the fence. Can you show me? Then you can fix it.'

'No worries.' Darryl grabbed tools and wire from the truck's tray. 'Chopper, you take the truck down the track, eh? I'll take the quad.'

They stood back as the truck slowly jerked away with its gears crunching.

'Has Chopper got a licence?'

'Nah, he's learning. Is he gonna get into trouble for driving, Sarge?'

'It's private property, Darryl. Not a public road.'

Darryl gave another short nod of his wide-brimmed hat, gunning the quad's engine. 'It's this way.'

In the squad car, Marcus followed Darryl down the well-maintained firebreak with the tall fence running alongside. The Peddlers were serious about security, with the fence ending deep within the river itself where you'd have to swim with the crocodiles to get around it.

Darryl pointed at the fence. 'That mongrel got in 'ere.'

'How did you spot this?' Marcus inspected the fence where the mesh matched perfectly.

'Footprints and cigarette butts.' Darryl pointed to the ground nearby. 'The dirty mongrel. Got no respect. Ol' Pop Peddler hated anyone throwing their butts out like that. It's a flamin' fire hazard.'

They were the same brand of tailor-made smokes Marcus had found at the house, now littering the neighbour's plot under a group of trees. There were a lot of them, all different ages.

'He's been here a bit, hasn't he, Sarge? Longer than Miss Wren's bin stayin' at the house.'

The realisation was like a spike of ice twisting along his spine. 'You didn't tell Wren this?'

'No. Only you. Here, see this?' Darryl pointed at the cut mesh where thin fibres were snagged. 'He wore black, just like that Felix from Sydney said.'

Marcus took photos and collected the evidence. Then he pushed against the fence, where it popped open like a swinging door. 'Well done for spotting this, Darryl. I wouldn't have seen it.'

Standing on the neighbour's property, their poorly kept fire break was nothing more than a dry, overgrown wallaby track. But someone had been regularly using it, to create a turning circle in the long grass to park beneath the group of trees. It was great cover to hide.

Looking back through the fence, Marcus faced the Peddlers' long golden paddock. In the distance the shed blocked the house from this location, with only the roof and attic window visible. The open field would've been hard to sneak across during the day, but from this spot you could watch people coming and going, to learn the occupant's routines.

'Can I fix this fence now, Sarge?'

'Here, I'll help.' Marcus pulled the cut mesh together as Darryl covered it with another patch of mesh to weave the wire through. 'Do you know why someone would sneak up to the house, Darryl?'

'Nope.' Darryl didn't even look at Marcus as he expertly used the fencing pliers and stood back to admire his work. 'I'm gonna put up one of Pop Peddler's signs here, like the one we got on the front fence, to let the fella know we know, eh?'

'Good idea. And you'll keep the gates locked?'

'Always do. I checked they were locked before I went to bed.'

'What time was that?'

'Ten o'clock. Same time every night.'

Felix raised the alarm at eleven.

Marcus reached inside the car for a manual, as Darryl put away his tools. 'Darryl, I'll ask you again. Do you know who would do this?'

'Wish I did. That's bad news scaring Miss Wren and that Felix fella. I promised her father I'd watch out for his daughter.'

'I'm glad you're here to do that, Darryl.' Marcus nodded at the Indigenous man, noting the worry lines deepening around his dark eyes. 'Here, this is for Chopper.' He held out the manual.

'What for?'

'For Chopper to get his licence. It's the road rules. The business card inside has my numbers. You call me if you see anything suspicious or if Wren's in trouble. Anytime.'

'No, worries. You goin' back to the house?'

Marcus suppressed his grin. Two-dollar Darryl did not want a policeman poking around the Peddler's property.

'I'll take a cast of the boot prints Wren found first, then I'll go back to the house.' Marcus wanted to be there when Wren spoke with Stewart, hoping her questions would help with all these little pieces that were starting to add up in his investigation.

NINETEEN

Wren heard his boots coming up the front steps, to then pause as he wiped them on the mat, the screen door creaked, and there he was, taking her breath away. Marcus.

'Coffee, Sergeant?' Felix stood in the kitchen doorway, playing the perfect host.

'Yeah. Thanks, Felix. You two all done?' Marcus dropped into the armchair on the far side of the room. 'How's the leg?'

'Fine. It's the bruising that's more of a bother.' She had to sit at an awkward angle to get comfortable, and her lower leg pulsed with heated pain. 'Did Darryl show you the fence?'

'He did. We fixed it. He's going to hang one of your grandfather's scary signs there.' Marcus winked at her.

Unexpectedly, she giggled. Her face flushed with heat, giddy at the sight of the sexy man in uniform who filled the room.

Stewart cleared his throat, removing a file from his bag. 'Marcus told me you wanted to talk about your father?'

'Yes.' Oh, she had questions, lots of them. 'For starters, can you explain Rowan's medical condition?'

Marcus sat quietly on the far side, listening as Stewart produced X-rays, blood tests, and various other tests, explaining the severity of Rowan's lung cancer, answering all of Wren's many probing questions that went on for a good twenty minutes.

'Did you do the autopsy?' Wren asked Stewart.

'Yes.'

'What about a toxicology test?'

'We found traces of assorted prescribed medications and alcohol in his system.'

She frowned. 'Wouldn't the mix of alcohol and medication be a dangerous cocktail? The perfect tool for a suicide or accidental overdose?' They were the toughest questions to ask, but she kept a cool head by imagining she was talking about someone else. She was just doing her research. And she was good at researching.

'Considering the condition of your father's lungs, Rowan was still smoking and drinking while taking the medication.'

Wren pointed at the report among the many, spread across the coffee table. 'But the toxicology report never showed he'd taken any significant amounts to cause any impact.'

'The type of medication Rowan was on, it's toxic when mixed with alcohol. I warned Rowan of the dangers of smoking and drinking while in his condition, especially while taking that medication. But he was very ill and I'd hoped that those meds would give him more time. It's what all terminal patients want, more time.' Stewart shifted in his seat, to flick through the pages of the file. 'Look, I also sought a second opinion with the coroner's office, who agreed with my findings. Here's the autopsy report.'

'Okay.' No, nothing about this conversation was okay, but she had to ask. 'Were there any photos?'

'Yes, but you're not seeing those.' Marcus's firm, commanding tone made her pause. They were the first words he'd spoken since this meeting began.

Marcus was right, she didn't need to see those photos.

The house phone rang. She made a move, but Marcus moved quicker.

'Stay there, I'll get it.' Marcus soon returned. 'It's for you, Stewart.'

Wren chewed her bottom lip, tempted to peek inside Stewart's medical file.

'Don't do it, Wren.'

She narrowed her eyes at Marcus, watching her every move from his chair. 'I have a curious mind.'

'I know you do; you asked some good questions.'

'Is that why you let me do all the talking?'

'This is your meeting, and you needed answers.'

Marcus was right. The coroner's report looked legit with its official stamp at the bottom, claiming: *Death by natural causes.*

So why was the house trashed? A letter hidden? And holes cut in the fence by a stalker staring at her through the window?

'I've got to head back to the hospital,' said Stewart, packing his bag.

'Everything all right?' Marcus checked his radio and phone.

'Clinic's about to begin.'

The way Marcus nodded at Stewart, it was obvious they were friends, or close workmates, with what they did as part of their job, and she'd taken up enough of their professional time.

'Thank you, Stewart, for your help. I'm sorry if I was rude to you earlier.'

'All good. How long are you going to hate me for giving you those needles?'

'Only until the bruises disappear.' Wren could only offer him a meek smile, because she was going to curse him every time the bruise hurt.

'Good. Once they do, I'll take you out to dinner.'

'Oh, um …' Her eyes flared in surprise. If Felix was there, he'd be nudging her to answer. 'Okay?'

Marcus wiped at his forehead, as if to wipe away his frown.

What was that frown for?

'Wren, keep an eye out for infections,' said Stewart, gently touching her upper arm. 'If it starts acting up or you get a fever, come and see me at the hospital straight away. No messing around.'

'I'll be fine.'

'I'm serious, Wren, you cut yourself in that mud.'

'It's just mud.'

'If it was the wet season, I'd be dosing you with antibiotics and keeping you in for observations.'

'Over a set of stitches?'

'There's a dangerous bacterium in the soil called *Burkholderia pseudomallei*, it causes Melioidosis. People have died from a simple cut on their fingers from that germ.'

'So it's not just crocodiles, snakes, and heatstroke I have to worry about, it's the soil, too?'

'Welcome to the Territory.' Stewart chuckled. 'I'll see you at the hospital in six days to remove those stitches. I've already booked you in, no excuses.' He passed her a card.

'I'll walk you out, Stewart. Wren, I'll be back to talk with you this afternoon.' Marcus led the way.

'Why?'

'Because all of that medication you tripped out on last night will be out of your system, and you'll have had time to think about what Stewart told you. Be here, in this house and not in the paddock somewhere, when I get back.'

'Hey—'

'Talk then.' Marcus closed the front door on her.

She scowled at the closed door. Just who the hell did Marcus think he was?

TWENTY

'So, what do you think?' Marcus asked Stewart as they headed for their cars. Hoping Wren was going to rest her leg, and stay inside that house. She was safe there.

'Gorgeous. Which of us do you think she'll choose?'

Marcus frowned as a surge of heat flared in his chest. There was no reason to be jealous over a woman he'd just met. Especially one who didn't listen to him, who was irritating and … And he had a job to do.

'I'm talking about what Wren asked you?' Wren was clever, using tactics similar to those he'd used himself to trip up an interviewee in an interrogation.

'Wren's questioning was thorough. Is Wren a lawyer or something?'

'No idea.' Marcus hadn't dug very far into Wren's past beyond her driver's licence and birth certificate.

'I'll ask on our date. It should make for interesting dinner conversation that doesn't involve cows or farming. Have you asked Wren out? Or is she ticked at you, too?'

'I can't. I won't.' Oh, he'd thought about it.

'Why not?'

'Work. She's involved with a crime.' Marcus couldn't date someone he may have to lay charges against while trying to keep her safe. It was confusing enough as it was.

'That stalker?'

Marcus nodded, keeping a tight lid on what else might be going on. 'Don't you have work ethics against dating your patients?'

'Not in a town this small.' Stewart shared that cocky grin the ladies loved. 'What do you think Wren's score will be on our dating-rating scale? Don't answer that because I'll let you know after our date.' Stewart tooted the horn, his car stirring up dust as he left the property.

It wasn't his business what Wren did. If she wanted to date the doctor, so be it. It had never bothered him before who Stewart dated. Yet he found himself struggling to shut off all these feelings for someone he couldn't have.

He had his job; he loved his job. As his mother would say, he was married to the job. There was no room in his life for anyone, especially someone like Wren. She was too clever, too pretty, and too stubbornly independent, with an inheritance that could land her sweet arse in jail.

He had to stick to his job, that was as black and white as it got. The law was the law.

TWENTY-ONE

Late in the afternoon Marcus returned to the Peddler farmhouse. Tanisha's car was still there, along with the handyman's van, and another car.

He groaned. It was Emelia's car.

'Welcome back, Sergeant.' Felix greeted him at the door. Gone was the pink apron and coffee mug, replaced with a cocktail glass. 'Did you see? We've got these chunky locks on the doors, and lights all around the house.'

'Good.' It's what Marcus asked for.

'I still want one of those vicious guard dogs that we can let out at night, but Wren refuses.'

'You have the fencing for it.'

'Good point, I'll try again.'

The kitchen table was filled with wine and women, while the handyman was packing up his tools in the living area. Ol' Pop Peddler would roll over in his grave at all these strangers in his house. 'Where's Wren?'

'In her office.' Felix pointed to the closed door at the bottom of the stairs. 'I'm happy to report Wren has locked herself away in that office ever since your meeting this morning. Well, mostly.'

'Good.' Marcus knocked on the office door. 'Wren?'

The women at the table were silent. He could feel their stares on his back.

'Come in, Marcus.'

Inside, Wren was nowhere to be seen. 'Wren?'

'Down here.' She was seated on the floor, behind the door.

'What are you doing down there?' She was cute, with her long hair down her shoulders.

'Hiding from everyone.' She raised her red wine glass. 'Care for a drink? It's a nice drop. Or are you still on duty?'

He was always on duty these days. 'How much have you had to drink? You're on medication.'

'The only medication I took was what you gave me this morning, and I'm only having the one glass. The bottle is on the cabinet with a spare glass, if you dare.'

Was this a peace offering of some kind? How could he refuse. 'Why are you sitting on the floor?'

'It was easier for my leg.'

'Fair enough.' He sat down beside her with their backs resting against the wall, facing the desk sitting before the large window, where a figure was drawn onto the glass panes. 'Who drew that?'

'I did. It's lipstick. I wanted to see what Felix saw.'

'Are you a private detective?'

'No, I'm just curious by nature. So, what's been happening in your world today? Anything interesting?'

'Work.' He sipped on the merlot. 'So, are you ready to talk to me about last night?'

'Are you going to share what you've learned?'

He didn't want to scare her.

Wren frowned at him. 'Hey, we made a deal. Remember?'

'We did.' He wished he hadn't, but he wanted to play

nice. 'Ladies first.'

'I found these today.' She held up a ziplock bag of cigarette butts.

'Riding around on the bike again?'

'No. These were in the shed. I was looking for a spot to store boxes and furniture.' She pointed at the bag. 'If you notice, they're of different ages and colouration. Have you had the others tested?'

'Yes, but we won't know the results for a few days. Are you sure no one else smokes around here?'

'Darryl and Chopper don't. No one else has been here but my father, who never threw his cigarette butts away like that, calling them a fire hazard. And he only smoked …'

Yeah, he knew all about the Peddlers' chop-chop.

Marcus stared at the image drawn on the window. 'What were you doing before you chased this guy?' He fought to stop his frown at her foolishness for doing such a thing.

'I was reading this.' She handed him a letter. 'I've set the desk and chair in the same position as last night.'

'You've recreated the scene?' Marcus was impressed.

'From the outside where that guy stood, you can see that it's a handwritten letter, but it's impossible to read the words.'

'Do you have any idea why he was here?'

'I'm guessing he's looking for something that Rowan had. Read the letter. I'm interested to hear your point of view, because he wrote it a few days before he died.'

'Toots?' Felix knocked, popping his head around the door. 'Aww, isn't this cosy?'

'Felix?' Wren's tone was laced with warning.

'The security guy has finished, and he needs you to sign off on something.'

Marcus helped her to stand, hating the sight of that

walking stick and how she hobbled.

'You stay there, Marcus. I'll be back in a minute.'

Marcus read the letter, then inspected the setting. Wren's attention to detail was remarkable.

'So …' Wren stood in the open doorway with her long skirt gently swaying. 'Want to see where I found that stalker's rubbish in the shed?'

Again, she read his mind.

'Bring your wine.' She re-corked the bottle, tucking it under her arm.

'Can I take this letter?'

'Sure, I made you that copy. That's part of the deal, right?'

'Where's the original?'

'In the safe.'

'I'll drive us up there.'

She tossed a frown at him over her shoulder. With the sun behind her, she was gorgeous.

'You're using a walking stick.'

'Fine. Only if you show me where Darryl fixed the fence.'

'We can check the gate's locked while we're in the car.'

'Deal.'

He'd never had to negotiate with anyone, not like this.

Marcus opened the passenger door for Wren to climb in, when her long skirt caught on the bandage, giving a flash of her cream legs, which made his mouth water.

But that bandage covering her calf was a stark reminder he was on the job.

At the fence, he helped her out of the car. 'I rarely walk around with a drink in hand while investigating things. Yet, it's becoming a habit in this place. This morning it was coffee and muffins, now this?' He grinned over the rim of the wineglass.

'It's a great way to do it, huh?' Wren inspected the repaired fence covered with a large sign that read:

**TRESPASSERS WILL BE SHOT ON SIGHT
AND FED TO THE CROCODILES.
WE'RE NOT KIDDING!**

She giggled. 'I like that sign.'

'Let's hope it does the job.'

At the shed, he pushed open the solid sliding door and followed Wren inside.

It was a large, sturdy shed, with a high roof and a mezzanine floor to one side. In the centre of the main floor stood a Landcruiser ute, which he recognised as Rowan's.

Parked to one side was a modern tractor. Her quad stood with two more motorbikes, assorted farming machinery, and a fancy ride-on mower were stored in the back. The Peddlers had some toys.

He followed Wren deeper into the shed's shade, to what he'd describe as an industrial area. 'Do you know what they used this equipment for, Wren?'

'Do you?'

'Why don't you tell me?'

'Do I have to?'

'So you know, huh?'

'I only found out yesterday. Swear it.'

'I believe you.'

'Well, believe me when I say they've stopped growing the tobacco. You've been driving around the place; you haven't seen any of it.'

Marcus didn't look too hard, either. 'Did Darryl tell you what they used this section for?'

'This is the chop-chop shop. They hung the tobacco to dry from those grids, then fed it into that chopping machine, then cured it for months. Some tobacco they'd cure it for a year or more. Then it got weighed, bagged, and sealed. Darryl said the tobacco planting and harvesting rotations were on a sixty-day cycle, with that long paddock sectioned off, giving them a regular supply. Apparently, this property's sandy soil and top end weather are the perfect conditions for tobacco.'

'I heard it was quite a large commercial operation.'

'You didn't see it?'

'Not in this shed, no. I only saw this place once, when they chased me away as a kid. It looked like fields of silverbeet to me. I was in Melbourne when they allegedly shut it down. But I never smoked.'

'Me neither. But for over two thousand years tobacco was used for cultural and religious ceremonies and even medicinal purposes.' Wren spoke as they walked around the silent machinery. 'Since the 1800s settlers grew tobacco that was used as a form of currency in this country.'

'Prison systems still trade in cigarettes.'

'True. I mean, tobacco was so commonly grown it was an industry supported by the Federal Government right through to the 90s. Then the Federal Government paid out all those farmers to stop growing tobacco.'

'For those *registered* as licenced tobacco growers.' No paperwork anywhere showed the Peddlers were commercial producers of tobacco. Did he dare ask her about the Sandfly Saloon? 'You did your research?'

Wren's clever eyes caught the light from the window. 'I enjoy researching and getting lost down rabbit holes of information. I lose hours discovering details on the net.'

'Any ideas on what you'll do with that machinery?'

'I haven't thought that far. I'm still dealing with the house, Rowan gone, and that guy ...'

Which is why he wasn't pushing her; she was still grieving.

'Here, this is where I found those nasty cigarette butts.' She led him towards the window, which gave them a clear view of the front and side of the house.

She opened the window to where women's laughter carried on the breeze.

'Are you worried about any of this?'

'I think Felix is doing enough of the poor, defenceless girly act for the both of us.' Wren pointed out the window. 'Upstairs, that left window was Rowan's room. Felix's is on the right, and I'm on the other side.'

'I know. I put you to bed last night while you were snoring.'

The colour brushed her cheeks as she ducked her head and returned to the main area of the shed. Getting a glimpse of her fragility was so unexpected, just as unexpected as his willingness to smile with her.

'Where's your hire car gone?'

'Around the back, by the kitchen door. I was going to give Felix driving lessons. I need some practise myself to drive this big thing.' Wren placed the red wine bottle and glass on the ute's back tray. 'Does that letter I gave you sound like it was written by a man who'd commit suicide?'

'No. But your father drank while taking that medication.'

'Rowan drank to help him sleep, to keep his nightmares away.'

'What nightmares?'

'He had them occasionally. This one time, while holidaying in Jamaica, we got plastered on their local rum. In our hotel suite, I heard him talking to someone else in the living room, but no one was there. He was so upset, blabbering something about Timor, I had to help him to bed.' Wren hugged herself, staring at the ground. 'I asked him about it the next day and Rowan said he didn't remember.

But he never drank dark rum again.'

Marcus leaned against the ute beside her. 'How come Rowan left the defence force?'

'He got injured on his last tour and received a compensation payout with a full military pension. He's got a load of medals and commendation certificates in the house.'

'I'd seen them.' Marcus sipped his wine, carefully preparing his next sentence. 'Wren, there is no evidence to suggest Rowan's death was suspicious.'

'If it was that obvious you would have been investigating a murder!' Anger sparked in her eyes.

'Okay, let's back up a bit. How do you know that letter is from Rowan?'

'It's his handwriting. I have other letters he wrote me to prove it. But Rowan knew I was coming. We'd made plans. Stewart said Rowan had three months left, not a matter of days. And if Rowan wanted to commit suicide, why didn't he use that loaded shotgun or consume all the medication in this house in one hit? Instead, he's found at the front door, beside a loaded shotgun, the house trashed, and this creep watching the place. Darryl may be right.'

'About what?'

She paused before answering. 'Darryl believes someone murdered my father. Darryl was guarding that letter, waiting for me to arrive.'

'Why?' He knew it. Two-dollar Darryl was keeping secrets and not just about Sandfly.

'I don't know. No one in town knew I existed, except for Darryl.'

'Why do you think Rowan did that?'

'Because he liked his privacy.'

'Think again, Wren. Come on, you're a smart girl.'

She sighed heavily, staring into her wineglass. 'Rowan hid me to protect me from something or someone.' She lifted her head and the pain in her eyes was cutting. 'Rowan knew this guy was coming. He had to. He could have given that letter to Otis, instead he had Darryl hide it, making him swear to only give it to me when I arrived. There's something more to that letter.'

'Like what?'

'I don't know yet. But Rowan had a habit of speaking in ways that could have a double meaning. He really played on innuendos, puns, and double entendres with his dry humour. He called it the Peddlers' code.'

'Like what?'

'Um …' She wriggled her nose. 'For a hangover Rowan called it a verandah. Money, as in cash, he'd call *pulp* for wood pulp for paper.' She then grinned, tapping the NT Police badge on his uniform's sleeve. 'Police he'd call *Lice* because they were always getting into his hair.'

'Hmph. Not the worst this uniform's been called.' Except she was darned cute with that grin, he had to grin with her. How did she do that?

Sadly, her smile disappeared as she tapped on the letter he'd stored in his top pocket. 'That guy was trying to read this letter. I don't know, call it a wild guess, but maybe there's a clue in there like those numbers on the bottom, I'm supposed to work out.'

'Like a clue for a treasure hunt?' Marcus stepped away from the pretty blonde clouding his judgement. 'What kind of treasure?'

'Yoo-hoo,' yodelled Felix, skipping into the shed. 'I'm not disturbing you, am I?'

'It's all good, Felix.' Wren narrowed her eyes at Marcus, annoyed at him again.

'I'm wondering if the sergeant would like to stay for dinner. It'll just be us.'

Marcus should leave now, while his sanity was intact.

'You should stay, Felix is a superb cook.' Her clear eyes were sexy as hell as she sipped on her wine, waiting for his reply.

No, he should go. 'Sure. Thanks for the offer.'

'Will we be having you or one of your officer's staying to watch over us?'

'That won't be necessary, Felix. The fence is fixed, Darryl and Chopper are nearby, and we've got new security lights and locks. And with the amount of police, we've had in the yard lately, the guy would be an idiot to return.' Wren scooped up her bottle and slid her arm around Felix's shoulders. 'Besides, the police are only a phone call away if you need them. We wouldn't want to waste their time on such trivial matters.' Sweet sarcasm dripped from her words.

Great. He'd upset her again.

'I'll set a place for Marcus. Dinner will be ready in five.'

Marcus pulled the shed door shut, the lock mechanism clicking into place. 'How long have you known Felix?'

'Since primary school, he's like a brother to me. We ran away together so Felix could watch his first Sydney Gay and Lesbian Mardi Gras. Don't worry, Felix will grow on you, you'll see. He's an amazingly generous and loyal person who doesn't judge people.'

Marcus hesitated at his police car. He should go.

Wren slid her hand into his and gave it a gentle squeeze. It was so soft and warm.

'Come on, let's forget about everything else going on. Come and be a guest at our table. You'll enjoy it.'

She was impossible to say no to.

TWENTY-TWO

Parking on the main street of Elsie Creek, Wren headed for the hardware store to pay her bill for the security work. Through the wide double doors, she paused at the largest ceiling fans she'd ever seen, effortlessly keeping the place cool.

'Well, if it isn't the long-lost Peddler, daring to grace us with her presence.' The elderly man pushed his thick glasses higher along his nose. He sat between two other men at the large card table. It was smaller than Sandfly's poker table, which had room for a roulette wheel.

Yep, she owned an illegal bar. Check.

That ran illegal gambling nights. Check.

While selling illegal chop-chop. Double check.

Should she change her nickname from long-lost Peddler to Rum-running Wren?

Her mother would spit pumpkin seeds while speed dialling for a priest and an airfare for Wren to get out of the place fast.

But Wren needed answers, hoping the three elderly men seated before her could help. 'Billy said I should come and speak with you.'

'That I did, indeed.' Billy came in behind her, tipping

his hat at her. 'Saw you pull up from the pub, Miss. I'm glad you took up my offer.' He pulled a chair out from the table for her. 'You mob, behave. This is Wren, the long-lost Peddler and she wants to learn about her family. Now that eagle-eyed old fool with the bottle-coke glasses, that's Jeffrey. Then James, better known as Jimmy, then Johnny on the other side.'

Wren shook their hands, then removed a slender wooden box from her bag. 'This is for you guys. I heard you liked your cigars.' Another thing her father had forgotten to mention—and that she hadn't told Marcus—Darryl had a special trunk full of hand-rolled cigars under lock and key.

'Is this a Peddler cigar? Smells like it.'

Wren admitted nothing. She wasn't selling these cigars, but offering them as a gift.

Oh no, she was just like her grandfather, swapping chop-chop for information!

'Your family made a fine tobacco.' Johnny opened the box, breathing in the tobacco aroma. He grabbed a cigar, then passed the box around. 'They had various grades.'

'Really?'

'You don't know?'

She shook her head, feeling like an idiot for not knowing anything. 'Only what Darryl's told me.'

'Well, your great-grandfather liked his cigars,' said Johnny. 'They'd sell the chop-chop to soldiers, the pub, and local supermarket here. They kept the good stuff for only those few in the know.'

'Were you one of them?'

'My father was. I remember the Sandfly Saloon was nothing but a tin roof, wooden crates for chairs, and an old tucker box he kept for beer. Goat Island has always been a good spot to watch the sun rise and set over the river, while fishing and having a quiet smoke, without the worry of responsibilities and crocodiles.' Johnny lit the cigar, puffed, then grinned. 'The Peddler's tobacco has got this signature scent to them. Every time I have one, it brings back memories.'

All four men sat back, smoking their cigars, with their playing cards face down on the table beside their coffee cups, and watched the wisps of cigar smoke curl towards those big-ass fans.

'Do you know much about my grandparents, about Pop Peddler?'

'Me, not so much.' Again, Jeffrey slid his glasses higher along the bridge of his nose. 'My family didn't mingle with the Peddlers. Billy, you would've known Pop Peddler through the pub?'

Billy poked up the brim of his old-fashioned Sunday hat. 'Yeah, I knew the man and he was one of a kind. Pop Peddler had this bowlegged walk, wearing his sawn-off shotgun, slinging it into his belt like a six-gun, with a long machete on the other side.'

'For what, war?'

'Nah, the shottie was for the crocs, and the machete was for harvesting the tobacco plants. And his Akubra had these slits on the sides to let the hot air out. He'd wear stained sun-faded jeans and that same blue long-sleeved shirt, with a cigarette always hanging out of his mouth.' Billy pointed at her with his cigar. 'You share the same colour eyes as a Peddler. But your grandfather and your father had a stare that could look straight through a man while he sized you up. Ol' Pop Peddler talked little, preferring to let others do the talking, but he'd usually end their conversations with *Nick off*.' Billy chuckled. 'And that was when he was being polite.'

'My brother did deliveries for the Peddlers after your uncles died in that flash flood,' said Johnny. 'My sister-in-law would get so mad at him for coming home late, reeking of rotgut. But all was soon forgiven when he'd empty out his pockets full of cash.'

'Did your brother work for the family long? Like Darryl?' Wren asked.

'Nah, Two-dollar Darryl's been there for a long time. The Peddlers considered him family. My brother only did it for a few years.'

'Your grandfather may have been a rascal to the coppers and to government surveyors, but he was all right,' said James, leaning his forearms on the table.

'What did they have against surveyors?' Wren asked.

'Rumour has it, your great-great-grandfather only paid for a hundred acres.' James and the other three grey-haired men chuckled behind their cigars. 'The thing was, Ol' Pop Peddler wanted more.'

'I've got papers to say it's a hundred hectares.' Which was almost two hundred and fifty acres. 'What's the catch?'

'The fences moved.'

'Huh?'

'Ol' Pop Peddler would regularly move the fences, increasing his perimeter,' explained James. 'They had no neighbours back then, so Pop Peddler had his boys help him shift the perimeter fences on both sides of the river a bit at a time until it included Goat Island.'

'Are you saying they just marked their spot and claimed it as their own? Surely someone would have said something?'

'I'm pretty sure Pop Peddler paid a surveyor to say it was a glitch in the paperwork, claiming that their original lot was always a hundred hectares and not a hundred acres.'

Wren sat back in her seat blinking at the table in astonishment. 'My family are con artists.' Adding stolen land to their list of illegal activities.

'They weren't hurting anyone, Wren. No one can contest it now, being squatters' rights and all. Back then there were no neighbours, and that government mob were glad to have settlers in the area.' Billy patted her hand in a fatherly manner. 'You should know that the Peddlers gave a lot back to the community, especially your father. Rowan paid for Karma's plush crocodile palace, where he'll live comfortably for the rest of his days.'

'Rowan helped me out, too,' said James. 'I'd had an accident with the tractor, the flamin' thing tipped on me. I was damned lucky Rowan and Darryl spotted the tractor belly-up, and carted me to the hospital.'

'You were out with that cracked collarbone and shoulder damage for a while,' Jeffrey said.

'Too long. I had crops to plant before the wet season kicked in, and I needed those crops to survive after suffering a few bad years. I was worried we'd lose the farm...' James leaned back in his seat, slowly turning the lit cigar in his fingers. 'Then my wife shows up at the hospital all smiles, telling me Rowan Peddler and Two-dollar Darryl drove over with their two flash tractors and worked day and night, sowing my fields, then gave my wife a handful of cash.'

'Why?'

'Because that's what Rowan Peddler did. He wouldn't take anything from me, no matter what I offered as payment. Told me to forget it, but I couldn't. He may have been a quiet man, your father, but he'd step in and just do stuff. Not like your grandfather. Now he was mean.'

'Nah, Ol' Pop Peddler was only a mean bugger to people who'd hassle them up at the house,' said Billy. 'He got sick of people begging for money, or trying to con something out of them. That's when the big fence went up.'

'Someone was nicking their tobacco, too,' mumbled Johnny.

James shook his head. 'I'd heard it was when the government said they needed licences to grow tobacco.'

'Whatever it was,' said Jeffrey, 'that mesh fence went up, topped with strings of barbed wire and signs to shoot anyone who dared enter, that the only way to speak with a Peddler was at Sandfly.'

'But then they'd just show up if you were in any kind of trouble,' said Billy, gently tapping his cigar on the edge of the ashtray. 'I'd seen it a dozen times where the Peddler's would help some farmer, stockman, or just a bloke down on his luck.'

'How?' Wren asked.

'Pop Peddler would rock up with your grandmother and their sons, carrying bags of clothes and tinned food for a family doin' it tough. And then Ol' Pop Peddler would just nod and pat you on the shoulder, while shovin' a wad of cash into a fella's pocket. He'd do it in a way where a bloke could still keep his pride, never asking for anything in return. Your father was the same. The Peddlers were good people, so don't let anyone tell you any different.'

Yet the law may say something else.

TWENTY-THREE

Wren sat on the floor in her father's bedroom, flicking through loose photos of Rowan as a boy through to his army days.

There were no photos beyond his time in the army. No correspondence. No outgoing calls on old phone bills, just a lot of medical bills for his mother. Then nothing. Until Wren reached out to her father, keeping every photo of their time together. It was easy to see how happy he'd been.

Rowan wore the same smile when he was a part of that group of eight in the army.

She picked up the phone. Was it too late to call?

'Elise Creek Police.' His voice was gruff, with a no-nonsense tone to it.

'Is that the detective sergeant speaking?'

'Wren? This is a surprise.' Marcus's voice softened. 'Is everything all right?'

'Yes, all good.' As good as expected. She cleared her throat. 'I have a question.'

'Shoot.'

'Were there any strangers at my father's funeral? You

were on the steps guarding the chapel's doors, it would have given you a bird's-eye view of everyone in the place.'

He huffed.

Duh, she knew what he was doing. Why did he assume she was dumb? 'So, was there anyone out of the ordinary?'

'Nope. Just you and Felix.'

'Did anyone from the military come?'

'No. I was expecting someone he may have served with to show, but you told me they'd lost touch.'

'That's what Rowan told me.' She angled her head at the image of eight military men, smiling, with their arms draped over each other's shoulders like brothers.

'What's going on, Wren?'

'I'm just going through Rowan's personal effects and found his old army photos. He was so happy. You couldn't fake the smile he's wearing. But there's nothing after that time.' She held up the last photo. 'Do you know anyone in the military?'

'I do, my mate Connor. Why?'

'Could you ask him, if someone they'd served with passed away, would they show up at his funeral?'

'Wren, we're in the outback. Remember how hard it was for you to get out here.'

'That's true.'

'Exactly where were you when you got the call about your father?'

'In Cuba.'

'For their tobacco, huh?'

She winced. 'No. nothing like that. I told you I didn't know—'

He chuckled.

Prick.

'What were you doing in Cuba?'

'Channelling my inner Hemmingway while perfecting

the art of being lost.'

'Huh?'

'I was cruising around in this amazing gas-guzzling vintage car, drinking an astounding amount of coffee, fresh from the plantations during the day. Then soaking up their rich sugarcane rum by night, while learning how to salsa.'

'Sounds like a holiday.'

'It was. They had beaches you could snorkel in and not worry about crocodiles, and waterfalls that filled emerald pools.'

'We've got some pretty spectacular waterfalls in the area.'

'You do?'

'Yeah. Some that aren't on any maps, where you can have the whole place to yourself.'

How romantic. 'Hard to find?'

'You'll need someone with local knowledge as there's a lot of country you can easily get lost in, if you don't know where you're going. I'll show you, but I won't be taking the police car. Your dad's ute would do it.'

'That'd be nice.' Everything about Marcus was nice and respectable while she was the bootlegger's daughter. But she liked the sound of his deep voice, as paper flicked in the background. 'Are you sitting at your desk in the office?'

'I am.'

'Why so late?'

'No one's here to annoy me, and the phones are usually quiet.'

'Oh, I'm sorry for disturbing you.'

'Wren, it's fine. Like I said, you're an exception to the rule.'

Oh brother, was she ever!

'So, what are you doing? Locked away in your father's room, going through his paperwork?'

'I am.'

'Are you sitting on the floor, resting that leg?'

'I am.' She grinned, peering around the room. 'When you say stuff like that, it's like you're standing right here.'

'The same way you read my mind and finish my sentences, huh?'

Her smile was so wide her cheeks ached. 'Yeah …'

'So, what else has been happening in the world of Wren?'

Didn't that make her smile widen. 'Well, I met the Triple Js …' They talked like friends, while carefully steering the conversation away from anything involving the Sandfly, chop-chop, and her father. It was a whole world of conversation.

'Well, I'd better leave you to it,' Wren said to Marcus. They'd been talking on the phone for over an hour.

'Yeah, I have a day job.'

'And more paper to shuffle?' She giggled, hearing the paper, imagining him closing files on that desk and flicking off the lamp.

'Hey, stop that.'

She laughed; it came so easily when in his company. 'Goodnight, Detective Sergeant.'

'Goodnight, Miss Sumney.'

She smiled at the phone.

Pulling herself off the floor, the sharp pain made her leg throb chasing away any tiredness.

Wren laid the photos inside the large cardboard box, keeping her favourites aside to frame, along with Rowan's service medals and military patches.

She frowned at the larger photo of eight men in army combat uniform. Handguns in hip holsters, rifles over their shoulders, and camouflage paint covering their faces.

Felix called it make-up.

Just like the man spying at her through the window.

She flipped the photo over, written on the back was *Timor 1999*. In the bottom corner was a faint watermark stating, *George Bridges, SMH.*

SMH? Was that a military unit?

She hobbled downstairs.

The night owl, Felix, had his music on while tinkering in the kitchen.

In the office, she opened her laptop and tapped in the photographer's name, *George Bridges.*

There were thousands of them.

George Bridges, photographer, wasn't much help either.

George Bridges, Timor, was a big zilch in the search.

She then typed in *George Bridges, SMH,* exactly as it stood on the back of the photo. And there he was, *George Bridges,* a reporter for the *Sydney Morning Herald.* Retired.

'Felix?'

'Yes, Toots.'

'Pack a bag. We're leaving.' She closed her laptop, slipping it into her trusty travel bag.

'Where are we going?'

'I'm taking you home to Sydney.'

TWENTY-FOUR

Stewart knocked on Marcus's office door, tossing a brown paper bag onto the desk. 'Are we still meeting for lunch today?'

'Damn, I forgot the time.' Marcus frowned at his watch. 'Thanks for the delivery. You can grab your shirt I borrowed the other night; it's over there.'

'Cleaned and pressed, I hope?' Stewart dropped into one of the guest chairs.

'If there's any complaints, speak to my mother. She does my laundry.' He unwrapped his hamburger.

'What are you working on?'

'Rowan Peddler's case file.'

'Has Wren got you working on it?'

'Wren has mentioned a few things that had me thinking, yes.' The beautiful woman he hadn't seen since dinner on Monday night. Their last phone call was such an easy-going conversation, covering all sorts of topics, he'd forgotten what life was like outside of work. He was tempted to take her to those waterfalls just to see her smile.

'I'll admit Wren made me take another look at my files, too,' said Stewart, unwrapping his burger.

'In what way?'

'Remember all that medication you had me collect from the Peddler property?'

'Hmm …'

'Well, the amount I brought back showed Rowan wasn't taking the correct dosages.'

'Too much?'

'No, too little. He hardly touched his meds. The medication in his system mixed with alcohol may not have been enough to cause any damage.'

Marcus's eyebrows rose in surprise.

'But Rowan did drink with those drugs, and if he was like Wren who has no drug tolerance…'

It was a cocktail for a never-ending coma.

'Here, what's your take on your autopsy photos.' Marcus spun the file around on his desk. 'The bruises across his arms and chest are in a straight line like someone tied him up. He's got the same on his wrists.'

'That's why I sought a second opinion from the coroner's office.'

'What did they say?'

'They suggested it was a combination of the ambulance gurney's straps, and the friction caused when being transported over the corrugated roads from the farmhouse to the hospital.'

'Don't they put those straps across the legs as well? And can a deceased body still bruise after eight hours?'

'Some do. Remember, Wren mentioned she bruises easily like Rowan. I saw the ones you made on her wrist, man. Nasty.'

'Not as bad as the bruise you put on her leg from that needle.'

'To think I wanted to put it in that cute arse of hers!' Stewart chuckled. 'Is Wren still ticked off at you?'

'Probably. We seem to have that effect on each other.'

Marcus bit into his hamburger, unsure what to tell Stewart. But he did value his opinion. 'Hey, can you tell me if you see any double meaning in this letter?' He ate while Stewart read the handwritten note.

'Wow, it doesn't sound like the letter of a man who'd commit suicide.'

'I agree. Rowan wrote that the day after you gave him the bad news, after organising with Wren to visit. They were planning on going through the house together.'

Stewart pointed to the bottom of the letter. 'What do those numbers *B1/ C13/ P47/ L8* mean at the bottom?'

'No idea. I thought they were his military serial numbers or a safe combination, but they're not. Does it sound like it has a hidden meaning? You spoke with the man?'

'When Rowan spoke it often seemed like riddles. What does he mean for her to *look outside the box* and to *see what others don't see*?'

Marcus shrugged, wolfing down his burger. He knew Wren had a knack for seeing things he couldn't see, and she was comfortable talking about murder and recreating crime scenes with lipstick.

'What did Wren tell you?'

'Nothing. I haven't seen her for a few days.' But he hadn't stopped thinking about her, even coming close to ringing her with some lame excuse about the job. 'Hey, Tanisha?'

Tanisha approached from the kitchenette, stirring her coffee. 'Yes, Sarge.'

'Have you seen Felix or Wren lately?'

'Not for a few days. Wren took Felix home to Sydney.'

His heart fell at the thought of Wren leaving without saying goodbye. 'Did Felix say why?'

'No. Although, Felix was worried Wren was going to dump him and run off on some secret mission.'

'What mission?' Marcus screwed up the lunch wrapper.

'Felix thinks Wren's searching for some of her father's old army mates, tying up loose ends at some military base. Felix wasn't allowed to go, so he was ticked about that.'

'When did you speak to Felix last?'

'This morning at the roadhouse on the highway.'

'They're coming back?'

'Wren's planning to be back in time to make your appointment, Doctor.' The phone rang; Tanisha left to answer.

'She remembered.' Stewart's grin was pathetic. 'I've never had a patient travel across the country to keep an appointment. Sounds like the girl is keen for our date.'

Marcus used the napkin to wipe away his grimace. Appetite destroyed.

The big-headed fool was still smiling. 'I'll let you seethe with jealousy on that one for a while, while I get ready for my date with the lady.'

Marcus scowled at the empty doorway. He had no right to be jealous of who Stewart spent time with. They were the same, never getting emotionally attached to any female, preferring to be married to their careers.

Even though Stewart was a good mate, he wasn't good enough for Wren. No one was.

Marcus glanced at the file before him. Wren wasn't coming back to see Stewart; she must have found something. But what?

TWENTY-FIVE

'TOOTS?' Felix hollered in the farmhouse hallway, 'Phone call.'

'Take a message. Tell them I'll call back later.' Wren had just finished re-arranging her desk to look out the window. Sinking into her office chair, she lifted her legs to rest on the desk, beside her father's open letter.

'But it was that gorgeous doctor for you,' said Felix, bounding into the office. 'He wants you to call him back. Which you will, won't you?'

'Probably not.' The trip back may have been shorter, after a direct flight to Darwin, but with a minivan full of people yakking, singing, and stopping for roadside tourist snaps, she'd had little time to think. Felix still hogged the front passenger seat, only this time filling the back with his entourage, dragging along his partner, Reggie, a pug dog called Coco, and their French bodyguard and club bouncer, Gabriel.

Now back in her office, her eyes kept getting drawn to the shed. Rowan had told her stories about that shed. She was desperate to remember them.

'That's enough!' Felix stamped his foot. 'You've been

like a mouse running around in the attic the way you're not sleeping. What's wrong?'

'Nothing.'

'Bull-diddly poop there's not, Toots. There's a gorgeous man asking you out and you say you don't care, that's not like you.'

'Excuse me?'

'No excuses, na-ah.' Felix wagged his finger at her. 'You need to find a man to distract you from all of this.'

She rolled her eyes, grabbing the letter she'd memorised. 'Leave my non-existent love-life alone.'

'No, I will not.'

'Fine, I'll leave.' She swung her legs down from the desk, so glad the stitches were taken out earlier today.

Felix blocked her exit. 'I'm not letting you pass until you tell me what's wrong.'

'Nothing is wrong.' She just couldn't share it with Felix. Not yet.

'Um, excuse me guys.' Reggie poked his head around the door.

'Go away, Reggie, my love. The Ice Queen needs to vent.' Felix pushed Reggie out of the room, closing the door.

'I do not need to vent.' She wasn't cold-hearted either.

'Well, something is wrong, or we wouldn't be yelling at each other like this.'

'You're always yelling or yodelling.'

'I'm a singer. I'm allowed to stretch my vocals, especially out here. *Who is going to hear us?*'

The glass on the windows vibrated from his voice.

'Well, I don't need you to set me up with some guy who sticks needles into me.'

'At least Stewart's bothered to make a move, unlike the sergeant. And you need something to stop you from becoming the ultimate Ice Queen. You've been so distracted, you're not indulging in the festivities of life, even at my club. If you won't do the doctor, do the sergeant, and get rid of what is killing your love of fun!'

'I have fun.'

'Not for a while, Toots. Just do as Father Felix commands and take either the doctor or the sergeant out for some fun. One of them has got to be doing it for you.'

'Oh, sure, why not call them both over and book me in for a threesome!' Wren tugged the door open only to come face to face with Marcus in the hallway waiting with Reggie, Gabriel, and Coco the pug staring at her. 'Are you kidding me?'

'Don't walk away from me. I haven't finished — Oh, hi Marcus. Been standing there long?'

'I tried to tell you that the sergeant was here.' Reggie scooped up Coco to smirk at them.

Marcus wasn't smiling, but his eyes were glimmering with humour.

The prick.

With head held high, she limped past them all and headed for the shed.

'Hey, I want to talk to you.' Marcus followed.

'Why? So you can amuse yourself with my unexplained theories.' Wren knew there was something inside the shed, some clue, and with Felix saying *mice in the attic* earlier it had her thinking. She reached the ladder that led to the mezzanine floor and started to climb.

'You're not going up there, are you?'

'You're not the boss of me.'

'Maybe you need one. You've only just got your stitches out and you're going up there. Why?' Marcus climbed up after her.

'Consider it none of your business because you'll think I'm stupid, anyway.' She faced the dusty area of old tools, boxes, and vintage toys.

'I don't think you're stupid. You just do stupid things. Reckless is what you are.' He climbed to the top, dusting his hands.

'What are you doing up here?' She pushed open the small window, letting in the cool breeze.

'I'm about to ask you the same question.' Marcus grabbed her arm, swinging her around to face him. 'We had an agreement. You'd tell me what you know, and I'd tell you what I know.'

'And I'm sure there's lots you haven't shared with me, Detective Sergeant.'

'You are the most frustrating woman I have ever met! You drive me insane; you know that.' His eyes darkened as his frown deepened.

'You don't think you affect me too? I can't think when you're around.' She couldn't believe she'd let that slip.

'Ditto.' Livid, he scowled at her with hands on his hips.

'I don't believe it.' The guy was controlled, serious and calm. He was everything she wasn't.

'Stuff it, you'll probably slap me for it, but right now, I don't care. But this is why …' Cupping the back of her head, his fingers gently slid into her hair. His other hand gripped her hip, pulling her into his chest as he leaned in to press his lips against hers. They were firm. Demanding. Sure. And commanding. She was helpless to resist him and his all-consuming kiss, which grew in confidence with each stroke of his tongue.

Teeth nibbled as their hot breath mingled until their lips were flush and completely connected. She moaned, gripping his shoulders, hanging on for the ride.

Her inner heat was so intense it flooded her entire body, she had to pull away from his kiss in order to breathe.

Every scrap of composure she had was gone. Along

with her ability to think. Speak. Stand. And breathe on her own.

Nothing about him within this moment, especially with that kiss, was a one-off. And that's what scared her.

And the way he looked at her ...

Marcus really looked at her.

He looked deep past her faults to see beneath the mask, exposing her, unlike any other man.

He was so much taller, stronger, and twice her weight. She tried to push away, but he didn't let her go, only stepping in closer until their eyes locked and an electric charge filled the air.

She held her hands up to brace against him for space. Instead, her fingers slid across his shirt where he was all hard and smooth like warm marble. With his chest rising and falling, his hooded lids only helped to darken his searching eyes.

'I should stop.' His breath washed over her lips barely millimetres away.

She held her breath, daring to dance into the world of desire that was so desperately filling her with an aching need to have all of him.

But did she dare?

'Do you hate me?'

She barely shook her head.

'I can't hate you either. I know we should stop, but I can't ...' He gripped her chin and controlled her mouth with possessive strokes of his tongue.

All she could do was dig her fingers into his shoulders and hold on, as the unexpected raw friction and intensity had her lost in the slow bump and grind of his kiss.

His fingers were on her hips, with an edge to his touch that she'd never felt before. He was all male, pure domination, leaving her with no mistake of who was in charge here.

But then he stopped and stepped back. Her body cooled away from his touch, but her lips were swollen and thirsty for more.

'We should get down from here.'

Blinking at the reality of where they were, it had her widening the gap between them.

'No.' He grabbed her wrist, pulling her against her chest, to wrap his arms around her. 'Don't do that.'

'Do what.'

'Don't walk away.' His voice was deep and hushed, it did something to her insides.

She struggled to remain sober. His job's integrity could be at stake just by being with her especially with her inheritance and the secrets contained within this Peddler's property. 'Marcus, you and me, we can't.'

'I know,' he murmured, with his lips brushing hers. His tender touch outlining her face and down her neck, only magnified her desire. He cupped her jaw in his hand and again their eyes locked. 'Wren?'

'Mm ...'

'It's your call.'

All her internal alarms were screaming at her to run as fast as she could. If he was affecting her like this now, what would she be like after a night together?

His mouth dropped to her neck, and in a slow motion, he made his way from her collarbone and up her neck, where his deep husky voice whispered in her ear, 'What's it going to be, baby? Hmm ...'

The single word freely tumbled across her lips. 'Stay.'

TWENTY-SIX

Seated in his office at the police station, Marcus tried to concentrate on the rosters, yet his thoughts kept turning to Wren. Rocking in his chair, the smile curled on his lips.

His phone rang, dragging him out of his daydream. 'Yeah?'

'Sarge, Mrs Bingle for you,' said Tanisha.

'Put her through …' He waited for the connection. 'Morning, Mrs Bingle.'

'Is that you, Marcus?'

'Yes, Mrs Bingle. How can I help you?'

'It happened again.'

'What did?'

'Someone ate my food. Half a loaf of bread is gone, as well as some tins of spaghetti, too.'

Marcus listened politely, still rocking in his chair. 'Are you sure you didn't eat it?' He had a soft spot for the octogenarian, who was a regular caller.

'Not the peanut butter, unless I fed it to my dog.'

'I'm sorry to tell you this, Mrs Bingle, but your dog is gone.' He'd helped bury the poor old pet, with Mrs Bingle's tears dampening his shirt. That was six months ago.

'Oh, I miss him so, Marcus. The house is so quiet without him.'

'I imagine it is.' He'd hate to be alone in a house that big.

When he glanced at the doorway, and there was Wren.

Good lord, she was like a ball of colour, brightening his world. His eyes dropped to her plump lips, and then up to her glistening eyes.

All she did was stare at him and his brain misfired, full of memories of last night.

And what a night.

He wanted to kiss her, to slam her up against the wall, to drag his mouth across her skin and ravage her neck. The sudden hunger led to a deep growl to stir within his chest.

'You there, Sergeant?' The voice hollered over the phone.

'Yeah, I'm here, Mrs Bingle. I'll get Porter to check it out.' He motioned for Wren to come inside.

'Oh, wonderful. Can you tell him to bring me some milk? Thanks, Sergeant.'

He arched his eyebrow at the phone. His favourite fifth grade teacher had just conned him again.

Marcus found the senior constable in the muster room, drinking coffee and flicking through a magazine. 'Porter? Can you check on Mrs Bingle about her imaginary house guest?'

'Again? What does she want this time?'

'Milk. And take out some bread, too. Mrs Bingle said she's missing half a loaf.'

Porter rolled his eyes. 'You know, the last time she said she was missing tins of baked beans, but they were all there.'

'If you're lucky, she'll make you lunch.'

'True. She does an excellent cake and coffee combo.'

'Do you make home deliveries often, Detective Sergeant?' Wren's voice was like silky honey.

He closed the door and gazed at Wren, leaning against his desk. Under the lights, her eyes were like crystal pools of a light sea-glass blue. Damn, she was beautiful.

He licked his lips in appreciation as his eyes freely roamed over every inch of her curvaceous body, which he'd intimately explored last night, worshipping her in the ways of a mortal man bedding a goddess.

'I wanted to say thank you for the flowers you sent me.' Her chest rose and fell, the air between them again crackled with electricity.

'You're welcome.' He'd never spent so much on flowers for anyone in his life, but Wren was worth it. 'Thanks for a great night.' For the first time, this morning, he didn't want to come to work.

'Oh, I wasn't going to just say thank you.' She grabbed the front of his uniform, pulling him towards her, she kissed him slowly, sensually, passionately, their chests pressed together with her heart pounding in time with his.

'Hey, beautiful,' he whispered in a husky voice, cupping her face. And again, his lips took hers, to kiss her slowly, tenderly, and intimately. Her tongue sliding in a perfect rhythm with his at just the right angle. It was deep and erotically tender, it was freaking perfect.

The phone rang again.

He hated that phone. He wanted to rip it free from the wall and toss it through the glass window, to then shove all the paperwork aside to lay the lady down across his desk.

Wren pushed against his chest, breaking their connection. She had a habit of pushing him away first.

He exhaled deeply, snatching up the phone. 'Yeah?'

'Oh, Marcus, it's me, Mrs Bingle.'

'You have my direct line now, Mrs Bingle?' He scratched at his eyebrow.

'That lovely officer, Tanisha, said it would help.'

'Tanisha did, eh?' Marcus gripped the phone tighter, already rehearsing his speech for Tanisha. 'Mrs Bingle, I've sent Porter to visit you. He's bringing some milk.'

'Oh, good. Is there any chance he could bring some bread? I was sure I had two loaves, but now I have none.'

'Porter is bringing out a loaf of bread with him, too. I thought you might need some.'

'Oh, aren't you just wonderful. Thank you, Sergeant. I'm sorry to take up your time, but it makes me feel so much safer knowing you're on the job. Take care.'

'You too, Mrs Bingle.' Marcus dumped the phone back into its cradle and gazed at the beauty before him. 'Do you want a coffee?'

Wren nodded, removing a large manila envelope from her bag.

He guessed she was here to talk about her father. They didn't do much talking last night, and he had no words to even describe what they'd done last night; but it was much more than just sex.

'Coffee, thanks.'

'Tanisha, can you make Miss Sumney and me a cup of coffee? Thanks.' He sat back at his desk. 'Is this where you share what you learned while you were away? I'm guessing one of your father's photos triggered your quick trip to Sydney.'

'Correct.'

'Here's your cuppa, Wren, probably not as nice as what you have at home.' Tanisha carried in their coffee cups on a tray. 'Sarge, can we get a coffee machine for the office?'

'Sure, just submit your request at our next budget meeting.' He grabbed his coffee from Tanisha.

'Really?'

'No. But thanks for the coffee. Close the door on your way out.' He waited a beat after the door shut. 'So, this photo ...'

Wren passed him the large manila envelope. 'Inside, there's a large photo of eight men. It was the last team Rowan served with before his discharge. They took this photo in late October 1999, in East Timor. Rowan was part of the Australian special force's unit sent over after the vote for East Timor's independence from Indonesia. Do you know much about that time?'

'Enlighten me.' Like the way she lit up the dullness of his office.

'Well, that independence vote led to the pro-Indonesian militia, the rebels, to go on a rampage killing thousands of unarmed farmers and villagers.'

'I remember now.' Marcus examined the eight men in combat fatigues, their weaponry at the ready, with full face paint on. But they were smiling with their arms around each other, standing near a village. He recognised Rowan Peddler.

'Out of that unit of eight men, only two men are still alive. Well, I think they're still alive. I couldn't locate them.' Wren wriggled to the edge of her seat and pointed at the men in the photo. 'Eight weeks ago, this guy had his life support switched off after suffering a stroke in the US.' She tapped on the next man in the image. 'That guy died after a heart attack in the UK. This one drowned after a boat accident in Queensland. Those two died in a car crash in Germany. And of course, Rowan ...' She sat back with her clear eyes full of concern. 'All of them died within the last six months. Pretty coincidental, don't you think?'

'Mm-hmm. I'm guessing you know why?'

'Don't sound so condescending. I don't have to share this, you know.' Her eyes flashed with annoyance.

'I'm trying to keep an open mind, but all you're showing me is a photo.'

'Here are the news clippings of their deaths, and the

timeline of events as my proof.' She pulled out more paperwork from the manila envelope.

'I'm to assume this is my copy.'

'Yes.'

Standing before him she laid out the paper trail of death notices, article clippings, Army service notices, and all sorts of proof of the eight men who'd died and served in Timor together. 'You're very thorough.'

'Because I knew you'd ask for this.'

'Now if only I could train those other people who wear police uniforms in this office to do this, I wouldn't have to work so late.'

'You do all the work around here because you want to, not because you have to.'

He sat back in his chair, frowning up at her. 'I like my job.'

'I know, that's why I'm sharing this with you.' She tapped on the paperwork. 'George Bridges took this photo. He was a reporter in Timor covering the independence vote and skirmishes for the *Sydney Morning Herald*.'

'And that's why you went to Sydney, to meet with this reporter?' He flicked at the media clippings she'd placed on his desk. 'What did he tell you? Did he remember, given how long it's been?'

'George remembered the incident well, because my father and his team were sent out on a drop ten minutes after that photo was taken.' She faltered, stepping away from him.

'Wren?' He grabbed her hand.

'George could never confirm it, but he was positive that those men were transported to the wrong area.'

'Say what?'

'It was a huge bungle that they tried to hush up. George claimed that where Rowan's unit had been sent, an entire village were found slaughtered. Innocent unarmed men, women, and children.'

'By whom? These men in your father's unit?'

'No one could confirm or deny.' She dug around in the paperwork and pulled out an article. 'This was George's piece on the incident. It was supposed to make front page news, but it got reduced to a mere notation hidden in the back somewhere.' She passed him the newspaper clipping.

Marcus read the paperwork and looked over the detailed map of the incident. It looked legitimate. 'But there's no confirmation?'

'The rebels blamed the security forces led by the Australian Defence, and the ADF blamed the rebels. But the major in charge left them there, without any support, forcing those eight men to fight their way through the jungle to survive.'

'What happened then?'

'They finally got back to base, where their entire unit was disbanded, all honourably discharged with large compensation payouts. That's when they scattered across the globe, never to see each other again.' Wren dropped into her seat, with her voice softening. 'That's why Rowan suffered from nightmares, telling me he'd never go to heaven, that he was destined for hell.'

'And you think all the deaths within this unit are connected? Including your father's?'

She nodded. 'As part of my research, I learned where the skirmish occurred was at a *Fatu Kuak* cave. It's part of their old religion to celebrate the passing of a loved one and their returning to earth's womb. They'd hold banquets near these caves as part of the ceremony.' She paused to sip on her coffee.

'Go on.'

'Well, during the time Rowan's unit arrived, the militia were burning down catholic churches. Priests were known to hide their church's most treasured possessions within these caves.'

'The looting got that bad?'

Again, she nodded. 'Those priests didn't really think about what they were doing, because for centuries the locals offered many gifts to wish their loved ones a good trip back to mother earth. Over time these caves kept many artefacts.'

'So they were loaded?'

'Ah-huh. It was also the supposed home to the greatest jewel of their region, *Ovo de Jade Diamante*.'

'What does that mean?' He loved the way it rolled off her tongue.

'The Jade Diamond. I couldn't find any photos, only sketches and clippings of its existence. But they say it's the size of an egg.' She cupped her hands to demonstrate. 'It's a jade-coloured diamond, decorated with strands of gold. It's said to be exquisite.'

'They didn't think to put it in a museum?'

'No. Some authorities suspected that the *Buan*, their ancient sorcerer, didn't know the significant monetary value of that stone. Yet, I think they must have because they hid it from any outsiders. After the rebels swept through the region, they never found any of their artefacts again. Here are my research notes and what George shared.'

'You're telling me someone's killing off this team of men for this—I can't believe I'm saying this—treasure?'

'Yes.'

'How?'

'Four of the men in this group were millionaires.'

'Back up a bit, here. Rowan didn't live like a king.'

'No, but he paid for my grandmother's medical bills with cash. He'd regularly fly around the world to catch up with me, and we stayed in some expensive places. Rowan gave me this gold watch when we were in Dubai, and this ring he had made for me when we were in Singapore. The emerald stone came from his mother's ring.' On her slender finger was a solitaire emerald stone, set with strands of gold crossing into a patterned Celtic weave to make up the band.

'I've never seen a ring like it.' It suited her delicate fingers. Hold on, if that was the case, Wren would be wearing property laundered from stolen goods.

Damn. Why did the one and only woman he ever wanted to be with come with a truckload of complications?

'It's specially made. I saw something similar in Ireland.' She then patted at her bare neck.

Last night he'd kissed her neck, fascinated by the goosebumps travelling across her soft skin.

'Rowan also gave me this cool compass, too. It was a black bauble on this long chain. I loved that piece, even if it never worked properly. The directions were all backwards.'

'Where is it now?'

'I gave it back to Rowan at the funeral. It's buried with him.'

'Why?'

'It was our in-house joke; I was always getting lost in the details, which is why he gave me the compass. Rowan would also tell me he'd never go to heaven, so I told him I'd bury him with that backwards compass so if it pointed to hell, he'd be destined for heaven.' She sighed, running her fingertip over her ring.

Did he dare voice his concerns of where her gifts came from, when they were playing so nicely together?

'Here, this is what I'm talking about …' She produced a drawing of a rock, the size of an egg, with smooth ends. The centre was a diamond, clear like white quartz, with the top and bottom encased in a green stone giving the diamond's centre a green tinge. 'Of course, there are many other versions of what the diamond looks like, but they all say it's a diamond the size of an egg. And that's what I believe the stalker is searching for.'

'And you think Rowan had this rock?'

'I don't know. Do you still think Rowan's death is accidental?'

'It's left a lot of unanswered questions.'

'What questions do you have?'

He hesitated.

'Don't you dare hold out on me.' She wagged her finger at him. 'You have no idea how hard it was for me to share this information with you.'

'Why?'

'I know how ridiculous all of this sounds. Military cover-ups and soldiers smuggling jewels out of a country. I get it. It took a lot for George to convince me, too, but he did.'

'So you believe him?'

'I do. And I know there's more in that letter Rowan wrote to me. I just haven't worked it out, but I believe I'm on the right track.'

Wren was a clever lady, who had made the effort to see him in his office, keeping up her end of the deal. Perhaps it was time to share. 'Stewart told me Rowan was hardly taking any of his prescribed medication.'

'Are you saying it wasn't an accidental death? Mixing his meds with alcohol?'

Marcus shook his head as he continued. 'There were bruises found in a straight line across his arms and chest, including his wrists. You told me your father bruised easily?'

'Yeah, we both do. What caused the bruising?'

'The State Coroner suggested it was from the straps of the ambulance gurney.'

'But you're not convinced, are you?'

Again, he hesitated.

She put her palm over his, lowering herself to meet his

eyes. 'Hey, it won't go anywhere.'

His fingers laced through hers, finding strength in her grip. She was a lot tougher than he'd given her credit for.

'There were traces of blood staining the left shoulder of his shirt. It was Rowan's. He'd been coughing up blood and wiped it on his shoulder, which makes me a little suspicious.'

'Why?'

'You told me Rowan was very particular about his dress. Is that true?'

'Yeah, clean clothes, polished boots.'

'So why would he cough and wipe the blood on his shoulder when he had a perfectly clean old-fashioned handkerchief in his pocket when he died?'

'You think someone tied him up?'

'Don't get too carried away here. It's just something I've been trying to work out.'

'But it makes sense.' She started pacing the floor. 'Okay, okay … So, he had alcohol in his system, and he didn't sleep. So, he must have napped or passed out and that's when he got tied up.'

'Hey, there are no facts to—'

'Shh, I'm thinking …' Wren continued pacing, chewing on her bottom lip. 'He was tied up, then given a tailor-made cigarette as his last wish, which made him cough up the blood that he wiped on his shirt.' She paused to demonstrate by wiping her chin on her shirt, only for her pace to quicken. 'And if this guy was interrogating him about the Jade Diamond, Rowan wouldn't surrender because he knew he was dying. Perhaps the other guy smothered him with a pillow. It wouldn't take much for his bad lungs to give out. Then he searched the house—'

Marcus had thought the same thing, even if it was all circumstantial.

'Oh no.' The colour drained from her face as she

collapsed into the nearest seat. 'Poor Rowan.'

Marcus swiftly moved to wrap his arms around her as she quietly whimpered.

The phone rang. Again.

Marcus frowned at the disturbance, surprised when it stopped. Tanisha must have remembered he had someone in his office.

Wren wiped away her tears. 'You've got work to do, I've already taken up enough of your time.'

'Are you sure?'

'I'll be fine. Thanks for listening, Marcus.' She gave his hand a gentle squeeze and paused at the door. 'We can't do this. You and me.' Her eyes were glassy, and he could see this was hard for her to say. 'You know I'm right.' She waved back at his office. 'You love your job, and you're good at your job, with a great reputation in this town. Yet, being seen with me, Marcus, it puts everything you've worked so hard for in jeopardy. Everything will be compromised, your integrity for your work, everything. I won't let that happen.'

He approached. 'Hey, come on, Wren—'

'No.' She held her hand up as a tear trickled down her cheek. 'You know I'm right—we had last night, but we have to stop now.' Her lips trembled.

He wanted to hug her, but she turned away.

'The thing is …' With her head lowered, her hand on the door handle, her voice wavered, 'I'm sorry, too.'

And she was gone.

Her perfume still lingered, as the outside world was shut out by his door clicking in place.

She'd left him alone in his big office, to do what he always did: his job. Yet in that single moment, it had never been a heavier and lonelier burden. He hated that she was right.

TWENTY-SEVEN

'Hello,' called out Tanisha. With Emelia beside her, they approached the farmhouse front porch steps.

On the phone, Wren waved at the visitors to come inside.

Felix, everyone's friend, skipped into the entranceway. 'Hello, luscious ladies, welcome. Welcome. Welcome. We're in the kitchen. Reggie and I have been whipping up some fabulous nibblies for tonight. Just go on through, I'll be right there.'

Wren hung up the phone.

'So who was that, Toots? It sounded like you were giving them the gentle heave-ho.' Felix grimaced as if in pain. 'You're not dumping Marcus, are you?'

'I was talking to the doctor.' She hadn't told Felix about her heart-breaking visit with Marcus yesterday. It was torturous. Especially after leaving the police station, she had to pull over on the side of the road and flat out ugly cry. And when she'd finally made it back home, all she could do was crawl into bed and hug her pillow, that still smelled of him, trying to soothe the pain in her chest that was crippling and so completely unexplainable.

'Did Stewart ask you out again? Did you say yes?'

'I told Stewart thank you, but no.' No more men. She was done.

'Wow, are you dating the babelicious sergeant?'

'Felix, it's complicated.' It was better to cut and run. If Wren hadn't committed herself to working on her father's matter, she would have bolted from Elsie Creek and the sexy detective sergeant. 'We can't.' A thick wave of gravity draped itself over her head and shoulders like a blanket. It was suffocating.

She had to let Marcus go. He was an officer of the law, and she had inherited an illegal bar, a stash of illegal tobacco, and was probably wearing goods bought by illegal means.

She'd seen Marcus's eyes flare over the jewellery, which made her rethink wearing the watch. But the ring, she knew the emerald stone came from her grandmother and she honestly believed that her father wouldn't do that to her. Rowan had stopped brewing the rotgut and growing chop-chop all because of her. She still believed he was a good man.

'Why not? Marcus is gorgeous and sexy and well, Toots, he must be good, or you wouldn't bother wasting your time.'

That's why it was so hard to say no to Marcus. They connected, not only mentally and physically, but on so many levels that he was emotionally addictive to be with, yet heartbreaking at the same time. It just couldn't be.

'Look, why not come and have a cocktail and forget all of that stuff.'

'I could do with a drink.' To drown her sorrows.

'Let's have some fun, shall we?' Felix hooked his arm through Wren's and steered her towards the kitchen.

They'd filled the round table with food platters and cocktail glasses, while the music played in the background, creating a party-like atmosphere in the kitchen where the conversation never stopped.

'Emelia, how come you're still single? Are the men blind in this town?' Felix emptied the last of the wine bottle into Emelia's glass.

'I try.' Emelia, the blonde-haired, blue-eyed beauty, dressed like a doll, huffed. 'I was nearly engaged to Kyle, but he broke it off to marry his childhood sweetheart, Kat. Since then, I've been chasing both Marcus and Stewart for ages, but I know Stewart is trying to ask you out for dinner, Wren. Did you say yes?'

'I said no, Emelia.' No more men. It was her new decree and Wren was going to stick to it.

'Why not?' The diamantes on Tanisha's nails caught the light as she traced the sides of her cocktail glass. 'Isn't Stewart good enough?'

'Duh, the guy stuck needles in my leg.' Wren grimaced at their laughter. 'Thanks for the sympathy vote, people.'

'You know, those two boys are always competing for everything,' Tanisha said, 'It's either football scores, darts comps, or women. It's just what they do.'

Emelia nodded. 'They have competitions with themselves to beat the other. I heard them call it their dating-rating game once, where they have a score system for the dates they go on. I think it's to do with the level of conversation topics that doesn't involve cattle?'

'No way.' Wren raised her eyebrow at Felix. 'They'd better not.'

Felix dived in with his thirst for gossip. 'Is that true? Tanisha? You'd know your boss ...'

Tanisha sucked on her straw so swiftly her cocktail glass was dry.

'Reggie, we need a refill for the lady, stat.' Felix whipped Tanisha's dirty glass away. 'Tanisha, what's it like working with Marcus?'

'He's an approachable boss. We could do more at the station if he'd let us.' Tanisha stirred her fresh cocktail with her pink flamingo swizzle stick. 'Considering he was such a rebel.'

'Oh, yes, Marcus was bad-bad-bad.' Emelia nodded.

'How is it possible for a bad man to become a sergeant? Don't they do background checks? Who wants a refill?' Reggie held up a large glass jug.

'I'll stick to my wine, thank you.' Emelia raised her near-empty wine glass.

'Honey, you'll stick with the program. You must indulge at least once in these cocktails. Felix is truly gifted with the flavours.' Reggie plucked the glass from her fingers.

'Don't do it,' said Wren. 'You'll get addicted.'

'I agree.' Tanisha took another deep sip from her glass. 'They're divine, even if I only came here for the books.'

'What?' Wren giggled, not expecting that.

'Your collection of Taylor Timm's novels.' Tanisha jumped up to pluck a paperback from the bookcase in the lounge. 'This is my favourite, *Lambert's Gold*. But I also love the company, too.'

'We only let you in for your chicken empanadas,' said Felix, with a straight face that soon shifted into a grin. 'Now can we get back to the hot gossip on Tanisha's sexy boss?' Felix patted Reggie's shoulder. 'Don't get jealous, lover. Tanisha, dish out some delicious dirt on Marcus. Was Marcus always going to grow up and become that super-sexy cop?'

'No.' Tanisha laughed. 'No one expected Marcus to become a police officer, considering how bad he was.'

'How bad?'

'Bad-bad-bad,' repeated Emelia.

Tanisha leaned her arms on the table almost hugging her cocktail glass. 'Marcus and his best mate, Connor, were big trouble in a small town. Stealing cars, street racing stolen pigs, doing tractor tug-of-wars on the train line, you name it, they were into it. They even had the Station Hand try and sort them out.'

'Who's the Station Hand?' Wren asked.

'He's this tough-as-croc-leather cattleman. An outback living legend.'

'Why?'

'Because he teaches people to become good stockmen,' butted in Emelia.

Tanisha rolled her eyes. 'He's much more than that. It was the Station Hand who wrestled with Karma, rescuing the croc from his son-in-law's dam.'

'Marcus and our new fire chief did that,' said Emelia. 'I saw the pictures, the Station Hand supervised with the new park ranger.'

'Marcus wrestles crocodiles?' Wren's eyes widened. 'Is that some sort of outback superman initiation the local men have to do to fit in?'

Emelia gave a dreamy smile. 'Marcus grew up here, and he was always cute, but bad-bad-bad. My daddy, who's the town's mayor, told me they were part of the lost boys.'

'Are we talking about *Peter Pan*?' Felix asked.

'I get lost,' said Wren, raising her straw in the air. It's how she found the best things, especially when it came to research.

'The lost boys were naughty boys whose parents would fly them in to get sorted out by the Station Hand.'

'How?'

'Allow me.' Tanisha sat forward, twirling her pink flamingo swizzle stick like a wand. 'We're talking the proper Territory outback, where these bad boys are dumped on a cattle station to meet the Station Hand. With nowhere to go they get a tough lesson on survival, dealing with extreme heat, flies, and the isolation, it soon sorts them out.'

'It sounds like a prison farm to me,' said Felix.

'For some, it is. Most of them end up loving the lifestyle so much it becomes their careers. Except for Connor and Marcus, because they made a run for it.'

The music got turned down and everyone leaned closer as Tanisha spoke. 'I remember that day … I was with my parents waiting for the bus in Elsie Creek to go back to boarding school, when this ute flew past us right down main street, heading for the central desert. It was Marcus and Connor, being chased by every cop car in town with their lights and sirens blaring. Marcus was driving.'

'Did they catch him?'

'Well, they found the Station Hand's ute dumped in the scrub, with a sorry note pinned to the steering wheel. But both Marcus and Connor disappeared for decades.'

'Connor only came back a few months ago. He helped Marcus defuse a bomb at the school and they both shot this guy who shot at Cecil our friendly water buffalo. Mm, this cocktail is delicious.' Emelia pushed her wineglass away.

Wren spluttered on her cocktail. 'So much for a quiet town.'

'Oh, that stuff never happens. It's rare.'

'So, how did Marcus become a police officer?' Wren had to ask.

Tanisha picked at the platter. 'After skipping town, Marcus hitchhiked to Melbourne to stay with his uncle, who was a policeman. It was through his uncle, that Marcus became a city cop, but he did the scary undercover stuff for the drug squad. He was good, too.'

'So why is Marcus not in Melbourne?' Wren asked.

'Oh, I know.' Emelia used her straw to scoop at her cocktail like a spoon. 'Marcus's father passed away, so he came back to help his mother and his aunt. They live in the same house together.'

'There's more to it,' said Tanisha. 'Marcus was only planning to stay until his mother was okay. But the old town sergeant, who was retiring, talked Marcus into staying with a promise to run things.'

'Marcus is the best sergeant this town has ever had; my daddy says so. He's the mayor, you know.'

Tanisha rolled her eyes at Emelia. 'I think it's because Marcus has done all those bad things in the past, no one can get past him. Marcus's first few months on the job, he really cleaned up the place. He shut down the illegal fighting pits, reduced the town's speed limit for Cecil. Oh, and he totally crushed the rivalry between the miners and stockmen.'

'Say what?' Wren asked.

'The miners and stockmen were always brawling at the pub—which is silly when half of them are ex-stockmen,' said Emelia.

'Marcus was brilliant!' Tanisha waved her flamingo in the air like an orchestra conductor. 'Marcus stepped into one of their infamous Thursday Payday Pub Brawls, to beat the stuffing out of both sides, single-handedly, bare knuckles too. It made him an instant legend that no one dares to take on this town's top cop.'

'Is Marcus strict when it comes to the law?' Wren had to know, considering her inheritance booty.

'*The law is the law*, he'll tell you,' Tanisha said. 'Marcus may be strict, but he's fair, and he does a lot of good for this town like the suicide prevention programs. He got the funding for a community bus to help the elderly go shopping and for their hospital visits. We're getting the firing range reopened, and a self-defence class starting for the ladies. But you can tell Marcus misses the excitement of the city. I reckon that's why he works so hard, keeping himself so busy at the station. But he lays down the law, even with us. We've got station rules too.'

'Like what?' Felix asked Tanisha.

'At his first staff meeting as station boss, Marcus said we had to be careful when it comes to dating and relationships while on his watch.'

'Why?' Felix gently nudged Wren under the table.

'Marcus told us he'd seen police stations destroyed because of someone having an affair with another officer's partner. So don't do it!' Tanisha shook her head with wide eyes. 'Marcus also said no one was to date anyone that they're working with, because he didn't want our emotions to interfere with the investigation.'

Wren sat back, crossing her arms over her chest. It's a good thing she'd stopped it before it started, because it'd ruin Marcus's respect for the rules with his own staff. Everything about being with Marcus was a bad choice—for him.

So why did it have to hurt so much, after only one night with the guy? She'd hate to think how she'd behave after a few months.

Gabriel, the large French bouncer from Felix's nightclub, came down the stairs. His broad shoulders, flat boxer nose, and buzz cut, gave the guy a menacing vibe.

Yet looking at Gabriel's beefy shoulders just made her miss Marcus more.

Gabriel motioned at Wren to meet him in the lounge room.

'Hey Gabriel, have you finished stargazing for the night?' The Frenchman was in love with the outback sky. He'd talked non-stop about the constellations and their mythologies, on their drive back to Elsie Creek. Gabriel never bothered to unpack his bags, keen to set up the special high-powered telescope he'd practically chained to the roof rack of their minivan.

'You're missing all the fun.' Wren had to admit the more she drank the more she forgot her misery.

The bouncer's serious face wiped the smile from hers.

'What's wrong, Gabriel?'

'You need to see this.'

TWENTY-EIGHT

With his boots resting on the edge of the station's old boardroom table, Marcus leaned back in the chair to watch the footy on the television resting on the fridge.

The front doors opened. It was Stewart, still in his white doctor's coat, carrying his trusty flask of coffee.

'Just what the doctor ordered: coffee.' Marcus gave his mug a rinse and grabbed a spare, putting them on the table as Stewart came round the large reception desk.

'How come you're stuck on night shift?'

'Porter's doing something with Tess.'

'So he's finally scored that date with her?'

Marcus shrugged.

'Why is Porter going to so much trouble for a date with our postmaster, Tess? She's got great legs, but…'

'Porter swears Tess is the one for him.' How did Porter know?

'Where's Tanisha?'

'Girl's cocktail night or something.' He knew it was at Wren and Felix's place.

Man, he missed Wren.

He shouldn't, and couldn't explain it, but he did. She

was invading his thoughts day and night, he'd given up on sleep to come in to work. 'I did the rosters, so I'm not complaining.' He was going to be here anyway.

The phone rang and Marcus scooped up the handle. 'Elsie Creek Police.'

'Oh, Marcus, is that you?'

'Yes, Mrs Bingle.'

'I've lost my milk and an entire tray of cookies. I'd just left them on the bench one minute, the next they're gone.'

'Cookies?' Marcus watched Stewart pour the coffee. It's rich caffeine aroma filling the room.

'Yes, Anzac bickies. I thought for sure the dog ate them, but then I remembered he's gone.'

'Mrs Bingle, when is your sister coming over to stay?'

'In a week, or is that two? I wrote the date somewhere ...' In the background drawers opened and closed. 'Oh look, there's my biscuits. I forgot I put them in the cupboard.'

'That's great news.'

'So sorry to bother you. Perhaps I'll get that nice Senior Constable Porter to collect them for everyone at the station. Do you think he could bring me some more milk? I'm going through it so fast these days.'

'Sure, Mrs Bingle.'

'Wonderful, have a good night, Marcus.'

'Goodnight, Mrs Bingle.' Marcus hung up the phone. 'Stewart, are you treating Mrs Bingle?'

Stewart nodded. 'She prefers my father. Got a crush on him. Is she getting worse?'

'She's calling about her food missing. But when we visit, we find it stashed in odd places. Porter is refusing to visit unless he's got Tanisha with him, because that last time he went out he found Mrs Bingle walking down the road in sunglasses and hat, with no clothes on.'

'I know, Porter called me. But, by the time I arrived, Mrs Bingle was lucid. She refused to visit the hospital for testing. Dad wasn't in town, and she'll only see him. But I do know her sister and niece will be arriving in a few days. I'm hoping to convince her to do some testing then. But she's adamant food is missing.'

'That we always end up finding. We've searched her house and property a dozen times and found nothing out of the ordinary. She's lonely, right? Living in that house all alone?' He'd hate that. Rowan Peddler lived the same. Was that why Mrs Bingle was ringing? Because of Rowan Peddler's passing, who also lived alone in a big empty house?

Stewart shrugged, toying with the handle on his coffee mug.

'I'll check on Mrs Bingle tomorrow, and I'll be putting her on a regular run until her sister gets here.' Marcus scribbled a note on the nearby pad, then picked up his coffee. 'Your night must be slow if you're here to annoy me.'

'Had one of the Merrick kids come in from a motorbike accident.' Stewart rocked in his chair as he watched the game.

'Mustn't have been too bad if I didn't hear about it. Which kid? They've got a few.'

'Three. Not as many as the Kimbles.'

'True.' The Kimble family had enough to start their own softball team.

'Little Ollie was hooning around on his dad's motorbike, fell off and rolled into a barbed-wire fence. They had to cut him off the fence and bring him in with the barbed wire still attached. The kid's more freaked out about his dad finding out about wrecking the fence and for damaging his dad's bike that no one is allowed to touch.'

Marcus frowned, he knew life was tough on the land, but still ... 'Where's his dad?'

'Doing a muster, not expected to be back for a few

days.'

'Really? You'd think he'd want to come in and check?' Did Marcus have to make the call?

'Don't worry, nothing bad is going on there. Ollie Merrick's father was barrelling through the hospital's doors wearing a load of worry on him like you do daily.'

Marcus scoffed behind his cup, taking a swig of the bitter brew. He wasn't a worrier. Warrior, sure why not. As for worry? Nah.

'The entire Merrick family is with Ollie, with Jenny organising beds for them to stay together for the night. The next fundraiser you do, can it be for camping beds for family members for the hospital? I don't like them driving for hours in the outback after dark, especially after the stress most of the patients and their family members go through. They're fatigued before they leave the hospital.'

'No worries, I'll see what I can do.' Marcus scribbled it down on the notepad.

'I bet ten the Tigers will win this game.'

'In your dreams. But I'll take your money.' He focused on the game playing on the small screen. 'Did you bail on a lame date, using the excuse that you had to see some patient?' They'd both done it, using their jobs to escape a bad date. It was the perfect barrier for never getting too close to anyone.

'I rang Wren and asked her out, but she had something else on.'

Marcus remained glued to the TV. 'Wren knocked you back, huh?' He steeled himself for the wrong answer.

'In the nicest way possible. I think she's still ticked at me for giving her those needles.' Stewart sipped on his coffee. 'I'll try again, though. I reckon I'll beat you on this one.'

'Why do you say that?'

'Because you don't date people involved with cases, especially when you're still chasing ghosts over her father's death.'

Marcus frowned at the mention of his own rule. He could never get personally involved with someone while on a case, especially if it interfered with the job. It was the one and only personal rule he swore to never break—because people he'd cared about had died.

'What do you think Wren will rate?'

'I'm not playing anymore, mate. I'm done with that stupid game.' With a foul taste in his mouth, Marcus headed for the office, only to turn and face Stewart. 'Wren's not a game, so stop asking her out, okay?'

Stewart blinked, only for his smart-arse grin to grow. 'Well, well, well. When did this happen?'

'Nothing happened.'

'Yeah, right? Look at you, pacing like a caged animal, getting all territorial on me.'

'Crap.' He dragged his hand down his face, all gritty-eyed and cranky. 'It's complicated.'

'Why? Because of Sandfly?'

'And all the other rules. Wren and I ...' Marcus squeezed his hand into a fist at the pure frustration of it all. 'We were so close—it felt so right.' Was this the same as what Porter was going through in his struggle to date Tess? 'But ...'

'But what?'

'Wren said no.' He dropped back into his chair to stare at the floor. 'The lady said no, and I can't argue with that.'

TWENTY-NINE

Wren followed the lumbering six-foot-four Frenchman up the stairs, while the rest of her house guests partied in the kitchen.

Gabriel flicked off the hallway light before opening the door to the spare room. 'I'll show you.'

She followed him into the dark room, to the large telescope. 'Find a new galaxy?'

Gabriel peered through the lens, then pointed. 'No. I was testing my new night vision lens, looking at the wildlife, when I spotted this …'

'Okay.' Wren peered through the lens and frowned. 'That son-of-a …' Through the lens she spotted a man, lying among the tall grass, watching the house with a pair of binoculars. He put them aside and lit a cigarette, to then resume spying on them.

Her body broke out in goosebumps.

'Gabriel? Can you go get Felix and Tanisha? Please keep the upstairs lights off so he can't see us.' Her icy glare darkened at the man in camouflage gear, now drinking from a travel mug while perving on them.

Sadly, his face was obscured by the grasses and

binoculars. She couldn't even tell his age. Was this their peeping Tom?

Was he connected to the eight men from her father's group in Timor?

'What's up, Toots?' Felix bounded through the door with Tanisha beside him. 'Why is it so dark in here?'

'Felix, I want you to look through Gabriel's toy.' Wren led Felix to the telescope. 'I want to know if that's our stalker?'

Felix released a husky choking sound, lifting a hand to his throat.

Wren gave him an encouraging pat on the back. 'You can do this, Felix.'

Hesitantly, Felix inched closer, leaning down to the telescope lens with his face screwed up as if he needed glasses. Then he gasped. 'That's him.'

'Are you sure?'

'Well, I think it's him. He's not wearing make-up, but he does sport the same cheekbone structure. It's hard to tell because this image is all red and grainy. I thought this would be a clearer lens?'

'That's the night vision lens,' mumbled Gabriel.

'It's brilliant. I see everything. Aww, look at the baby wallabies.' Felix swung the large telescope around like it was a laser-sight in a digital game.

'Tanisha, who owns that property?' Wren pointed to the vast lands opposite the farmhouse.

'It's the Folsom's property,' replied Tanisha. 'I'll go ring Marcus.'

'Good. Let's hope they can catch him.'

'Oh, good idea …' Felix gripped Wren's arm. 'What are we going to do?'

'Nothing. The police will round him up. Problem solved.'

Tanisha rushed back into the room. 'Marcus is on his way. He also told me to tell you, Wren, to not go running after the guy.'

'You'd better not, Toots. You can't leave me.' Felix's grip tightened on her arm.

'I promised Marcus I wouldn't.' Her heart tugged, missing the man who effortlessly filled the room with his presence. She wouldn't mind his presence right here, right now.

'Is that creep still there?' Tanisha asked.

Through the telescope lens, Wren frowned at the man, his face once again hidden by the binoculars aimed at the house. 'He's perving on us at this very moment. The nerve.'

'Can I see?' Felix now a little braver.

'Sure, everyone can look.' Wren stood back as they all took turns to watch the man watching their house.

'Hey, what's going on in here? Are you having a private party without us?' Reggie, with Emelia beside him, burst into the darkened bedroom. 'I can't see a thing. Where's the lights?'

'Don't—'

Too late, the lights came on.

'Bugger it!' Wren frowned at her reflection in the large window. 'We may as well wave hello. He's seen us.'

Which the drunken crowd did, waving at their reflections, with Gabriel shaking his head in the background.

'Sorry,' stage-whispered Reggie, 'what were you doing?'

'Gabriel spotted our stalker at eleven o'clock.' Wren flipped the bird at the window, doubting the guy was still there.

'It's the same man. He's so persistent.' Felix's face twisted in horror.

'Wren, you don't think it's like a real stalker?' Reggie

asked, scooping up Coco the pug.

'Why would you have a stalker?' Emelia peered around the room with picky eyes.

Wren didn't like being judged. Her skin prickled at the irritation of her privacy being violated on so many levels. 'Let's leave those questions for the police, while we all go downstairs and have some coffee.' As everyone filed out of the room, Wren gazed back at the window.

This stalker had to be the same person who'd searched the house while tossing cigarette butts around like breadcrumbs. He was after the Jade Diamond. She just knew it.

It had to be real. All of it.

It was time to stop feeling sorry for herself over Marcus. It was time to forcefully dump all of her emotions inside some trunk, then slam that lid shut deep inside her heart. It was time to play Ice Queen, to focus on beating this guy by finding the Jade Diamond first.

THIRTY

It was like the world had sped up and Marcus was stuck in a quagmire of muck going nowhere, making his grip tighten on the steering wheel all from worry.

Worry sucked.

Worry sucked even more when he worried over Wren.

Wren's house came into view as Marcus steered down the track. He'd been driving around in the dark for more than an hour hunting for that stalker. Sadly, there was nothing more he could do until the morning.

Marcus didn't even bother knocking as he walked inside the house. Fresh paint and fancy interior lights shone. Even though it'd been a long thirty-six and a half hours since he'd been here, he spotted the changes. Like Wren, he was also good at noticing the details.

'Sergeant, you're here.' Felix flounced in from the kitchen, no apron, no cleaning gloves, no cocktail glass, or coffee cup.

'Is everyone okay?'

Felix nodded, brushing arms over himself as if trembling with cold. 'It was the same man watching us that was watching Wren.'

'Where's Wren?'

'Well, after Tanisha called you, we all came downstairs and had coffee, while Wren went to her office.'

'Mm-hmm …' Marcus was known to have the patience of a saint, especially when dealing with the public, but Wren's office door was open and the room was empty. 'And then?'

'Wren grabbed some torches and said she'd be over in the shed.'

Marcus headed for the door. 'Alone?' That woman could be anywhere by now.

'I made Gabriel, our bouncer, go with her.'

'Good move, Felix. Stay here.'

Inside the well-lit shed, torches and coffee mugs rested on the ute's rear tray like the first night he'd been here.

'Wren?'

'Up there.' The accent had to be French.

'Where?'

By the ladder stood a hefty man pointing to the loft. 'I'm afraid of heights.'

That must be hard to admit for a man of his size. 'No worries. Why not head back to the house? I'm sure Felix would appreciate your presence.' Marcus climbed to the loft, where he'd shared his first kiss with Wren.

Assorted lanterns brightly illuminated the area where Wren was busily shifting vintage tools and toys aside. 'Did you find him?'

Determination had never looked so good on anyone — except for that sharp look in her eyes. Is this what Felix meant by Ice Queen?

Wren had every reason to be ticked at him, because he'd failed to deliver on catching the guy. 'No. We'll look in the morning. What are you doing?'

'I'm looking for a clue.' She rolled an old go-cart to clear floor space.

'Not this treasure hunting again.'

'You might think I'm letting my imagination carry me away, but Felix *thinks* it's the same guy who was peeking at the house. But I know it's him. I watched him dump his dirty cigarette butts in the dirt, littering all over the place, just like he did in this shed. And I bet he's searching for the Jade Diamond and I'm going to beat him to it.'

'Do you hear yourself?'

'Can you think of another reason why this perve is watching the house? I'm just ticked that I didn't get a good look at him. He's got to be one of the men who served with Rowan. Yet if I get Felix to look at that squad photo ...' She pushed a large wooden tea chest across the floor. 'I'd have to explain all to the delicate drama queen. Before you demand it, I'm not ready to put that burden on Felix. He worries enough already.'

Marcus blocked her path, holding the tea chest in place.

'Hey?' She frowned at him.

'I get it.' He held his palms up in a half surrender. 'It makes sense.'

She arched her eyebrow at him. 'Oh, really?'

'I believe you about the stalker, and your need for sensitivity when dealing with Felix. It makes sense. What I don't get is why you're pulling this place apart?'

'The letter ... it's a clue.' Wren held out her copy of the weatherworn letter bearing permanent crease marks along the folds. She pointed to the lined section of a paragraph and read aloud: *'I'm talking about some of those adventures and challenges that can start from your own home's front door ... in the place I told you I hung out the most!'*

'What's that got to do with the shed?'

'Rowan used to tell me that when his father, my grandfather, went on a bender, he'd hide up here as a kid. Pop Peddler couldn't climb. Apparently, he had a bad leg that made him bandy-legged?'

Marcus shrugged, barely remembering the man who'd worn a sawn-off shotgun tucked into his belt like a pistol.

'This was Rowan's safe space. He'd hide up here to skip chores, to get away from his big brothers, or his father when he'd done something wrong. I used to hide in the gap behind the back fence and garden shed whenever my mother was on the warpath. You?'

'In the crawl space under the house. I'd listen to my parents' rant, while pigging out on this stash of food and drinks I kept there.' He'd have no hope getting his shoulders through the gap now, and the junk he'd accumulated over the years, was it still there? 'So, you think Rowan hid something here?'

Wren leaned closer to the wooden floor slats ingrained with decades of dust. 'Rowan told me he used to lie on this floor watching people come and go in this shed. I'm looking for a peephole.'

'Like this …' With the toe of his boot, Marcus tapped at the wood's natural knot in the panel, its centre core gone.

'Great catch, I would've missed it.' She lowered herself to peek through the hole.

'What do you see?'

Wren wrinkled up her cute nose, using the back of her hand to wipe away the dust. 'Only the ute and the shed floor. You might see something I'm missing.' She sounded disappointed.

He lay next to her, peering through the hole in the floor, which gave a clear view of the shed, directly above the ute. 'Was that ute always parked there? Weren't you planning on doing some driving practise?'

'I tried, but the battery is flat. Darryl's getting me one tomorrow.'

'Have you moved it at all since you've been here?'

She shook her head. 'It hasn't been a priority.'

'Maybe we should see what's hiding beneath it?'

Her eyes lit up. 'Could it be that obvious?'

Downstairs, they both crouched beside the vehicle.

'There's a drop sheet underneath it, but the wheels are standing on it.' Wren tugged at the tarp, but it wouldn't move.

'I'll push it out of the way.'

Her eyes roamed over the muscles in his arms while sharing a sly grin. It was sexy as hell. 'Okay …'

Marcus removed the chocks behind the large all-terrain tyres, released the park brake, put the ute into neutral and pushed it towards the closed doors.

In its place stood an old oil tray resting on a large tarp. Wren shifted the tray as he peeled back the plastic sheeting to expose yellow letters painted on the cement floor:

LAMBERT

'You were right, Marcus.' She patted his upper shoulder.

Was this treasure hunt really happening? 'Who's Lambert? Is it someone you know? Or Rowan knew?'

Wren chewed on her bottom lip.

'Why is it painted in that yellow gold? It's an odd colour.' So was the word painted on the floor of a shed, it hadn't been there long.

'Gold. Lambert. *Lambert's Gold*!' Her tinkling laughter filled the shed, with her wide smile as bright as the rising sun. 'You're a genius.' She kissed him on the cheek, swiped her torch and coffee mug off the back of the ute, and headed for the house.

'What's *Lambert's Gold*?' He had to admire her determined stride, and the shifting hem of her dress giving glimpses of her soft legs.

'It's the title of a book.' Wren effortlessly jumped up the front steps and into the house, straight for the loaded bookcase in the living room.

'Ugh, not these, again.' He rolled his eyes at the books Tanisha had wanted to guard 24/7. 'You're saying the next clue is in one of these silly romance books?'

'Everyone is entitled to their own opinion. So, I'm assuming you've read them, in order to form your judgement?'

'Pfft. I'm flat out reading the station's paperwork. Any clues why someone like Rowan has these books? It's romance, right?'

'Lots of men read romance. And some of them are a lot tougher than you, so stop judging, Detective Sergeant.'

'What's the big deal? They're just books.'

Wren ran her finger along the many titles. 'They were gifts and, okay, Mr Macho—'

He frowned at her.

She matched it by raising her chin at him. 'Just because you may not like romance novels, it doesn't mean they're trash. It's like saying we all hate cops—'

'Careful, honey.'

'It's just a genre, like sci-fi and fantasy. If you made the time, what would you read? Wait ...' Her hand whipped up like a traffic cop, while she read him like an X-ray machine.

He didn't like being that exposed to anyone.

'You wouldn't read crime, because you'd pick out all the flaws and probably solve the mystery by page fifty.'

He barely shrugged, even if she was right.

'You'd read autobiographies. Am I right?' She poked her nail at his chest.

But he caught it, holding her soft hand, missing her touch. 'Yeah.' His voice was like gravel. She read him well. 'Are you going to judge me for that?'

'No. I read all sorts. Even the boring stuff on jar labels sometimes.'

'For your research, right?'

'Yeah ...' She pulled her hand free to scrutinise the bookcase. 'I can't find it. I know it was here ... Felix? Have you seen the copy of *Lambert's Gold*?'

Tanisha waved the book from the kitchen table, now clear of cocktails, exchanged for coffee and cake. 'It's with me in the kitchen. I've been drooling over it as usual.'

'Hey, what makes you think that the next clue is in this book?' Marcus spoke in hushed tones, grabbing Wren's arm before she walked away. He didn't think she'd want to advertise what they were doing.

'It's a romantic adventure novel that involves a treasure hunt.'

'M-hmm ... Did you read it a hundred times to know that? Are you a fan of this ...' He pointed at the bookcase, tilting his head to read the author's name. 'Taylor Timms?'

'I know that book better than anyone.' Wren tugged her arm free, anger flaring in her eyes as she headed for the kitchen.

'Yeah? How?'

'Because I wrote the bloody thing!' Wren swivelled to angrily stab her finger at the bookcase. 'I wrote all those books. I'm the author of what you call silly romance books!'

'*You're Taylor Timms?*' Tanisha's squeal was enough to shatter the windows into a million pieces. 'Oh my god, you're Taylor Timms.' Tanisha jiggled on the spot with the book pressed to her generous bosom, like a teenager standing in front of a boy band with backstage tickets at a concert. 'Taylor Timms, you're my favourite author!'

'Mine too!' Emelia and her blonde hair bounced up and down beside Tanisha. 'I have the entire collection. They're the next best thing to my bridal magazine collection.'

Marcus winced at the ear-splitting noise, imagining the migraine he was about to endure.

'Um-err … Felix? I can't deal with this …' Wren started backing away from the squealing pair of women in the kitchen. 'I need that book.'

'I'm on it, Toots.' Felix was stuck in a tug-of-war with Tanisha for the book, who was still gushing out an incomprehensible stream of words with Emelia over book titles, characters, and what he'd imagine were scenes.

'*Tanisha*! That is not your property.' Marcus's booming voice sliced through their squeals, instantly silencing them.

'Thank you, Marcus.' Wren whispered over her shoulder.

He winked at her, glad to help.

'Here's the book. We'll deal with this pair.' Felix passed the paperback to Wren, while Gabriel and Reggie blocked the kitchen doorway.

'Thanks.' Wren flicked open the book, brushing past Marcus to go into her office, slamming the door behind her.

The bookcase beside Marcus held an extensive collection of novels. He plucked a paperback from the shelf, peeling back the front cover to the acknowledgements, where there was a list of *Thank yous* to professors, doctors, universities, and other professionals that ended with … *most of all, thank you to Rowan*!

'Is Wren really Taylor Timms?' Tanisha asked Felix from where she was corralled in the kitchen.

'Yes. But Wren likes her privacy. She's quite shy.'

'Is that why she writes under a pseudo-name?' Tanisha asked. 'I thought she was a researcher.'

'Wren is always researching. She loves it. And the travels are all part of her research,' replied Felix.

'Like in the book *The Pharaoh's Lover*, did Wren go to Egypt?'

'Yes. She did the Amazon for *The Amazon's Alpha*.'

'Oh, what about the South Pole? Did Wren go there for *Antarctica's Thaw*?' Tanisha tapped on Emelia's arm. 'That's my second favourite to *Lambert's Gold*.'

'Yes, Wren went there, too,' replied Felix. 'Wren got to interview the scientists, but she had to stay for twenty-eight days until the next ice-boat arrived. I'd never been more worried.'

'Why?'

'The Ice Queen in the land of ice. Puhleese. And before you ask, all of Wren's characters are purely fictional.' Felix then wagged his finger at the pair of women. 'And don't you dare ask Wren to put you in one of her books. It's rude. I deserve to be there first, if that's ever going to happen. And Wren never bases the men on anyone. They're all purely made up.'

'The longest relationship Wren had with anyone was that ...' Reggie looked to Felix for the answer.

'Stupid he-man off-shore alpha a-hole miner.' Felix huffed, crossing his arms over his chest.

'What happened?' Tanisha asked.

Marcus's ears perked up, as he slid the book back onto the shelf.

'That pathetic macho male thought Wren's writing was stupid and gave her a hard time over her imagination. I mean, you should hear her sometimes—she'll come up with a fantastical story just based on a picture on Instagram.' Felix then sighed heavily, straightening his shirt. 'Anyway, I think he got jealous because Wren was so much smarter than him. But he also got embarrassed when his friends found out she was a romance novelist, so he dumped her.' Felix glanced at Marcus for a long second. 'He just wasn't man enough for her.'

'Why didn't Wren tell us she's a writer?' Tanisha asked

Felix.

'Because Wren doesn't like that sort of attention and likes her privacy. So none of you can make a fuss of this, okay? Wren hates it.'

'Is that why you said that Wren is being stalked?' Emelia asked. 'Because she's Taylor Timms?'

Marcus entered the office without knocking, to find Wren seated at her desk, flicking through the pages of the book with her father's letter open beside her. 'I thought you were a researcher or something?'

She barely gave him a side glance, keeping her focus on the book.

It was a big book, with a lot of pages.

Good god, she wrote a book. An entire book. A whole series of books, in fact. He knew how hard it was just to write out monthly reports, or court reports and charge sheets, but to write something that big took patience and skill.

'I'm sorry, Wren.'

'For what?'

He placed his hand on top of the book she was trying to read. His heart skipped a beat when her pretty eyes levelled with his. 'For saying they were stupid romance novels. You were right, I shouldn't have passed judgement on something I haven't read.' He had to step away from her to breathe. 'It explains a lot about you, though.'

'In what way?'

'Your use of imagination in *your uncanny ability to see things outside the box is a gift* ...' He tapped the open letter from her father, resting on the desk. She wasn't the only one who'd re-read it. 'Not only do you have a talent, but you're highly intelligent too.'

Her entire stance softened, right before him. Could the Ice Queen persona finally be melting?

'You've been able to use it to make something for

yourself, Wren, and you have every right to be proud of that.'

The brush of colour was so light across her skin, he was tempted to stroke her cheek through to her jawline and across to her dainty chin.

Stopping himself, he sat in the nearby guest chair. She'd said no, and he was going to play by her rules. 'So how did you come up with the pseudonym?'

'It was Rowan's idea.' She closed the book to display the cover. 'Rowan believed in me from the first draft. He actually submitted it to a publisher without my knowledge. I was so mad when I found out, but I wouldn't have the career I have today without his help. For ten years, he's been helping me with every book.' The sadness in her eyes was gut wrenching.

'Where did the name come from?'

A slight grin flashed on her supple lips as a memory passed. '*Taylor* is Rowan's second name and *Timms* was the name of the pub where we first met.' She gave a shy shrug as her thumb tenderly ran over the letters of the book cover.

'So that's why Rowan ended up with a copy of each novel.'

'The poor guy ended up being my advisor for the male perspective, as he wrote in the letter—'

'I am grateful to have had the privilege of not only being your friend and confidante, even if I was that grouchy old-fashioned advisor …'

'You memorised the letter?' She gazed at him in wonder.

It was Marcus's turn to shrug. 'Maybe I should read one of those books to form a proper opinion.'

Didn't that make the sun shine all over her smile?

Pity he was about to kill the mood. 'But we have more pressing matters, like the stalker. Did you find anything in the book?'

'Not yet, but it's there.' Wren dropped the book on the desk, rubbing her eyes, exhausted.

Marcus flicked through the pages trying to find an underlined section or something obvious, but the words were all a blur. 'You look as tired as I feel. Damn, it's one o'clock in the morning.'

She grabbed his wristwatch, tilting her head to read the time.

'Where's your watch?'

'I, um …'

He closed his hand over hers. 'You didn't take that off because of our conversation the other day?'

Her eyes were so big and conflicted with such a deep sorrow.

She'd done that for him.

'Aw, honey …' He stroked her soft hair. 'They were gifts from your father. You should wear them if they bring you joy.'

His reward was her meek smile.

'Toots …' Felix knocked on the door as he pushed it open.

'What's up?' Wren pulled back from Marcus.

'We've spoken to the girls and they're okay. They've asked a gazillion questions and had their fan-girl moment. They'll be fine now.'

'I hope so.'

'I'm sending the girls home, and the darling Tanisha said we can stay at her place until they catch the guy. Which won't be long, will it, Marcus?'

Marcus wished it were yesterday.

'I'll be fine here, thanks, Felix. But you should stay with Tanisha. You could have that pyjama party you've been dying to throw.' Wren slid the letter inside the book and headed for the main foyer.

'Tempting. But what will you be doing, Toots?'

'Sleeping.'

'Err, hello, I'm not under the influence of some outback fairy dust, I see what's going on. You'll be up all night reading that book, when you need some sleep.' Felix tugged on her shirt from the base of the stairs. 'Or Marcus could stay here again.' Felix nodded at Marcus.

Wren shook her head, turning for the stairs. 'That won't be necessary —'

'But it is.' Marcus inhaled the fire in his chest, hating to admit the truth. 'That way I won't worry about you all night and I can get some sleep, too.' He did worry for Wren, who could read him as well as he could read her. 'Most of all, I don't want to let you out of my sight, not until this whole situation is resolved.'

'Situation, huh?' She arched an eyebrow at him. 'Are you putting me under protective custody or something?'

'Don't get all Ice Queeny on Marcus, Toots, he's trying to help.'

'It's more than that and you know it, Wren.' Marcus stepped closer, holding her arm before she could walk away. 'This isn't some game, you know.'

Her eyes flared. 'Oh, I heard about you and Stewart's games. Am I part of that dating game? What was my score?'

Marcus frowned. *How the hell did she know that?* 'No game! There are no more stupid games, especially with you.' He scowled at the carpet that covered the stairs, wiping at his face, frustrated by his inability to express himself. There was no SOP manual, no law book for guidance, nothing that could help him now, only his gut.

'Dammit …' He went with his gut.

Bringing his hands to her face he cupped her jaw. Pulling her towards him, his mouth crashed against hers and he kissed her with hard lips that soon softened to join perfectly with hers.

Her breath caught as his fingers dove deep into her hair to cradle her head, controlling their kiss as it deepened.

He wanted to touch her, hold her, and breathe her all in. She was safe with him, because he was a man who'd kill for her, and he wanted her to know that, to read all he was trying to say in this one damned kiss.

Gasping for air, with his chest pounding erratically, he broke off their kiss. His thumb tenderly drew across her plump lips, wet from his kiss. 'You mean more to me than any game that's ever been invented—yesterday, today, or an eternity of tomorrows.'

Her dreamy smile barely curled on her lips. Finally, all that fear and fight against him was gone.

She cared for him as much as he cared for her. They were both feeling it, whatever this was. He could see that. Damn, his heart could bloody well feel it.

Still, he wasn't letting her go, holding her close where no one else mattered in his universe. Just her.

Why fight what felt so right?

'Wow, that was so hot!' Tanisha gushed beside Emelia, Reggie, and Felix holding a pug. 'So where are you staying tonight, Sarge?'

'I'm staying with Wren.' Marcus wasn't giving her an option, and for once she wasn't fighting him. As he took her hand and they climbed the stairs together, it felt like he'd finally come home.

THIRTY-ONE

The slow rise from sleep to wakefulness had Wren sighing deep into her pillow, having enjoyed one of the best sleeps, she didn't want to get out of bed.

A finger slowly and softly stroked her arm, and the body heat against her side made her crack open her eyelids to the vision of the magnificent male beside her. Marcus. Awake and watching her.

His tousled hair was so soft in her fingers. His eyes were dark, filled with an unseen power that drank her in with a gaze that skimmed over her body.

She'd never forget that look. Ever. It was how a man looked at a woman when every ounce of their being cared for her.

'Morning, beautiful.'

Oh, my word! She felt beautiful. Truly beautiful. That led to an unstoppable smile, starting from her soul to spread liquid sunshine throughout her body. She wanted to stretch and touch the sky. Except she stretched across the bed.

The bed was a mess. Sheets, blankets, and pillows were everywhere, as they'd slept in a tangle of limbs like long-lost lovers.

He ran his fingertips over her bottom lip, surprising herself when she licked at his finger with an urge to suck on it.

His dark eyes held hers, seeing past all her flaws, even the barriers she had yet to invent, he'd found a way past them, and still looked deeper.

'You are so beautiful,' he murmured. Pulling her closer, he cupped her face, covering her mouth with lips that were so deliciously gentle.

His hot mouth roamed over her collarbone, up her neck, and across her jaw, then back to her lips, where his tongue performed in soft strokes of perfection.

'I'd be a happy man if I woke up like this every day for the rest of my life.' He murmured against her lips, reconnecting with hers, and somehow connecting them on so many levels within this one deep kiss.

A shrill noise rang in the air.

'What is that?' She pulled back, blinking at the daylight flooding the room.

'My fricking phone.' He dug around the clothes and linen piled on the floor. 'Yeah, Marcus here ...'

She wrapped the bedsheet around herself, and with one last lingering look at him sitting on her bed talking on the phone, she turned and walked away.

Daylight had a way of removing the disguise of a daydream. They didn't call it a harsh reality for nothing.

Wren headed downstairs.

No one was around.

She put on the coffee and leaned against the kitchen counter, facing an enormous blue sky, with the gentle wave of native bushlands guarding the corridor of gold grass that made up the long paddock. It was a stunning scene from her window. Taking a big deep breath of fresh outback air, which was alive and pulsing with life, she could feel the world slow down around her.

She heard him coming down the stairs.

Her skin prickled as he approached. First, his fingers

kneaded her hips, then his lips nuzzled into her neck. The bristles on his chin a scratchy contrast against his warm breath, which sent chills down her spine. 'You got enough coffee for me?'

'I do.' She placed their steaming cups on the table, admiring his bare chest as he tossed his police shirt over the spare chair.

'So, tell me about this game you and Stewart play.'

He hung his head low, grinding the heel of his palm into one eye.

She sipped, watching him over the rim of her coffee cup. Why not ask the hardest questions first?

He gulped down a mouthful of his coffee, then let it rest on the table. 'It was something that happened over time. Betting on sports games, to dating – we only rated it on dinner conversations, that's it, I swear.'

'Why have a thing called dating-rating's game in the first place? It's creepy.'

He hung his head with a heavy sigh. 'It was a way to ensure we both never got involved with a woman for anything long term. Stewart's counting down the days until his contract expires. And for me, I've always focused on my job.' His voice was gravelly as he raised his eyes to meet hers. 'And no, I did not rate you with Stewart. I'm not going to. The dating-rating game is over. Permanently.'

'But, we, us …' She gazed at the slow-moving ceiling fans. 'How do I even begin?'

'With a question. You ask, I'll answer.' He reached across the table, his large hand warm and all-encompassing of hers. 'Wren, I want this. I know you do, too, and I know this comes with a tonne of complications, like your Granddaddy's speakeasy.'

She grimaced between pain and laughter at his unexpected terminology. 'What about the rule you have at your work?'

He frowned, pulling back. 'What rule?'

She pushed further. She had to. 'The rule where you told your staff about not getting involved with someone while working with them.'

'Not getting involved with a VOC.' He mumbled it like a rule he'd recited a gazillion times.

'What's a VOC?'

'Victim of crime.'

'Do you see me like that?' Wren didn't feel like a victim, never had. 'You said there was no crime involved with Rowan's death.'

'There's a guy stalking you, in this place.'

'So, you're here for your work?'

'Don't twist this around.' He pushed his chair back, raising his chin as if angered. 'It's not like that and you know it.'

She did. She felt it on all levels. He cared for her deeply, the way—if she had to admit it—she felt it, too. 'I'm sorry.' She reached across the table to stroke the back of his hand. It didn't take long for his fingers to become entwined with hers.

'That rule is there for a reason ...'

She waited, brushing her thumb over the back of his hand.

'Did you hear about my history?'

'About you being a bad-bad-bad man.' She barely kept a straight face, repeating Emelia's words.

He chuckled, shaking his head. 'Not that bad. Mischievous, rebellious ...'

'Naughty, huh?'

He nodded with tight lips, pulling his hand away.

'Everyone goes through a period of rebelliousness, it's nothing to be ashamed of.'

'Did you?'

'Yeah, I spat the dummy and ran away with Felix.'

'Why?'

'Felix's father had kicked him out of home when he told them he was gay. I'd been there for Felix way back when I used to guard the girl's toilet stalls for him, because he'd get picked on by the boys at primary school.'

'And you're still protecting him.'

'I do that for people I truly care about. Felix is family to me. So when he got kicked out, I wanted Felix to stay with us, but my mother—who is against all things fun—wouldn't hear of it. So, Felix and I did a sneaky lawn sale of our combined junk while my mother was at some church camp and used all that cash to skip hand in hand all the way to the train station. I heard you did the same with your best mate, Connor? Rebelled and ran.'

'Hmph. Connor had his own reasons for rebelling, like I did.'

'Connor came out, and you ran away to the circus together?'

'Pfft. Not like you did with Felix.' His scowl was short lived. 'I'm sure Connor's partner, Que, would have something to say about that. Just don't play cards with her unless you're willing to risk losing your dough. Que's fleeced me a few times.'

Sandfly had a card table. A big one, and a roulette wheel, too. But that was too big of an elephant to party with so soon in this room.

Marcus sat back, stretching his long legs under the table, toying with the handle of his cup. 'You know how you found out about your father, late in life.'

She nodded.

'Me too.'

'Sorry? I thought your parents were married?'

'The man who raised me was actually my uncle ...' He sniffed hard, shifting in his seat. 'And who I thought was my uncle was, in fact, my father.'

'The officer down in Melbourne?'

Marcus nodded.

'Did they have an affair?'

'Long before I was born.'

'Your uncle or your father? I'm sorry, I'm confused.'

'My mother was with my Uncle Tom, Thomas, first. She then had an affair and fell in love with Tom's younger brother, Henry.'

'That's why the rule of no affairs in your station?'

He scoffed. 'Did Tanisha tell you?'

She shrugged.

'It's no secret. But, hey …' His muscular body leaned over the table to hold her hand. 'What I just told you about my fathers goes nowhere.'

'Of course.'

'Nowhere, Wren.' His tone was harsh. 'Not in any book, nothing.'

'I wouldn't do that.' She scowled at him, crossing her arms over her chest.

They sipped in silence. She could feel him watching her every move. 'So, when you ran away from town, it was to be with your father?'

'Tom knew it was going to happen sooner or later. Even though he'd sworn to my parents that he'd never get involved unless I wanted to. I didn't know that my parents had run away to Elsie Creek for a fresh start.'

'They eloped?'

'Yeah. I'd been oblivious to it most of my life. I mean, there were no wedding photos at home like you'd see on the walls in people's places, but they were in love. Every day of their lives, my parents loved each other.'

'That photo on your office filing cabinet? It's of two men. One of them is wearing a police uniform, with lots of medals on his chest. Is that …'

'My two dads, taken at my graduation from the police

academy. It was the first time in decades that they'd been in the same room together. It was tense as hell, but Henry was always my dad. Tom told me he knew his younger brother would take better care of my mother than he ever could. But he'd made them swear to look after me well, which they did. I had a great childhood in this town.'

Yet Marcus had rebelled big time as a teenager. So something must have triggered it? 'They wouldn't let you see him when you found out who your father was.'

He gave a slow blink, that was soon followed by a frown. It was frightening.

She gave him a weak smile. Maybe she should stop reading him so easily, especially when she hated being judged herself.

But then he winked, and all was right with the world.

'No, they wouldn't let me see Tom, but I had to meet him.' He ruffled his fingers through his hair.

'And … was it as good a reunion as mine?'

'Was yours good?'

'No.' Wren laughed, hiding her face in her palms. 'It was awful. We were so nervous, suffering these long awkward silences. Even though I'd written this huge list of questions, we just sat there, complete strangers linked by DNA, with no clue how to talk to each other.'

Marcus snorted on his coffee, chuckling as he wiped at his mouth. 'Same. Except I copped a mouthful from Tom for how I ended up there.'

'So it's true that you ran away, stole a ute?'

'Borrowed a ute, and I made peace with the owner. Tom knew I was coming and gave me the welcome wagon I didn't expect.'

'What? Did he beat you—'

'We're talking about a senior detective.'

'Fine, did he use telephone books instead?'

His laughter made her smile. She was giddy and punch

drunk on sunshine and his smiles. What was going on?

'Close. Tom tore strips off me in the worst tongue lashing of my life.' Again, he raked fingers through his hair, gazing into his coffee cup. 'I needed it. This town's Station Hand is a puppy compared to that hard-nosed career cop who was used to brawling and dealing with city scum day in, day out.'

'You respect him.' She could see it.

'Tom was the best.'

'What do you mean *was*?'

'He died. On the job …' With an enormous sigh, his shoulders deflated as he cradled his cup with two hands. 'It was all my fault.'

'How?'

'Tom was worried about me. He died protecting me, when he should have been doing his job.'

'What? Why? How?' The questions rolled off her tongue.

'I was working deep undercover for this crew shifting drugs through nightclubs. I'd been there for almost a year, making my way up the food chain to working the docks, landing the big imports gig, when somehow my cover got blown. They were coming for me, and my uncle intercepted their car, which led to a shootout on the docks. He died from a bullet wound, but not before he took most of them down. The rest of the ops on the docks were done and dusted, we seized the shipment, stopping ten million dollars' worth of smack from getting onto the streets.'

'So they put away the bad guys …' Was she a bad guy? 'You came back to hide here, didn't you?'

'Huh?'

'That's why you're here in Elsie Creek. You can't work down there in case those bad guys find you, especially after a big drug bust that cost them millions.'

'Jeez, are you gonna predict my future too?'

'I didn't mean it like that.' She shuffled in her seat, wrapping her sheet tighter around her torso.

His breath was deep, as if exhaling a stream of smoke—if he was a smoker. 'You're right.'

She lifted her head and saw the depth of pain in his eyes.

'I'd always planned to hide out in Elsie Creek once we'd completed the sting. I was getting six months' paid leave to lay low. It just took a lot longer than I thought to get here, especially after my uncle's funeral and tidying up his affairs. I was only a half day's drive out, on the highway, when I got the call.'

'For …' She let the question hang in the air.

'My father, the man who'd brought me up, had died in a car accident. He'd been side-swiped by a fatigued tourist driving on the wrong side of the Kakadu Highway, forcing his car to roll, which led to Dad having a heart attack.'

'I'm so sorry.' She remembered his lecture on driver's fatigue when they'd first met, marching them from their vehicles on the side of the hot outback highway. 'To lose both fathers in such a short space of time must have been awful.' Her heart ached for him.

'It wasn't the best time.' Marcus scrubbed palms hard over his face as if ridding himself of the memory, only to dump his elbows on the table. 'Except, if Uncle Tom had only stuck to the protocols, the SOPs, like he'd trained me, like he'd trained his team, he would still be alive. But …'

'He let his emotions cloud his professional judgement, because you were his son.'

He didn't nod. He didn't even blink. Staring at her, as the realisation of what they were doing and why he had that rule of not dating someone while working a case. It was for a reason.

'Marcus, I don't want you to—'

'Stop. Don't say it.' Again, he reached across the table

to hold her hand. 'Let's talk about anything else but that.'

'Okay… Did your uncle accept you as his son?'

'Hell, yeah.' He grinned. 'We lived together like father and son, going to footy games, or yelling at the TV over cricket matches, having beers and barbecues. We'd bitch over who drank the last of the milk and whose turn it was to do the dishes. Except Tom chose to keep it a secret and not tell the outside world who I was.'

'Why?'

'To protect me because of his job. He had a lot of enemies.' Marcus paused, his frown faltering as his voice deepened. 'Like your father did with you.'

'I don't think so.' She shook her head.

'Hey, you said so yourself—no one in town knew about you. And it's a small freaking town for gossip like that. It's why I keep quiet about my two fathers. My mother doesn't need to be judged.'

'I won't tell anyone what you said. I swear it.' She screwed up her nose. 'Do you think this town will be judgey towards me when they find out what I do for a living? I mean, it's a town flooded with cowboys.'

'No idea. You're a novelty now as it is, and that's for just being who you are.'

'Which is?'

'The long-lost Peddler.' He glanced at the wall clock, gulping down his coffee. 'I've gotta bounce.'

'I'll walk you out.'

'In that sheet?'

'No one's going to see me.'

'Phew, lady, you have no idea what I see and what my mind wants to see—especially when it comes to you.' He playfully patted his palm over his heart as he walked backwards out of the kitchen, with a boyishly charming wide smile that shone in his eyes.

She grinned at him, feeling all goofy and giddy,

tempted to drop her sheet.

'Don't you dare.' His hand caught hers, keeping the sheet in place. 'As much as I'd love to stay and play all day …'

'Ah-huh …' Brushing his soft hair aside, her fingertips ran down his temple. 'You're so different away from the office.'

'Only the few see the real me. But I've always been me with you.' As he spoke, his eyes were steady as if staring through to her soul. 'Is that a bad thing?'

'No. It's a great thing. I really like this playful side to you.' His language and terminologies were so relaxed, compared to the rigid cop in uniform when on the job.

'You can stay if you want.' She stood on her tiptoes, feathering her lips against his, as her nails gently scratched across his bare chest.

'Well, aren't you the little temptress?' He inhaled deeply, as if to control his inner urges. 'Sadly, I've got things to do. Since we're talking about work, I'm putting you under police protection.' He peered through the front windows where a police car cruised along the driveway.

'What? Don't be ridiculous.'

'I'm serious, Wren. So I suggest you dash upstairs, have a shower, and put on something decent for the company you're about to receive.' He slid his arms through his work shirt, doing the buttons up as he headed for the front door.

Following him, she re-wrapped the bedsheet tighter around her body. 'Surely your department has much more important work to do than watch over me.'

'I'm not arguing with you over this, Wren. Porter is doing the day shift; I'll do the night shift.' He spun around, capturing her in his arms, to pull her against his chest. 'I don't think this guy is going to be daring enough to do anything in the daytime. But it'll give me peace of mind knowing you're being watched over when I'm not around.'

'Would I be receiving the same treatment if I wasn't Taylor Timms?' Her privacy was seriously getting a hammering, and she hated that.

'Yes. Elsie Creek has this unique quality where we look after our own. It's one of the reasons I love this place. So suck it up, Princess Peddler, and please stay home in your palace.'

'My what?' Unexpectedly, she giggled.

'Do you think you can try and do what you're told for a change, and stay put?' His muscular arms wrapped around her body, resting his forehead against hers. It felt like the safest place in the palace.

Then when he kissed her nose and then her lips, she melted against him.

'We good?' His hand paused on the front door as the police car stirred up the dust to park beside Marcus's much fancier patrol car.

'I'm not happy about the police protection thing.' She didn't want him to leave.

'But I am. When I come back, we'll talk about all of those other barriers that are stopping us from being together.'

'But—'

He pressed his finger across her lips. 'I want this, Wren, and I know you do, too. We may have a road-train load of complications, but I'm sure we can work through them, one step at a time. Because I get it …' He looked back at the police car, nodding at Porter clambering out of the patrol car.

'Get what?'

'You're the one.' His eyes were dark and hungry, giving her a look that made her blood hum in some sort of euphoric afterglow.

It made Time. Slow. Down…

'Wren?' His voice seemed far away as she swayed under the intensity of his stare.

She steadied herself against his chest, his strong heartbeat against her palms made her own skip. Did she hear right? 'One ... what?'

'The only one for me.' He leaned in, his large warm hands against her cheeks, his mouth grazing hers with a feather-light touch that soon became possessive, as if branding her.

She blushed inside and out, completely soul-deep naked.

'Whatever this is between us, I've never felt like this with anyone. I know it's only been a couple of weeks since I met you, and I'm probably damning myself for saying it, but I have to because time is a tricky fleeting beast, especially with my job.' He paused, swallowing hard. 'I think I'm falling in love with you.' In a rush, he kissed her, squeezing her so close to his body that she couldn't breathe, and then he was gone.

THIRTY-TWO

The shimmering haze across the sunburnt soil was a stark contrast against the shady verandah that surrounded the Peddler farmhouse. No, the palace. Wren liked it being called the Peddler Palace. It made her smile behind her water glass, while lounging on the outdoor couch, re-reading *Lambert's Gold*.

'There. It's done. What do you think?' Felix climbed down the stepladder, to smile at the assorted hanging pot plants he'd been eagerly planting.

'It looks good.'

'Tsk! You can do better than that, Toots.'

'Exquisite. You have created a delicate floating oasis that contrasts perfectly against the harsh outback skies. Better?'

Felix clapped, with the sun highlighting the sparkle in his eyes. 'Makes me want a garden now. Can't have plants in the club, people ditch their drinks and all sorts into the pots.' He slipped off his gardening gloves, which were as fancy as his dishwashing gloves.

Tucking the ladder inside, he soon returned with a bottle of white wine and two glasses. 'It's after lunch, Toots, let's celebrate. We are in holiday mode.' He handed her a glass. 'Can't believe this is winter, when it's miserably freezing back home. The queens in my club are complaining it's too cold for cocktails. Yet here we are, bare feet, and linen slacks …' He pointed to the yard, smiling at the open field. 'This dry season weather is glorious, it's like a warm spring. Tanisha was telling me it will stay like this for months, without any rain. Don't you just love it.'

'I can see you do.'

'Well …' He plonked onto the couch beside her. 'The shopping situation is a struggle. I've sent Gabriel and Reggie into town for milk and groceries, and that'll take hours.'

'You seem to cope. Are you going to admit you like it here?'

'Are you?'

'Um …' She paused to sip. 'I'm still digesting.' Along with everything else going on behind the scenes. 'You?'

'I like there's no stress here. The view isn't some pretty postcard, but the red-dirt-and-blue-sky look is growing on me. That sky is never the same and this whole Territory is so different to anything I've ever experienced.' Felix raised his glass to the scene that stretched effortlessly before them. 'Oh, as an FYI, Toots, Tanisha swears the townies will be more interested in what's going on between you and Marcus than this stalking-author thing. It'll settle down soon.'

'Okay …' Wait a second, was Marcus confusing lust with love? Could she be guilty of doing the same?

'Well, I'm happier now that we've got an armed guard on the premises.'

Wren peeked back through the kitchen window. 'Where is Porter? Still napping on the couch?'

'It's a hard day at the office for some. Is Marcus doing the night shift?' Felix playfully nudged her with his elbow. 'Maybe you should include this in another chapter. Doesn't have to be a biggie, just a line hidden in some back page in your next novel?'

'That's it!' Wren snatched up the book, opening the letter, to trace her finger along the last line. '*B1/ C13/ P47/ L8.*'

'What are you doing?'

'Felix, if I tell you something, can you keep a secret?' She hugged the book to her chest. 'Oh, and please don't think I'm stupid?'

'Don't insult me, Toots. I've never thought you stupid and I've always kept your secrets, like you've kept mine.'

'Well, this is my biggest secret ever.'

'What is it?' Felix leaned in closer as she opened the letter.

'You know how Rowan wrote me this letter?'

'Hidden in Sandfly by the dark and mysterious manager of a crocodile-infested island.'

She giggled. 'Two-dollar Darryl isn't mysterious. He's a nice man.'

'Go on.'

'This letter holds the clues for the start of a treasure hunt.'

'Oh, my GAWD.' Felix slapped his hand over his mouth as his words echoed across the long paddock. 'Sorry,' he said in hushed tones. 'Is that why you and Marcus were in the shed?'

She nodded. 'It's where we found the first clue that led to *Lambert's Gold*.'

'Oh, I thought you were just having sex.'

'In a dusty shed?'

'Hey, passion can be blinding, Toots. Ya gotta go with the flow when it comes in hot and heavy.'

Hot and heavy, with a whole backup choir singing out their hallelujahs and a double hell-yeah, it was heavy between her and Marcus. But was it real? Could it be sustainable for the long-term future?

Oh, great. Now she was dissecting her dating life like a business plan. Good thing Felix couldn't read her thoughts, or he'd be slapping her silly with his fancy gardening gloves.

'Why did Rowan pick *Lambert's Gold* as your first clue?' Felix tapped his chin. 'Is it because it's your first book? The tale of an estranged father and daughter team who go on an adventurous treasure hunt, where they both find love. I loved that book.'

'It was the hardest one to write. I wouldn't have completed it without Rowan's help.' She held up the letter, pointing to the bottom of the page. 'See those numbers?'

'Is that for a safe combination?'

'I'm hoping that you've given me the answer.'

'*Moi?*' His palm spread over his chest, giving his best performance as the drama-loving drag queen.

'B1 is book one. C13 is chapter thirteen …' She flicked through the paperback's pages. 'P47 is page forty-seven.'

'L8 is line eight.' Felix watched eagerly as she ran her finger down the page, counting the sentences. 'You mean this is a real treasure hunt?'

'Yes. Hmph, I lost count.'

'What's the treasure?'

'The Jade Diamond.'

'Ooh, sounds fancy.'

'It's this unique diamond, the colour of jade and decorated with gold.'

'How small is it?'

'It's as big as an egg.'

'Wow. Are you for real?'

'It's the reason I'm being stalked.'

Felix started to hyperventilate.

'Shh, no need for the dramatics, we're safe. And I need to read this line.'

Felix's cologne and his minty breath blended as he read

over her shoulder. 'What does it say?'

'The cellar door was the way down.'

Felix screwed up his nose. 'That's it?'

Wren repeated the line again and again, letting the words roll over her tongue. '*The cellar door was the way down … The cellar door was the way down.* It's a dumb sentence.' Not her best as far as her literary skills went as a writer.

'Remind me why there was a cellar in the story?'

'They were in her grandfather's house, it's where they found the map in the cellar. Remember? That's what started off the whole treasure-hunting adventure.'

'Well, this is your grandfather's home, but there is no cellar here.'

'It's the attic. Ha. I get it.' She could just burst from her skin with joy.

'I don't.'

'It's classic Rowan talk.'

'I'd never met the man.'

'Rowan would use words that had two meanings. He also had a habit of meaning the opposite when he spoke. It drove me nuts in the beginning, trying to work it out.'

'Why?'

'He called it the Peddlers' code. It was some form of family wordplay his father and brothers did when out in public.'

'Like a secret code, because they were bad-asses selling illegal tobacco and booze.'

Putting it that way, it made sense why Rowan spoke in riddles. Tucking the book under her arm, she stood up. 'I'm going inside.' The hunt was on!

'Ooh, I'm coming. Hey, if your family were such bad-asses, how is that going to affect your relationship with Marcus?'

She shrugged, choosing to keep her mind on the

treasure hunt.

'What'd I miss?' In his wrinkled police uniform, Porter sat up from the couch to wipe the drool from his cheek.

'Nothing, Porter. Go back to sleep. I'll be in the attic.' Wren swiped the rechargeable torch from the table by the front door and raced for the stairs.

'Not without me, Toots.' Felix clung onto the banister as he slid across the floor. 'There's fresh coffee and cake in the kitchen, Porter. Make yourself at home.'

'Thanks, I will.' Porter stretched as he stood up from the couch, his hair standing everywhere. 'That's a cool couch. No wonder the boss sleeps on it.'

Upstairs, Wren pulled down the roof hatch, setting the retractable ladder in place.

'Another ladder.' Felix whined from the bottom rung as Wren climbed.

'The last time you climbed a ladder was on that vintage train, and you saw the retro artwork covering the roofs over Elsie Creek.'

'Oh, I loved that. I wonder if Elsie Creek has postcards of their roof murals. I'd send them to everyone back home.' Felix fastidiously rolled up the sleeves of his shirt. 'I'm coming.'

'I'm here.' Wren waited up top to help her friend. Then, by torchlight, she searched for a light switch.

A single globe barely illuminated the roof space with its washed-out dome of yellow light. A small window covered in dust barely highlighted the many boxes, trunks of clothes, and Christmas decorations.

'It's a mess.' Felix dusted his hands. 'How can we find anything in here?'

'Think opposite … Cellar. Door.'

'Attic. Floor?'

'The roof?' She shone her torch at the ceiling, following

the heavy beams as they met the roof's lining.

Even though it was heavily insulated, there's no way they'd climb up here in the summer.

'What are we looking for, Toots?'

'The next clue.'

'Which could be anything,' said Marcus, climbing into the attic. 'Treasure hunting, I presume?' He smiled at Wren.

Her heartbeat paused, before an avalanche of emotions spooled through her bloodstream. It was like a warm rich honey seeping into her soul, making her light on her feet from just staring at the man who smiled at her. All she saw was big, beautiful, Marcus.

Was she falling in love, too?

'Isn't it exciting?' Felix clapped his hands in glee. 'We worked out the clue from the letter. It's up here somewhere.'

'You know, we could use the help of a professional trained to search for details. Got your torch handy, Detective Sergeant.'

His grin was stunning, sending her stomach off in a swirl of giddy goodness. And all Marcus did was smile at her, while unclipping the torch that lived on his fancy police belt.

They all stared at the roof, going over each beam and panel from one end to the other. Nothing stood out.

'I'm getting a sore neck.' Marcus rubbed his neck, stretching it from side to side. 'Can you read that sentence again?'

Wren flicked open the book. '*The cellar door was the way down.*' She shone her torch on the ladder that was a hole in the floor. 'Technically, this attic has no door.' And then she spotted it. 'It's the window.' Wren opened the window and started to climb onto its lip, but Marcus's large hands caught her, gripping her by the waist.

'What do you think you're doing?'

'It's not the roof, it's the window. It's the frame.' She

struggled against him, but he was too strong, pulling her back inside. 'I can climb.' She scowled at the guy.

'Wren did Mount Kilimanjaro. It's that dormant volcano in Tanzania. Didn't you, Toots. That was for your book—'

'I have no doubt that Wren is well skilled at many things, but I'm taller and stronger than the pair of you.' Marcus stood on the window's ledge.

Wren couldn't argue with that. 'Can you see it?'

'Yeah, I can.' He slid his torch back into its case on his police belt, then retrieved a sturdy pocketknife. It was like Batman's handy tool belt complete with pepper spray and gun.

'Well, don't keep us in suspense?'

Marcus opened the blade. 'Something's wedged tight between the roof tiles and the window frame … Got it. There you go, Miss Treasure Hunter.' Marcus passed down an old-fashioned film canister.

'I thought you said the diamond was the size of an egg. Could it be inside that?' Felix sounded a little disappointed.

'It's too light for that. I bet it's another clue.' Marcus swung inside and dusted himself off.

Wren opened the canister and removed a plastic bag containing a rolled piece of paper 'It's a map!' She smiled widely at Marcus and Felix, standing on either side of her.

'It's not old enough to be a treasure map, you know,' said Felix, pointing at the map. 'Where's the worn edges? The old-fashioned writing with a skull, and where's the X to mark the spot?'

Wren grinned at Felix. 'It's not a pirate map.'

'Well, this is the Peddler Palace. Who knows what Ol' Pop Peddler did after hours?' Marcus slid his arm over her shoulders, giving it a squeeze. 'Have you heard the rumour of how he claimed his hundred hectares?'

'There's nothing on paper to prove otherwise.'

Marcus's devilish grin was sexy as hell. 'So you did hear? Do your research on that one.'

'Look, it's a map.' Ignoring him, Wren pointed at the large pristinely white piece of paper holding a hand drawn map. 'That's the river running along the back of this property.'

'Is that the house?' Felix pointed.

'That's the town.' Marcus tapped on the far left. 'Church, pub, train station.'

'Where are the shops?' Felix twisted his neck around. 'And the police station? The hospital? The airport?'

Wren shrugged. 'Marcus, what's all that land mass? *Smoking Flat Lands* and *Watery No-Man's Land*.'

'I'd say that's everything out that window that we like to call the outback.' The man was adorable away from the station; he had Wren and Felix giggling at him. 'But I'd say those are reference numbers.' Marcus dragged his finger along the bottom edge of the page. 'Longitude and latitude.'

'Or it could be another book reference?' Felix asked. 'Not that I'd know how to read maps, but with Google maps, you need a beginning and ending for your destination.'

'Good point. Both of you guys are amazing. I'm impressed.' Wren rolled up the map and closed the window. 'Let's go downstairs, away from all this dust.'

'I'll go first and hold the ladder.' Marcus effortlessly jumped down.

'What brings you to our humble abode, Marcus?' Felix asked, gingerly climbing down the ladder.

'I wanted to ask Wren out to dinner, if she's not busy.' Marcus smiled up at her.

'She's free, so don't take no for an answer.' Felix waved with his fingers as if playing an air piano.

Wren frowned from the attic as Felix's cheeky laughter

disappeared down the stairs.

'Is this where you play Rapunzel or something?' Marcus asked. 'I'm not very good at singing, so I'm not gonna serenade you, sweetheart.'

She giggled, a proper girlie giggle. With a flushed face she fumbled her way down the ladder.

'I've got you, beautiful.' Marcus plucked her off the ladder and held her in his arms.

'Hi … And yes, dinner sounds great.' Or she could have her dessert now, and go for round three-hundred-and-forty-nine of the pleasure Olympics.

'Wear something sexy …' His tone was low, as his eyes roamed all over her. 'Not too sexy, or we'll never leave the house.'

Not that her jeans weren't sexy, but she was going to scour her wardrobe for an off-the-charts dress made for sinning. 'I'll see what I can do.'

'Hmmm …' The low rumble from his chest carried through to hers as his nose nuzzled into her ear. The air was pure sizzle, electrifying every cell in her body, to spark when his lips connected with hers. She swayed into his chest with her back arching as his arms tightened around her.

Her fingers brushed through his hair where she gripped him and took control to kiss him like a woman consumed within a thick, heady layer of lustful passion.

His radio crackled, breaking them apart.

'Saved by the bell …' She licked her lips.

'Any longer and I'd be playing caveman, tossing you over my shoulder and taking you back to bed.' He wiped over his mouth, taking deep breaths. 'Who taught you to kiss like that?'

'No one.' She dropped her head, as the heat rose from her neck to her ears. She'd gotten carried away. 'I've never kissed anyone like that.'

His fingertip lifted her chin, making her meet his eyes. 'And you will never kiss anyone like that except for me. And only me.' He kissed her hard, deep, and fast.

She struggled for air. 'Is this your way of asking for a copy of the map?'

He winked at her. 'You have set a precedent for your paperwork, and we have that deal.'

'We do.'

In her office, the printer got busy making copies of the map. 'Is there a reference library or some local historian in town? I want to compare this drawing to a proper town map.'

'Our library is part of the school. The Council office is a good start.'

'Where's that?'

'It's tucked behind the main street. Near the Ranger's station.' He rolled up his copy of the map. 'Do me a favour, Wren, don't show too many people that map, or we'll have a case of gold-rush fever in this town.'

'Good point.'

'Pity I'm going the other way, or I'd give you a hand.'

'I'm good, there's a new battery in the ute. Don't worry, you've already given me one ticket, I'll stick to the speed limits.'

'Hmph. Porter can take you. He could do with the fresh air after sleeping on your couch all day.'

She pursed her lips together, not going to get the guy in trouble, while locking the original map in her safe. She slid her copies of the letter and the map between the pages of *Lambert's Gold*, then tossed it into her large bag, flinging the strap over her shoulder. At the bottom of the staircase, she changed into her boots. 'Felix, do you want to come into town with me?'

'ABSOLUTELY.'

In the foyer, both officers winced as Felix's words

bounced off the walls.

'Let's go. Porter's playing taxi.'

'I am?' Porter screwed his nose up at his boss.

'I've got the front seat. Ooh, can we play with the sirens? And the lights? It'll be a disco party in the police car.' Felix flew past, slipping into his loafers, snatching up his man bag to bolt out the door.

'Don't you dare play with those dials! Before you think about it, Felix, the police radio is not a karaoke microphone.' Porter chased after Felix, who was stirring up the dust in his race for the police car.

'I feel sorry for Porter.' Marcus shook his head at Porter trying to control the big kid, Felix.

'Don't be. We'll spoil him.' Wren closed the house behind her, hearing the many locks click into place.

'Hey, you stay out of trouble, and I'll see you later for dinner.' With a quick kiss, a wink, and a sly, sexy smile, Marcus climbed into his squad car.

Sliding on her sunglasses, Wren couldn't wipe the smile off her face, even with Porter and Felix arguing like toddlers in a sandpit. 'It's a date, Detective Sergeant.' It had been forever since she'd been on a date and she was looking forward to it.

THIRTY-THREE

'Well, that was a crock. They knew nothing,' complained Felix, following Wren down the front steps of the town's tiny council building.

Porter looked up from his phone, leaning against the police car where he'd been waiting for them.

'At least we have a bigger map to work from. I just can't work out the layout of the town in the drawings. It's all twisted.' She turned the smaller hand-drawn map around, trying to find where it fit on the larger map she'd just bought. 'We need a large table to spread this out so I can work it.'

'Great idea, Toots.' Felix grabbed her wrist watch for the time. 'We can do that at the train station. The coffee van should still be open.'

'The what?'

'Coffee van. Tanisha and Emelia said it's an absolute gastronomic must-try, and they have tables there.'

'Or we could climb the train's roof again.'

'Now we're talking.' Felix hooked his arm through Wren's and approached the police car. 'Yoo-hoo, Mr Policeman.'

'You know my name's Porter, Felix. What do you want

now?' Sliding his phone away, Porter blocked off the car's front door. 'No more front seat for you.'

'Oh, come on, is that because I played with the siren?'

'And the lights. And the police radio. Marcus will have my head later.'

'But I had to know if Tanisha was coming for cocktail hour.'

'It's a police car. We do serious police stuff.'

'Whatever.' Felix waved at an imaginary fly. 'You can play chauffeur and we might shout you some coffee.'

'From the train station?'

'We heard it was good.' Wren tucked the map under her arm, keen for a decent coffee in one hand while she studied the map. The excitement was mounting, this was really happening.

'Lucy does a great job. Her stockman's breakfasts are brilliant.' Porter opened the back door for them. 'Go on, get in. Marcus would have a hissy fit if I left you alone for a minute.'

'You left us alone in the council office.'

'I could see you both through the glass doors.'

'In between texting your girlfriend,' Felix said with his tongue in cheek.

'Tess isn't my girlfriend. I wish she was.' Porter shared a long face.

'Have we met Tess, Toots?'

Wren shrugged. 'What's Tess like, Porter?'

'The best ...' Porter smiled as he talked all about Tess from behind the steering wheel of the patrol car, driving them down the main street of town. It was a quick trip to where the large pub towered on the corner, with the train station on their left.

'You mean you haven't gone on a date with her yet?' Felix asked Porter, parking near the vintage train, where assorted trucks and utes filled the car park.

'I've quit smoking for Tess. I shaved off my beard because she doesn't like beards, I'm even reading the books she likes. But she still won't say yes.'

'Why not?'

'I wish I knew. But at least Tess lets me hang out with her after hours in the post office.'

'Doing what?' They crossed the lawns to the food van, where the aroma of coffee filled the air. Assorted groups sat at the scattered tables shaded by large umbrellas. On the far side of the lawn, children squealed as they played on the vintage train.

'I help Tess to catch up on the mail. She works long hours as the post mistress. The mail never stops. All day trucks come and go, and then there's the train days and the mail plane.'

'All that from the small post office?' Felix pointed to the building beside the park that stood on the other side of the train tracks.

'Tess is a busy lady. I've been hoping that by hanging around she'll say yes.'

'I wonder where I've heard that before?' Wren arched her eyebrow at Felix, who had a sudden interest in the cloudless sky.

Porter continued. 'Only Tess boots me out when it's time to take her grandmother home for dinner. And I never get invited. I swear her grandmother hangs around the craft store like one of those chaperones.'

'If you were in that situation, and you were Tess, busy with a booming business …' Wren catching her friend's arm before he walked away. 'What would you want your future partner to do for you, Felix?'

Felix scowled at her.

'I could handle some advice, you know.' Porter

pleaded with them. 'I'm not getting anywhere. Stewart and Marcus tell me to forget it, saying it's too hard and too much of an effort for a date. Tanisha's says I've got to be patient. What more can I do?'

'Do you really care about Tess?'

Porter nodded. 'I can see us getting married and raising our kids in this town. She's the one for me.'

Wren's heart fluttered at the memory of Marcus calling her that only this morning.

'Hey Porter, won't be a moment,' called out a lady in an apron, clearing plates from the tables.

'No worries, Lucy.' Porter waved at her, then cleared his throat, facing Wren and Felix. 'Please, I'm open for suggestions.'

'Why don't you deliver Tess one of those decadent little cupcakes, with a coffee?' Felix pointed at the cakes displayed at the food van.

'And do what?'

'Nothing.' Wren grinned at the nodding Felix. 'If she's that busy, just pop it on the counter and say something like *sweet for a sweet.*'

'And then walk out like you're mega busy. That'll show her that you'd make the effort to hand deliver this for her. It'll speak volumes—especially when you're just as busy. She'll respect that.'

'That's great, Felix. Got any other suggestions?' Porter asked.

'I'm sure Felix can come up with something fantabulously extravagant later.' Wren wanted to unroll her map and work on her treasure hunt first.

'Oh, an outback date like no other.' Felix had stars in his eyes.

'Is that cheesecake?' Wren pointed at the glass display as Lucy climbed into the spacious coffee van.

'It's looks so lush. We can share a piece, Toots.'

'Sorry to keep you waiting. How can I help, Porter?'

'Lucy, can I get one of your best cupcakes and a fancy coffee for Tess? I want to deliver it to her. And an extra three coffees for me and my friends, Felix, and Wren. They'll take that cheesecake with two forks?' Porter pulled out his wallet. 'My treat, considering I've been drinking your coffee for days.'

'Are you the long-lost Peddler?' Lucy asked Wren.

'So they tell me.'

'Hi, I'm Felix from Sydney.' His wave flourished with his piano fingers.

'Welcome to Elsie Creek. Seen much of the place?' Lucy talked as she made their coffees, while Porter nervously fidgeted with his collar.

'We saw the painted roofs on our first night in town. The artwork was spectacular with that stunning outback sunset. Don't you agree, Toots?'

'I loved them.'

'You should check out our local museum. There are some amazing pieces in there. All locally made.' Lucy pointed through her serving window towards the train station itself. 'It's just through those bi-fold doors and into the old tea rooms.'

'Come on, Toots, let's take a squiz.'

'Um ...' Porter had a coffee cup in one hand, and the cake plate in another.

'Go and deliver that, Porter, we'll meet you back here.' Wren and Felix crossed the lawn for the Elsie Creek Tea House Museum.

Inside, their eyes adjusted from the bright sunshine as ceiling fans stirred the air. Overhead lights cleverly spotlighted an entire wall covered in images, outlining the history of the town. Along the other walls were artworks and sculptures.

'I like this.' Wren pointed to the rustic hat rack made entirely of horseshoes.

'That would look good in the front entrance at the Peddler Palace.'

Wren grinned at the name catching on for the house. The rugged hat rack *would* suit the hall, picturing Marcus hanging his many police hats there, while his boots rested right next to hers.

Hold the phone! Since when did she start thinking like some country music song, of hanging up hats and lining up boots, and calling it home?

She tried to shake the vision, which was so clear in her mind, while staring at assorted metallic sculptures made from tin cans, old tools, even cutlery, and corrugated iron.

Felix gushed, rummaging through his well-stocked man bag. 'I hope I've got my flash-the-cash have-to-spend credit card. I love that horse.' He pointed at the life-sized stallion completely made from spare metal parts welded together.

'Where would you put it?' She spied the bright open kitchen and its workbench.

'I don't know …' Felix did laps around the horse. 'But I want it.'

'Ah-huh … Think of the transport costs.' In the kitchen she unrolled the large map, then placed Rowan's smaller map over the top. With a pencil in hand, she tried to work out her bearings.

It was frustrating, like reading a nameless cake recipe missing half its list of ingredients.

She heard footsteps coming up beside her.

'Toots …'

'I've worked out some of the spots on the map. The titles to these places are great. *Southpaw's Salty Roost, Parley's*

Path, the *Smoking Flat Lands*, and *Watery No-Man's Land*. It's almost like your pirate map, Felix. Pity, it doesn't make any sense.' Her finger ran over the odd names. But where did they start? She tapped on the numbers on the bottom of the page.

'Wren?'

'Huh?' Felix only called her Wren when she was in trouble. She turned around and froze. 'Aw, no.'

It was him—the stalker.

THIRTY-FOUR

Marcus stared at his PC monitor, waiting on various reports. On any other day, emails flooded his inbox, but now, nothing.

'Are our NBN cables down again?' He yelled out through the open doorway of his office.

'No, Sarge,' Tanisha replied from her perch at the front desk.

'Are you sure we don't have some farmer digging up cables he's not supposed to? It's happened before.'

'Doubt it.' Stewart sauntered in, carrying a plastic container and thermos. 'You in?' Stewart asked Marcus. 'I've got this fresh lemon cake from the Merrick family.'

'The boy who pinched his dad's bike and decorated it with barbed wire?'

'Yeah.'

'Why did you bring it here when you have a hospital full of staff?'

'Staff?' Stewart scoffed. 'My old theatre staff is twice the size of what I work with in this town.'

'Are the nurses on a diet again?'

'How'd you guess? Give us that mug, you mug.'

'Sure. Might want to chuck that, it went cold hours

ago.' Marcus had been scouring hillsides for the stalker. He'd found tyre tracks, more butts, and empty cigarette packets of a brand that wasn't sold in town.

All clues showed that it was the same guy, in an unknown vehicle, in a town that had a back road to the tourist-attracting Kakadu National Park.

Of course, Wren would want an update as part of their deal. He just wished he had more to share with her.

Was tonight's dinner-date conversation going to be all about the treasure hunt, too?

He hoped not. He wanted this to be a real date. Not a skirt-chasing, call-you-later kind of date, either. He wanted the real thing.

Would Wren want to go to the pub? He rarely went to the pub himself, except in an official capacity. Last time was Rowan's wake, before that … He couldn't remember.

Was it too late to call Lucy at the coffee van and ask her to make him something special? But where would they go? There weren't that many options for dinner in this town.

While Tanisha chatted with Stewart, who was cutting cake and pouring coffee, Marcus texted his mate Connor: *Make any headway on that stuff I sent?*

He was waiting on various official channels, too. Keen to locate the final two men in Rowan's squad of eight, to confirm or deny if one of them was stalking Wren.

The station's front doors opened and in strolled the born-and-bred local, Alex Landers, carrying a box of beer. Alongside him was his heavily pregnant partner and local softball legend, Verily. The woman could pitch softballs faster than the highway speed limits, having clocked her fastballs using his speed camera. Those numbers didn't lie; her throwing arm was lethal.

Marcus met them in the doorway of the front counter. 'Look at you two …' Beer-brewing, truck-driving, Alex was about to become a father.

'Hey, Marcus.' Alex shook hands, putting the beer carton on the counter as Marcus kissed Verily's cheek. 'We're hoping you'll witness our signatures on some stuff.'

'No need for the beer, my signature is free. But I'll get my stamp.'

'I'll get it, Sarge.' Tanisha scooted back to his office.

'It's a new brew for your private police club out the back. We'd love your opinions on it.'

'Sure.' Marcus clicked his pen. 'What am I witnessing?'

'Our wills …' Verily spoke with her slight American accent. 'Before the baby arrives.'

Marcus arched an eyebrow in surprise at the mother-to-be. 'You know you'll have to change it once the baby is born and you've registered their name. You can wait—'

'My mother died from complications with my baby brother.'

All eyes turned to the doctor, cutting cake on the large table.

'Verily, you have Jenny looking after you, and she's the best midwife I have ever worked with.' Stewart put down his knife, tasting the cream on his finger. 'Do you need me to spout out my amazing credentials, too, because I'm only there to back up Jenny?' Stewart dished out slices of cake onto napkins. 'You are a healthy young mother-to-be, so don't stress. Enjoy this time. Put your feet up, get lots of sleep, and eat some cake.' He passed her a slice.

'Thanks, Stewart.' Verily smiled with relief, taking her cake. Between mouthfuls, she flipped open the file and laid out the paperwork to scribble out her signature. 'You've got Alex's passport application, too.'

'Are you going on a holiday?' Marcus watched Alex take his turn to sign the forms.

'Not until Nugget arrives, then we plan to visit Verily's

father in the states.'

'How long now, Verily?' Marcus provided his John Hancock, stamping his official credentials on all documents. They were organised for a young couple.

'Too long.' Verily rolled her eyes, rubbing her hands over her belly.

'Six weeks.' Alex smiled like a kid counting down to Christmas.

'I can't drive a truck anymore. I can't roll out of bed. I struggle to swing the softball bat properly, and my favourite bean bag has been banned from the cottage. I'm all belly.'

'And what a beautiful belly it is.' Alex leaned down to kiss her stomach. 'Don't you listen to your mother, Nugget. You're beautiful. You just stay in there until you're good and ready to come play ball with your dad.'

'So you're having a girl? No doubt a future softball champion like her mother.'

Both expectant parents smiled. Dear god, they were positively glowing.

His mate Connor was like that with his new family, too. Could Marcus ever have something like that one day?

'We've kept the gender as a surprise,' said Verily. 'It's killing Aunt Molly not knowing.'

Marcus's mobile rang. Speak of the dust-devil himself, it was Connor. 'Sorry, guys, I've got to take this.'

'Go on, Marcus. We know you're busy. I'll see you at Nugget's head-wetting at the pub?' said Alex. 'Six weeks, mate. Be there.'

'You're on.' Marcus closed his office door as he spoke over the phone. 'I thought you'd lost my number, mate.'

Connor's deep chuckle carried over the phone. 'You wish.'

'Or did you just forget to call me, now you're playing some old, retired dude from the military?'

'I swear I've got RSI from all the paperwork I had to fill out. But I don't mind retirement, if it means hanging out on my back verandah, drinking beer and watching the dog chase golf balls around that bog hole.'

'The one Que calls a pretty pond?' His chuckle matched Connor's.

'I know, she's a shocker. But I'm done with southern winters, can't wait to defrost.'

'I can relate. So, did you do any digging for me?'

Connor's rough voice softened. 'Yeah, I kicked over a few rocks.'

'Nothing too bad.'

'Um, well …' The sound of a door closed in the background.

'It's true, isn't it? They dropped those soldiers in the wrong place.' Where innocent unarmed people died.

'They're blaming intel for the wrong setting, but they were told to go for it too.'

'Really? Why?'

'The reports state they were fired upon, right in front of those caves. They were lucky to crawl through the jungle like they did because they saw some nasty dogfighting for such a small team.'

'Why was that team sent there?'

'The caves. Peddler's crew were specialists in bunkers, tunnels, and caves. They were legendary tunnel rats.'

'Really? Rowan was a tall, lanky guy.' Not built like a Mack-truck the way Connor was.

'Peddler had the perfect frame for it, skinny enough to burrow down tunnels. Crawling into small spaces, not knowing what was ahead, coping with snakes, trip wires, and close contact combat, all while mapping out tunnels they'd find and destroy. It's the reason Peddler and his crew were there.'

'Maps?' Marcus ran his fingers across his copy of Wren's map. It sat beside the copy of Rowan's letter, and a larger, more detailed map of the entire region.

'They were old school, dead reckoning, pencil scrawling mappers; not like the modern gadgets we use today. If Rowan Peddler was still around, I'd have a beer with the bloke just to hear his techniques on bomb defusing.'

Marcus would've punched Rowan Peddler in the mouth, then dragged his sorry arse to the watch house for what he was doing to Wren.

Sure, parents hid stuff from their kids, especially stories that made them look bad. Hell, he had a trunk full of his own junk that only Connor knew about. But Wren was now consumed with this treasure hunt.

And what the hell did he do if she found the Jade Diamond? Arrest her for being in possession of stolen property, to make her pay for her father's sins? 'Did you see Rowan Peddler's service records?'

'No. But he's well decorated for what he did. Rowan Peddler was well respected, ready for a promotion after his time in Timor. He was expected to be a lifer in the service, but then he up and quit with his entire crew after Timor.'

'Did you find anything on Timor?'

'No. And you never will. But I knew a guy, who knew a guy, who knew all about that incident in Timor and said it was hell. I don't know what I would've done if I was in their situation.' Connor cleared his throat, his voice dropping even lower. 'Did you know seven of those eight men are now gone?'

Marcus sat straighter, gripping the phone, shuffling through his paperwork. Wren only told him six were gone, not seven. 'Do you have the name of the one who's left?'

'No, sorry. But my mum emailed me about Rowan's funeral and the long-lost Peddler showing up. Are you going to tell me what this is all about, Marcus?'

'Not over the phone. When you get back, it'll be a bourbon-and-beer-chaser kind of conversation. My shout.'

'You're on. See you in a week and a bit. Just look for the overstuffed train carriage filled with all our junk.'

'How much shopping has Que been doing?'

'Nah, mate, it's all me and Billie. Que's complaining that Billie's grown two dress sizes just in the time we've been stuck down here.'

'Enjoy it while you can.' He'd never pictured Connor as a family man, but it suited him. His partner-in-childhood-crimes had found the perfect woman, now busily setting up home.

Could he have that with Wren?

Not without fighting for it first, and he hadn't even tackled their biggest conversation — the Sandfly Saloon!

He stared at Rowan's map sprawled across his desk. It was very sparse for someone who would've included details as a mapmaker. He recognised the pub, Sandfly, but *No-man's Land* was a whole load of space to cover. The man had given places nicknames he'd hoped Wren would understand. But where did they even begin?

'*Sergeant.*' Tanisha ran into the office with deep worry creases etched across her forehead. 'Porter's lost Wren and Felix.'

'What? How?' He flung out of his chair with his fists slamming onto his desk.

'They were at the tea house museum, ordering coffee. Porter ducked into the post office next door for just a second. By the time he got back, they were gone.'

Marcus ground his teeth, as he scrolled through his phone and tapped on Wren's mobile number. 'Pick up … pick up.'

'Porter's still searching and no one at the train station

saw Wren and Felix leave. I've been ringing Felix's mobile, and he's not answering.'

Wren's phone answered. 'This is you-know-who, and I'm probably who-knows-where, so leave your you-know-what ...'

'Wren, call me as soon as you get this. Please.' He disconnected it and then stared at the phone, willing it to ring.

Tanisha waved her phone. 'I rang Reggie, he hasn't seen them and he's back at the house with Gabriel.'

'Did anyone radio Sandfly?'

'Porter spoke with Two-dollar Darryl who says they're not at Sandfly, but he's going to check the property. It's like they've disappeared.'

His heart squeezed as his stomach curled into a rock. 'That bastard's got her.'

'The stalker?' Tanisha sucked the air in hard, even from behind her hand.

It was like the world slid away beneath his feet as he fell back into his chair with a thud. Fear spread like white lightning, slicing ice through his veins.

How was it that the only woman he truly, deeply cared about more than anything in the world, was in danger?

And on his watch.

In *his* town.

Hot breath pumped in and out. In and out. His chest tightened as a vein pulsed in his temple. 'That bastard!'

Fury flared violently through his chest. He pushed back his chair angrily, it slammed into the wall.

It was his worst nightmare. That one damned rule—to never get emotionally involved with someone on the job—which dictated that he stand aside. But he couldn't switch off the emotions flooding his bloodstream. And no way was he leaving this case up to someone else. This. Was. Personal.

Think. Think …

He'd had a lot of time to think over this too. It's why he had Porter watching Wren. But his mind drew a blank as pure fear for Wren clouded his vision.

Searching for an answer, his eyes landed on the photo frame, showing the image of his two fathers on the day when both men had been proud of him.

Beside it hung his bullet-proof vest with the words *Police* emblazoned across the front.

Sliding it on was like pulling on a shield, forcing him to focus.

He unlocked his gun safe and clipped both of his armour-piercing side-arms into the chest holsters, then snatched up his shotgun, fully loaded. He then emptied his entire ammo stash from the gun safe into his backpack. As he zipped it up, his mind cleared.

'Tanisha, call Ryder Riggs. One of his brothers owns a few retired sniffer dogs. Have them meet me at the train station to see if we can pick up a trail.' He gave out orders while rolling up the maps and his copy of Wren's letter on his desk.

He would not screw this up.

He didn't want Wren or Felix to get hurt. He wanted another sunrise holding Wren in his arms. He wanted a repeat of this morning.

How could the world have turned into a steaming pile of cattle crud in just a few hours?

Yet, this stalker was a stranger to the area, which gave Marcus the home ground advantage.

'Find a current photo of Wren and Felix to put out an APB to all police stations in the region. See if they have any officers spare to assist.' But that would take half a day, more, for any assistance to arrive. Which meant he was on his own, using whatever resources this town had. 'Send a copy of the photo to Jax. Ask our fire chief if his crew can block off the highway with their fire trucks like he did at Christmas with the floods. No one gets in or out of our district unless they've searched every vehicle. I'll call for a bush pilot to do an aerial search of the back roads.' There was only one main road through the town. Hopefully he could contain them with the limited resources he had.

Yet, the remotest and harshest country surrounded the town of Elsie Creek, in all directions. It's what made the outback the perfect place to hide.

THIRTY-FIVE

The annoying stuffy sack was ripped off her head, forcing Wren to wince as her eyes adjusted to the dim light in the small shed. The cool air was a relief against her skin, but she was dying of thirst from the rag tied across her mouth, making it impossible to swallow.

'Well, hello, Wren.' The guy crouched in front of her.

Finally, she saw his face. Her stalker.

Light blue eyes peered through deep suntanned wrinkles. He had a fit, lean build, and grey flecks through his blond hair.

She snarled. If she wasn't bound by the wrists and ankles, she'd give this guy what for.

'And I'm assuming you're Felix.' He removed the sack covering Felix's head.

Felix whimpered in terror, his face covered in sweat as he wiggled to hide behind Wren.

She wanted to tell Felix she was sorry and that it was going to be okay, yet she was unsure herself.

'I'll take your gags off, shortly. First, I'll fetch us some dinner while we wait for the sun to set. Back soon.' He ducked out a side door, leaving Wren and Felix alone.

Wren struggled and strained against the bindings that

bit into her skin, but they wouldn't give. With her heart pounding in her ears, sweat stinging her eyes, she scoured the dark corners of the shed for something to cut them free.

Felix kicked out at her.

She frowned at him, only to widen her eyes.

Felix's eyes were huge and white, his breathing erratic. Sweat streamed down his face as he struggled to breathe through his nose, with his mouth covered with tape.

Felix was having a panic attack.

'Breathe!' Wren screamed through her gag, getting onto her knees, pushing her face up close to his, holding eye contact. 'Breathe.' She demonstrated by taking a deep breath.

Felix hitched.

Pressing her sweaty forehead against his, she exhaled as loud as she could. Inhaled. Then exhaled. 'Breathe.' Dammit.

Ever so slowly, Felix followed her breaths, and calmed down, collapsing against her side to rest his head upon her shoulder.

With her hands tied behind her back she couldn't even hold him, as he silently whimpered. She wanted to cry and fall in a heap, too. But she couldn't afford to, for both their sakes.

Parked nearby was the hardware van they'd been shoved into at gun point. It was the same van that had been used to boost the farmhouse security. Had someone reported the van stolen yet?

By now Porter would've told Marcus they'd been kidnapped, which would've started a chain reaction.

God, she missed him.

Unable to wipe the sweat from her eyes, again Wren searched for a way out of this small shed. Along the far wall, assorted gardening tools, shovels and rakes leaned near a wheelbarrow. Twisting onto her knees again, she tried to get to her feet. 'Augh.' The prick had tied them to the shed pole.

She swallowed her frustrated scream. *No-no-no.* She didn't need to send Felix into another panic attack.

She wriggled on her bum, across the dirt to the pole, and tried to undo the knots.

'Here we are.' The stalker returned, carrying a tray. 'We've got roast beef sandwiches and cake.' He squatted in front of them. 'This is how we're going to play…'

Felix wriggled back against Wren, while she kept working on the knots.

'I'm only going to untie Felix's hands, but I will un-gag both of you. If you try anything, I'll kill Felix.'

'*What?*' She screamed through her gag, while Felix whimpered loudly.

'I don't need Felix. Only you, Wren.' The stalker was so calm about it, as if killing was his day job done in between picking up milk and collecting his dry cleaning. 'If you cooperate, I'll let you both live.'

Wren nodded at Felix, hoping he understood and hadn't gone into shock. She needed to keep him present.

Felix whimpered again, but finally gave the smallest of nods.

'Good. Just so you know, if you scream, I have no problem with inflicting excruciating pain to make you scream louder. We're in the middle of nowhere, and no one's going to hear you.' The stalker shared an evil grin. 'Now the boundaries for our agreement have been set, I'll play nice if you play nice. Felix first.' He whipped off the tape covering Felix's mouth.

'Ay-yay-yay-yay.' Felix yipped like a wild hyena, the tape marks red raw across his mouth. 'For the love of vodka and tomato juice, that's gotta be the worst form of waxing in my life.' He tried to blow at his face, in between heaving for air.

The stalker untied Wren's mouth gag. 'I can see Rowan

in you. You share the same eyes, shoulders too. I didn't know he had a daughter. Did Rowan?'

'We both found out later in life. Are you Steven Kempsey or Patrick O'Donnell?'

'Kempsey. Under normal circumstances, I'd say pleased to meet you.' He chuckled while untying Felix's hands, then dragged the tray to the floor space between them. 'Want something to eat?'

'I'm thirsty,' said Wren.

'Well, drinks all round.' Kempsey cracked open the water bottles, passing them to Felix. 'Nice little shed party we're having here. All that's missing is the music.'

Felix gulped heavily as he held the bottle to Wren.

Wren leaned at a weird angle trying to get her lips to the bottle to drink thirstily, with water trickling down her chin.

'Any guesses as to why you're here? Feel free to speak and share.'

'You're looking for the Jade Diamond,' Felix said, holding the bottle to Wren's lips.

'Felix!' Wren scowled as water spilled everywhere.

'Sorry, Toots.' Felix tried to mop up her shirt. 'Are you still thirsty?'

She nodded. They'd been stuck in that stuffy van for a long time, lying on the floor over corrugated roads, tied up, gagged, and blinded. It had been awful.

'Any luck in your search?' Kempsey cracked open another bottle of water for Felix.

'Rowan left clues and we've been trying to find them.' Felix again lifted the bottle to Wren's mouth. She scowled at Felix for giving away the details.

'Rowan was always an imaginative guy with stuff like that. He used to tell stories to amuse us when we were on patrol. It was Rowan who gave me the nickname Cammo-

Ken.' Sitting back on his haunches, Kempsey lit a cigarette, exhaling a thick stream of smoke towards the tin roof. 'Any guesses where I worked with your father?

'Timor.'

'Give the girl a gold star! So, what else did you learn?'

'Um ...' Wren licked her lips nervously. Did she dare tell all? Because what she'd learned wasn't pretty. 'I found out they dropped a group of eight men in the wrong place and they had to fight their way out to survive.'

'Ain't that the truth.' Kempsey dragged heavily on his smoke. Reaching for a bottle of bourbon, he took a deep swig. 'What's your knowledge of the Jade Diamond? Did Rowan tell you?'

'No. He told me nothing about his time in the military. But I know he suffered from nightmares. Bad ones.'

'We all did.'

'What happened?'

Kempsey studied her for a long time.

'Please. My father's gone; I have to know. And you said we're waiting for sunset ...' She tried to shrug with her wrists tied together.

'It's not like we hadn't told our COs a dozen times...' He inhaled deeply, staring vacantly at the ground. 'We landed in the jungle. It was thick, like nothing I'd ever seen, with steam rising from the heavy monsoonal rains. Rowan took charge, used to the weather from growing up here. We practically belly crawled up the side of the hill, looking for that ruddy cave. It was supposed to be in front of us.' Kempsey took a deep slug of his bourbon.

'Is that when you realised you were in the wrong place?'

He nodded. 'We'd radioed for confirmation when one of our crew spotted a cave. That's when Command ordered us to flush out any rebels hiding within those caves...' He frowned at the dirt, only to whip his head up with his eyes boring at her. 'They shot at us first.'

'Who did?'

'This group in the cave. The rain was coming down, visibility was poor, mozzies were in our faces, stuck in the late afternoon shade made worse by the thick jungle. We couldn't see them, only the muzzle flashes as they fired on us.' Kempsey's voice lowered as his head dropped to his chest. 'We didn't know it was a funeral celebration. Didn't see them until it was all over.' His breathing laboured as he whispered, 'Men … Women … Children.'

'That's terrible.' Felix covered his mouth with his hand. 'You must have felt awful.'

'We were doing our job.' Kempsey scowled, stabbing his cigarette butt into the dirt. 'Armed to the teeth, told to shoot an enemy where we didn't know who was friendly or not. We'd been given bad intel, fighting in a land where no one spoke English, where friendlies would sell us a bowl of rice one day and shoot at us the next. But that village damned us all. We knew we were destined for hell, that God would judge us for our crimes. We all swore to never tell a soul. Yet, here I am, the last of them, telling you …'

'What happened?'

'We were ordered to map out that cave and search for tunnels. That's when Tolser stumbled on the mother lode.'

'What did he find?' Felix asked.

'All sorts. We were used to that, finding anything from bats, snakes, wild pigs, rock art, and other stuff. But this …' Kempsey shook his head. 'Treasure. There were trunks of gold crucifixes, fancy candle holders, gold coins, plates, and goblets.'

'No way … Are you hearing this, Toots?'

Wren nodded. 'It was the stuff hidden from the churches.'

'You stole from the church?' Felix's jaw dropped.

'It wasn't labelled who owned the stuff. It was just sitting there.' Kempsey frowned, digging around for another cigarette. '*Finders keepers.* It's our unwritten rule for finding stuff in caves. Most stuff was just kept for souvenirs. We took what we could carry, hoping to buy out the locals or the enemy until we got back to base or found friendlies.'

'How long were you there for?' Wren asked.

'Eight. Long. Days. Of hell.'

They sat in silence, watching Kempsey puff on another coffin nail, butting it out with the others. 'We got back. Told our story, worried the brass were gonna pin us for murderous war crimes. If those people hadn't shot at us first, none of it would've gone down the way it did.'

'But you all survived?'

'Did we?' He narrowed his eyes at Wren. 'From our group of eight, two died in that jungle.'

'Did you leave them behind? That would've left evidence, right?'

'They were our brothers, so of course we dragged them back with us, including their treasure. Back at base camp, the six of us divided what we had left between us, because we were all going to scat as far as we could. What happened to those villagers wasn't our fault, but we didn't expect command to have our backs either, and I was done playing tunnel rat.'

'You kept the treasure as an insurance policy for yourselves?'

'Yeah. Smithy said we might need it to pay for lawyers.'

Wren shuffled in her spot on the dirt, getting numb in the leg. 'So why are you bothering with the Jade Diamond now if you had your own fortune?'

'I didn't even know it existed. None of us did. Or so I

thought.' He exhaled smoke, right at home seated cross legged in the dirt. 'I went to Thailand and lived like a king. But then them nightmares got to me. I couldn't sleep unless I was drunk or drugged. Eventually, I got hooked on heroin, got sloppy, and ended up in a Thai prison.'

Felix sucked in air, empathy coming off him in waves. 'Oh my, how did you survive?'

'I'd been there long enough to know how to buy my way out. It cost me everything.'

'That's why you're hunting the Jade Diamond, you're broke!' This was all to do with greed. 'How did you find out about the Jade Diamond after all this time?' Wren asked.

'When we split the loot, Rowan scored a jade block. He sold that box in Singapore, through one of my contacts. I always thought it was a block of jade, until my Timorese cell mate told me that the jade block was a box that held the Jade Diamond. He'd seen it as a kid. The *Buan*—'

'The what?' Felix cut in.

'That's the name of a local sorcerer who used the Jade Diamond as part of his *Klamar* ritual for funeral ceremonies,' replied Wren.

'Very good.' Kempsey nodded at her. 'The locals in that region believed that the souls of the dead, who couldn't leave this earth for some reason, would try to invade another person, like a ghost with unfinished business. The Jade Diamond was said to be good luck in helping those souls move on. It was my cellmate who told me it was like a heavy egg, with a green tinge to the diamond.'

Felix sat forward. 'The Jade Diamond is real?'

'It's real, it's priceless, and it's never been reported as stolen anywhere. Which makes it a clean slate under the *Finders Keepers Law*.' Kempsey squinted at Wren. 'So, now it's your turn to share.'

She clammed up.

Kempsey splashed tomato sauce and salt on a slab of meat, pressing it between two layers of bread. 'Or you can sit there and watch me perform a dozen forms of torture I learned while lapping up the luxury of a Thai prison.'

'I have no pain threshold.' Felix whimpered at Wren for help.

Kempsey pushed the tray towards Felix. 'Make yourselves some grub. We can chitchat while Wren's boyfriend rips the town to shreds searching for us.' He bit into his sandwich, carefully watching them as he chewed. 'It's your call on how you want to play, Wren. We could team up, where we can all walk away in the end.'

'Toots?' Felix pleaded, with trembling lips.

Wren exhaled deeply. She had no choice. 'In my bag is a book called *Lambert's Gold*. Inside, you'll find a letter from Rowan that holds the clues.'

'And the maps?' Kempsey rummaged through her bag. 'I saw you with that map, from the council office.'

'That's as far as we got—finding the maps.'

'Felix, make sure Wren has something to eat, we'll need our strength.' Kempsey unrolled the map across the floor.

'Do you want a sandwich? Or the cake, Toots.'

Wren wasn't hungry, but she needed the energy. 'Gimme the sugar. And more water.' She winked at her friend, hoping to put him at ease.

Kempsey tore at his sandwich while studying the maps.

If she helped Kempsey, they'd survive. She hoped. 'We haven't been able to work out the map yet.' She bit into the cake Felix held before her. It was a buttery lemon, sweet and light. 'Nice cake. Did you bake this, Kempsey?'

He didn't respond, finishing his sandwich, with his fingers tracing along the bottom of the hand-drawn map.

'We haven't worked out those numbers yet.' She took

another bite of her cake, hand fed by Felix.

'They're standard coordinates.' Kempsey dusted off his hands to dig around in his backpack, which was dumped next to her handbag and Felix's man bag. He pulled out a compass.

Angling his head, he frowned at the page, and then at the compass.

'You can read those numbers?' Wren nudged her leg against Felix's. 'Water?' Her throat was dry from the cake.

'Oh, sorry. Here.' Felix held the bottle to her mouth, watching Kempsey turn the smaller hand drawn map around the bigger map of Elsie Creek. 'Did we get the right map? The Council office didn't have too much.'

'You got the right map. It's just the numbers are all wrong.'

'Maybe your compass gadget thingy is out of whack?' Felix leaned towards the map, while pushing the cake at Wren's cheek.

'Felix? Watch what you're doing.' Icing smeared down her cheek.

'Sorry, Toots. It's just all too exciting.' Felix dabbed a napkin on her cheek. 'More cake?'

She shook her head.

'These numbers are wrong. I know this compass is calibrated correctly.' Kempsey held up his compass and the hand-drawn map. 'Rowan was gifted with his coordinates; he didn't mess this up. He's hidden it or there's some code or key to it and a starting point.'

Wren swallowed her silence.

'How did you find the map?'

'Oh, I worked that out.' Felix sat taller, pointing at the open letter. 'Rowan wrote clues in the letter, see ... on the bottom of the page. It was in the book, doing the opposite of what he says. Did he do that with you, Kempsey?'

'Yeah. It was annoying at first, but then it came in handy, especially when we were being grilled by the military police in Timor. Rowan called it the Peddlers' code.'

Wren just stared at Felix, freely sharing all.

Kempsey grinned at her. 'Thank you, Felix.'

'You're welcome. Want some cake?' Felix held up the plate, the perfect host, no matter the circumstances.

'I'm good.' Kempsey gave a low chuckle. 'Wren, being Rowan's daughter, I'm betting you want to find the Jade Diamond as much as I do.'

'How do I know you won't kill us once we find it?'

Kempsey's grin was evil. 'You don't. Yet, helping me only helps you both in this situation.'

Felix plucked at the cake crumbs, eating his feelings. If her hands were free, she'd be doing the same.

If she could drag out this conversation, or the search, hopefully Marcus would locate them. Even if she had no clue where they were, she had faith in Marcus.

'Can you read the letter aloud please, Kempsey?' With head down, she leaned back against the pole she was tied to, tracing her finger in the dirt while Kempsey read the letter.

'What do you think, Toots? What's our next move?'

'Shh, Felix. I'm thinking, okay? I usually think better on my feet.' She wriggled her boots, tied at the ankles.

'Forget it.' Kempsey sat back with the letter in hand. 'What's this mean *outside the box*? He's underlined that part.'

Wren dropped her head to her chest.

'Wren?'

'No. No. No.' She stared at the shed's roof where the shadows lengthened.

'What is it, Toots?'

'It's the compass.'

'What compass?' Kempsey asked.

'Rowan gave me a compass a few years back.'

'Wren never took it off.' Felix started plucking at the bread. 'Pity it was broken.'

'Broken how?' Kempsey narrowed his blue eyes at Felix.

'Wren said it never worked. It was backwards. Isn't that right, Toots?'

Wren wanted to thump Felix for giving away all their secrets.

'No. Rowan would have had it purposely calibrated to read backwards. He did that for a reason.' Kempsey tapped on the map. 'Where is this compass now, Wren?'

'It's in the box, just like the letter says.'

'What box? Is it in a jewellery box at the house—'

'The palace,' said Felix. 'We like to call it the Peddler Palace.'

'Do I look like I give a rat's—'

'It's—It's ...' Wren spoke up to stop them arguing; she didn't want to upset their kidnapper.

'Go on, Wren.'

She licked her lips. 'I-I gave it back to Rowan at his funeral. He's buried with it.'

'You're fricking kidding me?'

'I wish I was.'

'Why?'

'Rowan said he'd never make it to heaven.' She now understood why. 'I used to tell him that I'd bury him with that compass so he could use it to find his way to wherever he wanted to go.' Hoping he'd gone to a better place.

'Well...' Kempsey stood to brush himself down. 'Let's hope you don't believe in ghosts, because it looks like we're about to do some grave digging.'

THIRTY-SIX

It was in the early hours of the morning when Marcus collapsed back into his seat behind his desk at the station. There had been no sign of Wren or Felix, but they were still in the area. Had to be. The stalker was going after the Jade Diamond and using Wren to find it. But where?

The stolen van from the hardware store was still missing, last seen at the train station where Wren and Felix had disappeared. Now they were waiting for sun-up for aerial searches to recommence, but what could he do in the meantime?

And how desperate had this stalker become to do a daring daylight kidnapping?

Marcus unrolled the maps across his desk, searching for something, anything.

'Sergeant, this came in for you. It's from the Military Police and the Federal Police.' Tanisha placed the paperwork on her desk.

Marcus snatched up the sheet containing the mugshot of the last living member of the eight men from the squad of tunnel rats who worked together in Timor.

Wren had been right the entire time.

What he'd give to just hold her. He'd never let her go.

'This is the guy! The stalker. Tanisha, put an alert out on this Steven Kempsey. He's armed and dangerous.' He slammed the stalker's image onto her desk.

Tanisha quickly shared the intel over the radio.

Marcus skimmed the report on Kempsey's life and his time in a Thailand prison for heroin use. The man was an addict. That alone made Marcus's skin crawl. From his own experience in the drug squad, he knew all about addicts and Kempsey exhibited obsessive traits of an addict, the chain smoking, leaving cigarette butts everywhere, and the desperate move of snatching Wren and Felix in broad daylight.

No doubt Kempsey would be using Felix to control Wren, who had the map, the book, the letter, and the imaginative knowledge. But where were they?

He missed Connor, who would've helped him brainstorm strategies on this, especially with his military experience. Marcus couldn't trust just anyone with the details of what Kempsey was after, otherwise he'd have cowboys everywhere searching for treasure.

As for his team, Tanisha was busy manning the phones and radios. And he didn't trust Porter enough, not after he'd left his post and allowed Wren and Felix to get snatched in the first place.

'Hey.' Stewart tapped on the open door, dropping into the guest chair. 'Can I help with anything?'

Marcus arched an eyebrow, leaning back in his chair. 'You're going to think I'm mad.'

'Try me.'

'Close the door.' He was going out on a limb with this, but he trusted Stewart.

'Sounds serious.' Stewart closed the door.

'It's a treasure hunt.' Marcus showed Stewart the map and letter, explaining all he knew about Wren's hunt for the

Jade Diamond.

'No way.' Stewart gripped his fingers through his hair. 'This guy has Wren to help him find this diamond?'

'Yep. He's probably using Felix as leverage so that Wren will cooperate.' Even though Wren worked a lot on her own, she was also fiercely protective of Felix, like family. He understood that, rubbing at the fire in his own chest to help her.

'So, you're trying to work out the clues?'

'Yeah. Her father used codes. Wren understood it. The clues are for her …' He just wished he understood it. 'Which means Wren and Felix are still in the district.' And that's what gave him the greatest of hope in finding them in one piece.

He scrubbed his hands over his face, the stubble itchy on his chin. His brain hadn't stopped rolling on possible scenarios. He had the town's main roads closed, and even the back roads were being patrolled, keeping this guy contained within the area. But where were they?

There was a tap at the door.

'Come in.'

Emelia opened it up. 'I brought food and coffee for everyone.'

'Thanks, Emelia. I'm sure the team could do with a feed,' said Stewart, putting the paperwork back on Marcus's desk.

Marcus rolled up the map and letter and slid them into his bullet-proof vest for safekeeping. 'I could do with a coffee.' He'd lost count how many he'd drunk, but he wouldn't sleep, not while Wren was out there.

They joined everyone in the muster room, where Emelia was handing out plates of food to the various officers and volunteers. She then carried a tray of coffee to Reggie and Gabriel seated in the waiting area. Reggie sat up with hope in his eyes.

Marcus shook his head, wishing he had something more concrete.

The station phone line rang.

'Elsie Creek Police.' Tanisha's voice was terse, strained even, with worry lines exchanged for an eye roll as she spoke on the phone.

'Who was that?' Marcus asked Tanisha when she hung up.

'Mrs Bingle, again. She's claiming she's lost an entire cake and roast this morning.'

'Not her imaginary friend again,' said one of the officers.

The officer beside him chuckled. 'Not her dog, again.'

'There is no dog.' Marcus's voice cut through the chatter of the other officers. 'Finish what you were saying, Tanisha.'

'Well, Mrs Bingle cooked the cake for her sister's visit this morning. She swears she had it on the bench last night and now it's gone, along with a roast beef shoulder and a loaf of bread.'

'Did she check her cupboards?' Marcus asked her.

'Yes. And her drawers. She'd set an alarm for herself to make sure she put the food away if she napped and overslept. When she woke up, it was gone. The tray and everything.'

It was also unusual for Mrs Bingle to call this early. 'Can you check the phone logs back to when Mrs Bingle made her first call?'

Tanisha tapped away at the keyboard, as Marcus stood over her shoulder. 'About six weeks.'

Marcus scrambled through the paperwork on his desk for the reports on the age of the butts he'd found from the neighbour's fire break, where the hole had been cut in the Peddlers' fence line. The lab thought they'd been there for at least a month, maybe more.

'Dammit! Kempsey's hiding out there.' Marcus slammed the file shut, swiping his keys off his desk. How had he missed this?

'We've all searched there, Sarge,' Tanisha said. 'You did so yourself.'

'I know I did. Weeks ago. Back when Mrs Bingle made the first call.'

'And Porter's been there daily.'

Marcus had no faith in Porter to even search a shoe box properly, after what he'd done. 'Tanisha, call Ryder and the rest of the Riggs brothers for their dogs.'

'But they'd be long gone back to their cattle station.'

'No, they're in town. They went to Flo's for an early breakfast. Rigsy and his brothers keep a close eye on that old lady. Get them to meet me at Mrs Bingle's.'

Marcus climbed behind the wheel of his patrol car. Sliding on his seatbelt as the engine kicked into life, when Stewart clambered into the passenger's seat.

'What do you think you're doing?'

'I'm coming with you. Before you say anything, if you find them and they're injured, I can help straight away.' Stewart held up his chunky doctor's pack.

Marcus didn't need to hear that.

'Even if it is official police business, I want to help as your friend too.'

'Fine. Buckle up and keep a hold of your stomach, because this isn't a Sunday drive, Doctor.' Marcus slammed his tricked-up pursuit car into gear, and hit the highway to race out of town, with hope flaring in his chest. All he could do was hope.

THIRTY-SEVEN

The universe shared a spectacular display of stars to highlight the world below, where Wren craned her neck at Mother Nature's magnificent light show.

'Come on, stop wishing on a falling star.' Kempsey tugged at the rope hanging loosely around Wren's neck. The same rope ran was also looped over Felix's head and shoulders as he brought up the rear.

Gagged again, they stalked through open paddocks, silent mango orchards and assorted scrublands.

There was an eery screech directly overhead.

Felix's scream was muffled as he tugged on the rope, pulling on Wren's throat, dragging her to her knees. She couldn't breathe.

'It's just a fruit bat, Felix.' Kempsey hoisted the shovels higher onto his shoulder, shifting the large pack on his back, to roughly pick up Wren. 'Felix isn't used to the outdoors, is he?'

She shrugged, unable to answer due to the stupid gag.

A dingo howled eerily nearby.

Wren motioned for Felix to come up beside her. She couldn't hold his hand, but she could try to keep the rope from strangling her.

Tall spires rose from the earth like cathedral towers of mud. They were a marvel under starlight. But those ant mounds needed to be avoided, along with barbed-wire fences and unseen ditches as some of the hazards of their cross-country jaunt without a torch. Their destination, the town of Elsie Creek, shining like a metropolis in the outback.

'We'll stop here and take a breather. No screaming, Felix, or I'll cut out your tongue. Got it?' Kempsey dumped his heavy pack and shovels on the ground, handing out water bottles.

With her wrists now bound in front, at least she could drink for herself.

Felix guzzled his water. 'I've got to do more cardio. This midnight hike is killing me.'

Kempsey glanced at this watch. 'We've got an hour or more at this pace.'

They'd been walking for hours, struggling through tall brown grasses, cutting through fences, even skirting along the edges of sleeping herds of cattle.

She now understood why they were going cross-country under the cover of darkness, spotting assorted red and blue lights at various intersections of the highway. Marcus had strategically closed off the entire town of Elsie Creek.

A speeding car, with lights flashing, led a charge of more vehicles. Was that Marcus?

Sadly, he was driving the wrong way.

What she'd give to signal him right now. To hold him, and just breathe him in and not move for a week.

But then who was to say he wouldn't dump her, for all the trouble she'd put him through. She deserved to be dumped.

'Thanks to your boyfriend, it looks like we'll be taking the long way around to the church. Let's go.' Kempsey grabbed the cloth gag hanging loose around Wren's throat.

'Kempsey, before we do, please, can I make a suggestion?'

'Go on?'

'Can you untie Felix's hands.'

'Now, why would I do that?'

'To help him balance. You can tie a rope around his waist and connect it to me, and you can still keep the one you have at our throats.' The man was a brutal whizz with his ropes, but she hated being dragged like a row of donkeys. 'It'll allow Felix to hook his arm through mine and then he can match my pace, helping all of us to get where we need to go quicker.' She tugged at the coarse rope leaving marks on her neck. Already bruises were forming, not just on her neck, but on her wrists too.

'I'm so sorry, Toots. I don't mean it.' Felix whimpered.

'I know you don't.' At least she could squeeze his hand when she really wanted to hug the guy. 'We'll be able to speed up then.'

Felix nodded furiously fast. 'It's a good idea. It's something I can do. I can. I know I can.'

'Fine.' Kempsey untied the thick rope around Felix's wrists. 'Any funny stuff and I'll just chop off your hands, then we'll see how you balance yourself.'

What a bully! 'No need for that, Felix will stay with me.'

'Like glue.' Felix squeezed her arm. 'Can we please, please, please not do the gag thing?'

'Right now, this gag is muffling your squeals, Felix. But I'll leave Wren's off. Deal?'

'Yes, please.' She nodded at Felix. 'You okay with that?'

'Kempsey's right, I'll squeal. I don't mean to. Want me to put it back on?'

Kempsey shook his head, grinning as he secured Felix's gag in place.

With the rope loose around her neck, the connecting rope running from her waist to her wrists, then back to Felix, Kempsey dragged them along like dogs on a lead.

They trudged over low sloping hills that met the flat lands as the town's lights grew larger, circling to the far side where the dark church was cloaked in silence.

In the graveyard, Kempsey flicked on his torch, shining it over the various tombstones. 'Where is it?'

'Over there.' Wren pointed to the dark edges where all the Peddlers rested. What would her ancestors think of this?

'He hasn't been here long; it should be easy to dig.'

The flowers were gone, the mound of dirt not so big now.

'Felix, you'll dig. Wren, take a seat.' Kempsey dumped the shovels in the dirt.

She lowered herself onto the dew-covered grass, and Kempsey tied her ankles together. A shiver ran down her body.

'Cold? Or have you got goosebumps from someone running over your grave?' Kempsey chuckled. 'Your turn, Felix. Gag off?'

Felix ripped it off himself. 'I promise I won't scream. Unless a ghost happens to pop out, then I can't promise anything.'

'No one's around to hear you. They're all out looking for you, or fast asleep.'

'Can I help dig?' Wren wanted her hands on that shovel.

'Now, why would you do that?'

'Because Felix's has soft, pampered hands. He's not used to manual labour, and you might hurt him out of frustration.'

'It's true. I'm very particular about my hands. I wear gloves for everything. I make sure I moisturise them morning, noon and night, and I have weekly manicures.'

'Why?' Kempsey screwed his face up.

'Your hands age faster than your face. It's all those chemicals in detergents, hand sterilisers and hand washes, and—'

'Want me to put the gag back on you, boy?'

Felix gave a timid shake of his head.

'Zip it.'

'I will, I will. But I should warn you, I'm not digging up any dead people. I've never held a shovel in my life. I pay people to do manual labour.'

Kempsey rolled his eyes, huffing with annoyance. 'I bet you got beaten up a lot as a kid, too. Ah—' He pointed at Felix in a warning. 'Don't answer that. You and Wren can both dig.' He untied Wren's ankles, tethered them to the nearby tree, then passed out the shovels.

'In case you get any ideas, Wren, I'll be keeping my gun aimed at your friend.'

Oh, she was tempted to whack Kempsey right in the face with the shovel. 'Don't think, Felix, just dig.' She threw the blade of the shovel into the dirt, hoping to work off her anger. She was dangerously close to completely losing it.

'But, Toots, it's a grave.'

She patted his shoulder. 'Think of it as the treasure chest of gold. Your ticket to sunshine and paradise.'

'Like a real tropical island that doesn't look like Alcatraz, surrounded by crocodiles?'

'Exactly. Think of that as your next holiday.' She pushed the shovel's blade deep into the soil, trying to think of her next holiday, anything, and everything to occupy herself. They dug in silence under the glow of a super-city of stars.

Kempsey sat nearby with pistol in his lap, watching them dig. 'Wren, how long have you been dating that policeman?'

'Wren and Marcus were going to have their first date tonight, until ...' Felix dug up an eggcup's worth of dirt on the end of his shovel, then sprinkled over to the side like dusting cinnamon on a cappuccino.

Wren had been looking forward to that date. To have her hair done, to wear a pretty dress, heels, and even do her nails. But now her nails were ruined, chipped, and full of dirt from stumbling in the dark, with her hair everywhere, along with a collection of horrible bruises forming from the rope burn around her neck and wrists.

But she had found her rhythm, putting her back into it, making good headway, digging.

'It looks serious to me,' said Kempsey. 'You and this Marcus.'

'Excuse me? How is any of that your business?' She was sick of the invasion of her privacy from this stalking, peeping, bully of a creep. Kempsey had ruined her date night, her first real date with Marcus, aching to have him hold her right now.

She also hated herself for causing a mountain of worry for Marcus. This was not fair to him. Or Porter. Or Tanisha. Never mind the disruption she'd caused for the rest of residents of Elsie Creek.

Most of all that her poor best friend, her family, Felix, was being dragged into this.

Kempsey laughed at her.

Arsehole.

'Wren adores the man, and they get along so well.' Felix scooped up an ice cream scoop of dirt on his shovel and tossed it like crumbled nuts garnishing an ice cream sundae.

'Felix ...'

'I've known you for a long time, Toots. You just won't admit how you feel about Marcus. He's a wonderful man who challenges you on all levels, which is a great thing for someone with your intelligence. I believe he has a healthy respect for your job, and all he wants to do is protect you.'

This whole scenario would scare Marcus away from her for good. He'd broken his own rule of dating a VOC. Oh, she was most certainly a victim now. A kidnapped victim.

'It's Marcus's job. It's what he does, especially with what's been going on.' She nodded at the stalker sitting in the grass, cradling a loaded pistol.

Marcus should back-pedal his cute behind as far away from her as possible when this was all over—that's if Wren and Felix survived the night.

'It's more than that.' Felix leaned on his shovel, dabbing fingertips at his temples. 'There's passion. Fire. And sparks between you two. Why fight it, I say.'

'You've got to admit, there's definitely some chemistry from what I've seen.'

'See, Kempsey agrees there's more to it,' said Felix 'You just won't admit it because you're scared of getting hurt, that's all.'

'Scared? Felix! We're digging up a grave. In the middle of the night. At. Gunpoint.'

Felix's face fell in a sweeping wave of fear.

'I'm sorry, I shouldn't have said that.' She dropped her shovel and hugged her friend.

'Oh, brother.' Kempsey climbed to his feet. 'How freaking sentimental. Can we please get back to digging?'

Wren needed to distract herself as she dug deeper. It was eerily quiet. 'Just out of curiosity, Kempsey, are you the last of the eight men from the group who teamed up in Timor?'

'Yes, I am.' He sighed heavily, leaning against a neighbouring tombstone. The name etched into the stone was *Patrick 'Pop' Peddler.*

Wren had to grin at the irony. Her devious grandfather,

who wore a sawn-off shotgun tucked into his belt, probably wouldn't bother too much over having a criminal, holding a pistol, leaning against his tombstone. Was this karma coming back at her for her family's past?

'How did they die?' She looked up at the man who wouldn't hurt her, not until he had that diamond. That knowledge gave her the strength to dare ask. 'Out of that group of eight, how many died at your hands or were their deaths coincidental?'

'Get out, Felix, you're useless with that shovel.' Kempsey retied Felix, securing him to the tree. 'Do you really want to know the stories of dead men?'

'I'm curious that no one else noticed.' Wren found it easier to dig with Felix out of the way. 'Didn't you like them?'

'They were like brothers to me.' Kempsey stood like a prison officer, and she was part of the prisoners' chain gang, with blisters forming on her hands.

'But they died … The first two members of our squad died from injuries caused in the jungle. We were cursed after that trip.' Kempsey rummaged through his pack and removed a hip flask. 'Here, you deserve some of this.'

'I won't say no.' She took a sip out of the flask, the scotch warming her throat. Even covered in dirt, the early morning chill was cooling against her sweaty skin. 'What happened to the rest of the men?'

Kempsey took a deep swig of his flask. 'Two passed away in a car accident while I was in prison. Smithy, he had a heart attack in front of me. He could never calm his nerves after Timor.' His sorrow was visible in the softening of the wrinkles around his temple. 'Tolser fell out of a boat and sank like a rock. He couldn't swim to save himself, so he drowned. O'Donnell was in hospital with cancer, I just gave him a higher dose of his meds and he slipped into a peaceful coma to never wake again.' He then paused, taking another swig of his flask, putting it away.

'And Rowan?' Wren held the shovel, facing the man towering over her.

'I felt sorry for the guy, coughing up blood like he was. The pills he was taking were just making him sicker. Look, Wren ...' He skimmed a palm over his hair. 'Rowan looked ill, knew he was ill because he asked me to help him, even telling me how he wanted it done.'

'How?'

Kempsey leaned against the tree, beside Felix, with his gun at the ready. 'I thought a lethal cocktail of that strong medication he never took, mixed with his favourite bourbon would take him quick. I even had a smoke with him, like old times watching the sunrise together, until I smothered him.'

Two-dollar Darryl was right, her father had been murdered.

'Why? Because he didn't give you the bloody diamond?' The anger was low and heated in her voice as she gripped the shovel tighter.

'Believe it or not, Rowan wasn't scared to die. After the many times we stared death in the face as tunnel rats, death didn't scare us.'

'How dangerous was it? Rowan never said much of his time in the army.'

'We were tunnel rats, sandpit tunnellers, dealing with cave-ins, tripwires, or snakes. We knew how dangerous our jobs were. Death didn't scare us, it's what kept us going in the jungle for those eight days. We believed in living for today, living in the moment, because we could all die tomorrow!'

The man was preaching, while she shook with fury, digging into the dirt.

Thud.

'I think we're there ...' On hands and knees, she brushed the dirt aside. 'Oh, no.' She scrambled out of the hole, fast. 'I can't, I'm sorry.'

'Get back in there.'

Felix rushed to his feet, putting his body between her and Kempsey. 'Are you stupid, man? You can't expect Wren to open her own father's—'

'Don't say it. Just don't say it.' She didn't even want to think about it. 'I can't.'

'Fair enough. I'll tie you back up.' Kempsey roughly clasped her wrists together behind her back, securing her to the tree beside Felix. 'Sit.'

Kempsey picked up the shovel, jumped into the hole, flicking on his flashlight. 'What am I looking for, Wren?'

'It's a large marble, on a long gold chain. It's in his hands, which are crossed at mid-chest.' With her own hands behind her back, she felt around the dirt until her fingers found a stick.

Kempsey worked in the hole where dirt brushed against wood, then there was the whoosh of an opening door.

Wren kept her head down. 'Felix, don't look.'

'I'm not, Toots. I'm thinking he's just opening a fridge.'

'Yeah, that'd work, getting a beer from the fridge.' They even grinned at each other. 'I could do with a beer or two, maybe one of your cocktails. One with lots of ice and rum. I've got a taste for rum.'

'I want one with cream. To overindulge in the comforts of carb-loaded cream, ice cream with whipped cream.'

'Like a sundae.'

'Yeah …'

As Felix described a decadent cocktail creation, Wren kept scratching the stick in the dirt.

'Got it.' Kempsey laughed, holding his hand in the air like he'd scored a trophy. It was her compass, dangling like a black bauble from the chain between his fingers.

She really was a grave robber now.

Kempsey crouched on the grass, rolling out the maps to work out the coordinates with the compass. His eyes shone with excitement under the torchlight.

Felix, on hands and knees, crawled to the edge of the map. 'Is it working?'

'It is. The compass isn't broken, or backwards, it's been calibrated specifically for this.' Kempsey tapped at the hand drawn map. 'Wren, do you know where we're going?'

She nodded. She had to keep going, they'd live if they did. 'To *Southpaw's Salty Roost*.'

THIRTY-EIGHT

Marcus and half a dozen men swarmed Mrs Bingle's property. 'Search everything. The attic, the roof, corners of the sheds and behind machinery, everything.'

Ryder Riggs approached with a terse nod of his black Akubra. Ryder had proven himself to be cool under pressure, unafraid when it counted. Hell, the guy helped a kid hold onto a broken hand grenade to stop it from exploding, and never broke a sweat. 'Tell us where you want the dogs to start, Marcus.' Ryder tossed his thumb back to his brothers clipping harnesses onto their dogs. All five of the Riggs brothers were here, as well as many other volunteers.

'Start from the kitchen's back door. The guy's been stealing the old woman's food.'

'Sergeant, you're here.' Mrs Bingle opened her front door, completely stark naked. 'I told you stuff was missing.'

'You did, Mrs Bingle. That's why everyone is here to do a proper search.' Marcus turned back to the doctor. 'Stewart, can you attend to Mrs Bingle, please? Call her sister and see how far away she is.' Marcus didn't care that it was three o'clock in the morning. Mrs Bingle needed attention and shouldn't be left alone. 'I'll be leaving an officer here until her sister gets here, unless you see fit to take Mrs Bingle to the hospital.' He'd failed the old woman.

'Good thing I'm here, huh?' Stewart slipped off his jacket, slipping it around the elderly woman's bare shoulders, and guided her back into the house.

'Oi, Sergeant.' Ryder stood at an open shed door, motioning to Marcus.

'What did you find?' Marcus ran to the garden shed; the stolen hardware van was parked to one side. He put his hand against the bonnet, it was cool. *Dammit.*

'They were camped here for a bit. Probably waiting for sunset.' Ryder pointed to the tray containing a half-eaten roast and cake remnants, swarming with ants.

How far ahead were they?

'Can someone ask Stewart to bring out Mrs Bingle?' Marcus called out. 'I want her to tell us if anything's missing.' Thick red dust lay undisturbed in areas of the shed. But by the door there were a lot of scuff marks.

He shone his torch on the floor, the roof, the walls, pausing when something reflected from the edge of the wall near the pole.

His heart squeezed, wiping his hand over his mouth.

It was a gold watch.

Wren's.

It was the watch Wren didn't want to wear around her delicate wrist, when she thought it'd been bought from the proceeds of stolen goods. *Jeez, Wren.*

He was about to scoop it up when the torch highlighted shadows in the dirt, barely visible.

It was a message written in dust …

N

RIP **+** **Dad**

S

That beautiful, courageous, intelligent woman had left him a clue.

'Ryder, we're on the right track. Wren and Felix have been here. They must have gone cross-country. See if the dogs can pick up a scent.' If he could get an idea of their general direction, that'd help.

With his phone, he took a photo of Wren's message written in dust.

Stewart spoke in soft tones with Mrs Bingle, now fully dressed, and hopefully with some clarity to remember things.

The woman wasn't well, Marcus knew that. But he wasn't a doctor either.

Marcus scooped up Wren's watch. *Where are you, Wren?* He peered out into the darkness.

'All my husband's shovels are gone,' said Mrs Bingle. 'Roger isn't going to like that. He's very particular about his tools, you know. Where is Roger?'

Marcus put a tender hand on her arm. 'I'm sorry, Mrs Bingle, but Roger passed away.'

'When?' A frail hand clutched the cross on her necklace.

'Over six years ago. I'm sorry.' Marcus nodded at Stewart. 'I think that's enough for her, don't you agree, Doctor.'

Stewart nodded towards the driveway. 'That's why I've got the ambulance coming.'

'Why is the ambulance here?' Mrs Bingle asked.

'Your sister is going to meet you at the hospital. My father, Doctor Mannen, is waiting for you.'

'Really? He's a handsome man, your father.'

Marcus watched Stewart load Mrs Bingle into the ambulance. Guilt still burdened his shoulders for not believing her. But he'd been in this shed, he'd searched all the sheds on this property, the first time she'd called.

But Mrs Bingle lived in a big house, on a large property. The stalker, with his military skills, could have been camping in the hills, or deep in the gullies, and no one would have known.

Then the dogs started barking excitedly, pulling hard on their harnesses.

'Sarge?' Ryder pointed to the darkness where a hazy glow shone in the distance. 'The dogs found a scent. They're heading back to town.'

All the pieces whirled into place. 'I know where. Pack up, Ryder. I might need you and those dogs yet.'

'Where are we going?' Stewart rushed over, with the ambulance now cruising down the long dirt driveway.

'Everyone, meet me at the church. Head for Rowan Peddler's gravesite.'

In the car, Marcus showed the photo on his phone to Stewart. 'RIP DAD. *North. South.* Look at it, the way it's set out. Wren's gone for the compass to read the coordinates on the bottom of the map.' Marcus put the car into gear and hit the road, effortlessly overtaking the ambulance. 'Rowan gave Wren a compass.'

'Where is it?'

'She buried it with him, and Mrs Bingle's missing some shovels, which means they've gone to dig it up.'

'Why dig up a compass?'

'Wren said it never worked property, but I bet Rowan had it calibrated to read backwards. It's a theme with this whole hunt, everything seems opposite. Rowan knew this guy was searching for the diamond, he wrote that letter to Wren as a failsafe.'

'Where was the letter?'

'Hidden at Sandfly where Two-dollar Darryl had been sworn to secrecy. Rowan told Darryl to only to give it to Wren when she arrived, if Rowan didn't make it. No one in this town knew Wren existed, except for Darryl, who always believed someone had murdered Rowan.'

'Is that why you never closed the case?'

'And it won't be closed until I say so.' Marcus put his foot down and sped back to town. *Hang on, baby, just hang in there.*

THIRTY-NINE

Wren's legs were killing her. The chunky rocks that made up the railway line weren't easy to walk on. With Felix beside her, gagged and bound, they stumbled in the dark. Skipping along the wooden rails, or balancing on the long singular steel beams, was a game they'd given up a long time ago.

Yet, by sticking to the train tracks they'd been able to walk right past the roadblock, to stroll through the heart of town.

On the far edge, they crossed the one and only highway, following the fence line around to a large open paddock that led them to the back of the Elsie Creek Hotel.

The two-storey pub towered before them, its balcony swamped in yellow lights, while hot white spotlights shone from the corners of the building. The combination of lights spread far across the extensive property, including parts of the rear beer garden.

'Where do we go from here?' Kempsey waved the rolled map, as they stood on the edge where the beer garden's lawn met the rubbly dirt of the surrounding scrub.

With her wrists bound, Wren had to use her head to point towards the area opposite the large picnic tables, set beneath clusters of palm trees that cast long shadows across the lawn.

'Okay, this is how we're going to play it.' Kempsey pulled out his sharp knife. 'I'll quietly slit your boy's throat if you even dare raise your voice.'

She gulped, nodding.

'Good girl.'

The patronising prick!

He pulled down her gag. 'So, what are we looking for? The coordinates are pointing to that meshed area. What is that?'

'Haven't you been here before?'

'No. Fill me in.'

'Southpaw, as you know, is …'

'A left-handed person.'

'And a salty is what the locals call a saltwater crocodile. The Southpaw, I'm guessing, is to do with Karma, who has no left foot.'

Kempsey screwed his nose up. 'They keep a crocodile at the pub?'

'Yeah. He's some fortune-telling mascot,' Wren replied, with the gagged Felix nodding beside her.

'And the roost? Crocodiles don't roost.'

'No …' She leaned against the cool mesh of Karma's enclosure that was hidden in the shadows. 'The roost is that cave.' She pointed. 'Rowan built that cave.'

'How do you know?'

'When we came here for Rowan's wake, Billy, the yardman, told us that my father built the cave for Karma. It was something about rocks helping the crocodile to digest his food.' But why build a cave for a cold-blooded animal that needed sun, not shade. 'Anyway, Rowan planted those bromeliads on the roof. Brom's are shallow-rooted plants. It's where we might find our next clue.'

'The coordinates says it's here. So where is this creature?' Kempsey narrowed his eyes at the pen, with its pond glistening silver from the pub's lights.

'Karma's probably in his pond. It's deeper and bigger than I thought it was.'

'How big is this croc?'

'Massive. How are you going to do this?'

'You are.'

'Am not.' Her tone was harsh but hushed. 'Crocodiles can jump. This barbed-wire fence is here for a reason—it's a man-killer.'

'Or we can send in your friend.' Kempsey patted Felix on the head like a schoolboy.

'*Hm mmh wer-mrr.*' Felix mumbled through his gag, while wriggling on the spot like he wanted to pee.

'What's he saying?'

'Remove his gag, and I'm sure Felix will politely tell you.'

Kempsey grinned. 'You're getting snarky, young lady.'

'I'm tired, my feet hurt, I'm hungry and I'm thirsty. What more do you want from me?' This was not how she'd expected to do a treasure hunt. What was her father thinking?

Kempsey lowered Felix's gag. 'What do you want?'

'In my man bag—'

'What about it?'

'I've got Billy's homemade beef jerky in there.'

'Oh, I'm starving.'

'Not for you, Toots, for Karma. Remember? Meditating Crocodile. Throw it out, and he'll do his thing, while you do your thing.'

Wren narrowed her eyes at her friend.

'What's that evil eye for, Toots?'

'You do realise I have to go in there now?' Her best friend had just signed her death sentence.

Felix gasped for air.

Kempsey rummaged through Felix's bag. 'There's so much junk in this bag. How many hand creams do you have?' He dumped tubes of cream onto the ground.

'Hey, that stuff is expensive.' Felix hurriedly tried to scoop up his precious creams.

'I'm still not going in there.' Wren started to back away.

'I could shoot it,' mumbled Kempsey, still digging around in Felix's man bag.

'Don't do that. It's a rescued disabled animal. Karma has done nothing wrong.' Wren didn't want to hurt anyone, human or man-killing beast.

'Karma has yet to predict if I should marry Reggie.'

'You're kidding.' Now beyond cranky, Wren was surprised at the selfishness of her friend, who was more worried about his hand creams.

But then she realised, Felix was desperately trying to hang onto his sanity from the terror of this entire event. It was how he was coping, by grabbing his hand creams off the grass.

She only wished she knew what her own coping mechanism was to survive.

'Got it.' Kempsey held up the plastic pouch of jerky, taking out a dark strip. 'Hey, this is good stuff.'

'Don't I know it?' Felix dumped his hand creams back into the open man bag. Then he held out his open palm. 'May I? It'll help keep my trap shut.'

'Sure.' Kempsey opened the bag releasing the pungent aroma of beef, pepper, smoked hickory with a hint of molasses. 'Wren? You said you were hungry.'

'Absolutely.' Her mouth was watering as she plucked a piece, pointing at the silvery ripples of the pond. 'He's coming.'

'I wonder if he can smell it? Like through the water?'

Felix leaned in next to her. 'Here, kitty-kitty.' Felix even smiled, playfully nudging her arm. 'He's coming. Look.'

The long, scaly snout barely breached the surface, his marble eyes peering just above the waterline.

'Kempsey, be a good man, and throw all of that jerky to the bottom of that shade thingy —'

'The cave I'm supposed to climb.' Wren tore angrily at the last of her jerky.

'Listen, Toots, Karma can't jump around corners, only in a straight line. If he's eating under the lip of the roof, you should be fine.'

Or she was croc toast for that salty's breakfast.

'I've never fed a crocodile before. Here goes.' Kempsey hurled a wad of jerky sticks over the tall fence. They arced over the pond, hitting the manmade rock wall, to fall like brown confetti across the concrete.

Karma slowly glided across the pond to the edge, hoisting his large body out to scoop up a few pieces of dried flavoursome meat in his mouth. Then he sighed, with mouth open, staring up at the stars.

'That is cool,' Kempsey said.

'I know.' Wren nodded, chewing on her jerky. She wanted to chill out and meditate like Karma to watch the stars and forget this nightmare.

'Right, off you go, Wren. Felix and I will stand watch.'

'And how are you going to warn me if that beast jumps?' Calm on the outside, the terror started prickling up her spine. All her internal alarm bells were screaming at her to not climb that fence.

'With the flashlight. Go on.' He held the knife to Felix's cheek.

'Be safe, Toots.'

'I didn't sign up for this. What the hell was Rowan thinking?' Trying to summon her courage, because she had no choice, she turned to Kempsey. 'Got any wire cutters, handy?'

'Nope. Improvise. Find something to cover the barbed wire and climb.'

She craned her neck up at the fence, topped with three strings of barbed wire. It was just like the fence surrounding the Peddler property.

Figures. Her father paid for it, after all.

In a huff, she grabbed a nearby plastic chair from the outdoor tables and a large floor mat that ran along the cement edge between the back verandah and the beer garden's lawn.

She positioned the chair against the fence, climbed up and heaved the thick rubber mat at the barbed wire.

It took a few goes to get it into place, but it was enough to protect her as she hoisted herself over the fence.

Her boots landed with a noisy thud on the top side of the concrete's domed cave. Rocks shifted beneath her feet as she dug around in the dirt.

The torchlight flashed in her eyes.

She froze.

Peering over the lip's edge of the cave's roof, she saw Karma lying in wait, directly below her. Mouth wide open, strips of jerky lay across his tongue, Karma was staring right at her. Or was he meditating?

So why did Kempsey use the flashlight?

She shrugged in Kempsey and Felix's direction, where they were crouched down, pointing behind her.

That's when the backdoor of the pub opened.

She flattened herself against the rocks.

It was Billy.

The yardman flicked on a bank of fluorescent lights that ran along the length of the large verandah. Whistling some tune, he opened a metal cabinet and dragged out the fire hose.

Wren jammed her fist to her mouth, stopping her intense need to scream for help to the old man in the Sunday hat, flicking his suspenders higher up his shoulders.

But the flash of the steel blade that pressed against Felix's throat killed all her courage. She didn't dare risk the lives of Felix and Billy, including the life of a man-eating crocodile.

The whoosh of the large firehose came on. Keeping his back to the gardens, Billy hosed off the area near the bar.

This was her only chance.

Not even bothering to roll rocks out of the way, she burrowed her hands underneath them like a worm digging through the soil. Hands scratched, nails torn, she spread her arms wide, like a face down snow angel kissing the dirt. The bromeliads' jagged-edged leaves pricked her skin, bugs and other creepy crawlies brushed her fingers, as rocks scratched and bruised her hands. Finally, her cold, grubby fingers snagged on a metal box the size of a rectangular pencil case.

She pulled it out of the dirt, still flat on her stomach, and opened it up.

It was another rolled piece of paper and something else. Using the light from the pub, she could just make out the words through the plastic sheet protecting the note ... *key*.

She'd found the key.

Throat dry, adrenalin pounded in her ears as she crawled backwards down to the fence line, while keeping an eye on Billy and Karma.

'Psst ...'

She froze.

Kempsey was motioning at her to aim for the dark paddock that ran alongside the haphazard group of parked utes.

He was pointing to the stables.

She nodded at Felix. She would not let her friend

down.

Practically kissing the cold rocks, she waited for her chance, as Billy continued to hose off the verandah. Now facing her, he shifted chairs while whistling as he methodically worked along the one strip.

With no choice but to wait, she opened the box to try and read the note through the plastic.

She knew where to go, but couldn't move, not while she was in Billy's direct line of sight.

Kempsey held his palm up, signalling for her to stay still.

She wasn't about to argue.

While waiting, she carefully cleared a cache of rocks to scrawl in the dirt. She had to hope Marcus was finding her clues.

Marcus was her coping mechanism. The big, beautiful, strong man, picturing him so clearly, she drew on his strength. Through him, she'd survive. She had to.

Kempsey hustled Felix towards the neighbouring stables, while Wren waited for his signal.

Billy crouched under the pool table.

This was her shot.

She leaped at the fence and threw herself over it. Landing heavily in the grass, she rolled, skidding to her knees, before she could unsteadily clamber to her feet and race across the lawn.

The hose turned off behind her. 'Who's there?'

Wren dropped her body flat across the wet grass, making herself as small as possible.

A deep guttural growl permeated the air, making the hairs on the back of her neck stand on end.

'Karma, behave.' Billy scoffed, poking up the brim of his hat. 'I'll hose you off soon enough. You know I've got to do this section first. Be patient, big fella.' The hose turned back on with a whoosh, and Billy resumed his whistling.

On her belly, Wren crawled across the dew-covered grass until she was deep in the shadows where the lawn kissed the red rubbly dirt.

A large hand roughly dragged her to her feet, with the other covering her mouth to stop her scream.

'Shh.' It was Kempsey, taking her to the far side of the stables, where Felix was waiting, tied to the stall like a horse. 'What did you find?'

'The key.' Under torchlight, Wren opened the metal box with her dirt-caked hands. Her clothes were wet, smeared with grass stains and red rubble, with grit spilling inside her shirt. She was desperate for a shower.

Kempsey shook the contents of the plastic bag. 'What is that?' He held out a rectangular white object that stretched across his palm to his fingers. 'Looks like an odd-shaped bone.'

'It's the key to something?'

'What does the note say?'

'They're coordinates. And a poem.' She read aloud the note:

Dare to visit the watery no-man's land to visit the King, you must walk the planks to the parley table to play with the key.

'None of this makes sense.' Kempsey unrolled the maps, dragging the backward compass from his pocket to work on the coordinates. 'But I know where we're going. You do too, Wren.' His finger tapped at the spot on the map. 'But how can this thing be a key?'

Felix wriggled around in some weird sixties jive.

'What?' Kempsey removed Felix's gag, untying him from the stables.

'It's the Sandfly Saloon.'

'We know that.' Kempsey rolled his eyes, putting the compass and map away.

With bound wrists, Felix pointed at the object in Wren's hands. 'That really is a key. It's the key to their piano. It's ivory.'

Wren wanted to hug her friend. 'Felix, you're a legend. The Sandfly Saloon's piano is missing a key.'

'Well then, let's go,' said Kempsey.

'You can't expect us to walk back,' whined Wren. Her feet were killing her.

'No. We'll be taking that.' Kempsey pointed to an aluminium boat on a trailer attached to a single-cab ute that was parked on the side of the road. 'We'll be visiting the *watery no-man's land*.'

'What's he talking about, Toots?'

'The river? In the dark? There are crocodiles everywhere. I've seen them. And they're wild. King is called King for a reason. He's dangerous with his harem of crocodiles.' Wren had enough of crocodiles for one day, thank you.

'Your boyfriend may have cut off the roads around this town, but he hasn't cut off the riverways.' Kempsey flicked open a switchblade to effortlessly jimmy open the driver's door.

'Stop calling Marcus my boyfriend.'

'What do I call him then?'

'Detective Sergeant Moore.' The man deserved respect for the hell she was putting him through.

'Let's go.' Kempsey tossed his pack with her handbag and Felix's man bag into the back of the ute before bundling Felix into the middle of the ute's bench seat.

Through the bug-splattered windscreen an extraordinary palette showed on the distant horizon—rich mauves blending from a light purple into a vibrant strip of orange. Dawn was coming to a sky filled with stars.

She thought of her father, who'd sat with the knowledge of watching his last sunrise. Was this going to be her last? 'It's going to be a beautiful day ...'

FORTY

Using the car's spotlights, Marcus lit up the gravesite to find shovels cast aside and white cigarette butts littering piles of freshly dug soil. And one big open hole.

Holding his breath, which collided with his heart in his throat, he peeked into the deep ditch. The relief at finding it empty was intense.

Empty, except for the casket.

Everyone else around him pulled up in their haste to avoid that big hole in the ground.

The stalker wouldn't hurt Wren, he had to believe that. Wren was going to be safe while hunting for clues, which meant Felix would also be unharmed to keep Wren playing the game. Or …

'Dammit.' He had to look. Or he could get the doctor to do it?

'Don't even think about it.' Stewart held up his hands. 'These are surgeon's hands, I don't do dirt, officer.'

'Wuss. You'd probably twist an ankle or stub a toe. Maybe even bite that tongue that never stops sprouting off how good you are.' Dropping into the open gravesite, Marcus blocked his nose then lifted the casket's lid.

It was exactly who should be there, undisturbed.

Again, another wave of relief swamped him, and he quickly climbed out. 'Stewart, call Tanisha and have her alert the church about this open site. Everyone else, I want you to spread out in this immediate area and search the ground for a message written in dust.' Marcus furiously took photos before they disturbed this crime scene. 'I'm hoping Wren's left us another clue.'

How far behind was he?

Marcus peered back in the direction of Mrs Bingle's property. It would've taken anywhere between three to six hours for them to hike cross-country. Then the time to dig would've been at least an hour. He couldn't picture the stalker digging, he'd leave that to Wren, while keeping Felix close.

Surely, he wasn't that far behind them.

Or was he?

And where the hell were they now?

He pulled out the map tucked into his bullet-proof vest. Only a few places were marked on the hand-drawn map, but which path did they take? He didn't have the manpower to cover such a large area. Now that the stalker had the compass they could be anywhere.

'Sergeant, over here. The dogs have found something.' Ryder pointed to the nearby tree.

Marcus loved those dogs.

Near the base of the tree trunk, on a cleared patch of dirt lay an emerald and diamond ring. Its gold band had an intricate Celtic pattern.

'It's Wren's ring.' Hope flared in his chest, recognising her dainty ring.

Beside it, scratched in the dirt were the letters:

K A R M

'What's Karm? As in calm?' Stewart scratched at his

blond hair while a few of the men milled around muttering suggestions.

Marcus took more photos on his phone, then scooped up Wren's ring, putting it safely in his pocket beside her watch. Determined to give them back to her.

'Ryder, have the dogs see if they can pick up a scent and see which way they went?' Marcus tapped in the letters K A R M into Google.

The search results showed *Karm* was the name of a band, some sort of music, and a store. It was also the Hindu noun for *doing*.

Wren may be a word player, but it didn't quite fit. What was she trying to tell him?

Again, the dog's barks rose with excitement.

'Where, Ryder?' Marcus swiftly followed the dogs, as they eagerly pulled on their harnesses, through the back fence of the church. They scrambled up the rocks and hit the train tracks.

'They've headed back to town.' Ryder pointed ahead. With noses down, tails wagging, the dogs leaped with excitement to race along the tracks.

From the rise on top of the train tracks, Marcus spotted the tallest building in town. In the distance it was like a lighthouse shining in the never-ending sea of sky and dust that made up the outback. It was the Elsie Creek Hotel.

'It's *Karma*! They've gone to the pub.' Chunky sun-bleached rocks tumbled as Marcus scrambled down the embankment in the race to his car.

Phone to his ear, he dialled the publican, the one the locals called God. Samantha could see all from her roost, which was the top floor of the Elsie Creek Hotel.

'Where are we going?' Stewart asked, climbing into the passenger seat.

Marcus pointed at the hand-drawn map. '*Southpaw's Salty Roost.*'

FORTY-ONE

Thick curls of mist rose from the surface of the slow-flowing river. Pastel colours of Malibu blue to dusty seashell pink skies perfectly contrasted against a shimmering deep azure blue river.

Dragonflies hovered over enormous pink wild lotus flowers, and spotted emerald frogs jumped from leaves the size of small coffee tables. The boat putted around the wide, sweeping corner of the river where large trees towered along the bank, hedged with wild bamboo that softly waved like feathers in the breeze.

Kempsey steered the boat, keeping it in the centre, as daylight grew stronger.

Wren and Felix huddled together on the floor, bracing against the crisp morning breeze.

'I'm freezing.' Now dry, mud and grass stains caked Wren's shirt and jeans. Annoyingly, with her wrists still bound she couldn't even hug herself. 'Didn't think I'd get cold in the tropics.'

'It is winter. But isn't this just glorious?' Felix smiled at the scenery. 'Look at where we are, Toots.'

She didn't have the heart to tell him they were floating towards their doom. Surely someone would have alerted

Marcus of their trail of muddy breadcrumbs by now.

The boat took another sweeping bend where a tree stood full of screeching nocturnal black fruit bats. They swirled in thick hypnotic waves around the massive tree to then hang upside down among the branches as their place to rest.

Daylight was almost here.

Further ahead in the river, a large *plop* caused rippling rings to spread from the centre. Again, another *plop*, only this time it was from a huge silver fish breaching the waters to chase a smaller fish.

The water started to bubble in the area where the creek met the main river.

'What is that?' Felix pointed at the water that swirled and bubbled. 'It's like boiling water.'

'That's bait fish. They must feed on the change of the tides.'

'Where did you learn that, Toots?'

'Rowan. We did some fishing up in Far North Queensland and through the Torres Straits. He'd promised to take me fishing here ...' The river system was truly beautiful. One moment it was wide open flatlands of dried flood plains, to lush tropical monsoon thickets, completely untouched by man, and it was all part of the Peddlers' property. This was the *Watery No-Man's Land*, where crocodiles rested on the far muddy banks waiting for the sun to warm their cold bones.

Ahead stood Goat Island.

As if hovering above the mists, the Sandfly Saloon's glass windows reflected the sky. It was a simple place on stilts, a safe harbour among the river's wilderness, yet gorgeously rustic from this view.

Kempsey switched off the boat's engine. 'You two lay down here until we reach the dock.'

Wren and Felix crouched on the boat's floor, as the

riverbanks rose higher.

'Do you think he's awake?' Wren whispered to Felix.

'Who?'

'Two-dollar Darryl or Chopper.' She could barely make out the roof of Darryl's home from their flattened position on the boat's floor.

The boat clunked against the tall pylons that made up the small pier. Kempsey tied the boat to the staircase. 'Ladies first.'

They climbed clumsily up the steep metal stairs to the wooden decks that surrounded the Sandfly Saloon. It was a magnificent view this time of the morning, a perfect spot for a coffee to watch the wakening world. Goat Island was high enough away from the crocodiles in a splendid position over the water.

'Why do they call it Goat Island?' Kempsey dumped his heavy pack and their bags onto the deck.

'Because only a goat would want to fish among the crocodiles.' It's what Darryl had told her.

A large sea eagle flew overhead, its massive white wings extended to skim across the water, its large lethal talons poised to effortlessly scoop a fish straight out of the silvery surface. Then with large heavy flaps of its broad wings, it pushed the eagle higher and higher, to the tree on the opposite riverbank.

'That was incredible.' Wren smiled at the magnificence of that eagle.

'I know.' Felix gave her arm a squeeze. 'Goat Island is growing on me.'

'Me too.' Was she finally understanding why her family had kept this place for so long? A tranquil secret away from tourists. She wanted to sit right here on this deck and cast out a fishing line and watch the shadows shift with the sun.

'Wren, do you have any keys in your bag?' Kempsey held out her handbag.

'I think so. I've never had to unlock the place before.'

Kempsey tipped out her bag across the wooden deck, scooping up her chunk of keys. Bits of paper, her purse, and a stash of pens rolled in various directions to slip through the cracks. 'Hey, they're good pens and we're not littering this place.' Wren scrambled to her knees to catch papers and pens, like Felix had done with his hand creams.

'Can't you see we're in Mother Nature's theme park?' Felix pointed back to the water. 'Hey, where did all those crocodiles go? They were just there a minute ago.'

'They're here, somewhere.' She didn't want to think about those prehistoric killers. Especially King, the scary mob leader.

'And here we are.' Kempsey unlocked the roller door, lifting it up. It didn't even make a noise.

Bugger. She wanted it to scream to get Darryl's attention.

Was Darryl even home? She leaned over the railing, hoping to see his house.

Kempsey cut off her view. 'I'd say your manager is out looking for you.'

'How would you know?'

'There were no lights on inside his shack. And your bar manager takes his truck into town at daybreak to collect the mail and hit the supermarket at six.'

'How long were you spying on everyone? I found your filthy cigarette butts in the shed. You really have a nasty litter habit.' She picked up what she could in pens and papers, with Felix helping her to shove her trash back into her bag.

'Too long.' Kempsey herded them into the Sandfly Saloon. 'Drinks are on me.'

'For the love of vodka and vodka, it's vodka, good

man.' Felix pointed to the glass bottle on the bar shelf

Kempsey chuckled from behind the bar. 'Top-shelf bourbon for me. Here, help yourselves.' He plonked the bottle of vodka on the countertop. 'Any mix? Ice?'

'You look quite at home behind that bar,' Felix said.

'I did my time as a bartender. I've never been inside this place. It's cool. Yours, Wren?'

'Apparently so.'

'There's nothing on paper about this place existing. Which means this is an illegal bar. And you're dating a cop! How does that work?' Kempsey's laugh was nasty. 'And here we have it.' He lifted the upright piano's fall board to expose the long row of ebony and ivory keys. 'It really is missing a key.' He removed the rectangular piano key from his pocket. 'Who wants to do the honours.'

'Me.' Felix raised his tied wrists in the air. 'I've been studying YouTube videos on how to replace that key and tune the piano.'

'You play?'

'*Do I play?* Bah.' With head held high, Felix swaggered towards the piano. 'Untie my wrists, handsome, and I'll play a tune that'll make birds jealous.'

'That confident, huh?' Kempsey untied Felix's wrists, where Felix promptly took the key, lifted the lid, and carefully started to put the piano back together.

'Felix's mother was a piano teacher. He's been playing since he was two.' Wren sipped on her vodka. Even if it was only daybreak, it'd been a long night.

'Oh, what a sweetheart. Two-dollar Darryl found me a tiny flathead screwdriver.' Before Kempsey could react, Felix had his head down into the piano's body, using the small screwdriver to tune it up, tapping on the key. 'It works. We have music.'

'I'll take that.' Kempsey pocketed the screwdriver.

Flicking back his imaginary coat tails, Felix sat on the piano stool, then stretched out his arms to crack his knuckles. 'Any requests?' His fingers floated across the keys to play the scales. 'Oh, I know, something from Kempsey's era: Billy Joel's *Piano Man*.'

Music soon filled the Sandfly Saloon.

'He's pretty good,' said Kempsey.

Wren nodded. 'Felix is brilliant. The drag queens in his club get jealous whenever he hits the stage with his baby grand.'

'His own club, huh?'

'Yeah.' As she took a seat at the large card table, Kempsey sat beside her and plonked the vodka and bourbon in front of them.

She could do with another shot, a hot shower, a fabulous feast and then sleep for a week. Even better if she was lying beside Marcus, holding his big hand.

Felix finished the song and turned on the stool. 'Any requests—oh, hello.'

It was Chopper in the open doorway.

'Morning, Miss. Did Felix from Sydney fix the piano?'

'*Chopper, run!*' Wren tried to get in Kempsey's way, but he was too quick. Sliding across the table, he dragged the kid back inside by the shirt and held the gun to his temple.

'Leave him alone. Chopper's only a kid.' Wren hit at Kempsey with her two hands like a club.

Kempsey dragged the kid further inside. 'Where's your uncle?'

'In town, looking for Miss Wren and Felix.'

'Why are you here?'

'T-t-to open the bar, and to keep watch in case Miss Wren came back.'

'I'm so, so sorry, Chopper.' Wren wanted to cry. Too many people were now involved. Chopper didn't deserve this, he was a sweet kid.

'Wren, stand by the bar. Felix, pick up your rope and tie up Chopper's hands behind his back.'

Wren wanted to smash the glasses at the bar and fling them like a thousand knives at Kempsey. But he had a gun, and you never took a knife to a gunfight.

Wren pinched her lips together, rubbing at the ropes on her wrists. Her jaw ached from gritting her teeth, as her overwhelming frustration blended with stress.

From the corner of her eye, she spotted Chopper's fancy knife that looked like a lighter. It was seated on the side rail among the pens, drink pads, and straws.

Before she lost her nerve, she slid it into her jeans pocket, pulling her crusty shirt over the top. It was sharp enough to cut cardboard boxes like butter, so it could certainly cut the ropes at her wrists—if she got the chance.

'Okay, kid, this is how it's going to play out.' Kempsey pressed the gun to Chopper's cheek. 'This isn't for kicks and giggles, see.'

'There is no need to hurt Chopper.' She scowled at Kempsey, stalking towards him, suddenly braver for carrying a concealed weapon. 'Felix and I have been cooperating with you this entire time. We've been helping you search for the stupid stone.'

'And you'll keep helping me. Now, no more fun and games. That piano key isn't the key, is it?' Kempsey left Chopper to sit on the floor by the open doorway.

Wren rested her bound wrists on top of her head, closing her eyes. She was desperate for a solution out of this nightmare, one where everyone survived. But Kempsey was becoming dangerously desperate the closer they got to the Jade Diamond.

'What's it going to be, Wren?'

No longer bothering to conceal her hatred, she gave the

glare of a thousand deathly daggers all aimed at her captor. 'You'll need to re-read the last clue.'

'Fine. You two, take a seat at the table.' Kempsey herded Wren and Felix to the table, where he emptied the metal case and unwrapped the note. *'Dare to visit the watery no-man's land to visit the King …'*

'That's the river, and the crocodile called King. Go on.' She stared at the grains that made up the large wooden table.

'… You must walk the planks to the parley table to play with the key.'

'This is the parley table.' With bound wrists, she patted the tabletop that had its own roulette wheel. The fortunes it must have won and lost, and the secrets and stories shared by those who'd dared to take a seat at this gambler's table.

'Why?'

'Parley is a term for conversation. Pirates used the term as a meet-and-greet peace-talk sort of deal.'

'I knew this was a pirates' treasure map.' Felix smoothed over his hair, free from any ropes, and somehow immaculately clean. 'So, what's the planks, Toots?'

'The planks are the path Chopper came from. It connects Goat Island to the mainland.' Wren pointed her hands to the open doorway. 'I'm so sorry, Chopper.'

'All good, Miss.' He gave her a nod, trying to be brave.

'Concentrate, Wren.' Kempsey warned her. 'What is the next clue? The key?'

'I don't know.' She dropped her head onto the table, its cool wood comforting against her cheek. She gazed out the wide-open doorway that could have been her path to freedom. 'What about the map?'

Kempsey cleared the table of glasses and bottles to unroll the maps. 'There is only one spot left… *The Smoking Flat Lands.*' He tapped on the page. 'Know where that is?'

'Yeah.' She pointed down the path. 'It's that long

golden paddock out there. It's where my ancestors grew tobacco for almost eighty years.'

'I bet that bugger's buried it out there.' Kempsey stood in the doorway as the sun breached the treetops, spreading golden sunshine across the water.

'Golden hour,' muttered Felix, his wide eyes reflecting a world shining gold.

'What did you say?' Wren sat straighter.

'Reggie's all about taking photos lately, especially since we came out here. He loves this time of day, calls it golden hour. All those big photographers talk about it on Instagram.'

Wren followed the sunshine streaming through the door, leading a trail directly to the piano. But it wasn't the piano.

She pushed her chair back and followed the beam of sunlight across the room.

'What are you seeing, Wren?' Kempsey's shadow stretched across the floorboards, mindful to not block the sunbeam as it hit the wall, like a spotlight.

And there it was. Right before her. The picture of Wren and her father at the bar where they'd first met. 'It's the picture.'

Carefully, she removed it from the hook on the wall and turned it face down on the parley table. On the back of the photo frame was a thick wad of black tape holding down a slim package.

'Good girl.' Kempsey pulled at the sticky electric tape.

Wren took her shot. She moved back from Kempsey, stealthily removing the knife from her pocket to drop the knife onto her boot and then onto the floor without making a sound. She paused, watching Kempsey, before kicking the knife across the room, noisily dragging a chair over the floorboards to disguise the clunky sound.

But it stopped in the middle of nowhere.

Oh, no. She side-stepped to block Kempsey's view as Chopper swung his legs, his sneakers kicking the knife towards his waiting hands.

'What have you got there, Miss?' He nodded at her, adjusting his seat.

She could breathe. 'It's a treasure hunt. I'm so sorry, Chopper.'

'Quiet. Sit down, boy. This has nothing to do with you.'

Chopper sat back against the wall as Kempsey tore open the plastic covering.

'And here we have it.' Kempsey held up a steel key, and another rolled piece of paper. 'The key and the last coordinates.' Kempsey unrolled the notepaper, dragging the compass out of his pocket. He went through the coordinates on the paper then on the map, only to frown.

'What's wrong?' Wren asked.

'It doesn't make sense. The numbers he's given us take us off the map.' Kempsey checked and rechecked the numbers again. 'What am I missing? Any ideas, Wren?'

'Rowan wouldn't leave a simple set of numbers and a key for anyone with a compass to work out.' She pointed to the empty frame clearly outlined on the wall. 'So, what if you superimposed the numbers then used the backward compass? Would that work?'

'Hmmm… How many pens did you save before they went overboard?' Kempsey rummaged through her handbag to retrieve a pen. He then scribbled down the numbers onto a beer coaster. Again, her trusty compass—the one she had thought was broken—showed him the spot and Kempsey marked the area with an X on the map.

'It worked?' Wren's heart was in her throat, it was hard to differentiate between the excitement blending with terror.

'Come on, let's find this diamond.' He dragged Felix by the arm, stopping to stare down at Chopper.

'Leave him, please. Chopper can't go anywhere.' Wren pleaded with Kempsey, putting herself between Kempsey and Chopper. 'Didn't you ever find yourself in the wrong place at the wrong time?'

'Yeah, Timor and everything else after that.' He stared down at Chopper. 'But he needs to stay here a little longer.' Kempsey wound a spare piece of rope around Chopper's chest, tying him to the side pole.

Wren was terrified Kempsey would discover the knife. It looked like a lighter, and Kempsey was a smoker who'd snatch it up quick smart.

'Keep your nose clean, kid.' Kempsey tapped the kid's baseball cap. 'Felix, Wren, let's go cross the planks to the *Smoking Flat Lands*.'

Shutting the gate to keep King the crocodile out, Wren gazed back at the Sandfly Saloon. They were now on the last run home. So where was the cavalry?

FORTY-TWO

It was utter chaos in the beer garden, and the pub wasn't officially open yet. But there were stockmen, miners, farmers, and fishermen all shouting over each other at the back of the pub.

On the edge of the arguing group of men stood Marcus, with his officers and Stewart beside him.

'*Oi!*' His authoritative voice shut the mob up and they turned to stare at him. 'What the hell is going on here?'

One man spoke, jabbing at the air. 'Someone's been at Karma.'

'Mongrels. I'll bloody kill 'em,' said another cowboy.

More men complained as they stabbed at the air, whining and whinging at the crocodile pen.

'All right, all right.' The female voice rose above the din to silence them. 'Let the officers through, they're here to help.' The crowd of men parted and there stood Samantha, Australia's youngest publican, sipping on her coffee. 'Morning, Sarge.'

'What's going on?'

'They want to lynch whoever poked their noses into the crocodile cage and upset Karma.'

'You're kidding?' Stewart said, 'It's a crocodile.'

'They're very protective of Karma, who happens to have a gift at predicting winners of football matches.'

Marcus understood that Karma was worth a pretty penny to the crowd who'd bet on anything from running ponies to cane-toad racing.

'Billy.' Samantha waved the grey-haired man over. 'Billy can tell you firsthand, considering he's got a special relationship with the beast.'

'Where is Karma?' Marcus peered into the wide pond.

'Hiding,' replied Samantha. 'Wouldn't you if you had all this mob shouting at you first thing in the morning?'

'That long-lost Peddler did this. Just like a flamin' Peddler to cause mischief like this.' Billy wagged his stubby finger. 'And that fella Felix from Sydney was in on it, too.'

The crowd's grumbles grew with a lot of men frowning in Marcus's direction.

'BACK OFF YOU LOT.' His voice cut through the crowd that took a step back from his steely stare. The protective fire he had for Wren was barely containable. 'Unless you are directly involved with this matter, I suggest you go wait by the pool table, so I can find out what is going on.'

Marcus stared down the men in assorted hats, their grumbles barely audible, as they slinked off to the back of the bar.

'If you ever decide to quit your day job, Marcus, let me know. I could use your skills in crowd control.'

'You can control this crowd without even blinking, Samantha. Why did you let it go on?' After all, the locals all called her God.

'The men are so worked up over this, they've started passing a hat around to pay *me* to upgrade my own security system. Do you think I'm gonna stop that?' Samantha gave a wry smile.

'Now, Billy.' Marcus adjusted his cap and stared down at the cranky yardman. 'Why do you think this was Wren?'

'Because only you, the long-lost Peddler girl, and that Felix fella from Sydney, knew about Karma's taste for my jerky. That was good jerky I'd given 'em and they threw it all over the place, wasting it.'

'You do know Wren and Felix have been kidnapped, right?' Normally Billy had an amazing amount of empathy for anyone. Yet Billy also went to bed earlier than the average person, starting his day job in the middle of the night.

Billy's crinkles softened as he stared up in wide-eyed wonder, turning to Samantha, his boss, who nodded in confirmation. Billy tore his hat off, wiping a palm over his snowy hair. 'No, I didn't. I'm so sorry I ever said a bad word about the pair of them.'

Marcus patted the old man's shoulder. 'Besides the jerky, what else is out of the ordinary with Karma's pen? There has to be more to it to upset everyone like this.'

'I'll show ya.' Billy hoisted his suspenders higher along his shoulders, leading them to the rear of the enclosure. 'They used a chair and the mat to shimmy over the barricade. But look at the mess they'd made of the garden. Rowan Peddler planted that garden, Wren knew that.'

'It's a clue.' Marcus gripped the mesh to peer at the mess of rocks and plants shoved aside. There were letters in the middle, but the way the sun was hitting the soil it was impossible to read.

'Bugger it.' Marcus hoisted himself up and over the fence. He needed a closer look.

'Are you crazy, Marcus?' Stewart shouted, with Samantha and Billy gripping the fence. His officers rushed to assist.

'I've already wrestled with Karma before.' But he'd done that with Jax, the fire chief, under the supervision of the

Station Hand and the local croc wrangler. 'Besides, I'm fully armed with three pistols, a taser, and a can of pepper spray.' But for Wren to do this unarmed, she must have been terrified, making his guts churn with worry.

Why would a father do this to his daughter, putting Wren in terrifying danger like this over a stupid treasure hunt?

'Can someone please watch that beast in the pond?' Marcus knew crocodiles were at their most lethal in the water, with the agility to jump the full length of their body clear of the water. And Karma did it daily for sport.

Marcus's shadow covered the clearing of rocks and plants on the side of the concrete mound. There was no jewellery to be found, only the most precious jewel of all, her imprint. It was Wren's height, her arm lengths, her shape, pushed into the soft soil, like a snow angel, but in dirt. It was another message written in dust.

In the middle, near the chest area, the letters were smeared:

A N D F

'What does it say?' Stewart asked.

Marcus understood that Wren had to keep the clues cryptic, especially in such a public place. He admired her strength and determination to leave him clues while inside a crocodile cage.

Damn, the woman had grit.

Marcus took photos with his phone, then hauled his butt back over the fence. 'A N D F.'

He showed the image on his phone to Stewart.

'Sarge! Sarge.' Bottle Shop Luke jogged over with one of the bar's duty managers. 'Someone's nicked our boat.'

'Where was it?'

'Parked by the paddock next door. We'd only come in to unload the delivery truck before we went fishing, but now it's gone.'

'How long has it been missing?'

'We've been inside less than two hours, if that. This isn't to do with Wren's kidnapping, is it?'

The pieces fell into place. 'It's not *and*—F it's *Sand*. That dirt angel is for fly. He's taken them in Luke's boat to Sandfly. He's taken Wren and Felix home.' Marcus led the chase to their patrol cars with hope flaring in his chest. He knew that it was much quicker to get to the Peddler Palace by road than by boat, so now he had a real chance of closing the gap.

FORTY-THREE

With his pack over one shoulder, Kempsey rechecked his coordinates against the compass and map. Beside him Wren, still bound at the wrists, with Felix hooking his arm through hers, they trudged along with their boots crunching on dead grass and red powdery soils.

The sky was a light summer blue, endless in its depths, without a cloud to be seen. The perfect accompaniment to the long paddock that rolled ahead of them like a cream blanket under the sun. This one paddock had so many different colours to it, depending on the time of the day, like it was a living breathing artist's palette.

Kempsey slowed his pace. 'Well, according to the map, it's under our feet.'

'Where?' Wren scuffed her boots on the dry, red dust. 'Are you sure?'

'I'm sure.'

'What, *here* here?' Felix stamped his loafer on the ground causing a small puff of dust to rise and fall.

It echoed.

'Did you hear that?' Wren rushed over and knocked her knuckles on the turf. It was hollow.

'I think we have ourselves a hidden bunker.' Kempsey smiled, dumping his pack to the ground. 'You two sit there. It's my turn to dig.' From his pack, he removed his army-issue fold-out shovel and carefully removed two inches of dirt in a rectangular shape to reveal a door.

'What's a bunker?' Felix asked.

'It's an underground cellar separate from the house. Some have wood holding up the sides, or they're made from concrete,' explained Wren. 'Some people use them for cyclone shelters.'

'Very good, Miss Wren. They're also a common military tool. We used to make them and destroy them as part of our day job as tunnel rats. And here's a door with a lock.' Kempsey pulled out the metal key, twisted it in the keyhole, pulled down the recessed handle, and lifted the metal door that had grasses growing on its panel. 'I hope you're not claustrophobic.' Kempsey helped Wren to her feet.

'Don't think so. But if you untie my hands I can climb down.' Wren scowled at the stupid ropes, encrusted with dirt, sweat, and dried blood from the wounds they'd made around her wrists.

'Not on my shift.'

'Why does Wren have to go down there?' Felix whined, also being hauled to his feet.

'Don't worry, you'll be right behind her. I'm not leaving you two up here on your own.' Kempsey loosened the rope he used to tie Wren and Felix together.

Wren peered down the hole. It wasn't deep, but there was no ladder.

At the far end of the flat paddock stood the large farmhouse. She had a clear view of the attic window and the front verandah. But without the map, you wouldn't have even known the bunker was here. Were there more bunkers hidden within this long corridor?

Kempsey gathered the rope into a loop, securing it around her waist, positioning Wren on the edge. 'Done any rock climbing?'

'I'm more of a hiker, but I have done some rock walls in the gym.'

'Good. I'm going to lower you down. Easy as.'

Wren held the rope, walking backwards into the hole. It was about two metres deep. She wriggled herself free of the rope around her waist. What she'd give to get rid of the ones around her wrists. 'I'm down.'

'Here comes Felix.'

'I'm right here, Felix, just take one step backwards, like climbing a ladder.'

'I can't. I don't … *Augh*.' Felix fell back into the cavern, knocking Wren to the ground.

'Felix, I love you like a brother, but you weigh a bloody tonne.' Wren struggled to get out from under Felix's weight. Her whole body ached, seriously depleted of energy.

'I'm so sorry, Toots. I'm just not an outdoorsy person.'

Kempsey effortlessly jumped down, leaving the ropes hanging from the ceiling. He pulled Felix off Wren. 'Are you okay?'

Her ankle throbbed, along with all the other aches within her body. 'I think he twisted my ankle.'

'Come on, up you get.' Kempsey, again, pulled Wren to her feet.

'Ow-ow-ow.' She winced, using his shoulder for balance, the sharp pain was unbearable. 'It's my right ankle.'

'I'm so sorry, Toots. Can I do anything?' His hands free from any bindings, Felix rubbed her shoulders.

'Just stay here, with me.' She hooked her arms over his, to clutch their hands together like they'd done as small children, facing their fears together. She had to believe they'd get through this.

Kempsey used his flashlight to survey the simple rectangular room. It was small. And empty. 'There's nothing here.'

'There has to be.' Wren frowned. 'Rowan wouldn't have made this bunker for nothing.'

'Well, Toots, your family did cook up illegal booze and chop-chop as their day job. Having something like this is perfect for hiding their stash from police raids.'

Wren hadn't considered that. Her family secrets were endless. But in the pit of her stomach, something didn't feel right.

'Toots, have we done all the clues?' Felix asked.

'I think so.' They'd come full circle, ending where they'd begun this journey.

Why did her father send her around the countryside like this, when you could clearly see the bunker from the attic window? How come no one at the house spotted them? Where was everyone?

'Do you think we missed something?' Kempsey tapped his knuckles along the wooden panels lining the walls.

'No. All paths have led us here.'

'Do you think your father sold it?' Felix asked with a meek shrug.

'Why would Rowan write me that letter with all those clues if he had sold it?' Led by her own frustrations, she clawed along the wall, keeping the weight off her throbbing ankle that hurt a lot more than just a sprain, the bone ached. But she didn't have the luxury of surrendering to her pain. 'It's here. It must be here. I did not climb into a crocodile pen or dig up my father's resting place for nothing.' Her bitter words bounced off the walls.

'All right, Wren.' Kempsey held his palms up to calm her down. 'Let's go back over the clues. We'll start with the letter that helped you find the map.' Kempsey's torch highlighted the letters on the page. 'How did you find the map?'

'It was a clue we'd found in the book, *Lambert's Gold*, using those numbers there ...' She pointed to the bottom of the letter. 'But we're missing something.' The walls and roof were smooth, and there were no hidden doors. Nothing.

'What's the book about?' Kempsey asked.

Felix brushed himself off. 'Oh, well, it's an adventure romance that involves this amazing treasure hunt.'

'What was the treasure?'

'A chest of old pirate's gold from a Spanish galleon.'

'Have you read the book, Wren?'

'Read it?' Felix laughed. 'Wren wrote it!'

Kempsey arched his eyebrows at Wren. 'Did Rowan read it?'

'Rowan helped me. We used to have these brainstorming sessions drinking rum. It was our tradition. We went through almost a bottle trying to work out how to hide that treasure to really stun the readers.'

'Where did you hide it?'

'In the book I hid the gold within the ship ...' Her eyes travelled around the room. 'It wasn't out in the open. In fact, when they first found the ship, it looked completely empty.'

'Like this room?' Kempsey shone his flashlight at the corners.

'Yes.' Could it be?

'So where was this Spanish gold hidden?'

'Within the walls. The pirates had built a false wall in their cargo hold, trapping the gold inside.' Wren tapped on the wooden panelling, all her aches and ails momentarily forgotten. 'It's in the walls! Look for a slightly raised board, one that's not flush like the rest of them.' Wren pressed her palms against the walls. 'Feel for a bump or a bend. Something that's slightly imperfect from the rest.'

'I think we have it.' Kempsey rapped his knuckles on a warped board. 'Stay there, I'll get the shovel.' He hoisted himself up the rope, tossing the fold-out shovel down.

Wren ran her palm over the curved board that stood out further than the others. 'I think you're right.'

'You two, go stand under the open doorway, in case there's a cave-in.' Kempsey used the shovel's blade to pry the board loose. It creaked and groaned as dust spilled from the cracks in the ceiling, until the board finally came away, landing on the floor with a thud, revealing a hole within the dirt wall.

Leaning the shovel against the wall, Kempsey shone his torch into the round plastic pipe. 'There's something in here.' He dragged out a large object wrapped in a cloth. 'What do we have here?' Kempsey set the torch down to unwrap the parcel.

'Is it the diamond? Let me see, let me see.' Felix stumbled.

'Ow, watch my ankle, Felix.'

'Sorry, Toots, I just have to see it.' Felix crawled across the dirt on all fours. 'What is it?'

Kempsey unrolled the cloth to reveal a bottle. Around its glass neck was a note wrapped in protective plastic.

Her heart sank. Not another note.

'Is it in the bottle?' Felix asked Kempsey.

'I don't know this brand … It's rum?' Kempsey held up the bottle to the light. 'It's just rum.'

Her heart sank even further recognising the brand. 'It's Cuban rum, the Havana Club Máximo. They only make a thousand of those bottles per year.' She sighed, sharing a slow shake of her head. 'It's my favourite, ridiculously expensive, rum.' She'd shared a nip with Rowan when her first book had hit the shelves. It was the rum that started the next story, soon becoming a tradition. It was a rarely found rum, but, oh boy, didn't she drag out her credit card to just have a taste if she ever spotted it at some bar on her travels.

'How expensive?' Felix the club owner asked.

'About three thousand dollars a bottle. Which means that letter is for me.' Her father had made this whole adventure for her. They used to share a lot of adventures together, coming to rely on each other, especially when abroad.

Wait, she really hadn't been flying totally solo, not as much as she'd thought. She'd had Rowan, and she had Felix. But with Rowan gone, who would be her travelling companion now? Grief gripped at her heart, truly missing her father who had been a big part of her world.

'Is it another clue?' Felix asked.

Kempsey opened the letter and read it aloud by torch light:

Dearest Wren,

Well done for making it this far. I thought the adventure would be something you'd enjoy as you took on the challenges of these clues.

But alas, the diamond is gone. I'm sorry, kiddo. I really am.

I know it must fill you with shock and horror for what I'd put you through, but it's true.

When I found out about my illness, I didn't think I had time to make amends, so I posted the Jade Diamond, by slow boat to Timor. I'm hoping the consulate will have it by the time you read this.

I know you'll be disappointed or furious at me when you read this, after all I'd put you through, but I had to send it away. I had to make up for all the bad things I'd done in my life. Originally, I was planning to do this with you, to come clean with all of my sins, where we'd take the Jade Diamond back to its rightful home together as my final hurrah.

Sadly, if you're reading this, time ran out sooner than I'd planned. But hey, I'm used to living in the moment and so should you.

So in place of the diamond is your favourite rum. I know how much you enjoyed this drink. I had hoped we'd share it together to watch the sunset from my favourite spot, discussing your next adventure in the world of words. It's a tradition I adored sharing with you.

As for this treasure hunt, I did this to give you one last adventure to remember me by.

Be safe, kiddo.

All my love

Rowan (AKA Dad)

PS. I'm being straight with you and not writing the opposite in what I'm trying to say, there is no Peddlers' code to uncover from here, because the adventure is over! You made it.

'What a load of crap!' Kempsey screwed up the note. 'That bastard.' He punched at the wall, to then pace while muttering a furious list of expletives. 'That sick prick knew all along that he had it and sent it away.'

He scowled at Wren. 'Are there any clues in this letter?' He waved the scrunched-up letter in her face.

Wren shook her head.

Kempsey roughly grabbed her arm. 'Are there?'

She wanted to cry, the fear overwhelming. 'No. It's gone. It's all over.'

'That prick!' He shoved her aside.

Wren slammed against the wall, crying out in pain. Her boot was cutting off the circulation to her throbbing ankle.

Kempsey kicked at the rum bottle, sending it spinning in circles across the floor.

As the bottle slowed to a stop, Kempsey stopped pacing.

'What are you going to do now?' Wren tried to swallow down her fear, with her pulse whooshing in her ears, and her body trembling.

Felix wasn't much better, cowering in the corner.

She dragged herself up to limp towards him. She had to protect Felix.

'I'm getting out of here, that's what I'm doing.' Kempsey tugged on the rope hanging loose from the ceiling.

'You can't leave us here.'

'Watch me!'

'No.' Wren tripped past her fear, unable to flee for her life. It was time to fight—or die trying.

As Kempsey started climbing, she threw herself against his back to slam him against the wall. Screaming through her pain, she kicked at his knee, lashing out erratically with her hands clubbed together into one fist.

Kempsey grappled with her, laying in some punches, then threw her against the wall to lash out with his boots.

Wren tried to protect herself with tied hands, but something crunched, cracked, and popped. Her vision soon filled with stars as the sheer blinding pain screamed at her, along with the metallic taste of blood filling her mouth.

'Stop it! Just stop it!' Felix went to lunge.

'Sit back down, boy.' Kempsey stood deathly still with

a straight arm aiming his deadly pistol at his hostages. He tugged on the rope and without another word, Kempsey climbed to the top.

'Just so you know, in a few hours you'll run out of oxygen, and no one will know where to look for you until it's too late.' Slamming the door shut, it sent a rain of dust to smother Wren and Felix in complete and utter darkness.

FORTY-FOUR

Marcus gunned his vehicle, hitting the dirt road at breakneck speeds. The red dust churned high into the air like a ferocious storm, hiding the following cavalcade of cars flashing their police lights.

In the passenger seat, Stewart held on with white knuckles, looking positively green.

But Marcus wasn't slowing down for anything.

His phone rang. It was the station's number. Why weren't they using the radio?

He punched the speaker. 'What?'

'Sarge, Tanisha. I just had Two-dollar Darryl on the phone. He's just spoken to Chopper, who's at Sandfly. He's seen Wren and Felix. *They're alive.*'

The hope was like freaking sunshine, sending prickles across his scalp. 'Where's Wren?'

'Still with the stalker.'

'Where?'

'Chopper doesn't know. They tied him up and he said they're on a treasure hunt, that's why they're digging for clues, Sarge.'

Which was why Tanisha chose to not blast this

information across the airways when they had a lot of locals who were glued to the radio. Well done, Tanisha.'

'How did Chopper get away?'

'Wren secretly snuck Chopper a pocketknife to cut himself free from the ropes. As soon as he did, he called his uncle.'

Wren was a freaking hero. Damn, he wanted to hug her so badly.

Tanisha continued, 'Chopper raced down to the house and said they've gone but doesn't know how. The vehicles are still there, the shed and the house is locked up, and the boats are still docked at Sandfly. But Wren, Felix and their kidnapper have disappeared.'

Marcus frowned, gripping the steering wheel tighter. 'They couldn't vanish like that.' But then they'd escaped him so far, using train lines and going cross-country. 'Where's Darryl now?'

'At the Peddler property, he's opening the gates for you. Darryl's radioed the fishermen to keep an eye out for any strangers on the river systems. But he hasn't said anything to them about the treasure hunt.'

'Good. And thank you for not sharing it over the radio.'

'They're my friends, too, Sarge. Is there anything you need me to do?'

Marcus leaned over the steering wheel staring at an infinite blue sky. Did that bastard know how to fly? He hoped not, or they were screwed.

'Tanisha, radio for Monet. Get her to do an aerial sweep over the Peddler property. And ask Mickey at the airport to monitor the radar and airwaves. I want them both to keep watch for any suspicious planes or muster choppers in the area.'

'Got it. Anything else, Sarge?'

It was a long property, with scrublands on both sides

making up a hundred hectares, that included an intricate river system to hide in. The Peddler property wasn't a walk in the park.

'Call Darryl and tell him to do a sweep of the fence line, to search for another hole. The kidnapper may have another car stashed on a nearby firebreak.'

The diamond had to be on the property. It's the only reason they were there. 'Tell Darryl I'm five minutes away.' *Hang in there, Wren.*

FORTY-FIVE

'Toots? … Please wake up.' Felix whimpered, nudging at her shoulder. 'I know we said we'd always die together, but not like this. You're not allowed to die like this.'

Everything. Hurt.

Lying on the dirt floor, it hurt to breathe as pain layered upon pain weighed her down. Wren moaned, unsure if her eyes were open. If they were, she couldn't see anything in the thick blackness.

She tried to move, but her shoulder spasmed in a horrific wave of cramps up and down her arm. Her lungs squeezed as if a thousand knifes were stabbing at her ribcage.

She cried out, her voice sounding foreign. She tried to roll onto her back, but with her leg twisted and her ankle throbbing, she saw stars again.

'Toots?' The fear in Felix's voice was a whole new level of fear.

It was enough to bring her back from the brink of unconsciousness. With her cheek pressed against the dusty floor, she could hear his breathing and feel his body heat. He was close. 'Felix.'

'Toots, you're alive.' He hugged her.

'Augh.' The pain bit at her from all angles. She writhed in the dirt, screaming. 'Don't touch me.'

'Breathe. Just like you did with my panic attack. Breathe through the pain, like women in labour. *He-he-he* then *ho-ho-ho* …'

Oh, she hated him right now, but amazingly it worked.

Teeny tiny, quick breaths helped her to focus on her breathing, as the bulk of the pain subsided.

Then the main issue came to light, because they were staring into a black void. Trapped in an underground bunker where no one knew they were there.

'Felix?' She didn't have the energy to sit, so she just lay there, breathing slowly, barely moving her lungs at all.

'What do we do?'

'Listen, Felix.' She licked her lips, tasting the dirt and blood from her split lip. 'Come closer …' She didn't have the energy to shout with her head pounding fiercely.

'I'm here.'

She gripped his fingers tightly as tears squeezed from her eyes. His hands were free! 'You've got to be brave, Felix. I need you.'

'I'll try, but what can I do?'

'Find the shovel. Kempsey left it leaning against the wall. I want you to use it to prop open the door. We need air.'

'Oh, good idea.' Felix groped around the floor of the cavern, stirring the dust that tickled her nose.

If she sneezed, she'd black out from the pain. She couldn't and wouldn't do that to Felix. She needed to focus, to find a way out of this mess.

'Ow.'

'What?' Hot and thirsty, Wren tried to swallow, to wipe the dust off her face, but her wrists were still bound together. Bruises pulsed and swelled all over her body, including her cheek in the dirt.

'The shovel fell on my hand. But I've got it, Wren. I did it.' The joy in his voice soon disappeared. 'But I don't know where the roof is. I can't see a thing, and all the walls feel the same.'

Her breath was raspy, something nasty was rattling in her weighty chest. 'Feel for the missing wall panel. Then, put your back to the hole, walk dead ahead until you hit the other wall. From there the door should be directly above you.'

Felix shuffled his shoes while patting blindly at the walls. 'Ow, for the love of vodka and cold drip coffee, I think I've got a splinter.'

She huffed, her lips even curling into a slight smile. Trust Felix the fabulous to take her mind away from her own pain. Some people would've found it irritating, but she knew he did that comic act to help her.

'You okay, Felix? Want me to get you a hot towel?' What she wouldn't give for a cold towel to wipe at the horrendous heat coming off her in waves.

'Oh, Toots, you treat me so well … I found the other wall.' The shovel banged on the roof, spilling dust.

She couldn't remember if Kempsey had closed the latch, praying he hadn't. 'Push. Felix …' They needed air.

'It's so heavy.' Felix groaned, as his shoes shuffled in the dirt.

It was only a peep, a small slither of light that grew.

Then it was gone.

'I'll try again. You stay right there, Toots. I've got this.'

She could just picture Felix rolling up his sleeves, smoothing down his hair, just like the time he'd climbed the ladder on the vintage train.

Again, there was a hard thud against the roof. A soft shuffle of shoes, and then a deep groan.

The stream of light was glorious. Complete with dust particles floating on a sunbeam, pushing cool air against her hot cheeks.

'Toots, I did it. We have air.' Felix was so proud. His cheesy smile spread across his face as he greeted the sunlight. 'Do you think they'll find us soon?' He looked at Wren and his smile fell. 'Oh my god, Wren.'

She looked in his general direction. Dark crimson blood was pooling around her. *Oh crap*. Her heart fluttered, the panic swirling in her limbs. If she was panicking, there'd be no holding him back. 'Felix, no—'

'AAAHHHHH ...' Felix screamed. Only to inhale to let out the mother of all screams, which bounced like a sonic boom within the bunker, she winced with her eardrums in pain.

BANG.

'Was that a gunshot?' Felix asked.

Wren didn't have the strength to respond.

'Maybe Chopper can hear us?' Again, he bellowed louder than a sonic jet breaking the sound barrier. Her ears ached.

When Felix stopped, she could hear him thinking as her whole head pounded.

'Toots, if that was a gunshot, do you think it was Kempsey, coming back for us?' Felix gasped, backing away from the door, dropping the shovel to plunge their world into darkness.

She shivered as another wave of cramps burned her arm and shoulder, her ankle throbbed all the way up her leg, as her lungs squeezed fire.

Good luck if Kempsey was coming back to finish her. She was done.

'I'm so sorry, Felix. You know I love you like family, so believe me when I say I'm so sorry you got caught up in this mess,' Wren whispered with the tears flowing, as her head pounded louder. 'Tell Marcus, that big, beautiful detective sergeant …' She licked her cracked lips, her throat raw.

'No. You can tell him yourself. You have to.'

'Tell him—tell Marcus I love him. I was such a fool to not even recognise it, and an even bigger idiot to not fight for it. I should have fought harder, seized the day …' She was the one who'd pushed Marcus away, when all she wanted to do was hold him, one more time.

What sort of romance writer was she when she didn't even recognise what love was in her own story?

Pity it was too late.

It was all too late.

FORTY-SIX

The police car fishtailed down the dirt drive. Marcus grit his teeth, pushing the accelerator pedal to the floor, and the car flew through the open gate with its rows of barbed wire glinting in the sunlight.

Around the bend the Peddler Palace rose from the red dirt. What he'd give to see Wren standing on those front steps to greet him, even with Felix flouncing out behind her.

But there was no one, only a group of hanging pot plants.

Then he spotted a lone figure limping across the field.

'Who is that?' Stewart pointed.

Marcus leaned over the steering wheel and sneered.

He slammed on the brakes, spinning the car to the side. In one quick fluid motion he unclipped his seatbelt and dragged the doctor out with him over the driver's seat, throwing his friend to the side of the car.

Stewart cried out. 'What the hell do you—'

The first bullet smashed the passenger window, sending small pebbles of glass across the dirt, its shot only now echoing in the surrounding air.

'Stay down.' Marcus pulled a pistol from its holster. Cold in his palm, he aimed it over the car bonnet and let off a fast and furious round of shots, spraying dust around the feet of Steven Kempsey. And those were his first and final warning shots.

The other patrol cars pulled up behind him, more guns pointed at the lone man in the paddock where red dust swirled like smoke across the flat lands.

The *Smoking Flat Lands*. The last spot on the map.

But where were Wren and Felix?

Hobbling to a standstill, Kempsey dumped his heavy pack in the dirt and wiped the blood from his nose and at the deep scratches across his face.

Someone had put up a hell of a fight.

'Drop your weapon and put your hands in the air, Kempsey.' Marcus had him in his gun's sight, his finger resting on the trigger.

Kempsey took a long, sweeping look at his surroundings.

Then a mighty scream carried across the field, sending birds fleeing in all directions, it made the hairs on the back of his neck stand.

'That's got to be Wren and Felix,' whispered Stewart, his back pressed to the side of the car.

'It's Felix.' Felix was the only one with that sort of lung capacity, the guy had made house windows rattle just calling for Wren.

'One of them must be hurt.' Stewart opened the back door to drag his doctor's bag out of the car.

'I said put your hands up, arsehole.' Marcus couldn't move. Not yet.

Kempsey swayed in his boots. Stuck between the house, the shed, his freedom, and with no hostages to hide behind.

'You've got nowhere to go, so drop your weapons. NOW.'

Kempsey tapped his handgun against his leg, then against his head, muttering to himself.

Marcus gripped his pistol tighter.

Not even a bird moved. The wind died. And the world crawled to a halt.

Kempsey then stood deathly still and smiled. 'I've stared in the face of death so many times ...'

'Don't do it.' Come on, arsehole, let's dance.

'Reckon they'll let someone like me into heaven ...' Kempsey lifted head to face to the sun. 'Or hell...' He took a deep breath and went for it, raising his gun at Marcus.

But Marcus was more than ready, pumping a tight cluster of bullets into Kempsey's chest.

Before the smoke had even cleared, Marcus bolted. His boots kicked up dust as he sprinted across the field, to grab Kempsey by the bloodied shirt. 'Where is she? Where's Wren and Felix?'

Another almighty scream echoed, as if from beneath the earth itself.

Kempsey's head rolled. A trickle of blood spilled from his evil grin. 'You won't make it. They'll run out of air in the hellhole they're in ...'

'Where?'

Stewart checked for a pulse. 'He's gone.'

Marcus dropped the body. 'Did anyone pinpoint the direction of that scream?'

'Sarge, it came from over there.' It was Chopper rushing over from Sandfly, as more officers rushed forward.

Two-dollar Darryl ran to meet them from the opposite fence line. 'That way, they're down there somewhere.' He pointed to the long rolling field.

'Everyone, spread out in a line,' called out Marcus. 'We're looking for a hole, or a bunker. Look for anything out of the ordinary in the dirt. It's only recent, so there'll be freshly disturbed soil and tracks. Hurry, they're underground and running out of air.'

Time crawled as the sun rose higher. A watery haze of heat rose from the golden field that seemed to roll on forever. A group of men, spanned out in a line, searching the field. But they had too much ground to cover and not enough men.

'Over here, Sergeant. They're here.' Two-dollar Darryl and Chopper raised a large metal door out of the dirt. It was a bunker.

Inside, on the dirt floor, blinking up at the light, was Felix cradling a bloodied Wren in his arms.

'Wren?' Marcus's heart stopped.

'Wren won't wake up.' Felix shook his head with tears staining his cheeks. 'She won't wake up.'

Marcus jumped down into the bunker.

'He was going to kill us, but she fought him, and he …'

'It's okay, you're safe now, Felix.' Marcus carefully took Wren from Felix. Unsheathing his knife, he cut the coarse rope from around her dainty wrists, deeply bruised and bloodied.

'Stewart, get down here. Someone call for an ambulance, now.' Marcus held his frail, beautiful Wren to his chest, wiping the bloodied, tangled hair from her precious face. Her lip and her eye were swollen, and there was a nasty bump on her forehead. But where was the blood coming from?

He felt for a heartbeat. It was too slow, with a death rattle deep within her lungs. She was barely breathing.

'Stay with me, baby. You're going to be fine.' Marcus rocked her in his arms in the dark hole in the ground. 'Don't leave me. Not when I've just found you, Wren. I love you, Wren, you hear me. Please, baby, please, stay with me.'

FORTY-SEVEN

Beeps, blips, and sterile smells, mixed with a swirl of floral fragrances. It was confronting and confusing.

Her eyes struggled to open, but the world was fuzzy.

Wren blinked, and blinked again, her body trapped. She couldn't move.

Oh no, was she still tied up and held hostage?

The beeping over her head grew more insistent. It was irritating as she struggled to move. Squeezing a hand. A big warm hand.

It was Marcus.

The beeping slowed down as tears filled her eyes. She tried to hug him, hold him, but couldn't. He was asleep, his head resting near her leg, which was bound in a thick white plaster cast.

Aw, crap!

'Hey …' Marcus lifted his head, his hair messy, with a three-day bristle covering his strong jawline. The whole package was gloriously sexy. But the concern in his dark eyes only made her fear for him.

'Marcus …' The tears flowed freely now.

'I'm here, babe, I'm not going anywhere.'

'I just want to hold you.' She blubbered into a flat-out ugly cry. She didn't care how it looked, she needed him. 'It's all I wanted the entire time was to hold you.'

'I have to be careful of your injuries.'

'Don't care. I'm not letting go.' She used her fingertips to pull at his shirt. It wasn't a police uniform, only a T-shirt and jeans. No guns. No cuffs either. And no annoying phone to interrupt them.

'I've got you.' He lifted her ever so gently, resting her head on his shoulder. She just breathed him in. 'How do you feel?'

'I hurt. But I'm good.'

His chuckle made her want to smile. 'How can that be good? I can call the doctor for more painkillers.'

'No, just stay here.'

'I'm not leaving.'

'But what about work?'

'I've got Porter running the station. It's his penance for leaving you two alone.'

'Hey, it—'

'Shh.' He put his finger across her lips, leaning in closer. 'Don't argue.'

'I won't. Especially when it comes to security. I'm just sorry I didn't listen to you sooner.'

He winked at her. 'But you're okay, aren't you?'

Her two hands cupped his hand. 'All I wanted was this.'

'My hands.'

'And what they're attached to … Marcus, I know I look awful …' She felt awful and the hospital gown's starchy white was never her colour. 'But I have to say it now, before anything else gets in the way.' She tried to take a deep breath, it hurt, but it didn't stop her from saying, 'I love you.' She blubbered, 'I love you.' The words were not nearly powerful enough for the overwhelming emotions filling her chest.

'I know. Felix told me.' His grin was stunning.

Oh, how selfish of her to not ask about her friend. 'Where's Felix?'

'He's fine. Not a scratch on him. You, on the other hand, have issues.'

She winced. 'How bad.'

'Dislocated shoulder, broken ribs, punctured lung ...'

'Sheez.'

'... a hairline fracture in your ankle, and a concussion to go with the stitches in the back of your head.' He then leaned down to tenderly kiss her bandaged wrists. 'And lots and lots of bruising. But I got him. He's gone.'

Her fingers raked through his soft hair. He was so handsome, just the sight of him made her heart soar. 'And I'm still here ... I heard you.'

He looked up.

She gave him a soft smile. Nothing was holding her back now. Time was too precious to waste. 'I heard you. In the bunker.' She squeezed his hand. 'You never let go.'

'And I don't intend too anytime soon.'

'But what about ...' She lay back on the pillows, her thumping headache was clouding her thoughts.

'Hey, chill out. You're stuck in here for a bit.'

'How long have I been here?'

From his pocket, he pulled out her gold watch. 'Thirty-four hours and twenty-five minutes.'

'You found it?'

'And your ring. I'll keep them with me until they unhook you from all these gadgets.'

Again, the tears welled in her eyes. 'You found them. You read my clues?'

'I did. I understood them, too.'

He truly understood her. How rare a gift was that! 'Are

people upset by what I've done?' She'd torn up the town, had roads blocked for her, all sorts.

'It wasn't your fault.'

'I'm responsible.'

'No. Felix told us how Kempsey murdered your father. Wren, you were kidnapped, none of this is your fault. However, if your father was alive, I'd certainly be having something to say to the man.'

'Get in line.' Why did Rowan send her on a treasure hunt for a diamond that was never there?

'The town is more shocked over you daring to climb into a crocodile pen. You've earned your place in this town's gossip books as a proper Peddler now.'

'Oops.' That was a memory she didn't want to think about.

'Hey …' He stroked her hair. 'That's nothing compared to what I got up to as a kid looking for kicks. You had justifiable reasons for your extraordinary actions. I admire your grit and courage, not many people would do what you did.'

She didn't feel very courageous. 'When do you go back to work?'

He shrugged. 'I'm taking time off. I've got plenty of leave saved up, especially with the overtime I earned this past week. I'm finally taking the time to kick back and read some books.'

'Yeah?'

'You might know the author.' He lifted a copy of *Lambert's Gold*.

'You're not?' She pulled the sheet over her head to hide. 'You can't read that in front of me. That's not allowed.'

'I'm almost finished. It's pretty good.'

'You're just saying that.' The cocoon from under the sheets only radiated the heat from her cheeks.

He pulled the sheet down, brushing her hair away. 'I'll never lie to you, Wren. I like it. Don't tell too many people though, it might ruin my reputation as a cop who shoots first and asks questions later.'

'Are you in trouble for, you know, for taking out the bad guy? And me ...'

'Nope. Unless being in love is trouble.' He grinned, pressing her hand to his lips. 'But right now, we have no phones, and strict visiting hours, so we can finally talk uninterrupted. I'll even order in some decent food. But I think you might want to leave off the cocktails for a while.'

Her smile mirrored his. 'Is this where we get to map out our own future?'

'You bet. On top of our list of topics is that little thing you inherited called the Sandfly Saloon.'

FORTY-EIGHT

The world of red dust and blue skies whizzed past as they followed the string of wire fences that dared to contain an endless countryside. Wren leaned against the window of the ute, so glad to finally be out of hospital and on her way home to the Peddler Palace.

Home?

Mixed emotions of joy and fear swirled inside her chest at the thought of returning to the place where so much had happened. It was her father's home, which had been in her family for generations. The home where her father had died, where she had dealt with a stalker and where she'd nearly died herself.

'Are you okay?' Marcus gave her thigh a gentle squeeze as he steered the ute down the dirt roads.

'This ute suits you.' It was her father's ute, which she still had yet to drive.

'I thought it'd be easier for you to climb in with your cast. Can't speed in this.'

'When do you get your police car back? Did they fix it up from the bullet holes?'

'Waiting on the driver's window. It'll be there when I return to work. No rush is there?' He gripped her hand.

'No complaints from me.' She squeezed his hand, never

wanting to let it go.

'Hey, are you sure you're not in any pain?'

'I'm done with needles, thank you very muchly.'

'You'll never get over your hate of needles, huh?'

'Doubt it. It's worse now.'

'Reckon you'll hate Stewart forever?'

'Only until the bruising goes down.' She flipped down the visor. Her skin was puffy and yellow around the eyes, worsened by her paleness, and her wrists were still black from the bruises. 'I look awful.' Bound around her chest were tight bandages that were an immense help for her ribs, healing fast.

'Hey, you still look beautiful to me.' He gently brought her hand to his lips.

Wren couldn't help but smile at him. Marcus hadn't left her side since she'd woken up in the hospital. And now she was going home.

'Where's Felix?' She'd expected him to be at the hospital today, like every other day, promptly showing for visiting hours, to fuss over the flowers in her room while kicking out Marcus to go shower and change.

Fabulous Felix had postponed everything—his return to Sydney, even seeing Karma for his marriage prediction to Reggie—until Wren was back on her feet.

'I think Felix has organised a homecoming party for you.'

'As much as I'd love a drink, I hope he hasn't invited the whole town.'

The wide gates topped with barbed wire stood like tall sentries guarding the red dirt driveway, and around the bend there rose the Peddler Palace beneath a cobalt blue sky.

Unexpectedly, she smiled, as a soothing warmth spread through her limbs as the stress left her shoulders, just from looking at the two-storey farmhouse. 'Home.'

It felt like a home. Her home.

But there were too many cars out front. 'Can't we sneak into my room and have a picnic?' She spotted Darryl's truck towing the freezer trailer, now sporting a large yellow 'L' plate on its back panel.

'Did Chopper get his permit?' Chopper had been studying whenever he'd visit her in the hospital, with Marcus as his tutor.

'He did. Perfect scores too.' Marcus barely nodded, but she could tell he was proud of Chopper's achievement.

'Did Felix set up a bed for me in the office, or on the couch?' She tapped her leg's plaster cast. 'Or are you going to carry me up the stairs?'

'Gotta get my exercise in somehow, especially when your coordination on those crutches sucks.' Marcus chuckled, slowing down the vehicle to park by the front door. 'Don't worry, Felix said it's only family.'

Wren didn't have that big a family.

The front screen door whipped open by Felix, who skipped down the steps with Reggie, Tanisha, and Coco the pug dog following.

But it was Two-dollar Darryl and Chopper she hugged the hardest. 'Are you guys okay?' They were the backbone of this place, they were family.

'We're all good, Miss. Sarge said we're heroes,' said Chopper.

'You are in my books. I mean the official books.' The Sandfly Saloon was now an official business.

'Felix has been teaching us all about running Sandfly legit. I'm assistant manager now.' Chopper's grin was glorious against his dark skin. 'We've even got proper hours now, too. Sarge there helped us get a liquor licence.'

'Maybe I'll finally get a drink in the place,' said Marcus.

Two-dollar Darryl shook his head, poking up the brim of his Akubra. 'Only bugger is we've now gotta pay tax. Your grandfather hated paying tax.'

'Now everyone, let's get the lady inside.' Felix bundled Wren into the house where the festivities of her homecoming began.

At sunset, Wren limped away on her crutches to sit at the small table on the front verandah. She dumped the cloth bag, containing a box Felix had given her, onto the table.

Inside the box she found the bottle of Cuban rum, two shot glasses, all of Rowan's letters, notes, maps, and her compass from the treasure hunt. A treasure hunt that had no treasure.

Even though it was all wrapped up in a neat little box, it was going to niggle at her forever. Where was the Jade Diamond now? She hadn't seen any news of it turning up in Timor. It was as if it had vanished.

Cracking the seal, she poured herself a shot of rum from the ridiculously expensive bottle they'd found in the bunker and sat back in the cane chair.

Before her the sunset shared a spectacular display of reds, golds, and orange, spreading across the cloudless sky, making the long gold paddock shine a deep reddish gold.

Gazing at the floorboards, disappointment still nagged at her for not finding the diamond. Did Rowan mean what he wrote in the letter?

'Hey, what are you doing out here?' Marcus poked his head out the front door.

'Escaping from the rabble-rousers inside.' She smiled softly as he gently kissed her hand, then took a seat beside her.

'Two-dollar Darryl told me this is where Rowan always sat, exactly where you are, to watch the sunset. But he'd have his bourbon and smokes. Here, try some of this.' Wren poured the bourbon man a shot of rum.

Marcus sniffed at the glass before sipping. 'Nice.' They sat back and just took in the view while savouring the rum.

She'd missed this view, glad to be finally free from the

constant air-conditioning and the hospital's white walls. It felt good to be home.

Again, her eyes fell to the floorboards at her feet. 'This is where you found him?'

'Yeah …' Marcus leaned back, crossing one leg over his knee. 'With loaded shotgun leaning against the door frame. Rowan must've known all about Kempsey.'

'I agree.' When a thought hammered home she sat iron straight in her chair, which wasn't easy given the restrictive bandages strapped around her ribs.

'Oh, no. You've got that look, like you did with the whole treasure hunt.'

'Marcus, Rowan knew. That's why he went to such extremes with the clues, only to suddenly change his mind like that. Rowan wouldn't let me dig him up, but he knew Kempsey would do anything to find it. He made the hunt so hard, making the clues almost impossible, hoping Kempsey would get caught.'

'Hold on a second, why would Rowan put your life at risk?'

She shrugged. 'I don't think he meant to. He'd never do that to me on purpose. I know that. And he said sorry in his last letter, which means he must have known Kempsey was coming for him. So what if Rowan put the Jade Diamond somewhere safe?'

'Rowan's letter said he mailed it.'

'You know the post mistress. Does she remember seeing it? Or Rowan?'

'No, Tess doesn't.'

'So, what if Rowan put it in the most obvious of places? What if he said exactly what he meant in his letters and not the other way around?'

Marcus shook his head. 'Sorry, you've lost me with that translation.'

'Kempsey knew what Rowan was like. Kempsey knew

to look for the opposite. He knew the Peddlers' code, from when they were interrogated over the Timor incident.' She rummaged through the box and pulled out the letters. Straightening the pages, she read aloud:

'... I'm talking about some of those adventures and challenges that can start at your own home's front door. As your grandmother would say, home is where the heart is, especially in the place I told you I hung out the most!'

She then flicked to the last letter that had been found tied to the rum bottle:

'So in place of the diamond is your favourite rum. I know you'll enjoy this drink. I had hoped we'd share it together to watch the sunset from my favourite spot, discussing your next adventure in the world of words.'

'Which means?' Marcus asked her.
'Wait, there's this part ...'

'I'm being straight with you in not being the opposite in what I write or say.'

She folded the letters. 'I don't think Rowan mailed the Jade Diamond. There's no way I'd send something as priceless as that by snail mail. I think he hid it somewhere else.'

'Where?'

'Here!' She tapped her good foot tenderly on the floorboards.

'Where?'

'Here, here.' Wren used her crutches to tap on the floorboards. 'You, Chopper, and Darryl, all told me this is where Rowan would always sit. It was one of his favourite spots. Like you said, I bet Rowan was sitting here the night he died, he was on watch, guarding this space with a shotgun.' She slowly lowered herself to the floorboards.

'What are you doing?' Marcus gently held her back.

'I have to see.' Wren pushed the chair aside. 'Look!' She pointed to the slight gap in the floorboards, where a dark shadow sat directly beneath the chair. 'There's something down there.'

'Yeah, it's called dirt.'

'Didn't you tell me you had a hidey-hole under your house as a kid?'

'I don't believe this.' He raked his fingers through his hair. 'Fine, I'll get underneath. But only if you sit back in that chair.'

'Deal.' It's not like she could crawl under there anyway.

'Don't move. I'll get the torch.' The front door swung open, he caught it before it even closed, flicking on the torch. 'Good thing my mother does my laundry. By the way, my mother and aunt are coming over for lunch tomorrow to meet you.'

'What?!' She touched her hair that was in dire need of a cut and deep conditioning. 'I look awful.' Especially with her multiple wounds.

'You can't avoid her, now you're free from the hospital. You'll be fine. Mum already loves Felix.' Marcus jumped off the verandah and squatted beside the house. 'You're right, there is something down here.'

'Tell me it's not a snake.'

'Thanks, babe. I'm about to crawl into the belly of the beast for you.'

'Sorry.'

Marcus's laugh followed him as he crawled under the floorboards that made up the verandah. 'I found something.' He crawled back out and brushed the dirt off himself, to hold up a small black sack. 'You don't think it's a bit too simple?'

'Totally. We all went for the most difficult solutions because that's what we'd expected.' Wren opened the bag and carefully unwrapped the thick black velvet material inside. It was heavy and small.

'Oh my … Marcus.' Wren's eyes widened as she held within her palms the Jade Diamond. Its diamond centre was so clear with a pale jade hue. Delicate gold strands ever so delicately weaved inside its core like veins making it a natural phenomenon so unique to this world. It was the size of an egg, sparkling like a Swarovski crystal, catching the sun's rays to radiate a dazzling display of rainbows across the house.

'We found it.'

'You did,' he said.

'*We* did. I'm not flying solo anymore. Here.' She handed him the exquisite stone.

Marcus gazed at the stone in stunned silence, his eyes reflecting the priceless gem.

But to Wren, Marcus was a thousand times more precious than any buried treasure.

'You're looking at me weirdly again, like your imagination is going into hyperdrive.'

'I was just thinking that you're more precious than any treasure.'

'That's better than being so hot I could start bushfires.'

She giggled, wanting to belly laugh, but afraid it would hurt.

'What's going on out there? Toots, are you playing with a mirror in the window? I can get you a bell if you need my attention, because that dazzling light is distracting. I need sunglasses.'

'Come and look, Felix. We found it.'

The front door swung open, and Felix paused mid-flounce. 'Is that— No. That's not … Is that the Jade

Diamond?'

'It is.'

'Can I touch it?'

'NO.' Marcus laughed at the shock on Felix's face. 'Here, you hold it, it's heavy.'

'I must show everyone. Yoo-hoo, Reggie, get out the champagne and your camera, we found the Jade Diamond.' Chairs shifted around the kitchen table as their guests rushed to meet Felix in the lounge area, where he stood cradling the diamond like a baby bird.

'So, what are you going to do with that rock?' Marcus asked, carefully wrapping his arms around Wren, as they watched Felix through the window, showing off the Jade Diamond to everyone in the house.

'I'm going to take it back to Timor. It's what Rowan wanted to do; he just ran out of time.'

'Timor, huh? That's just across the pond. Sounds like an adventure.'

'Want to come with me?'

'Really?'

'Aren't you overdue a proper holiday that doesn't involve hospitals?'

'A holiday sounds good. But not just any holiday.' Marcus turned her around to face him. 'How about we make it a part of our honeymoon?'

Did she hear right? 'You haven't even taken me out on a date yet—or even to dinner—and you're already planning a honeymoon?'

'Okay, how about a dinner date, wedding ceremony, and honeymoon all in a week?' He laughed at her reaction. 'It'll happen eventually, so why wait? Time is a tricky thing, especially with my job.'

'So I found out.'

Marcus gently held her chin, lowering himself to meet her eyes, with his thumb barely brushing over her healing lip.

'I thought I'd nearly lost you, Wren, and I will not waste another minute on protocols and rules when it comes to you. Remember, you woke up, just wanting to hold me.'

'I did. I still do.' She gripped onto his shirt, with the same need to hold him close.

'So let's stuff tradition and elope. My parents did it.'

'Are you serious?'

'Want me to get down on one knee?'

'Wow, I'm speechless. I have absolutely no words.'

'That's a change.'

'But I could do with a permanent travelling companion—'

'Your silence didn't last long.'

'—and a male advisor for my books.'

'It can't be any more dangerous than what we've just gone through. Listen, Wren, I chose to not play it safe for my work, never hesitating when it came to tackling the dangers of my job. But in my private life I always played it way too safe to never get involved with anyone—especially when it came to love. I was doing it all wrong.' He took a step back to rake fingers through his hair. 'What I'm trying to say is that I'm going to be playing it much safer on the job from now on, because I don't want to miss anything with you. It's a job I don't want to be married to anymore.'

'But you love your job.'

'I do. But I love you more. Uh-uh, let me finish …' His finger pressed softly over her lips. 'I don't want to play it safe with how I feel about you and what we do as a couple. So, what do you say we break all those rules about love and make our own? I know you've changed your world for me. I know what it's cost you to legitimise the Sandfly Saloon and the money you've lost getting rid of the chop-chop.'

'I did that for you. For us.'

'There you go. You made the biggest move first. You also said you don't want to go solo anymore, and well, babe …' He slid his arms around her waist. 'This is my big move for you. Marry me.'

She just stared at his earnest eyes, feeling the love radiating from him in a look that saw past her layers. Only this time she didn't feel ashamed to show him.

'Besides, don't all your books have a happy ending? The guy gets the girl, and they confess their undying love for each other and live happily ever after, right?'

'How many of my books did you read?' Because she hid under the bed sheets in her hospital room whenever he cracked open a book. It was embarrassing having anyone read her books in front of her, she still got shy over it.

'A few. Jenny has a collection of them she keeps at the nurses' station at the hospital. They're good. But, you know, those sex scenes, I'm sure we can do way better than that.' He nuzzled into her neck, sending a cascade of goosebumps to run across her spine.

'Okay.'

'An okay is not good enough. This is a big deal, it deserves a yes or no response, Miss Sumney.'

'I'm thinking of changing my surname to Peddler. After all, this is the Peddler Palace.'

'Call yourself whatever you want, but I'll be the one to call you … mine.' He gripped her hip and stepped in, drawing her into his chest, to lean in and press his lips against hers that were firm. Demanding. Sure. And oh so heavenly commanding.

She was helpless to resist him and his all-consuming kiss, which grew in confidence with each stroke of his tongue. Their lips were perfectly flush, deliciously connecting them on so many levels that went so much deeper than the flesh.

She inhaled sweet air, her vision a blissfully dreamy world where only Marcus mattered, with her voice a sleepy murmur, 'Did I say yes?'

'That's better. I hope you're not expecting me to get

you a rock as big as that Jade Diamond for an engagement ring?'

'No, it weighs a tonne.'

'We could always knock off a chip to make you one.'

'Is that legal, Detective Sergeant?'

'Don't know, don't care. All I care about is the woman I love, and I love you.'

'Aw, I love you too.' She wrapped her arms around his neck, listening to his strong heartbeat, inhaling his divine aroma. She'd never get sick of holding him.

Her gaze followed the long paddock that rolled on like a carpet of gold beneath a spectacular sunset.

This was home.

The perfect place to sit at her laptop and write in front of that glorious view, in a place filled with love, adventure, and unique history. It was the perfect place to heal, to grieve for her father, to grow, to play and to watch over her own family

Inspiration swirled inside her. She wanted to capture the poetry of life, with a sudden itch to put ink to paper and write the best story ever. His. Hers. Theirs.

Wren smiled up at her one true love, and then at one of the most spectacular outback sunsets she had seen in years. It wasn't going to be her last, but it was one she would forever remember as the long-lost Peddler who had finally found home.

THE END

For now …

A PLACE WHERE
ELSIE CREEK
SUMMER NEVER ENDS

I have a gift for YOU!

Learn the secrets of

ELSIE CREEK

Exclusive to Elsie Creek Readers!

Simply go to:

https://melarowe.com/elsie-creeks-secrets/

Did you like the story?

If so, *your opinion* matters to me!

I'd love to read your review on
GOODREADS, or BOOKBUB.

I'd also be doing my own *dance-in-the-dust* if you shared
the cover of this book on social media for me to see how
far this story has travelled!

Please add *#Escape2HEA* for me to find you.

With much gratitude,

mel
A. ROWE

ACKNOWLEDGEMENTS

Thank you

Thank you for reading this story of the fictitious town of *Elsie Creek*. She may not exist, yet there is a part of her found in the Northern Territory townships, roadhouses, dusty sports grounds, crocodile-crowded boat ramps, and even in the rural pubs sparsely scattered across northern Australia.

Thank you to the amazing Handbrake for the technical military terms and for not disowning me whenever I burrow down into a new story. Maybe you'll read one of my stories one day, just not in front me.

To the publicans of the Sandfly Saloon – thank you for keeping the beer cold and the conversation flowing for many a fisherman who washed up on your shore.

Thank you to all those I had served with, and to those who continue to serve as a member of the Northern Territory Police—it's a job unlike any other. And again, many thanks to the amazing Detective Sergeant Vanessa Barton for your help and friendship.

Thank you to my online writer friends and to the amazing editing Deb team at DNP. Thank you to Eliza Maas for a conversation about small towns and their stories. To Clare Burns for having a sharp eye, and the Fabulous First Readers team for their support, I am truly blessed to have you all join me on my writing journey.

I'd also like to thank the quirky, colourful, and exceptionally extraordinary people I've met while working and living throughout northern Australia. The experience has been—and continues to be—priceless.

Most all, thank you to you, dear reader, I am so grateful to you for taking the time to read my story and for supporting this outback author. It means the world to me.

Until next time,

A. ROWE

australian bestselling author

ABOUT THE AUTHOR

Australian bestselling author, Mel A ROWE, creates escapes for today's busy women to enjoy from the comfort of their home.

Delivered with a dash of drama, witty humour and quirky family units, Mel is known for reinventing romantic versions of home, taking her common characters on uncommon journeys that lead from boardrooms to billabongs as they try to find their own HAPPILY EVER AFTER.

Living in Australia's Northern Territory, Mel enjoys random outback road trips, fumbling with her camera, annoying her family with her bad singing, and making new friends in the middle of nowhere—except for water buffalos. She's been chased by a few.

Feel free to contact Mel, as her word journey
continues, at

MelAROWE.com

Receive *free* exclusive insights, and news

on upcoming releases by joining:

https://melarowe.com/newsletter/

Also by Mel A ROWE

Australian Bestselling <u>ELSIE CREEK SERIES</u>:

The ART of DUST

DIAMOND in the DUST

CAKED in DUST

XMAS DUST

MUSTER in the DUST

ROLLED in DUST

WRITTEN in DUST

Standalone Stories:

Avoiding the Pity Party

Unplanned Party

The Football Whisperer

Winter's Walk

Run Beautiful Run

Watch for more visit: <u>MELAROWE.COM</u>